HOLLY BOURNE is an a[...] feminist education began when she read Caitlin Moran's *How to be a Woman*, but it was working at an advice charity for young people and her own experiences of blatant everyday sexism that drove her to write critically acclaimed *Am I Normal Yet?*. Followed by *How Hard Can Love Be?* and now *What's a Girl Gotta Do?*, the trilogy is an incredibly honest and hilarious insight into the complexities and contradictions of being a teen feminist. Holly has appeared at #FeminisminYA panels across the UK and Ireland. She is a 2016 World Book Night author and was shortlisted for the YA Book Prize.

www.hollybourne.co.uk

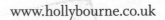 @holly_bourneYA

@hollybourneYA

HOLLY BOURNE

AM I NORMAL YET?

USBORNE

~~RECOVERY~~ DIARY
Normality

Date: 18th September

Medication: 20mg Fluoxetine

Down from 40mg — whoop whoop!

Thoughts/Feelings: Am I normal yet?

Homework:

- Touch the rim of the kitchen bin, don't wash your hands for 10 minutes afterwards
- Eat 3x meals a day, plus snacks
- Keep up the good work, Evie!! :)

(What? No sticker?!)

Evie's homework:

1. Don't let anyone at college find out about you-know-what
2. Begin a life of normal, and catch up on what you've missed over the past three years.

   Normal at 16 =
   * College
   * Friends (who won't dump you because you're too annoying)
   * A boyfriend? A first kiss at least?
   * Parties? Fun?

One

It started with a house party.

This wasn't just any house party. It was also My First Date. Like first EVER date. In my entire life. Because, finally, following all the crap that had gone down, I was ready for boys.

His name was Ethan and he liked the Smashing Pumpkins (whatever that is) and he'd managed to grow real stubble already. And he liked me enough to ask me out after sociology. And he was funny. And he had really small, but cute, dark eyes, like a ferret or something. But a sexy ferret. And he played the drums *and* the violin. Both! Even though they're, like, totally different instruments. And and…

…and – oh, Christ – what the HELL was I going to wear?

Okay, so I was stressing. And obsessing. "Obstressing" times a million. In an utterly deplorable way. But this was a big deal to me. I was doing something NORMAL for once. And I reckoned I could just about pull it off. And I *did* know what I was wearing. I'd run through every possible clothing combination in existence before opting for tight jeans, black top and a red necklace, i.e. what I reckoned to be the safest date outfit ever.

I was going to be normal again. But I was going to step back into it safely.

The outfit

Jeans = Cool, just-like-everyone-else, and I-won't-sleep-with-you-right-away-so-don't-even-think-about-it-mister.

Black top = Slimming – yes, I know…well it was a first date, and my drugs had made me a bit…puffy.

Red necklace = Hints of sexiness underneath, for when you've been a good boy, and in six months' time, when I'm ready, and you've said you love me, and lit some candles and all that stuff that probably doesn't actually ever happen to anyone…

…Oh, and you've been deep-cleaned and put through ten STI tests.

Nice. Safe. Outfit.

Put it on, Evie. Just put the damn thing on.

So I did.

*   *   *

Before I get into how it went and how it was the beginning of *something*, but not the beginning of Ethan, I guess you'll want to know how I met him so you have some emotional investment.

Bollocks. I just gave away that Ethan and I didn't work out.

Oh well. Whoever had a great love affair with a guy who looked like a sexy ferret?

How Evie met Ethan

New college. I'd started a brand new college, where only a handful of people knew me as "that girl who went nuts". Despite my tiny collection of mostly-home-educated GCSEs, the college let me in to do my A levels because I'm actually quite smart when I'm not being sectioned.

I noticed Ethan in my very first sociology lesson. Mainly because he was the only boy in there. Plus, the sexy stubble ferretness.

He sat across from me and our eyes met almost instantly.

I looked behind me to check who he was staring at. There wasn't anyone behind me.

"Hi, I'm Ethan," he said, giving me a half-wave.

I waved back with a flap of my hand. "Hi, I'm Evelyn… Evie. Always Evie."

"Have you done sociology before, Evie?"

I looked at the crisp new textbook on my desk, its spine still utterly intact.

"Erm, no."

"Me neither," he said. "But I heard it was a Mickey Mouse subject. An easy A, right?" He did this big grin that caused all sorts of stuff to happen to my insides. So much so that I had to sit down in my chair – except I was already sitting in it, so I just sort of wiggled awkwardly, panicked, then giggled to cover it. "Why are *you* taking it?" he asked.

A question. You can answer questions, Evie. So I smiled and said, "I thought it was safer than psychology."

Oops. *Think.* You think before you answer questions.

His face wrinkled underneath his mop of unruly hair. "Safer?" he repeated.

"Yeah, you know," I tried to explain. "I…er…well… I didn't want to get any extra ideas."

"Ideas?"

"I'm very impressionable."

"What sort of ideas?" he leaned over the desk with interest. Or confusion.

I shrugged and fiddled with my bag.

"Well in psychology you learn about all the different things that can go wrong in your brain," I said.

"So?"

I fiddled with my bag some more. "Well, it's more to worry about, isn't it? Like, did you know there's this thing called Body Integrity Identity Disorder?"

"Body Identi-what-now?" he asked, doing the smile again.

"Integrity Identity Disorder. It's where you wake up one day, convinced you shouldn't have two legs. You suddenly hate your spare leg, and you really want to be an amputee. In fact, some sufferers actually *pretend* to be amputees! And the only way to cure it is to get a limb hacked off illegally by this special leg-hacker doctor. People don't usually get BIID, that's what they call it, BIID, until their early twenties. Either of us could get it. We don't know yet. We can only hope we stay emotionally attached to all our limbs. That's why sociology is safer, I reckon."

Ethan burst out laughing, making all the other girls in my new class turn and stare.

"I think I'm going to like doing sociology with you, Evie." He gave me a tiny wink and a cheeky head tilt.

My heart started beating really quickly, but not in its usual trapped-insect way. In a new way. A good way.

"Thanks, I guess."

Ethan didn't do anything other than stare at me for the rest of the lesson.

That's how we met.

I looked at my reflection. First up close, my nose pressed against the mirror. I stepped back and looked again. Then I closed my eyes and opened them really quickly to surprise myself into an unbiased reaction.

I didn't look bad, you know.

From my reflection, you definitely couldn't tell how nervous I was.

My phone beeped and my heart did a little earthquake.

Hey, just on the train. Looking forward to seeing u tonight. x

He was coming. It was real. Then I saw the time on my phone and panicked. I was seven minutes away from leaving late. I chucked everything into a bag, then ran to the bathroom to brush my teeth and wash my hands.

Just as I'd finished, it happened.

BAD THOUGHT

Have you washed them properly?

I nearly doubled over. It was like someone had stabbed me in the guts with a knitting needle.

No no no no no.

And then another came to join the party.

BAD THOUGHT

You should wash them again, just to make sure.

I did double over then, holding onto the edge of the sink as my body crumpled. Sarah'd warned me this could happen. That the thoughts may come back when I cut down my dosage. She told me to expect it. It would be okay though, she said, because I had "coping mechanisms" now.

My mother knocked on the bathroom door. She'd probably been secretly timing me again – anything over five minutes was a warning sign.

"Evie?" she called.

"Yes, Mum," I called back, still knotted over.

"You okay in there? What time do you need to leave for your party?"

She only knew about the party. She didn't know I had a date. The less Mum knew, the better. My little sister Rose knew, but had been sworn to secrecy.

"I'm fine. I'll be out in a sec."

I heard her footsteps thump down the hallway and I let out a slow breath.

Logical thought

You're okay, Evie. You don't need to wash your hands again, do you? You only just washed them. Come on, up you get.

Like a well-trained soldier, I straightened myself and

calmly unlocked the bathroom door. But not before one last
brain malfunction muscled its way in for a parting shot.

BAD THOUGHT

Uh oh, it's coming back.

Two

After a dismal summer of constant frizz-rain, September had been on its best behaviour. My leather jacket swung over my shoulder as I walked to the train station. It was balmy and light still, with kids rollerblading down the pavements and parents sitting in their front gardens with evening beers.

I was so unbelievably nervous.

I hadn't wanted to meet him by myself. But Jane – TRAITOR – was getting a lift to the party with Friend-Stealer...sorry, I mean Joel.

"You don't really need me there to pick your date up," Jane had said, in a sickly-sweet voice. "Isn't that a little... immature?"

I, personally, thought it was more immature to dye your naturally-blonde hair jet black as an act of rebellion against your perfectly-nice parents – like Jane had. But I didn't tell her that. I just stared at my feet so I didn't see the patronizing crinkle at the sides of her kohl-covered eyes.

"I just thought it would be cool, like, if we all rocked up together?" I replied. "You and Joel. Ethan and me. You know, as a group?"

"Hon, he'll want it to be just you and him. Trust me."

I used to trust Jane…

I used to trust my judgement.

I used to trust my thoughts.

Things change.

And, today, things were spiralling.

What if Ethan didn't turn up? What if it was the worst night ever? What if he could tell I was mental and lost interest? What if I never found anyone who could put up with me? I mean, yes, I was better, but I was still… well…me.

I remembered what Sarah told me about dating.

What Sarah told me about dating

"I got a date," I said to her.

I sat on my favourite chair in her office, twirling a stuffed bunny in my hands. Sarah did Family Therapy too, so there were always loads of toys to play with when she told me things I didn't like.

It's impossible to surprise a therapist – I'd been with her two years, and I'd learned that early. Yet Sarah did sit up in her big leather chair.

"A date?" she asked, her voice all neutral and therapyish.

"This weekend. I'm taking him to a house party." The bunny spun faster and I couldn't help but smile. "I guess it's not like a date date. I mean, there won't be any candles or rose petals or anything."

"Who is this date with?"

Sarah jotted notes on her big A4 pad, like she always did when I said something interesting. It felt like an achievement, when she got the Bic biro out.

"Ethan from my sociology class," I said.

"Right, and what is Ethan like?"

My tummy bubbled and my smile spread out wider, like margarine.

"He plays the drums. And he thinks he might be a Marxist. And, he finds me funny. He actually said yesterday, 'Evie, you're so funny.' And…"

Sarah broke in. With her classic question.

"And how does that make you feel, Evelyn?"

I sighed and thought about it a moment.

"It feels good."

The Bic biro moved again.

"Why does it make you feel good?"

I dropped the bunny back into the toy bin and stretched back, trying to work out the answer.

"I never thought a guy would fancy me…I guess. What with everything up here…" I tapped my brain. "And, it would, you know, be nice to have a boyfriend…like everyone else…" I trailed off.

Sarah narrowed her eyes and I braced myself. Two years had taught me narrowed eyes = a blunt question.

"It might be nice, but do you think it's the healthiest thing for you right now?"

I stood up, instantly mad.

"Hey! Why can't I just have one normal thing? Look at how much better I am. I'm coming off my medicine. I'm going to college every single day. I'm getting good grades. I even put my hand in a bin last week, remember?"

I slumped back down again, knowing she wouldn't rise to my dramatic outburst. Sure enough, she remained composed.

"It's normal to want something normal, Evie. I'm not denying you that, and I'm not saying you can't or shouldn't do it—"

"You couldn't stop me anyway, I'm a free person."

Silence to punish my interruption.

"All I'm going to say, Evie, is that you're doing brilliantly. You said so yourself. However…" She tapped her biro on her pad, rolling her tongue in her cheek. "However… relationships are messy. Especially relationships with teenage guys. They can make you overthink and overanalyse and feel bad about yourself. And they can make even the most 'normal' –" she made the quote sign with her fingers – "girls feel like they're going crazy."

I thought for a moment. "So you're saying Ethan is going to mess me about?"

"No. I'm saying boyfriends and girlfriends in general

mess each other about. I just want to make sure you're strong enough to cope with the mess, alongside everything else."

I crossed my arms.

"I'm still going on the date."

It was a bit of a walk to the train station. The sun set gradually, making the sky an inky purple. There is lots of sky about where I live. Most houses are detached, with big sprawling gardens. The town centre has a Starbucks and a Pizza Express, a few pubs and all the other usuals, but it's still just an island of buzz in a vast sea of suburbia.

Ethan sent another message, telling me when his train was due to arrive. He lived a couple of towns over. It was exactly a nineteen minute train journey.

BAD THOUGHT

What if he holds onto a pole on the train?
What if someone with norovirus sneezed into
their hands, and then held the same part of
the bar before Ethan?
What if Ethan then holds my hand?

I stumbled on nothing and almost fell flat. Dating *did* bring a whole load of new mess into my brain. But, as ever in my brain, it was never "normal" mess.

Things I reckon it's normal to worry about before a first date

- Will it be awkward?
- Will they fancy me?
- How do I look?
- Will I like them?

I'd had all the above, on a recurring merry-go-round of neurosis ALL DAY, but I'd also had stupid stupid bad thoughts about stupid stupid bacteria. As bloody always.

To distract myself, I replayed how Ethan and I had got to this first date.

How Ethan and I got to our first date

He'd come into our second lesson looking pretty damn pleased with himself.

"Hey," I said, shyly, as he sat opposite me.

"Alien hand syndrome," he answered, nodding cockily.

"Huh?"

"It's a new thing for you to be scared of. Alien hand syndrome."

He'd remembered our conversation! And he'd done his own research! I grinned and tilted my head. "Oh yeah? And what's that?"

Hang on… WHAT THE HELL IS ALIEN HAND SYNDROME? WILL I CATCH IT?

"It's proper weird." He waved his hands about all crazy. "It's a neurological condition where your hand, like, grows its own brain and does crap all on its own accord." He grabbed his throat and pretended to strangle himself.

"What, even jazz hands?" I asked, trying to make light of it through my inner doomness.

He made his fingers jazzy, waving them in my face as I laughed nervously. "Yeah, maybe. But alien hand randomly slaps people, or chucks stuff on the floor; it might even try and strangle someone else. Here, I'll show you."

He got out his phone and pulled up a YouTube clip, checking our sociology teacher still hadn't arrived, leaning right in close so we could watch together. It was the closest a guy's face had ever been to mine and I felt all panicky, in a good way. Ethan smelled of bonfire, in a good way. I could hardly concentrate on the hand video.

I drew back first, and got my textbook out. "I don't believe it," I said. Not wanting to believe it.

"It's real, honest."

"How do you get it?"

Ethan put his phone back in his pocket. "It's usually a side effect of an operation to cure epilepsy."

I let out a big, real, sigh of relief. "Oh, good. I'm past the age where you develop epilepsy."

Ethan burst out laughing again, just as our teacher arrived and shushed him.

Class began. Our teacher paced in front of the interactive whiteboard, introducing us to Marxism and Functionalism. Ethan kicked me under the desk. I looked up and he held my gaze intensely, before retreating back under his hair, a small smile on his rounded dimpled face. I withheld a grin and delivered a retaliatory kick. When he looked up, I held eye contact for only a second.

Best game ever. Kick, stare. Kick, stare. Goosepimples stood to attention all over my body as our teacher's lecture faded into background noise.

I didn't have one bad thought the entire lesson.

In our next class, I was ready for him.

"Capgras Delusion," I said, before he'd even sat down.

He threw back his hands. "Aww, man, I've got one too. I wanna go first."

I shook my head. "Nope. Mine first."

"All right, all right. What's Capgras Delusion?" he asked.

I put on an authoritative voice. "It's when you suddenly believe someone close to you, like your husband, or your sister or something, has been replaced by an identical imposter trying to take over their life."

"Woooooah. No way."

"I know."

"Like an evil twin?"

"I guess."

"That is so cool."

"I guess." I'd already checked on Google and I wasn't in the high-risk category.

Ethan threw his bag down and stretched back in his chair. "Pica," he said.

"Whata?"

"Pica. It's an eating disorder where you love eating inedible objects with no nutritional value. Like rocks, and laptops and stuff. You're just compulsively hungry. You're always in and out of hospital because you've eaten stuff you shouldn't."

I was about to open my mouth but he stopped me.

"Don't worry. You're unlikely to get it. It's linked with autism."

I nodded happily. "Cheers."

We smiled at one another but were, once again, interrupted by our teacher, daring to teach us.

Over the next few lessons, we took it in turns to share a new disorder we'd discovered. Until suddenly one day Ethan seemed intent on actually learning. I watched him scribbling in his notebook as we were introduced to Karl Marx's big revelation that poor people aren't treated right by rich people. I tried to concentrate too, opening my own pad to make notes.

That was, until his notepad slid across my desk.

Can I ask you out?

My breath ran out of me and I smiled the entire lesson. I wrote back only one word…

Maybe…

The bell rang and everyone stood to reload their bags. "So," he said, sitting on my desk right in front of me. He was *so* confident. I liked it.

"So, what?"

"Are you about this weekend?" he asked. "I like you, Evie, you're on the cute and kooky side of weird."

KOOKY!? I'd finally made it down the weirdness spectrum to merely kooky!

I flicked through my plans. "I'm going to a house party on Saturday. There's this girl in my form, Anna. She said her mum is really cool and lets her have house parties. Her first one is this weekend."

"Cool. Can I come? With you I mean?"

OHMYOHMYOHMYOHMYOHMYGODDDDDDDDD.

"Sure," I said, as nerves and goodness went crazy in my bloodstream.

"Great, where is it?"

I reached the platform two minutes before the train was due and tapped my foot whilst waiting. I allowed myself to get excited. Like, really excited. Was I going to fall in love? Was this the start of it? Had I managed to find a nice sexy boy in my very first attempt at dating? Was this karma making up for the crap my life had been for the past three years?

Yes. Maybe. No, hell, yes.

The train was coming. Ethan was coming. For once, finally, I was living my life as it should be. For once I was going to catch a break.

The train doors opened… Ethan appeared amongst a crowd of passengers getting off…and tripped over his feet, landing flat on his face. An empty two-litre bottle of cider rolled out of his hand.

"Bollocks," he yelled. He tried to stand but fell again, rolling onto his side and laughing.

This wasn't supposed to happen.

I took a tentative step towards him. Passengers sidestepped us, giving us both dirty looks.

"Ethan?" I asked.

"WOAH, EVIE, I NEED YOU TO GIVE ME A HAND HERE."

He reached out for my arm, and I took his body weight – staggering under it as he righted himself. He absolutely stank. Of cider. And maybe a bit of sick.

"Ethan…are you pissed?"

He fell back a couple of steps, stopped his fall and broke into a proud-of-himself boy grin.

"Don't worry, love. I've got plenty left for you." He reached into his backpack and retrieved another two-litre bottle. Only half of it was left.

I realized Sarah might've been right.

Three

It was only a short walk to the party but, with an intoxicated Ethan, it took much longer.

"Out of the road," I said, steering him away from oncoming traffic. He took my hand-holding to mean something else entirely and squeezed mine tight. His felt warm and clammy.

I tried not to think of the germs. I failed.

He stumbled over his feet. "Whoops, wow, you have good reflexes."

His body weight shifted and swayed under my arm; I was practically dragging him to the party. He kept stopping to glug back more cider. Half of it went down his Smashing Pumpkins T-shirt, and some dribbled down the sides of his mouth. Could I run away? Was that fair? Or had I just met my match in weirdness? Was this the sort of behaviour the Love Gods had seen fit to pair me with? I couldn't leave him: I'd definitely been stranger than this in the past.

Ethan chucked the second empty cider bottle over a fence, right into the middle of someone's front garden.

"Go and get it."

"Okay." He didn't even argue.

We turned down Anna's road.

"Almost there…" I said, like I was taking my child to Disneyland.

Ethan ran ahead, then turned round so he was walking backwards, facing me. "Hey, guess what?" His smile was so wide I couldn't help but smile a bit too. Those treacherous dimples.

"What?"

He looked at his hand, then stretched his mouth into a horror scream and pretended to strangle himself, like in sociology. "LOOK, IT'S THE ALIEN HAND, IT'S OUT OF CONTROL."

Despite myself, I giggled.

"WHAT'S IT GOING TO DO NEXT?" He slapped his face. "Oh no, it wants to jump bodies." And he reached over and grabbed my boob. I looked down at my chest in horror.

"HONK HONK." Ethan beamed at me. I slapped his hand away.

"Did you just grab my boob?"

Too pissed to pick up on the scary in my voice, Ethan smiled wider.

"It wasn't me. IT WAS THE ALIEN HAND."

How? How was this happening to me?

I pushed past him and stormed through Anna's front door into the party. Ethan lurched behind yelling, "WAIT, THE ALIEN HAND IS SORRY."

Rock music blasted my eardrums the moment I got inside. I stopped at a people blockage in the hallway. There were groups of college friends everywhere, spilling up the stairs like bubbles in an exploded bottle of champagne. The bass made my heart beat faster. I looked around for anyone I knew. Ethan caught up with me.

"Hey, you ran off." He looked all lost and cute. I melted a bit and let him take my hand again.

"No more alien hand, okay?" A sentence I never thought I'd say.

"Okay."

We pushed through the crowds, saying "hi" to people as we passed. Jane – TRAITOR – was on a sofa in the living room, surgically attached to Joel. Somehow she found it in herself to stand up and hug us both hello.

"Evie, you guys made it!"

I gave her a weak hug then pulled away, examining her face. A new piercing dangled angrily out of the bottom of her face.

"Wow, Jane, you've had your lip pierced."

And your personality eaten by your soul-sucking boyfriend.

"I know, right?" she said, all thick and girly. "It hurt like a mofo, but Joel says he loves it."

I raised my eyebrows at Joel.

"Some gal you got there," I told him.

"I know, isn't she the greatest?" He pulled at Jane's leg like she was a puppy that needed controlling.

"Aww, Joel," she simpered.

To distract myself from the mini-sick in my throat, I gestured to my date. Hoping like hell he could control himself.

"Hey, guys, this is Ethan."

Joel waved, not even bothering to stand and say "hello". Joel didn't bother with many people. "WOOOO," Ethan yelled, like a frat boy at a stag do. "GREAT PARTY."

I leaned over to Jane and yelled in her ear over the music. "Jane. He's really, really drunk."

"I can see that."

"What do I do?"

Ethan made the metal sign with his fingers and jumped up and down on the spot. Everyone stared, bemused.

Jane looked like she was about to offer advice but then Joel pulled her back onto the sofa and kissed her urgently. I stood alone for a moment, contemplating what to do. Distance. I needed distance from the situation.

"I'm going to the kitchen to look for alcohol," I yelled over at Ethan. He stopped mid-headbang.

"Will you get me some cider?" he asked.

"Are you sure you've not had enough?"

"You can never have enough cider."

"I think you're living proof that you can."

"What?"

"Never mind."

Why Jane was a traitor

Jane and I. Me and Jane. It has always been us against the universe. Well, us against secondary school at least. We met in Year Eight and bonded immediately over our mutual disregard for everyone else.

"Hi," she'd said, sitting next to me – all bag banging on the table in an I-don't-care way. "I'm Jane. I'm new. I hate everyone in this room."

I looked round at the gang of popular girls preening in the corner, the boys all making fart noises in their armpits, the goody-two-shoes craning their necks in the front row.

"I'm Evelyn. I hate everyone too."

She flicked me a wicked grin. "Great. So we can be friends."

I'd never known closeness like it. We spent almost every waking second together. We walked into school, spent lunchtimes huddled and gossiping, drawing stupid pictures of our classmates, making up our own in-jokes. After school we'd go round to each other's houses – watching films, making up silly dance routines, gobbling up one another's deepest darkest secrets.

In Year Nine, I got sick.

Then I got worse.

Then I got whatever is worse than worse.

Jane was always there.

Always there with me in the school toilets, calming me down, shushing me as I scrubbed my hands so raw that blood poured into the sink. Always there at my door after school, on Bad Days, when the thought of even stepping outside was unimaginable – with my homework clutched in her hand and the latest gossip to tell. Always there at the weekends when I couldn't do anything, or go anywhere, because everything was terrifying. She never pushed. She never judged. She never complained. She just let me lie on the sofa in her living room whilst she played the clarinet.

When I got better we were stronger than ever. She fought my corner when people called me a weirdo. She didn't mind that I freaked out last minute and couldn't make it to prom and we'd watched *Carrie* instead. On our last day of Year Eleven we jumped up and down, hugging outside the gates.

"We're leaving, Evie, we're actually finally leaving," she said. "College is going to be so different and amazing and brilliant. We can be completely new people."

"I won't be 'the girl-who-went-bat-shit-crazy' any more."

She smiled her sparkling smile.

"And I won't be 'that crazy girl's mate.'"

We were euphoric the whole summer – planning our new lives, our future happiness, with the same determination of a crazed bride-to-be.

Jane met Joel on our first day of college.

She ran up to me at the end of the day – her face red,

her hair flapping in the wind behind her. "Oh my God, Evie, there is the most incredible guy in my philosophy class. His name's Joel."

I giggled and did a gorilla voice. "Me Joel, you Jane."

She didn't laugh.

"I'm serious. He stared at me, I swear, like the entire first half. And then we got paired up to answer this question and, oh Evie, he's so deep. He like GETS Aristotle. And he's the lead guitarist in this band. And he's got tattoos, but, you know, like good ones…"

She rambled on while I analysed the peculiar feeling forming in my stomach. An uncomfortable lurching, a rush of sickly…

… Jealousy.

I wanted to be happy for Jane. She deserved happiness. She deserved a "well done" for being so perfect for so long. I made all the right noises when she gushed on about him. I pretended I didn't want to cry when she announced he'd asked her out only two days later. I helped her pick out an outfit that didn't resemble anything she'd ever worn before. Seriously, Doc Martins. From the girl who played Grade Eight clarinet and owned the *Now That's What I Call Disney* album.

In return, for the past three weeks, all I'd had was missed phone calls. I got messages saying "Joel walking me in this morn, soz" and I wandered to college many mornings alone. She spent every lunch on the green, decamped in Joel's lap, piling her tongue into his mouth. I sat to the side of them, making awkward small talk with Joel's friends as my friend fell in love quicker than I'd ever known was possible.

Her cute vintage dresses became band T-shirts with ripped denim mini skirts and Converse. Her beautiful blonde hair turned jet black overnight and she didn't even ask me to help her dye it. Eyeliner was ladled around her eyes. She worshipped bands that sounded like bears having sex in an explosion of All The World's Noise.

She hadn't just given her heart to Joel, but her entire personality, her entire…Janeness. So quickly, so willingly. She must've been desperate to get away from me. I must've been so annoying she was willing to morph identities, just so she could escape me.

What I couldn't handle wasn't the dropping of me as a friend – although that stung like an African Killer Bee – but the selling out of who-you-are and what's-important-to-you just because a boy likes it. To me that made you a traitor against girl kind…against yourself. But maybe I was just lonely…or jealous. Or both.

The kitchen was bursting with alcohol. Piles of beer cans, half-empty bottles of wine and a few own-brand bottles of spirits dominated the black laminate countertop. Joel's best friend, Guy, was pouring a beer into a red plastic cup.

"All right, Evie," he nodded, concentrating on getting the foam right. We'd been forced into an awkward friendship since his best mate and my best mate had become love's young dream.

"I'm okay. Sorta. My date is, like, really drunk."

Guy looked up from his beer. "You brought a date?"

I deliberately jogged his beer, making some dribble over his hands.

"Don't sound so effing surprised."

Guy smiled and wiped his hands on his jeans. He was the one half-decent thing about Jane's transformation into a pod person. He and Joel were in the same crappy band and yet Guy was okay. Funny, sharp, just that little bit self-aware. And attractive, I suppose, if you're into that whole messy hair, ripped jeans sort of thing.

Pity he was a massive stoner...

"So how drunk is he?" he asked.

I sloshed some red wine into a cup and took a careful sip.

"He's headbanging. And pogoing at the same time – which I didn't know was possible."

"*That* guy's your date?" Guy's thick eyebrows went all sarky.

I laughed. "You've seen him?"

"Yes. Man, he IS drunk."

"He pretended he had alien hand syndrome on the way here, used it as an excuse to grope my boob."

I regretted telling him instantly, as saying the word "boob" automatically makes boys look at yours. Which is exactly what Guy did. Blatantly. He smiled his wicked grin again and took a pull of his beer. "Can't say I blame the guy."

"Hey."

"I'm just saying."

"Well don't." I crossed my arms over my chest.

The dull thud of the music made the glasses in all the cupboards tinkle. We stood there for a moment just giggling at each other before Guy drained half his drink. "So do you like this guy?"

I shrugged. "Yeah…I guess. He told me he liked the Smashing Pumpkins and I googled what that was."

"Geez. Girls actually do that?"

"What? It's just a google! So you wouldn't google something for a girl you like?"

Guy looked down at his chest and puffed it out. "I'm perfect, I know everything."

The top of his T-shirt sleeve rode up, displaying his half-arsed biceps. I spotted a scab.

"Wait! Have you got a new tattoo?" I leaned over to examine it as he rolled his sleeve up properly, looking all pleased with himself.

"I got it done last week. It's at the scabby stage."

I wrinkled my nose. "Delightful."

He traced the twisted black design lightly with his finger. There was still a red outline, blushing angrily from where the ink had hijacked his skin.

"It's tribal," he said, proudly.

I rolled my eyes. "People always say that about tattoos. What does it even mean?"

"You know. Like, from a tribe."

I glanced sideways. "But what tribe?"

"Well, you know, just tribal." There was an edge of irritation in his voice.

"You can't just get 'tribal'," I told him. "There's not just like this one big 'tribal'. Which tribe? Where from? What's the tribe's name? What does the tattoo mean?"

"Screw you." He finished his drink and plonked his cup down with a loud *clack*.

"What's that in tribal?"

And, despite himself, Guy laughed. "At least I'm not dating a premature alcoholic."

Just as he said it, Lottie – an old friend from primary school – walked into the kitchen with another girl. Lottie and I used to be close, but she was a genius and got a free scholarship from Year Seven to Eleven at the local private school so we'd lost touch. She was at my college now and I'd seen her a few times – her long, dark hair cutting its way through the corridor.

"Oh my God, Evie, is that drunk guy with you?" Lottie interrupted, not even bothering to say hello.

I hugged her, then withdrew and took a medicinal sip of wine. "What's he doing now?" I said. I'd only been five minutes. Ethan couldn't have got that much worse in five minutes.

"Relax, he's just, er, dancing a lot, that's all." Lottie started sorting through the bottles of booze. "Oh, this is Amber," she gestured to the girl beside her. "She's in my art class. Amber, this is Evie, we went to primary school together."

I turned to say "hi" but was struck by how…intimidating this Amber was. She must've been six feet tall, with long red hair. She was absolutely stunning and yet had her arms around herself, like she was trying to block herself out.

"Hey," I said, smiling.

"Hi," she replied.

"Wooooooooooooooooah," Guy stared upwards at Amber's face. She was at least four inches taller than him. "You're like…huuuuuuuuge."

Amber hugged herself tighter. "No I'm not." Her voice didn't match her body language at all. It was strong and bossy. "You're just a midget."

I decided I liked her immediately, though Guy looked stunned. He was a bit short…bless 'im.

"Don't worry about him," I said quickly, keen to impress her. "He's just permanently tattooed a complete mystery onto his body for ever… In 'tribal'." I pointed to his tattoo.

Amber laughed while Guy chewed his lip, fuming.

"Whatever, I'm going for a smoke." He took another beer with him as he left the kitchen.

"Boys," Amber sighed.

I sighed back.

"Tell me about it."

Four

I delayed returning to my drunken date. I chatted to Lottie and Amber and took my time pouring out some apple juice I'd found in the fridge, hoping Ethan was pissed enough to think it was more cider.

Brandishing two glasses, I returned to the packed living room where I'd left him.

Ethan wasn't there.

The space he'd cleared for himself with his dancing was now full of people playing a drinking game. Joel and Jane lay half-horizontal on the sofa, shamelessly appreciating each other. I inched around the cheering circle of drunks towards them, scanning the shadowy faces for Ethan.

"Jane?" I asked the back of her head.

No answer. Just slurping noises.

"Jane?"

She untangled her tongue from Joel's and pulled away. I imagined the noise of a plunger being yanked out of the loo.

"What?" She didn't hide her annoyance.

"Have you seen Ethan?"

"Who?... Joel...stop it," she giggled. He was stroking the tops of her legs.

"Ethan. My date," I said.

"Dunno. Maybe he's gone to the loo?"

Without hesitation she returned to Joel's mouth. His hands inched round her back, pulling her on top of him.

I bit my lip to hide my annoyance and tried to work out where he could be. Jane was right. I should try the toilet. Maybe he was sicking up all the cider? I manoeuvred into the hallway, asking everyone if they'd seen a very drunk boy wearing a Smashing Pumpkins T-shirt. Nobody had any useful information. The music was louder. People were wasted. The party was really kicking off. Nobody cared about my very first date going AWOL. I found the downstairs toilet door and tried it. Locked. I banged on the door.

"Ethan? You in there?"

"Who's Ethan?" a voice called back.

"Never mind."

I retraced my steps to the kitchen, peering inside. He wasn't there. He wasn't in the dining room either, where an elaborate game of poker had been set up – boys using Monopoly money as chips. I saw people had spilled out onto the back garden patio and tried there. I bumped into Guy as I slid through the glass doors.

"Evie, where you off to?" There was only the teeniest

bit of white left in his eyes. The rest were pinky red. His pupils were huge.

"Hey, druggie. I've lost my date."

"He's run off already?" Guy burst into frenzied giggles that didn't stop. I strode past him, leaving his hiccupping laughs behind me. Bloody stoners. I wrapped my leather jacket around myself as the now cold air hit me, letting my eyes adjust to the dark. A group passed a dubious-looking cigarette around in a tight circle, arguing loudly about retro children's TV programmes. Past them, I saw two figures sitting under an ivy-covered gazebo.

Lottie and Amber.

I grinned and walked over, trying not to twist my ankle in the gravel. "Hey again," I said, sitting next to them on the bench.

"Hey," Lottie said, moving over to make room. "Where's Ethan?"

I let out a big sigh. "He's gone missing."

"Seriously? You can't find him?"

"Nope. I left him with Jane when I went to the kitchen but when I came back he'd disappeared."

Lottie rolled her eyes, putting a cigarette between her lips and lighting it. "Let me guess, she was too busy sacrificing her entire being on to the altar of Joel to do anything else?"

I let out a giggle, immediately feeling guilty for being bitchy. Lottie'd never been one to mince her words.

"How do you know her?" I asked.

"She and Joel are in my philosophy class. She was pretty cool at first. Then, well…within a week she'd got with Joel. How do you know her?"

"We're best friends…" I sounded like a child. "Well, maybe, we were in secondary school. She is a little…in love, I guess."

"In love?" Lottie passed her lighter to Amber who also had a fag hanging out the side of her mouth. "She's in love with herself."

"Lottie…"

"Ahh, come on, it's true. All she ever talks about is herself. Or Joel. I didn't even know you were friends, she's never mentioned you."

That hurt, but then I thought of Jane's hand in mine, clutching it reassuringly, as I bawled in the school toilets after having a panic attack in assembly.

"She's been a good friend…" I awkwardly tried to change the subject. "I didn't know you smoked?"

Lottie looked at her cigarette like she'd only just noticed it. "I don't usually. We've started tonight, haven't we, Amber?" She bumped her tall friend.

Amber took a shaky puff, coughed, then looked at me. "So where do you think your date's gone then?"

I sighed. "I don't know. The whole night's a mess. He's obviously not interested."

Amber exhaled, blowing a clumsy plume of smoke into the night. "I bet he only got so drunk because he's nervous. Have you looked upstairs?" she asked.

"No."

"Then go upstairs, find him, and suck his stubble off."

"Eww. But thank you."

I left them to their cigarettes. Inside, the stairs were littered with clumps of people as I picked my way upwards, shouting "sorry". Music shook the walls and my eardrums thrummed in time to the beat.

I tried a door.

Bathroom. With a puddle of vom next to the loo. Grim.

Good thought

But you saw some sick and you didn't freak out, did you, Evie?

I tried a couple more doors but no joy. The last door was Anna's bedroom – strictly out of bounds – she'd been yelling at anyone climbing the stairs, "Don't anyone shag in my bed."

But she hadn't forbidden anyone curling up in there in a drunken ball to pass out – like I reckoned Ethan had done.

I rattled the door handle and turned it. It was dark.

There were noises. Sex noises.

"God, sorry," I mumbled, blushing as I realized what I'd interrupted.

Light fell over the half-naked entwined couple.

Ethan's face emerged from behind Anna's hair.

So *she* was allowed to shag in her bed… It made sense I guess.

I turned and left.

How it began

On. Our. First. Date.

On. Our. First. Date.

"On. Our. First. Date."

"I know, honey," Lottie said in a lullaby voice, gently pushing my head into a taxi. She and Amber climbed in after me.

"Can you take us to the top of Dovelands Hill?" she asked the driver.

He turned round to protest. "Isn't it a bit dark?"

"We're big girls. Just drive."

I stared out the window as the darkness sped past us, stunned. Bad thoughts, followed by worse thoughts, mounted up in all my available brain space.

BAD THOUGHT

You can't even keep a guy for a
whole first date.

BAD THOUGHT

It's because you're ugly and stupid and disgusting and you'll never get a boyfriend.

WORSE THOUGHT

He could tell you were mental. He just used you to get an invite to a party so he could meet normal girls.

I didn't notice Amber stroking my hand, the sympathy in her eyes. Or Lottie paying the fare and dragging me out onto some scrubby grass. Not until they sat me on a bench overlooking the town and offered me a cigarette.

"No, thanks, I don't smoke."

"Tonight you can," Lottie said, shoving one between my lips.

"I don't even know what to do."

"Just suck it. It's horrible. I think I'm only going to smoke this weekend, then give up."

I huddled over her hands as she lit the fag and sucked as hard as I could. A coughing fit followed. "That. Is. Disgusting," I announced.

"I know, right?"

"But I do feel more…dramatic. Maybe in a good way?"

Amber laughed then choked on her cigarette too. She spluttered and coughed while I sat back on the bench, feeling slightly happier by the fact I'd made a potential friend laugh.

It was a stunning view. The town stretched out below us in an ocean of yellow and red dots of light. So cold my bones ached, but beautiful. I felt a bit of the angst in my stomach dissolve like a throat lozenge. The bigness of the view stood Goliath-like next to my worries, forcing them to run into hidey-holes and think about what they'd done.

Lottie banged Amber's back until the choking subsided.

"Thanks, guys," I spoke out to the darkness. "For, you know, taking me away from the situation."

Lottie stubbed out her cigarette a quarter of the way down. I followed suit, glad for her lead. "Don't worry about it," she shrugged. "I would want to get out of there if it happened to me."

"And it was a shitty party," Amber joined in. "I felt like I was on a rejection conveyor belt – being sexually rejected by every guy there."

"I'd rather that, I think," I said. "Rather than them leading you on a false first date so they could get pissed, humiliate you, then boink someone else."

Amber wrinkled her nose. "True... Did you just say 'boink'?"

"It's retro. It's funnier than 'shag', less cringe than 'make love', and less offensive than 'fuck'."

She nodded. "Fair enough."

"I watch a lot of old movies...and people just talked nicer back then."

My phone vibrated madly.

"DON'T ANSWER IT," both of them yelled as I searched through my bag.

"Why not?"

"It will be him," Lottie said. "With an excuse."

"A lie," Amber added.

"A manipulative lie."

Amber put on a gruff boy voice. "I'm sorry, I just fell into her mouth."

Lottie joined in. "I just got scared of my feelings for you, but it made me realize how much I care."

"Yikes," I said. "Have you guys created a boy excuse dictionary or something?"

"Did you just say 'yikes'?" Amber asked. "Seriously? Are you, like, from a time warp?"

Lottie, sandwiched in the middle, put her arms round the both of us and talked out at the view. "Amber and I may sound bitter, but we're not. We're just realistic. About boys..."

"...and how crap they are," Amber finished.

Lottie patted her head. "I met her in art and she was crying over some bell-end on the football team. We bonded over drawing his untimely death."

"What did football guy do?"

Amber's face ducked behind her sheet of auburn hair. "Stood me up."

"God, that's awful. I didn't know people actually did that in real life."

"They do to me."

"Hey," Lottie said. "It could be worse. Like me. I just have guys 'boink' me, then lose interest straight afterwards. Usually when they discover I'm smarter than them."

Lottie *was* smarter than them. She wasn't being big-headed, just honest. She was smarter than everyone. At primary school she'd gone to special classes with the headmistress to be more "academically challenged". She'd read textbooks, for fun. And she was definitely going to Cambridge. Even though we were two years away from that.

A miserable silence descended upon us. My phone went off again. We all ignored it. I saw the tiny light of a car in the distance driving slowly away from our town, surrounded by night. I wished I was riding in it, escaping my disappointment. I thought again of this night, and what it was supposed to be. My first ever date… My first step into the world of normality. I'd just wanted to be like everyone else, and yet my attempt had turned out weirder than even my weird head could've imagined.

Finally I spoke. "You guys?"

"Yeah?"

"Is it…because I'm ugly?"

"Don't be ridiculous," Lottie said. "You're not ugly."

"Yes I am. I'm Louise and everyone else is Thelma." I threw my hardly-smoked cigarette into the mud dramatically.

"I wouldn't say Susan Sarandon is ugly," Lottie said again.

"Fine then, I'm Jane Eyre."

"Jane wasn't *ugly*, she was just plain," said Miss Going-to-Cambridge.

"Fine then. I'm the Elephant Man."

"You're not a man," Amber pointed out.

"Stop ganging up on me."

Their laughs punctuated the darkness.

"Anyway…" Lottie started. "I'm not exactly an oil painting."

"Don't be stupid," I protested. She was gorgeous and she knew it. Men's eyes practically goggled out of their faces when they met her. Her long dark hair, her everything-in-the-right-place face.

She smirked in reply. "If I were in a girl band, I would be the one that nobody fancied…"

"Hey," Amber butted in. "That would *so* be me instead. I'm the ginger one! Nobody ever fancies the ginger one in bands."

"Fine then. I'm Mary out of the Bennet sisters."

"Well if that's true," I stood up. "I'm…I'm…Mr Collins," I yelled, and the three of us dissolved into hysteria. We huddled together on the bench, chuckling and yelling "Mr Collins" until our tummies hurt and our teeth chattered from the cold.

"I really liked him," I half-whispered, remembering far too soon why we were sitting in the middle of a field, gone midnight. I needed to message my mum actually; she would probably be freaking out.

Lottie cuddled me into her. We'd not sat like that since we were eleven.

"I know you did," she replied. "Shitty, isn't it?"

Amber gatecrashed the hug, giggling as she made room for herself between our heads.

"Screw guys," she said. "Let's meet for coffee tomorrow and spend the entire afternoon talking about everything other than boys."

"Amen," I replied.

And that's what we did.

RECOVERY DIARY

Date: 25th September

Medication: 20mg Fluoxetine

Thoughts/Feelings: Will anyone ever love me, or am I too much of a freak? I can't even get a date to stay on a date with me...

Homework:
- Continue eating meals 3x a day plus snacks
- Try and spend ten minutes a day doing mindfulness breathing to help "stay" with unhelpful thoughts, before letting them go

Evie's homework:

Stay normal!

Five

By Monday I was ready and raring to see Ethan again.

I'd had so many dialogues with him in my head. They all ended with him on his knees, sobbing: *"But I'll never feel this way for anyone, the way I feel for you."*

Lottie and Amber firmly believed I should ignore him.

"Why waste time on him?" Amber'd said, the day before, at our first coffee meeting as friends. She slurped up her cappuccino. "He is not worth your H_2O."

"Oxygen is O_2," Lottie corrected.

"Oh, shut it, Einstein."

"I just want him to be a tiny bit sorry," I said.

"He isn't...otherwise he wouldn't have done it in the first place...I bet..."

"HUSH," Lottie yelled across the table, cupping her mug of weird herbal tea. "No talk of guys, remember? Let's discuss world domination instead."

Thus all talk of Ethan, footballer-stander-upper guy, and

all Lottie's conquests ceased, and we chatted about ourselves instead. I learned Amber wants to go to art college. How she hates her little stepbrother because he calls her "Ginger Pubes" and her dad won't do anything because he is whipped by her evil stepmum, so she put hair-removing cream on her stepbrother's eyebrows whilst he slept. Then Lottie filled me in on everything I'd missed since we were eleven, laughing about how she'd almost been chucked out of her posh school after getting arrested at a May Day protest. "But Mum and Dad were really proud," she said. She updated me on her hippy parents... "Dad is refusing to wear anything on his bottom half when gardening and the neighbours keep calling the police."

I listened and laughed and sipped my latte, downplaying any question they fired at me about my life.

I didn't really have any shareable anecdotes. That's the thing about anxiety – it limits your experiences so the only stories you have to tell are the "*I went mad*" ones. I drank all my coffee as they giggled and shared and I wondered what they'd do if I leaned over and said:

"The funniest thing happened when I was fourteen. I, like, completely stopped eating because I thought all food was contaminated and would make me sick. Hilarious, huh? I dropped, like, two stone initially. Great diet, I know! And then, there was this one time, when my mum tried to force-feed me. She held me down and globbed mashed potato around my face, crying, and screaming, 'JUST BLOODY EAT, EVIE.' But I wouldn't. And then I collapsed and they took me to hospital and misdiagnosed me with anorexia. So funny, right? And then I was super thin and still wouldn't eat so they, like, SECTIONED ME. And it took them, like, WEEKS to finally diagnose me with OCD and Generalised Anxiety Disorder. So, anyway, have you guys ever been sectioned?"

I couldn't really tell them that, could I?

Especially as I liked them so very much already. And telling them was a certain way of wrecking the friendship.

Don't argue. I'm right about that. Trust me. I mean, look at Jane. She'd run the first chance she got.

They allowed me five minutes of Ethan analysis as we walked back to our respective houses.

"It's simple," said Lottie. "Just look him straight in the eye and say, 'You are nothing to me.'"

"Erm. Isn't that a tad dramatic?"

She shrugged. "Maybe. But imagine how much it would hurt if someone looked you in the eye and said that?"

BAD THOUGHT

Someone might look me straight in the eye
and say, "You are nothing to me."

"That, my friend, is a fair point."

*   *   *

I had sociology and my Ethan-altercation first thing. I was supposed to be walking in with Jane, but she cancelled again. To go in with Joel. Again. She didn't even ask how my date went.

Both Amber and Lottie – however – messaged on my way in.

You go girl. Remember he is NOTHING to you. – Amber

Good luck today! Let's celebrate with an all-day breakfast afterwards. They do one in town for only three quid. You have second period free, right? – Lottie

Ethan was already sitting in the classroom. In his usual spot, watching for me to arrive. He looked sheepish. I smoothed down my T-shirt.

You are nothing to me.

His eyes followed me as I wobbled to my chair and concentrated on getting my book out of my bag. We were both early and the only two students there.

"Evie," he said, all urgent and pleading.

You are nothing to me. You are nothing to me.

I gave him my best ever glare. "I am nothing to me."

Darn it!

"Huh?"

"I mean, you are nothing to me," I corrected myself.

"That's not what you just said."

"Yes it is. Shut up."

"Have you been practising that killer line all morning and now delivered it wrong?"

I felt my face burn. Ethan's eyes were almost dancing with the hilarity. Git.

"No. Why would I waste brain tissue thinking about you?"

His look softened and he leaned over and clasped my hand. I looked at it. "Evie. I'm so sorry about Saturday night."

I pulled my hand away. "Which bit? Getting completely bladdered, sexually assaulting me and blaming it on a rare neurological condition? Or, I don't know, GETTING OFF WITH SOMEONE ELSE ON OUR FIRST DATE?"

A girl walked into the classroom, midway through my yelling. She heard what I said and glared at Ethan. Solidarity. That's what girls need more of. Solidarity.

"All of it. I'm sorry for all of it. But mostly I'm sorry I've messed things up with you."

"Or just sorry that you've been caught?"

"I really like you, Evie…"

I dared myself to look at him again. His hair fell into his eyes. His dimples lay dormant but you knew they were there…

"Yeah, well, your penis seemed to really like someone else on Saturday."

"My penis likes you too."

He was smiling. Like it was all a big hilarious joke.

I took a deep breath. "Please just leave me alone."

More students trickled in, buzzing with their own conversations, emptying the contents of their bags onto desks. Class started in five minutes.

"Won't you at least hear what I've got to say?" he begged.

Although it wasn't protocol, I figured I may as well hear him out. Besides, I was curious… "Go on then…"

"I'm being serious now…Evie…" He took my hand again and I reluctantly let it stay there for a bit. "I'm actually worried about myself. I think I'm a…a…sex addict."

I laughed so hard actual spittle flew onto our entwined hands.

"Seriously," he protested, not noticing the spit. "Why are you laughing? It's not funny. It's a very serious condition."

I tried to calm myself. "Well, technically, it's not been confirmed as an actual medical condition (*the things you learn from fellow patients*), but I'll go with you for a second… why do you think you're a sex addict?" I giggled on the last two words, but Ethan looked positively devastated.

"I'm telling you, I'm really scared of myself, Evie. I, like, literally can't stop thinking about sex. I think about it all the time…" He lowered his voice to a whisper. "I like you…I really do…but I get the impression you're not…you know… easy…and then this girl, Anna, was all over me when you went off, and I thought…I need to get my fix…"

I very deliberately removed my hand and wiped the back of it on my jeans. "Ethan. You're not a sex addict. You're just a sixteen-year-old boy."

"No, I have a problem! I watch porn all the time."

"Which is disgusting and probably not very good for you, but, again, unfortunately for society as a whole, totally normal."

"Will you forgive me? I'll get help. For you, I'll get help."

I'd always been so mad at myself for missing out on dating, so keen to catch up. I'd always mourned the years lost where I was supposed to be getting touched up at parties, and getting songs dedicated to me by spotty boys at the ice-skating disco, and kissing other mouths and enjoying how they felt rather than mentally calculating how many billions of bacteria must be on their tongues... Anyway... I'd really felt I'd missed out on boys. Now...now I was beginning to wonder what the fuss was about.

"Ethan, you don't need professional help. You just need a wank, and what you really need is to leave me alone, for ever."

"Evie, please?"

"Just leave me alone."

Six

Amber cut a piece of sausage and examined it glistening on her fork. "Coming out for breakfast is possibly the best idea you've ever had, Lottie," she said. Then she ate it.

"I told you it was amazing," Lottie replied, poking shiny scrambled egg onto a spoon. "May this become our new Monday ritual."

"I still can't believe he told me he was a sex addict," I said.

"Shh," Lottie said. "Not in front of the eggs."

They'd taken me into town in our joint free period, promising fried food was the answer. We were in a grotty cafe, one that Lottie promised actually did amazing food. She was right, but eating a delicious breakfast with a plastic knife and fork ruined it a bit. Bacon had helped, to some extent, but I still felt this burning desire to discuss and analyse every molecule of what had gone down with Ethan. Preferably on a loop. Over and over.

"I hate him," I continued, showing no respect for the eggs. "I hate him and yet I still feel this burning desire to discuss and analyse every molecule of what's happened. Preferably on a loop. Over and over."

"Welcome to the world of boys," Amber said, puncturing another sausage.

Lottie put on a sugary voice. "I hate you, and yet I want you to like me, and I want to know everything about your brain."

I smiled weakly, took a bite of toast and pushed my plate back. "I hate myself. One date and look what's happened to me."

Lottie pushed the plate back towards me.

"Which is why you must have restorative meat and friends who won't let you talk it over on a loop."

"He's an arsehole though, right?"

"We've already agreed that he is."

"And, he's not really a sex addict, is he?"

"Evie!"

"Okay, okay."

My appetite for discussing Ethan was still vastly undented, but Lottie had just used the word "friends" and it made my stomach goo more than Ethan's smile ever had.

"Let's change the subject. How's the smoking going?" I asked Amber.

She shook her head and swallowed. "It's not. I gave the rest of the cigarettes to my stepbrother."

"AMBER," we both yelled.

She didn't even try to look guilty. "What? He's the Antichrist. I'm doing the world a favour."

"How old is he anyway?"

She blew a wisp of reddish hair out of her face. "I dunno. Ten, maybe younger?"

"AMBER!"

"He'll be fine." She batted our protests away with her fingers. "I don't want to talk about him. So, you two… How did you become friends?"

Lottie and I looked at each other. "We went to the same primary school," I said.

"Yeah." Lottie smiled at the memory. "We had to do extra lessons after school together because we weren't challenged enough in the classroom."

Amber pointed an accusing finger at me. "Wait, you didn't tell me you're a genius too, like Lottie here."

"I…"

I had been. Clever, I suppose. Once. Now I had barely any qualifications to my name, and I'd ruled out almost all A level subjects based on their potential to trigger a relapse.

A levels I couldn't do

Geography – Out of the question. Learning about volcanoes? And earth crust? And ice ages? And all the other geological phenomena I couldn't control and could kill us all dead? Are you kidding?

Biology – Oh, cancer. Let the person with diagnosed Generalised Anxiety Disorder and OCD learn about cancer? Next!

French/Spanish/German – Why bother learning a language when it's highly unlikely you'll ever be well enough to leave your own country? I'd barely left the county... Only that one time for a cousin's wedding where I completely lost it at the finger buffet and Mum and Dad had to drive us home through the middle of the night...

Philosophy – Don't even get me started on what existentialism does to my mind.

Psychology – We've already discussed this.

And so on and so on and so on, until I took sociology, film studies and English language. Nice and safe. No scary ideas.

"She's well clever, aren't you, Eves?" Lottie asked, disrupting my inner ramblings.

"I'm okay. I guess." Sarah once said it takes quite a high level of intelligence to dream up every worst-case scenario for every situation. Ever. Like I can...

Amber mopped up her beans with her stiff triangle of white toast. "So did you guys not stay in touch when you were at different secondary schools?"

"I..."

Lottie interrupted. "I tried. But after Year Eight, Miss Snooty Knickers here fell off the planet and stopped answering my calls."

She said it friendly enough, but a bit of hurt was there.

"I…I… Sorry, Lottie. Secondary school kind of swallowed me up whole…"

"And spat you back out again?" Amber finished for me. "That's what happened to me. I hated school so much. I'm so glad I'm at college. You two are the first people I've met in a long time I actually like."

We all beamed at each other, though inwardly I felt queasy with guilt…and grease. I hadn't meant to ditch Lottie. I just…ditched life, and Lottie was part of that. What was I supposed to do? Answer her calls and say "Sorry I can't come out tonight, I'm writing the sell-by dates of every food item in my house into my special OCD diary"?

She wouldn't have understood. Or worse, she would've pretended to understand but then got annoyed when her support didn't magically cure me and buggered off.

Just like Jane.

"Right, I'm stuffed," I announced. "And film studies beckons."

Amber narrowed her eyes. "Lottie. You said the girl was smart. And she's off to film studies?"

"Hey! I'll have you know we have to write essays!" I protested.

"Yeah, yeah. About what?"

"*Casablanca* and stuff?"

"Cassawhatta?"

"I'll pretend you didn't just say that," I said.

We all chucked our money on the garish tablecloth and

scraped our chairs back to leave. An autumn chill hit us as we trundled back to college.

Guy was just leaving as we got to the gates. He was smoking a suspicious-looking roll-up, his hair stuffed into a grey beanie hat.

"Evie," he said, far too pleased to see me. Definitely a suspicious cigarette. He held out his hand for a high-five. "How was your date in the end?"

I high-fived him back unenthusiastically. "Not great. He went upstairs and shagged someone else."

Guy tried and failed to hide a burst of laughter. "On your first date?"

"He's a sex addict," I explained. "Well, that's what he told me anyway."

This time he didn't even try to hide his giggles. He bent over, clutching his ribs. The roll-up dropped out of his mouth onto the pavement. Guy didn't notice.

"Seriously?" he asked, his head still upside down.

I looked to the others for support. They just gave me "we're talking to this loser again?" looks.

"Seriously. That was my weekend."

"Christ, you make me laugh." He got himself upright again, realized he'd dropped his joint, and ducked to pick it up off the floor.

"Yeah, well, at least I'm not plucking a soggy roll-up out of a gutter with an indeterminate tribal scar forever etched onto my body."

"Fair enough." Guy was waterproof against insults once

he'd had a smoke. "Anyway, you got class now? Bye, ladies." He re-lit his smoke and sauntered off.

Amber didn't look impressed as we watched Guy cough his way down an alley. "That's the guy from the kitchen, right?"

"Yeah, Guy. He's okay really. He's Joel's best mate."

"And Joel is?"

"Jane's boyfriend."

"Ahhh, Jane." Amber gave Lottie a knowing look. I tried to read into it but the bell went.

"See ya," I yelled behind me and I ran off to class and *Casablanca*.

"See ya."

Seven

I was almost late for film studies and sat down all a-bluster, grabbing my notebook out my bag and rushing to get to the right page. My rush was wasted though as our teacher, Brian, walked in wearing shades and bashed his head face-down on the desk.

"All right, class? I'm hung-over as sin," he told the wood. "Take it easy on me today."

From what I could tell, Brian was a frustrated director with a drinking problem. Yet he was worshipped by the rest of my class for his tendency to yell "NO YOU'RE WRONG" and smash the table if you dared suggest *Forrest Gump* deserved that Best Picture Oscar over *Pulp Fiction*.

"So…" Brian continued to address the desk. "As I need to spend most of the next hour focusing on not vomming my guts up…" I felt sick, instantly sick. "Here is a very easy task for you. For some unknown reason, the examining bastards have decided to add noughties films to the exam syllabus. I haven't read which ones they're testing you on yet, so turn to the person next to you and discuss your favourite three films since 2000. Then report back at the end of the class. GO."

I counted around the circle of desks to work out who I was paired with.

One…two…one…two…one… I looked to the left of me, and found myself staring into the most impressive pair of cheekbones the world has ever known. They were attached to this guy, a smiling guy, as he'd already worked out we were partners.

"Hi, I'm Oli," he said.

"Oh, hey, I'm Evelyn…well, Evie."

He smiled again. The cheekbones. The almighty cheekbones. His face looked like it had been chiselled out of butter by the gods, and yet he was all shy and looky-downy. *Ding ding ding.* My innards were lighting up like a slot machine. I promptly forgot all about worrying I'd fail my AS level due to Brian's teaching.

"I've not seen you in class," I said, knowing I certainly would've noticed THOSE cheekbones before. "Did you just switch AS levels or something?"

He coughed and his smile dropped slightly. "I…no… er…there was a problem with my admission…" His voice went up like it was a question, and he carried on. "They thought I was staying on at my old school's sixth form… paperwork muddle. This is my first full week."

I nodded. "Oh okay. That's…er…weird. So, you like

films, huh?" I gestured towards the screen at the front of the classroom, and then cursed myself for stating something so obvious.

"Yeah. I'm not much of a reader, I prefer my stories in visual form. How about you? You're, like, the only girl in this class, have you noticed?"

"Oh, am I? Right…" And we both blushed, his sculpted cheeks and my normal puffy cheeks each glowing red. "But, yeah, I love films…they're escape, aren't they?"

Escape was undermining it. Films had been my saviour over the past few years. The roll of opening credits the only thing that could distract my brain when it swan-dived into the neurotic abyss. I must've watched hundreds of movies during my meltdown. Locked in my sterilized room, a tiny TV in the corner, I was able to lose myself in the stories and get caught up in the characters. For two hours at a time, I could forget all the whirring non-stopness of gut-twisting anxiety. I could merge myself into the lives of people capable of leaving the house, capable of having storylines.

"I guess they are," Oli said. "So, anyway, shall we do this assignment then?" He couldn't quite hold eye contact. Which was a shame because his eyes were a shocking green colour. Like basil, or something more romantic-sounding than basil. But basil is a pretty lovely shade of green to have eyes made out of.

"Yes. Sure." His shyness made me shy and I found myself playing with my hair. "So what are your top three films since 2000?"

"Well, *Fight Club*, obviously," he started, ticking it off on his finger. He didn't even need to think about it. He'd obviously honed the list loads of times in his head. I was impressed. "Then *Pan's Labyrinth*, and, well, *Donnie Darko*. Of course."

I nodded, secretly correcting him in my head. *Fight Club* came out in 1999, but he seemed too shy for me to say so. "Donnie's my number four. He doesn't quite make it into the top three though."

"Ahh, so what are yours?"

I didn't need to think about it either. "*Amélie, Eternal Sunshine of the Spotless Mind,* and *Big Fish*," I reeled off.

It was his turn to nod, and it was an appreciative one. "Interesting choices…for a girl."

"And that's supposed to mean?" I asked.

"Well…er…" Oli realized his mistake and he spluttered and stumbled over his answer. Shy shy shy shy SHY. "It's just…erm…well…not a regular girl's top three, I guess… in a good way…seriously…in a good way…I meant that in a good way." His basil eyes downturned and I could see him hating himself internally. It felt weird, making someone else nervous rather than being the nervous one. Quite powerful. I liked it. He was so shy though that I dropped his "good film choices for a girl" comment. Maybe I fancied him a bit.

"So what film got you into film then?" This is a film-person question. We've all got one. The film that made films a way of life, rather than just passive entertainment.

"*The Godfather, Part II.*"

I burst out laughing and Oli's cheeks burned brighter.

"What's wrong with *The Godfather, Part II*?" he asked, a bit mortified.

"Nothing's wrong with it – it's a great film. It's just also the biggest gender cliché ever of a bloke's favourite movie. And you just made that comment about me having good film choices for a girl."

"But, it's Al Pacino…" His eyes didn't meet mine and I let it drop. Again. I really did fancy him, I guess.

"Never mind. I like *The Godfather* too."

"Oh…cool…" He stared at the desk. "So what film got you into films then?"

I smiled, recollecting the first time I'd seen it. "It's a weird one. *Edward Scissorhands*."

"Really?"

"Yes, really."

The first time I saw Edward Scissorhands

I'd just started to get sick, and no one knew why or what or how yet. Mum had tried to force me to go to school again, but I'd barricaded myself into my bedroom by pushing all my furniture against the door.

Have you ever barricaded yourself into a room? Honestly, it's the most definitive way of confirming that, yes, maybe you have gone mental.

And that confirmation unleashes the emotional landslide – where, suddenly, after fighting for so long, your brain gives up and erodes in on you, spiralling your thoughts into monsters who seize the city and tell you nothing is going to be okay ever again. That this is your new life now. Fear, and pain, and confusion. And your mum hammering at the door, screaming that she's calling the police for your truanting, and you don't even care – just as long as you don't have to leave the house.

Eventually Mum gave up – thinking if she stopped "giving me attention" I would "snap out of it", because that's what every parent of someone who gets head-ill believes at some stage.

I was left in peace.

To ruminate into madness.

The problem with that is, there's only so much delirious spiralling you can do before your brain gets a tad bored. Not bored enough to move the furniture, open the door and say, "I'll go to school now." But sustained crying was exhausting and, without drinking, due to the barricade and such, it got hard to keep producing tears. So eventually I started looking for things to do and found an old DVD Jane'd lent me – she'd been going through a Johnny Depp obsessive period – and shoved it into my laptop.

Films had never been a huge deal to me before. They were things in the background in a friend's room, or a way of passing time on Christmas Day when the family is bored of one another. But the moment *Edward Scissorhands* began, with its haunting music and blizzarding snow and magical fairytaleness, it did the impossible. It made me forget what was going on in my head. For one blissful hour and a half I was distracted by this story of an odd boy who didn't fit in, in a boring town just like mine. It was like going on brain holiday. And it was so beautiful and poignant and perfect. That was the film that did it.

And for the following years film was my only escape. I chased gorgeous story after gorgeous story, usually old romances, my film pile growing ever bigger and my movie knowledge ever greater as my brain got gradually worse, and then much worse, and then better.

"So why *Edward Scissorhands*?" Oli asked, his basily eyes wide with interest.

"Oh. I just like Tim Burton," was my reply.

Eight

Sarah couldn't wait to hear about my disastrous date. Naturally.

"How did it go?" she asked, before I'd even sat down. Her pen was already poised above her notepad.

I picked up the dilapidated rabbit. "Aren't you going to ask me how I am first?"

"How are you?"

"Fine."

"So how did the date go?"

I shook my head. "You're getting it all wrong. We're supposed to sit here in awkward silence first, because obviously I'm not fine, that's why I'm in therapy. Then we make small talk for at least five minutes before I open up."

Sarah narrowed her eyes. "You've imposed rituals into therapy, haven't you?"

"No," I said sheepishly. Maybe I had a *bit*. "It's just you're not saying stuff in the order you usually do."

"And does that make you feel uncomfortable?"

I narrowed my eyes back at her. "I'm in therapy for an anxiety-related disorder. EVERYTHING makes me uncomfortable."

Sarah let out a small laugh. "Fair enough. Let's do this the usual way."

"Thanks."

"Do you have this week's Worry Outcome survey?"

I rummaged in my bag and plucked out a wadded ball of paper. It took a moment to flatten out the creases on my knee. "Here it is."

"Thanks." Sarah leaned over and took the paper, fanning it out, scrutinizing it.

A Worry Outcome survey is a therapy thing – a thing you only get to know about if you've been through The System.

I remembered the first time Sarah asked me to fill one out.

My first Worry Outcome survey

I was rocking in the chair, my foot buckling back and forth on the carpet, riding through the relentless adrenalin surges. Everything looked dangerous. Even Sarah was dangerous. I'd spent the car journey convincing myself she was actually a serial killer, who earned trust from her patients before killing them and making it look like suicide.

"Now, Evelyn," she'd said, putzing about on her computer. She hit enter and a sheet of paper slid noiselessly out of the attached printer. "I'm going to give you something called a Worry Outcome survey. Have you heard of them before?"

I shook my head.

"It's just like homework. Nothing scary." *Like she knew what scary was...* "But I want you to take this sheet around with you..." *Around where? My bedroom, i.e. the only place I spend my life?* "And whenever you get a worry, I want you to fill out the first three boxes."

She held out the sheet. I didn't want to touch it. Where had it been? Where had her hands been? What if Sarah'd been to the toilet before our session and not washed her hands afterwards with soap and water? I pictured the bacteria multiplying on her fingers. I could almost see their luminous glare in real life. I whimpered away from the sheet.

Understanding, for this session at least, she put it on the table. "Let's look at it from here, shall we? You can pick it up with gloves later."

I thanked her with my eyes.

"Now...as you can see...the first column is the date. So note down the date you get that worry..."

The paper had a giant table on it. It looked like this:

Date of worry	Worry topic	Worst perceived outcome of worry	Did this outcome happen?	How well did I deal with this worry?

"So, I'm what? Supposed to fill it out when?"

"Whenever you have a worry," Sarah replied.

"Every single one?"

"Every single one...well...if they start to repeat themselves...just tally it. Then we can see each week if your worry came true and, if not, it may help you challenge some of these unhelpful thoughts. Now...do you think you can do that?"

I nodded slowly. It sounded a lot less scary and a lot more manageable than the other crap she'd tried to get me to do since I was unsectioned. Like only wash my hands ten times after going to the loo instead of fifteen times. And drinking fresh milk rather than those tiny capsules of long-life milk that can survive a nuclear holocaust.

"Great." She beamed and pushed the piece of paper over. I stared at the one lonely sheet of A4, looking all hopeful on the mahogany table.

I started laughing. Really laughing. A snort even happened. Sarah looked around self-consciously. "What is it?"

"Are you kidding me?" I asked, gesturing towards the paper.

"What? What's so funny? I don't get it."

Bless her, she looked genuinely baffled. I guess I didn't laugh much in that room. More sobbed. And wailed. And yelled, "NO YOU CAN'T MAKE ME."

I laughed myself out and pointed to the paper.

"You've told me to list every worry I have, as it happens, and you've only given me one sheet of paper?" I snorted again.

Getting it, she smiled. "Do you not think one sheet is enough?"

"I think you should print out some more."

She smiled more broadly, and hit the keyboard. Another survey slid out.

"And again."

Another slid out.

"And again."

And one more.

"Surely that's enough?" she said, after the fifth sheet was added to the pile.

"You have no idea what you're dealing with."

At the next appointment, I presented her with my filled-out survey. This is what some of it looked like. Not all of it – I don't want to be personally responsible for the death of the rainforest.

Date of worry	Worry topic	Worst perceived outcome of worry
May 5	Washing my hands. HHT HHT HHT HHT HHT HHT HHT III	If I don't wash them properly, I'll get really ill, then have a painful death and possibly infect my parents and little sister and they'll die too.
May 5	Cleaning my room. HHT HHT HHT HHT II	It's all I have and if I can't clean it it'll get covered in germs and then I'll get sick and maybe die, or maybe make my family sick.
May 5	Can't go to school. HHT HHT IIII	It's too full of people touching everything and I'll get sick and even if I did go back they'd all call me a freak.

Date of worry	Worry topic	Worst perceived outcome of worry
May 5	All food must be cooked completely through. No raw food. ‖‖‖ ‖‖‖ ‖‖‖ |||	I might get a stomach upset and be sick and then I might get worse and I'll die.
May 5	My therapist is a serial killer. ‖‖‖ ||||	She's going to gain my trust and then kill me and make it look like suicide.
May 5	Touching people.	People are disgusting and don't wash properly and I can't know for sure they have washed so if I have to touch someone I might get sick and die.

On and on it went. Pages filled after pages. I'd even started writing on the backs of them. I'd got a lump on my finger from the non-stop scribbling. Every single thought, over and over, sillier and sillier, and yet scarier and scarier as those days went by.

When I handed it in, Sarah took one look and said, "So, yeah, you did need all those five sheets, didn't you?"

And so it went on.

But not any more…

Present day again: I hand my new Worry Outcome survey to Sarah. Only one side of paper. Never, ever, did I think I would see the day when I only used one side of paper. For a week. A whole week! Oh the pride in being normal.

Date of worry	Worry topic	Worst perceived outcome of worry
September 22	Date won't go well.	He won't fancy me. He'll realize I'm mental and/or unfanciable and I'll ultimately die alone.

Date of worry	Worry topic	Worst perceived outcome of worry
September 24	Men are repulsed by me.	Ethan didn't fancy me and slept with someone else so all boys won't fancy me because I'm mad and I'll die alone. Is that different from the first one, Sarah??? I never know.
September 24	I'm going mad again. It's all going to come back.	I've started having bad thoughts again. I'm going to lose it again, lose everything I've worked for. And end up back where I was...
September 24	My new friends will find out about my illness.	They won't get it...

Every single session I was amazed how blasé Sarah was with my Worry Outcomes. She'd just collect them like they were art homework and, if we had time, we might go through one of two of the worries at the end.

"So," she said, scanning this week's. "Take it the date didn't go well then?"

"You could say that."

"So let's fill out the rest of the columns…" She grabbed her pen. "You were worried the date wouldn't go well… and…it didn't. So would you say the worry came true?"

"He slept with someone else, Sarah. On our first date. Would you call that 'the date going well'?"

She mumbled something.

"What was that?"

She didn't make eye contact as she repeated herself. "I did warn you…"

I crossed my arms. "You're going to lecture me on boys? You are an NHS Cognitive Behavioural Therapist. Tax payers are spending a fortune for you to help me get better so I can become a functioning member of society. Are we really going to go down the 'boys are no good' route? Can't I just charge that to my new friends?"

She always changed the subject when I got difficult.

Effortlessly, she looked down to the bottom worry. "Ah, yes, your new friends. You're worried they'll find out about…about what?"

I gestured to the therapy room. The beige walls, the box of crappy toys, the nondescript desk… "About this. Being here.

Why I have to come here."

That prompted a scribble in the pad. "And what's wrong with coming here?"

A lump trampolined up my throat, as it always did when the topic came up. My eyes prickled with Yet. More. Tears.

"You know…it's embarrassing. They won't get it."

"What won't they get?"

"Any of it."

I crossed my arms and made the "I'm-not-going-to-talk-about-this-one" face and she let me off this time.

"All right…we can discuss that one later. You've written here that you're scared you're 'going mad' again?" She tapped the sheet with the end of her pen. "What's that all about?"

I thought of the knitting-needle-in-my-guts moment before the date. The bad thoughts. Immediately my tummy began to swim in the extra adrenalin.

"Before the date…" I started. "I was…washing my hands…just the once…but then I wanted to wash them again…and again…" I remembered touching Ethan's hand and winced. "And again."

Unperturbed, Sarah asked, "What else was going on before the date? How were you behaving?"

"I dunno…I was a bit jumpy, I guess. Wound up. My brain did that thing where it stepping-stoned from place to place and my heart was beating all hard. But it was okay… but then I wanted to wash my hands. I've not felt like that in a while…" The throat lump soared up on the trampoline again, wedging itself just behind my tonsils. I tried to swallow. She gave me a moment to compose myself. They're never "there there", Cognitive Behavioural Therapists. They're more like having a strict teacher that you know cares about their students deep down somewhere. The most sympathy I've ever got out of Sarah was a silent passing of the tissue box.

"We've discussed this, Evie, remember? That these thoughts could come back now you're reducing your medicine?"

I nodded, looking at a scuff on the carpet. "I know. But I just sort of thought maybe that wouldn't happen and I would get lucky or something. I must get lucky at some point, right?"

"What's important to remember is that you've got all the techniques now, to deal with these thoughts when you have them."

"Can't I just never have bad thoughts? Can't they just go away for ever?"

And, for once, there was a bit of sympathy in her eyes. Because that wasn't going to happen. She knew it. I knew it. I just wished I didn't know it.

Nine

Mum was cooking dinner when I got back – wearing the apron of doom. "Doom" because her cooking evoked fear in even the strongest-stomached of people. She heard me slam the front door and peeked round from the kitchen, over the top of Rose, who was engrossed in some awful music video on TV where none of the girls seemed to be allowed to wear clothes.

"How was your appointment?" She nodded her head towards Rose and gave me a stern look.

Rose didn't even look away from the screen. "Yeah, Evie," she said. "How was therapy?"

"It's not therapy," Mum butted right in. "Is it, Evie? It's just a check-up?"

"Oh for God's sake, Mum," Rose said, turning round on the sofa. "I know she goes to therapy."

I leaned against the wall and held my breath.

"Well…yes… but we don't all have to call it that, do we?"

"Why not?"

Dad bowled into the living room then, brandishing a large glass of red wine. The smiley stain around his lips suggested it wasn't his first. Dad tended to self-medicate himself before Mum attempted cooking. "All right, Evie?" he asked. "How was your therapy session with Sarah?"

"It was…great," I said. As I always did. "Very…umm…" I looked at Rose who was pulling a face, and laughed. "Very therapyish." And Rose laughed too.

Mum's lips went all tight and she disappeared into the kitchen.

"Good, good, well I'm just going to read the news before we eat." And Dad tapped me slightly affectionately on the shoulder before withdrawing to his study. I slobbed down next to Rose.

"She'll tell me off later, you know," I said, looking at the half-naked stick insects on the screen and immediately regretting eating a Mars bar at lunch. Stupid music video.

"I know. How was it anyway?"

"I'm not allowed to talk to you about it, you're too impressionable." I ruffled her hair with a cushion and Rose "oi"ed and batted me off.

"Anxiety isn't chlamydia."

"You, missy, are far too young to know about chlamydia."

"I'm twelve. I have internet access. And boys at school who accuse each other of having it."

"I'm scared for your generation."

"Everyone's always scared for someone else's generation."

"You are far too wise, little one. Far too wise."

She was, Rose. Wise, I mean. I never really believed in the wise little sister thing – thought it was just a narrative device in indie films. Then Rose grew up and started spewing out wiseness like it was bogeys in cold season.

"I'd better go make peace with Mum." I stood up and stretched.

"Why? You've not done anything wrong."

"Ahh, dear Rose. But an easy life. Anything for an easy life. Plus you know how much she worries."

The smell of spag Bol, slightly burned, wafted up my nostrils as I entered the kitchen. "Mmm, smells great."

Mum frantically stirred a pan and didn't turn around. "Evie, do you mind boiling the kettle for the pasta? Oh God, the sauce is too thick. How do I make it less thick?"

I steered past her to grab the kettle. "Just add more water and keep the lid on."

She did as I said, but all clanging and banging with the pan. My stomach turned. Having Mum cook always made me stressed. She got in such a state about it, like every meal was as important as Christmas dinner. It was so much easier when we just heated up fish fingers.

"Dad's home from work early," I said.

"Yes…yes…" she muttered, now lifting up the lid to peer at the sauce with genuine fear. "So, how *was* your appointment then?"

"Okay. The usual." I flicked the kettle on to boil.

"Did Sarah give you any homework I should know about?"

I shrugged, even though she wasn't looking at me to see it.

"Just the usual. *Don't go mad again.*"

She whipped round and a bit of sauce flew up and splattered her apron. I didn't tell her.

"Don't talk like that when Rose is around."

"What? She's watching TV. And she knows what's going on!"

"Yes but still…she's very young, Evie. It's best not to… you know…make her more aware of it?"

"OCD isn't chlamydia," I said, copying Rose. "It's not like she's going to catch it off me." Though there was some research to suggest OCD could be triggered by learned behaviours. They asked about my mum a lot when I went through psychotherapy on the ward…

She bashed the pan down, splattering more sauce. "Evie, that's disgusting! I'm just saying, we don't have to rub it in Rose's face now, do we?"

I took a deep breath, knowing arguing only made her worse. Then she'd start crying, or blaming herself, or overcompensating for the guilt by following me around the house like a prison inspector, making sure I was following Sarah's homework to the T.

"Can I help any more with dinner?" I asked, offering it like a peace pipe.

Mum pushed some hair back from her face. I tried not

to think about the hair getting into the spag Bol. I failed.

"Do you *want* to help with dinner?"

"Yes, Mother. That is why I asked." Another deep breath.

"All right then, can you lay the table too?"

I dutifully got out all the relevant cutlery and only released my big sigh once I was in the dining room. My mum – oh the issues. I know saying you've got issues with your parents is about as groundbreaking as saying "Hey, I have to poo most days", or "You know what? Sometimes I get bored" but that doesn't make the issues any less true. Oh, I love her. Of course I love her. And she's a good person. I'd even go as far as to say she's a great mother – until it comes to my "mental health problems" – then she's... well...how exactly do I put this...?

... She's a nightmare.

Okay, well, both she and Dad are, but she's worse. Like, I'm sure it was very traumatic and all, to have me go just so very mad. But they're so...scared of me now, that I feel almost like a shared science project between them – the "Let's-never-let-this-happen-again" project. To be fair, in one of our family therapy sessions, the CBT lady at the unit told them they had to be "strict" with me, "for my own good". Because us OCDers can be quite the manipulative bunch, getting everyone all worried about us, convincing them our fears are totally valid, becoming puppeteers of everyone around us, emotionally guilt-tripping them into behaving how we want them to so we don't freak out and ruin the day. Mum and Dad were told not to "indulge" my worries. I just wish they hadn't taken to it so enthusiastically. I know it sounds stupid, but it feels like they're being mean. Like they're against me. And it doesn't help that Mum keeps twitching about Rose – worrying I'm going to break the only perfectly-functioning offspring she has left.

We ate dinner. It tasted of burnt. Yet we all pretended it was yummy because Mum kept asking, "Is it okay? Is the sauce too thick? It's too thick, isn't it?" while Dad drank a bit too much wine. Once I'd finished, I carried my plate to the sink then went up to my room. Washing up was something I hadn't quite conquered yet and Mum, thankfully, didn't force the issue if I helped cook or lay the table. I just couldn't stand washing up. The fact that all the bits of food come off the plate into the bowl and float about, waiting to attach themselves to the next thing you put in there to be washed? How did that clean anything? And don't get me started on the number of germs in every kitchen sink. Honestly, you'd rather lick a toilet if you knew.

I sat at my desk and mucked about on my *Casablanca* essay for a bit, but I couldn't focus. Sarah's appointment was bothering me.

Why couldn't I tell Amber and Lottie about my issues? What was I really scared of? Surely they wouldn't dump me? As long as I stayed normal enough not to piss them off…

Yet I just knew I couldn't. Mainly because they seemed to like who I was and I didn't want to tarnish the illusion.

And also, well, what if I told them and they reacted in one of the ways I hated?

What really pisses me off about people and mental health problems

I don't really "get" angry. If I'm going to be emotional, I do sad. Crying. Not swearing and yelling and punching walls.

Apart from about this.

Sarah once told me about the "dark ages" of public awareness, where people didn't really know much about mental health problems. And what they did know was mostly wrong. There was loads of MISINFORMATION and STIGMA and it was really terrible and everyone suffered in silence for ages, not knowing what was wrong, and not seeking help because they didn't understand what their brain was doing to them and why.

But then we decided we needed to CHANGE THE WAY WE THINK about mental illness. Huge awareness campaigns were set up. A few soaps gave their characters depression and whatnot, following each episode with a voiceover saying, "If you've been upset by anything seen on this programme, go to this website and yadda yadda yadda." Slowly, but surely, mental health eked its way into the public consciousness. People began to learn the names of conditions. People began to understand the symptoms. People began to say the oh-so-important phrase "it's not their fault". There was SYMPATHY and UNDERSTANDING. Even some politicians and celebs came out, as it were, and told national newspapers about their own suicide attempts or whatever.

We couldn't stop there, could we?

I can say, with some confidence, that it's gone too far the other way. Because now mental health disorders have gone "mainstream". And for all the good it's brought people like me who have been given therapy and stuff, there's a lot of bad it's brought too.

Because now people use the phrase OCD to describe minor personality quirks. "Oooh, I like my pens in a line, I'm so OCD."

NO YOU'RE FUCKING NOT.

"Oh my God, I was so nervous about that presentation, I literally had a panic attack."

NO YOU FUCKING DIDN'T.

"I'm so hormonal today. I just feel totally bipolar."

SHUT UP, YOU IGNORANT BUMFACE.

Told you I got angry.

These words – words like OCD and bipolar – are not words to use lightly. And yet now they're everywhere. There are TV programmes that actually pun on them. People smile and use them, proud of themselves for learning them, like they should get a sticker or something. Not realizing that if those words are said to you by a medical health professional, as a diagnosis of something you'll probably have for ever, they're words you don't appreciate being misused every single day by someone who likes to keep their house quite clean.

People actually die of bipolar, you know? They jump in front of trains and tip down bottles of paracetamol and leave letters behind to their devastated families because their bullying brains just won't let them be for five minutes and they can't bear to live with that any more.

People also die of cancer.

You don't hear people going around saying: "Oh my God, my headache is so, like, tumoury today."

Yet it's apparently okay to make light of the language of people's internal hell. And it makes me hate people because I really don't think they get it.

"Oh, you have OCD. That's the thing where you like to wash your hands a lot, right?"

It annoys me that I've got the most clichéd "version" of OCD. The stereotypical one. But it's not like I chose it. And, yes, I do like to wash my hands a lot. Or did. Well, I still want to, every second of the day, but I don't. But I also lost two stone because I refused to eat anything in case it contaminated me and I died. And I have a brain on a permanent loop of bad thoughts that I cannot escape so I'm technically imprisoned in my own mind. And I once didn't leave the house for eight weeks.

That is not just liking to wash your hands.

No, you don't have OCD too.

If you had OCD, you wouldn't tell people about it.

Because, quite simply, despite all this good work, some people Still. Don't. Get. It.

Mental illnesses grab you by the leg, screaming, and

chow you down whole. They make you selfish. They make you irrational. They make you self-absorbed. They make you needy. They make you cancel plans last minute. They make you not very fun to spend time with. They make you exhausting to be near.

And just because people know the right words now, doesn't mean they're any better at putting up with the behaviour. They smile and nod and say, "Oh, how awful, yes I watched a programme about that, you poor thing"… And then they get really pissed off at you when you have a panic attack at a party and need to leave early. When they actually have to demonstrate understanding, they bring out the old favourites like "come on, try harder" or "it's not that bad" or "but that isn't logical" – undoing all the original hand-patting and there-there-ing.

That's why I can't tell Lottie and Amber. That's why I have to hold it in.

Because if any more people don't get it… Don't get me… Then I don't think I'll be able to take it.

Ten

Lottie stared at herself dreamily in the mirror and straightened a section of her hair.

"When I was a little girl," she said, in a bedtime story voice. "I always dreamed of growing up and going to a metal gig held in a church hall."

Amber and I giggled.

"Church halls are totally rock 'n' roll now," I told her. "It's like, ironic or something…well, that's what Jane said."

"Or…in translation…Jane's boyfriend's band can't get a gig in a real venue?" Amber suggested.

I giggled again, wonking up my perfect eyeliner cat flick in the process. Sighing, I reached for a tissue. Joel's band was headlining a gig tonight. In a local church hall. It was all Jane had been talking about. And, dutifully, I'd agreed to go to it. With Amber and Lottie as backup, of course. Amber had provided her house as getting-ready headquarters.

"Let me get this straight," Lottie said, shoving another

clump of hair between her GHDs. "Jane asked you to go with her, and yet is now meeting you there?"

I nodded. "Yeah. She said Joel needed her to help set up or something."

"Do you remember when you were a little kid and your mum used to say, 'And if so-and-so asked you to jump off a cliff, would you'?"

"If Joel asked Jane to jump off a cliff she'd be vaporized already," Amber said, waiting patiently for her turn in front of the mirror.

"Yeah. Seagulls would be eating her brain," said Lottie.

I didn't join in the laughter this time.

"Come on," I said half-heartedly, "she's not *that* bad."

My friendship with Jane was the continuing subject of minor conflict in my blossoming relationship with the girls. Quite simply, they didn't like her. They found her devout worship of Joel scornful. Plus, as decent mates, they didn't appreciate how much she blew me out. Though I agreed with pretty much everything they said, I couldn't join in with the bitching. Despite everything, I still felt I owed her…

"What's going on with you and this bloke, Oli, then?" Amber asked, spritzing some vanilla perfume onto her wrists and rubbing them together. I'd told them about his cheekbones…and him of course.

I pulled a face. "Still the same. He's so shy. Which is good, because Ethan wasn't shy and look what happened there. But it's, like, impossible to get him to chat about much.

And he's not in college very much. He misses loads of lessons."

"Really? Why?"

"I dunno. Colds, I guess. It's that germy time of year, isn't it?" Like I didn't know…

After another half-hour of preening, we were ready. None of us knew what to wear to a gig in a church hall so we all chose a little bit of black. Lottie had ironed her hair into harsh vertical lines but softened it with a demure black top. Amber, trying to make herself smaller, wore a black strapless top and black jeans. And I was wearing a black tea dress covered in polka dots. If you squinted, we looked like a gaggle of witches.

We bumped into Amber's demonic little brother on the stairs on our way out.

He took one look at his sister.

"You look like a boy," he yelled at Amber, a cheeky yet evil grin on his face.

Amber bristled. "At least I'm not adopted."

His nasty face dropped and went red. "I'M NOT ADOPTED, YOU TAKE THAT BACK."

"You'll just have to talk it through with your mum and dad." Amber pushed past him, dragging us with her, and slammed the door shut.

She didn't talk for a bit when we got outside – all of us pretending it wasn't that cold, and it wasn't that awkward.

Lottie broke the ice by producing a bottle of cherry Lambrini from her bag.

"Seriously?" was all I had to say about that.

"Aww, come on, we're going to a gig. In a church. Cheap shite alcohol is needed."

She untwisted the top of the bottle – always the start of a classy night – and took a slug. "Mmm," she said. "Tastes like wrong." She handed the bottle over to me and I took a delicate sip.

"MORE," Lottie demanded. I sipped again. "MORE."

"Jeez – peer pressure much?" I handed the bottle to Amber, thinking now wasn't the time to tell them I wasn't supposed to drink much because I was on brain-altering medication.

Amber wrapped her coat round herself about ten times, as if trying to erase who she was. She grabbed the pink bottle and chugged half of it, before wiping her mouth and announcing, "My little brother is such a cock."

"Families suck," I said, thinking of my mum. "And he'll always wonder if he's adopted now. It was the ultimate comeback, Amber."

She put her arms around us and brought us in for a girly hug – always tricky with boobs in the way. "What would I do without you guys?"

I knew how she felt.

The church hall was rammed, like Midnight Mass, but with more eyeliner and pierced lips. We even had to queue to get in, which was pretty funny as everyone else there was about thirteen so we towered above them.

"So what's the name of their band again?" Lottie asked in the line.

"Erm…Bone Road? They used to be called Road of Pain, but it was patented by some guys in America."

Lottie's face creased up as she struggled not to take the piss. "And Bone Road means?"

"Er…" I tried to remember Jane's explanation. "Something to do with capitalism is killing us all slowly, and soon all that will be left of our souls is a road of bones?"

That seemed about right.

The crowd surged and Amber, who'd got split from us in the queue, rode the wave crest of people back over to us, like King Poseidon or something. I had at least twelve pairs of elbows jabbing into my body and kept trying to twist away from them. If a church hall event was this crowded on a Saturday night, there was something seriously wrong with this town. We definitely needed a Nando's.

"But souls don't have bones," she objected.

"Jane said that's the point."

"The point of what?"

"The name. It's existential, apparently."

Lottie sighed. "There better be a bar."

Using our fully-matured elbows, we barged to the front, paid our three quid, got our hands stamped and bought some drinks from the makeshift bar. A warm-up band was already playing in the hall on a dusty stage. A crowd stood below the stage, half-listening to the screaming…sorry…

I mean music. The hall ceiling was so high that – even with the huge turnout – it felt they were playing to nobody. A pink helium balloon stuck in the rafters, emblazoned with "Happy 5th Birthday" did nothing to improve the rock 'n' roll feel.

Jane appeared – wearing a mini dress so revealing I could see the frilly edge of her pants. "You guys! You made it! They've had to stop letting people in, isn't that amazing? Fire hazard."

Within seconds, Joel was at her side, snaking his hands around her waist.

"All right?" He nodded at us, then kissed the top of Jane's head.

"All right?" we chorused back.

"It's mad in here," I yelled at him over the music, in an attempt to make polite conversation. "You guys excited?"

Joel shrugged. "It's a good crowd."

"Yeah, isn't it?"

Joel didn't reply as he was kissing all the way up Jane's arm. Amber rolled her eyes at Lottie, just as a pair of hands covered my eyes.

"Guess who?" a gruff voice growled in my ear.

I pulled the hands off and whipped round. Guy was there, grinning at me.

"Guy?"

"All right, trouble? Brought your nympho boyfriend with you?" He held a beer and, from the way he was inanely grinning, it wasn't his first.

"No. He's in a recovery clinic," I deadpanned. More inane grinning. Guy banged bottles with Joel.

"You ready, man?" he asked.

Joel removed Jane from his person and they smooshed their knuckles in that boy way. "Mate, I was born ready."

Jane, not sure what to do with herself, wrapped her arms around her exposed chest and rocked on her feet.

"What song you guys starting with?" she asked.

"'Die Bitch Die'," they both said. With no trace of humour on their faces.

Amber spat out half the warm wine she'd been drinking from a plastic cup. They all turned but Lottie covered while Amber choked behind her.

"Wow. Powerful title," she said. "Is it based on any real-life experience?"

Joel didn't notice the sarcasm. "I wrote it about my ex-girlfriend after we broke up."

Lottie widened her eyes and nodded. "Wow, Jane better not piss you off."

"That's what happens if you fall in love with a musician."

Jane simpered and curled herself back round him, like Joel had said something romantic, rather than creepy and sinister.

I looked around the hall to try and stem my inner laughter. The lead singer of the support band was wailing now, grasping his microphone to his lips so close you could hear his spittle echo about the speakers. A few of their friends, obviously there for moral support, stood near the front, nodding their heads, punching the air. The usual stuff. My ears already buzzed from the noise, which wasn't helped when Guy leaned over and yelled right into my face.

"What are you looking at?"

I turned away from his mouth to protect my eardrum. "I know you're onstage, and so you see it from a different angle," I said. "But don't people 'appreciating' music look odd to you?"

"What do you mean?"

I gestured towards the group I'd been analysing. "Like that lot. Why can't everyone just stand round quietly and listen? Why does pushing each other, or chucking half-filled bottles of beer in the air, or flicking your long greasy hair over each other, or making that devil worship sign with your fingers…why does that mean you enjoy the music? If I was in a band, I would want everyone to listen quietly and concentrate."

Again Guy laughed. I always seemed to make him laugh. He pushed his dark hair off his face and shoved a sweaty arm around me.

"You don't really understand metal, do you?"

"I understand that Joel got dumped and needed to get over it by calling the girl a bitch in a song…which kinda makes him a dickhead. Is that metal?"

He laughed again. "Nah, that's just Joel. I didn't think we should open on that song anyway."

"So why are you agreeing, you're the lead singer, aren't you?"

"Because it's got a kickass bassline."

I nodded to the side. "Oh, okay. That makes me feel so much better about some poor girl being publicly called a bitch in a song, just so Joel can make his willy feel bigger."

"You're really something? You know that?"

I was? He didn't say it in the nicest way. There was a bit of awe in his voice…but a bit of disdain too. "Anyway, you going to watch me from the front?" He puffed his chest out.

"No. I don't like touching too many other people. I'll stand at the back, and if you see me standing real still, and concentrating, it means I'm enjoying 'Die Bitch Die' in my own special way."

I disentangled myself from his sweaty armpit and joined the girls on a last-minute dash to the toilets.

We squeezed back into the hall just as the support act finished. Personal space wasn't an option anywhere and my chest tightened as I tried not to think of how much germy breath was exhaling into the stuffy atmosphere. Jane found us and pulled us through the crowd.

"Guys," she yelled. "Over here. I've got us a spot."

"That's odd," Amber said. "Joel's gone and she's suddenly all friendly."

"Shhhhh."

We crammed into her tiny gap. Bits of my body touched all different parts of other people's bodies. I took a deep breath and concentrated on my ribcage going up and down to distract myself. Jane rambled on about the band's chances of a record deal to an unimpressed Amber and Lottie.

Everyone pushed to the front of the stage, causing tidal crowd surges to disturb the rest of us. An out-of-place looking bunch of lads stood to our left. They were smartly dressed and drinking the most expensive bottles of beer the pop-up bar provided. They stood out more than us. Not just 'cause they were our age, but they were blatantly posh too.

"I'm so excited," Jane stage-whispered to me. "I've never seen him play live before." She grabbed my hand and I studied her face. It was filled with utter adoration. Her eyes were distant and dewy, her cheeks pink, her smile was practically tattooed on. Despite everything, I gave myself a moment to feel happy for her. My best friend was in love – I had to be glad for that much at least.

BAD THOUGHT

Even if no one will ever love me...

The lights dimmed and Joel, Guy and the others shuffled onto the stage and the screams from the audience began. Guy kicked over the microphone stand whilst simultaneously grabbing the mike out of it. He clutched it right over his mouth and stood with his leg up on Joel's guitar amp.

"This," he said, in a voice much gruffer than usual, "…is 'Die Bitch Die'."

I was engulfed with noise. What can only be described as "a din" blurted through my eardrums, ripping holes through them, filling my brain with "oww". The crowd surged forward but I stood firm against the tide, grinding my heels into the dusty wooden floor.

"Let's go closer to the front," Jane yelled.

I crossed my arms and shook my head.

"Why not?"

"No. Just no."

She looked to Amber and Lottie for support, but they looked as bemused by the whole gig as me. Amber's arms were also crossed, a puzzled look on her pale face. Whereas Lottie was just sort of...sneering.

"You gotta die now...DIE...DIE. DIIIIIIEEEEEEEE!" Guy's voice took on a monstrous quality. Like the Gruffalo was hidden in his ribcage holding a spare mike. However, everyone else seemed to love it, and it spurred the mob on. We held our own against the crush and were somehow shoehorned to the back. That was perfectly fine with me.

Gangs of girls screamed whenever Guy opened his mouth. He did look kind of sexy up there, I guess. What with the sweat, and the cockiness, and the attention. He caught my eye briefly and winked and my knees went a bit funny. But then he launched into their next song – the opening line of which went: "I hate you so much for breathing. I wish I could make you stop."

And I promptly lost interest again, staring instead at the "JESUS LOVES YOU" banner hanging limply above the stage.

As they catapulted into their next song – a really REALLY angry one – the audience rose to a new level of mass insanity.

We were pushed and jostled from all directions and I began to really not enjoy myself. The random posh blokes kept bumping into us, and then falsely apologizing. Amber gave them her very best evil eye but they didn't seem to care. Then one of them pushed the other, and he pushed them back, and before we knew it...

...*Whoosh*...

A bottle of beer whistled through the air and emptied itself all over Lottie's everything.

For a moment, she just stood there. Dripping. Her hair mangled. Her make-up smudged. Her clothes drenched.

"Oh my God," one of the boys said, moving forward from the group. He was tall and very clean-looking and his voice was the poshest thing I've ever heard. "I'm so sorry. Are you okay?"

Lottie glared at him. "Was this your fault?"

"Yes. I'm dreadfully sorry. The boys, well, we got carried away."

He leaned in so Lottie could hear better but she pushed him away.

"Get off. I'm SOAKED."

"I'm so sorry."

"Good. You should be."

"Hang on, Lottie, is it?"

"How do you know my name?" she demanded.

Her face was so full of venom even I was scared. Posh Boy backed off a bit.

"Didn't you used to go to my school?"

She nodded slowly.

"I'm in the year above you, I think. I remember seeing you around but I've not for a while, did you leave?"

Lottie was still glaring at him, but I could see her thawing a bit.

"I'm sorry," he continued, still waving his hands, all posh. "Let me make it up to you… Can I get you a drink?"

"You know what? I'm doing okay on the moistness front."

"Some peanuts then?"

Lottie gave him a look.

"Crisps?"

She looked to the band and back again. Joel was in the middle of a five-minute guitar solo whilst Guy lay on his side, pushing himself round in a circle using his legs. Lottie swept her wet hair off her face. "Yes. Multiple bags of crisps might do it."

Posh Boy steered her through the crowd towards the bar whilst Amber and I looked at each other and shrugged. Jane, oblivious to all the drama, screamed, "I LOVE YOU, BABY!" through her hands. Posh Boy's mates didn't bother trying to make small talk and were swallowed by the crowd. The guitar solo made way for a five-minute drum solo…

I was getting bored. This was a problem. Boredom leads to worrying.

The clashing of the cymbals twitched my brain. The banging of the drum sped my heart. I imagined everyone's breath coming out into this airless hall. The spent carbon monoxide, the droplets of germs floating through the air after people coughed. My heart started giving the drummer a run for his money.

Most bugs aren't airborne. Most bugs aren't airborne.

But most are carried by touch. And it felt like half a million people had touched me in the last half-hour. I pictured the bacteria multiplying on my exposed arms, spreading down to my wrist and up my palms and fingers.

My throat went tight.

Trying my best to hide my inner wobble, I leaned over to Amber's ear and yelled, "Can we take a break?"

She smiled. "I thought you'd never ask."

Leaving Jane in a love-struck trance, we elbowed and jostled our way out. My heart thudded the whole time and it seemed to take ages. But eventually we pushed through the double doors into the lobby and were engulfed in calm. There was space. And oxygen. And clean air streaming in from the entrance. I shivered with relief and delight.

"Where's Lottie then?" Amber asked, her voice a bit too loud, not yet adjusted to the lack of screaming music.

I looked round for her. "I dunno. Probably killing that guy somewhere. Did you see how wet she got?"

"I'm just jealous she had a reason to leave sooner."

"Music not to your taste?"

Amber winced, making her freckles blodge together on her nose into one brown lump. "No. Not at all. Do you ever worry you're being a teenager wrong?"

I thought of the last three years. "I KNOW I'm being one wrong."

"I mean, what's wrong with finding songs glorifying domestic violence offensive? What's wrong with finding live music too loud? What's wrong with a nice cup of tea and a chat?"

I giggled. "You sound like my mum."

"You see! I'm doing it wrong. But sometimes, like tonight for example, I really don't bloody care."

We made our way to the bar slowly, taking our time so we could delay going back in. There wasn't a queue – just some underage drunk girl half-passed out on a giant cushion in the corner, being forced to drink water by the staff.

"I can't see Lottie," I said. "Isn't that guy buying her crisps?"

"Maybe she's drying herself under the hairdryers in the bathroom?"

We went back to the toilet. She wasn't there.

"Outside?" Amber suggested.

The air was even cooler and crisper outside. A hint of autumn winged around me, making goosebumps ripple up my arm.

"Lottie?" I called softly.

Getting a bit nervous, I called again. No answer. What if the posh drink-chucker was actually a psycho and the drink-chucking was an elaborate ploy to get Lottie away from her friends? What if he was killing her right now?

We crunched in the gravel round the car park, towards the church, and my worries were stopped in their tracks.

Lottie's body was pressed up against the wall. By Posh

Boy's body. Lottie's face was pressed into Posh Boy's face. Lottie's hands were on Posh Boy's arse. An unopened bag of crisps lay at their feet.

I looked at Amber, who'd spotted them at exactly the same time.

"Looks like she's forgiven him," Amber whispered.

"Looks like it."

We turned away and crunched back alongside the church, which was all lit up in eerie beauty by floodlights.

"Evie?"

"Yes?"

"Would you think I was being a teenager wrong if I said: 'Can we go home now, please?'"

"No," I said. "I'd think you were a legend."

So we sent a message to Jane and an otherwise-engaged Lottie to let them know we were leaving.

RECOVERY DIARY

Date: 16th October

Medication: 10mg Fluoxetine   *Duh, duh, DUHHHHHHH!*

Thoughts/Feelings: I dunno, the usual?

Homework:
- Start to "own" your bad thoughts, using the Worry Tree exercise we talked about
- Be extra vigilant about keeping Worry Outcome surveys now your dosage has been lowered again
- Tell me if you experience any severe anxiety symptoms

Eleven

Lottie was loved up. Since the band night she'd had a heady glow about her, and her phone kept going off. She disappeared some lunchtimes to meet Posh Boy (Tim) in the graveyard and would come back with leaves stuck in her hair. In that time, Ethan had stopped giving me Labrador eyes in sociology and now chatted everyone else up. I'd begun looking forward to film studies instead. Brian's lack of professionalism made it easier to get to know Oli better – we now traded film recommendations like children trading football cards. And I'd dropped another 10mg on my medication. I was now down to only half a pill. HALF! I used to take three a day, plus benzos, a tranquillizer-type drug that made me sleepy all day.

"You know," Amber said to Lottie, as we prepared to pay for another breakfast at the dodgy cafe. "You are allowed to talk about Tim. We're your friends. We're happy for you."

Were we? I'd privately been more sad for myself that yet

another friend had procured a boyfriend whilst I remained unlovable.

"Yes, tell us," I said. Jealousy would get me nowhere.

Lottie blushed and ducked behind her dark hair.

"God," Amber said, with a bit of disgust in her voice. "You're proper loved-up, aren't you?"

Lottie went redder and moved the dribbling sauce bottles about on the sticky tablecloth.

She mumbled something.

"What?" we both asked.

Lottie emerged from her hair. "I said, I feel bad talking about it."

"What? Why?" Amber asked. "Evie and I can handle your gushing, can't we, Evie?"

I nodded and put my hand on Lottie's to stop her playing obsessively with the sauce. "Of course we can."

"But I don't want to be one of those girls…" Lottie put her head on the table briefly before raising it again. "You know, like Jane."

Jane had got much worse since the gig. It was like she'd morphed into a mini version of Courtney Love overnight – backcombing her dyed hair, talking loudly in the canteen about wanting to get her nipple pierced. I'd even talked her out of getting matching tattoos with Joel. Tribal ones.

"Lottie, you are nothing like Jane," I reassured her. "For one, you've not blown me off three times in the last week."

"I know…I know…but I'm scared that if I talk about Tim with you guys then I'll fail the Bechdel test."

"The what?" I asked, whilst Amber nodded wisely. "Nah, you won't. Don't be silly."

I was confused. "What's the Bechdel test?" Was this something else I'd missed from school? Was it a test I was supposed to be revising for?

Lottie saw the panic in my eyes. "Calm down, Evie. It's not an actual academic test." She patted my hand. "It's a feminism thing."

"Feminism? There's a test for that?"

Would I pass? I quickly scanned my thoughts and feelings to check them for feminismness. The pay gap makes me cross, and yet I wear make-up. I feel sick whenever I look at the front cover of *PHWOAR* magazine, and yet I also look at the model's boobs and feel bad mine don't look like that. I hate that Jane ditched me for a boyfriend and that Joel is all she ever talks about, and yet, I would really quite like a boyfriend myself...

... My brain hurt.

Oblivious to my inner conflict, Amber explained it to me.

"Have you really not heard of it? I thought you would've done it in film studies. It's like a feminism litmus test for films and books and stuff. Basically, in the eighties, this super cool illustrator who I LOVE called Alison Bechdel realized that all female characters do in fiction stuff like films and books, is talk about men. So she made this simple Bechdel test. And, to pass it, a film's got to have at least two women in it—"

Lottie butted in. "And they've got to have at least one conversation about something other than men. Just one conversation, that's it. And it's passed."

"Ooooooh, okay." I thought through all the hundreds, possibly thousands, of films I'd watched, thinking it would be easy. Two minutes later I had nothing. Nothing but a dawning realization of how broken the world was. "Hang on…umm…surely…surely there's got to be some?" I said to them, feeling like my whole love of cinema had just dissolved around me, seeping into the plastic chair I was sitting on.

Lottie shook her head. "There are some films, but barely any; it'll take you ages to work them out. Like none of the Lord of the Rings films pass, and none of the original Star Wars. Even the last Harry Potter film doesn't have two girls having a conversation in it. It's screwed up, isn't it? Like, women aren't worth a storyline unless they're discussing men and what men do." She wrapped her arms round both of us, dragging our heads towards the table and dangerously close to our remaining breakfast. "Still so far to go, ladies, still so far to go."

I mulled it over some more whilst removing myself from her embrace. I didn't like my face being so close to a dirty plate.

"Okay, I get it. But we've just spent half an hour discussing the best way to eat eggs. And before that, we argued about which song from a musical best sums up our lives. And, just yesterday, you were explaining *The Female Eunuch* to me…

so, surely we've earned the right to discuss your new boyfriend?"

"Ahh, yes," said Lottie, patting my head, like I was the dunce student. Which I was, compared to her, who basically snorted academia in her spare time. "But if we were in a movie, then they wouldn't show any of that. They would just cut straight to this breakfast, to the moment you guys ask me about Tim."

Whilst I sat there with my brain still throbbing, Amber reasoned with her.

"Come on, Lottie. We're your friends, we care about you. We're interested in Tim because he's something in your life, not just because he's a guy. I promise that you can tell us how deliriously happy you are without pooing on the sisterhood."

"Eww."

"So...is it love?"

Lottie visibly melted before us, her face softened around the edges like she was in a dream sequence. "He's...he's..." She went quiet and started playing with the bottles again. "He's really thick..."

"Umm, Lottie?" I said. "That's not very loved-up sounding."

"But he's totally cute with it," she protested. "And I'm not being a bitch – he told me himself he's a bit thick. Everyone at my old school calls him 'Tim Nice But Dim' from that old TV show or whatever...but he is very sweet and I'm smart enough for both of us anyway. And...oh God, this is going to sound REALLY bad but he's a proper man's man, you know? Like HURR, or something. He's all muscly and protective and macho and sporty and everything I am technically really against, but actually, am annoyingly attracted to."

"I hate that," Amber said, nodding. "I know I'm supposed to fancy nice guys who only watch Ethical Porn or whatever, and will never treat you badly blah blah blah…but then… well, I fell for that football standerupper twat, didn't I? Because he made my loins go fluttery."

Lottie and I sniggered at the use of the word "loins". I turned to her.

"You seem really happy, it's nice. I can't wait to meet him properly."

She pulled a face. "I guess. But it's early days, isn't it? And I'd much rather spend this wonderful breakfast time chatting to you guys about stuff other than my boyfriend." A grumpy waitress came over and took our empty plates. "Anyway, what's going on with Joel and Guy's band then?"

"You're talking about men again," I pointed out, as I rummaged for a tip in the depths of my purse.

"Damn it. This Bechdel test is harder than you think."

Twelve

The following lunchtime, I found myself alone.

Jane and I were supposed to be going for a coffee, but she'd once again cancelled. And Lottie and Amber both had an art coursework deadline and had holed themselves up in the studio. I went to the cafeteria and plonked some food on my tray, wondering how embarrassing it would be to eat it by myself. Very, I reckoned. But I was hungry.

I paid and stood with my tray, scanning the place for somewhere to sit. There were clumps of people everywhere, almost all the tables were busy and would therefore involve me perching at the end like a huuuuge loser.

Panic panic panic panic…

And then I saw Oli sitting in the corner. He had a whole table to himself, with his knees resting up on it. His headphones were plugged into a small screen balancing on his lap. I grinned – something about him just made me feel all…cute. I walked over.

He looked up when I put my tray down.

"Hey," I said. "I'm friendless today. Can I sit here?"

His head jerked backwards, making his headphones fall to his chest. "Bollocks," he said, and went to grab them, his screen sliding off his lap. "Ahhh, nuts." I smiled as he collected up his things, muttering swear words under his breath. Finally he gestured to a chair near him. "Of course. That would be...erm...great. Sit down. Sit, sit."

Seriously, the guy could be awarded a medal in Shyness.

I sat and watched him watch me with his nervy jumpy eyes of basily goodness.

"You've got a nice spacey table here," I said to him.

He looked round at it, almost in surprise. "I guess... Nobody ever sits in the corner. Have you noticed that?"

"Not until now." I took a bite of my sandwich, chewed for a bit, then pointed to his technology. "What you watching over here, all by yourself, anyway?"

Oli turned the screen round and I saw Jack Nicholson frozen in his iconic white hospital costume. "*One Flew Over The Cuckoo's Nest*," he said, though he didn't need to. I'd watched it countless times, comparing it to my time spent sectioned. Thankfully, things had changed since then.

"Classic," I said, impressed.

"You wanna watch some with me?" he stuttered.

I put my sandwich down. "Sure."

I budged over to the seat next to him and he handed me one of his earphones. The intimacy of it made me all quivery. There was something about sharing headphones, creating your own auditory world together that others couldn't hear, that I thought was so romantic. It helped that we had to practically rest our heads on one another, restricted by the short cord between each headphone. I tried to concentrate on the film, but Oli's close proximity was distracting. He was so twitchy! His leg jumped up and down, making the screen rock. He also smelled amazing which didn't help my attention span. We sat like that for ten minutes or so, watching Jack Nicholson's amazing performance, until my tummy grumbled and I flicked the earbud out so I could concentrate fully on my sandwich.

Oli paused it. "You like the film then?" he asked.

I took a sip from my Coke bottle. "Yeah, I do… I like all that 'what is madness?' stuff."

I didn't tell him why, obviously.

But he gave me a huge cheekboney smile, like he totally got it. "Me too, me too. There aren't enough films about it. Being mad, I mean."

I returned his smile. "There so aren't. And the movies only focus on the really 'exciting' mental illnesses, like schizophrenia or personality disorders where the main character needs to have sex a lot."

"Where are the boring ones about depressed people who just don't get out of bed?"

"Exactly! They should make a film about depression where it's just one person, lying in bed, staring at the ceiling for an hour. Then it'd be authentic."

"Yeah…" Then he went quiet.

I took a bite of my sandwich, struggling to digest as being around him made me feel all warm and cottonwoolly. Though his nervousness did make me more nervous. I wondered if he liked me. He certainly looked at me a lot during lessons. He wasn't looking at me now, rather scrunching his hands up in a ball, squeezing his fingers one by one. I was about to try and break the silence but he spoke.

"Do you ever wonder," he asked, "how we decide what's mad and what isn't? There's so much crazy stuff in the world – everything's a mess most of the time – but then people who can't handle it are called mental and have films made about them... But what if they're just reacting to the weirdness of the universe? Isn't it more weird to just think everything's okay, when it clearly isn't?"

I drummed up the courage to move my chair closer to his, to show I agreed with what he'd said. He still wouldn't look at me.

"You know..." I said. "I think they're re-releasing this at the cinema soon, so young people like us can see it on the big screen."

In other words: *Ask me out please, ask me out please, ask me out please.*

I watched his face as he dropped his earphones again, and ducked down to pick them up. Then he looked at me. Something passed, something good.

"I...I..." he said, and I urged him on with my eyes.

Please ask me out. I really like you.

"I…I…" And when his face dropped I knew he wouldn't.

"I… It's a pity we've just watched it then, isn't it?" he said.

"Yeah," I said, still smiling. "It is."

Thirteen

My phone beeped from under my body. I turned over on the grass and looked at the screen.

"Who is it?" Jane asked, from behind a pair of sunglasses.

I grinned. "Oli."

"Has he asked you out yet?" Joel asked, from under Jane. She was lying on top of him – her head on his head, like they were a sandwich.

"Umm… No, not yet."

Autumn had slid back into summer for one last gasp before winter snatched all sunshine away for six months. It was mild and bright and lovely. Half of college sprawled out over the grounds, huddled in groups of not-so-new-any-more friends. I was sunbathing with Jane, Joel, Guy, Lottie and Amber. Although Amber was attempting to use her sketchbook to shield her face from the rays.

"I'm so jealous of your skin, Lottie. You tan so easily,

whereas I'm going to have to spend my entire ginger life plastered in factor 30."

Lottie arched an eyebrow. "Yes, but think of all the wrinkles you won't have when you're older?"

"Annnnnd, I'm going to stop complaining now."

Lottie smiled. "Never stop complaining, Amber. It is why I love you so very dearly."

Guy snorted. "Who is this guy any way?" he asked, an unlit fag dangling from his lips.

Lottie tilted her head up from the cushion she'd made out of her jumper and answered for me. "He's this super sweet guy from her film class. But he's so shy it's ridiculous."

"He's not shy," I said, defending him. "He's just…umm… shy."

Guy lit his cigarette, took a deep drag then exhaled deliberately into my face. I coughed and glared at him.

"He sounds like a pussy."

"He's not a pussy!"

"Oh yeah?" he said, tauntingly. Then, with no notice, he grabbed my phone out of my hand.

"Hey," I said, clambering to get it back but he fended me off with his cigarette.

"Hey, what animals do you like? I've always wanted a monkey," he read off the screen. He made a look of utter disgust and chucked my phone back at me. "See, told you. Puss. Ay."

I collected my phone off the grass and dusted the mud off it. "He's just making conversation. I like monkeys too."

"Whoop whoop, why don't you just marry the guy?"

Amber sat up and joined in. "He has a point," she said. "Did he honestly just message you about animals?"

"Just this one time."

"And what else does he message you about?" Lottie asked. I had everyone's attention and I didn't like it. I felt defensive of Oli, and his cheekbones, and our future children's cheekbones.

"Umm. Films sometimes."

"Anything else?"

"Er. What we did at the weekend?"

Guy finished his fag and stubbed it out in the grass. "And yet he's never said, 'Why don't we do something this weekend?'"

I didn't reply, just looked at his fag butt. Wanting so badly to pick it up, carry it over to the bin and then wash my hands twice. Maybe three times.

My phone beeped again. I looked at the screen and broke into a huge grin. "HE'S ASKED ME OUT," I yelled, waving the phone at all of them.

Lottie and Amber shrieked and ran over to read the message. Lottie read it aloud.

"'Fancy cinema this weekend?' Aww – finally! I'd about given up hope."

I beamed at everyone, then quickly stuck my tongue out at Guy. A date! With a boy! To the cinema! Like people do!

BAD THOUGHT

You'll have to sit on a cinema seat that's already been sat on by hundreds of thousands of dirty people.

BAD THOUGHT

He'll want to buy you popcorn. How can you explain that you won't be able to eat the popcorn?

BAD THOUGHT

What if he realizes within minutes that you're a massive weirdo freak and runs out leaving you alone to fester in the germs?

"So...?" Lottie said, examining my suddenly pale face. "Are you going to message him back?"

"Shouldn't I wait a while?"

"Yes," Guy said.

"No," Amber butted in, ignoring Guy. "Message him back. He's shy, he'll be dying by now."

I flicked through our plans for this weekend. "Isn't Anna having another party on Saturday? Should I invite him to that?"

Amber thought about it and shook her head, sunrays bouncing off her hair. "Hmm. No... See how the cinema goes and then, if you still madly fancy him, you can tell him about the party and invite him along."

"Perfect," Lottie joined in. "And then if the date is terrible, you can tell us all about it at the party."

I couldn't hold in my smile as I shot back a message.

Sure, cinema sounds great. Sat during the day? X

"Argh," I squealed. "I've sent it. I have a date."

Lottie and Amber pulled me in for a bear hug and, surprising us all, Jane unearthed herself from Joel's grasp and joined in on the hugging action.

"I'm so excited for you," she squeaked.

Guy and Joel rolled their eyes at each other in an *erghgirls* way and I felt a bit silly. I broke apart the hug. "Come on, girls, calm down. Bechdel test, remember?"

Jane scrunched her eyebrows in confusion. "Bechdel what?"

"Oh, don't worry, Jane. It's not a test for you," Amber said.

"Huh?" she asked as Lottie and Amber burst out laughing. Bitchily. My stomach twisted for Jane. I would always defend her...when it wasn't me complaining about her or calling her names in my head. My phone beeped with Oli's reply, breaking the awkwardness.

Sounds good. See you Saturday.

And we did more squealing.

The college bell rang in the distance and the others groaned and picked up their bags and litter. I lay back in the grass, a mixture of euphoric and petrified about the impending weekend.

Lottie stood over me, blocking out the sun. "You not got class?"

"Nope. Free period."

"Lucky bugger. You staying around here?"

I yawned and stretched. "Nope, don't think so. I think I'm just going to walk home."

"Not fair. Anyways, come on, love birds," she said to Jane and Joel. "We're late for philosophy. See yas."

I waved them all away. All of them apart from Guy who, to my surprise, still sat next to me on the grass.

"You not got class either?" I asked him.

He shook his head. "You say you're walking? Whereabouts do you live?"

"Ashford Road."

He stood up, shaking grass from his band T-shirt. "That's right near me. I'll walk with you." It was a statement, rather than a question. He held out his hand to pull me up off the ground. I took it gingerly.

"Okay, I guess," I said, wondering what the hell we were going to talk about for the thirty minute walk.

For the first ten minutes, apparently absolutely nothing...

We veered along the pavements in a hazy sunshiny stupor. The awkward silence hung heavily over us like a cloud of conversational napalm. It only dispersed when Guy brazenly lit up a cheeky spliff and I sighed dramatically.

"What is it?" he asked, blowing out the smoke slowly.

"Don't you ever wanna, like, live in reality?"

He looked bewildered for a sec, before looking at the small rolled-up flaming paper in his hand.

"This is reality. It's natural!"

"It's a mind-altering substance."

"It's a plant."

I sighed again. "Whatever."

The fragrant smell floated past me on the wind and I tried not to cough. Silence descended once more and I wondered why he'd walked with me. Especially as he seemed a bit pissed off. He spoke first.

"So, you looking forward to this date then?"

I gave him a sideways look. "I guess."

He took a drag and giggled a bit under his breath. "And this one's not a nympho?"

I glared at him. "Not that I know of... No."

"He's just a pussy."

My glare intensified. "I object to that word."

"What word? Pussy?"

"Yes. It's sexist. And vulgar. What's having a vagina got to do with not having any courage? You're a misogynist."

"I'm an a-what-a-nist?"

"If you don't know what it means, then you definitely are one."

He giggled again in response. "You're funny."

"I'm not trying to be funny. I'm trying to be angry."

"That's what makes it so funny."

"It's only funny to you 'cause you're high. Alone. On a Thursday."

He laughed again, his eyes already red. "I'm not alone, I'm with you."

"That's not what I'm telling the police if they pull over and arrest you."

His laughter got more and more amplified. I let him giggle himself out and watched him finish his joint and flick it into a bush. Younger girls had started crushing majorly on Guy since the big church gig. I'd heard some girls from the local secondary school, my old school, discuss his fitness in the fish and chip shop, and some of them followed him and Joel around in town. I examined him now. The sun lit his face from behind, giving him his own little golden lining, detailing his unruly mop of hair. He was attractive, I *guessed*.

He muttered something under his breath.

"What was that?" I asked.

"I said, I'm not a misogynist."

"I'd believe you more if you weren't laughing as you said it."

He ignored me. "Anyway, the context of the word 'pussy' isn't in relation to a vagina. It's pussy as in 'pussycat'. Put that" – he flicked out his hand towards my face – "in your pipe and smoke it."

I gave a wry grin in defeat. He was right. Pussy came from pussycat. "I can't smoke it. You've smoked it all."

And I lost him again in splutterings of laughter.

The sun beat down on us. The leaves were glowing golden, our jackets hung off our arms. As we neared my house, we conducted an epic game of "Would You Rather?" which had us both tearing up with hysterics.

"Okay, okay, okay," Guy said, hands flailing dramatically, barely able to talk. "If you HAD to…would you rather have two bollocks the size of watermelons, or twenty the size of grapes?"

I snorted. "That's disgusting. I don't even know what it's like to have balls in the first place."

"Oh, it's great. Trust me."

I suddenly found myself thinking of Guy's balls, and went a bit red. "Umm…two the size of melons, I guess."

He pointed at me. "Why?"

I shrugged. "I dunno. They'd be easier to tuck into my boxers?"

It took a while for him to calm down. It was hard to tell with Guy how much of his laughter was my natural wit, and how much was his cannabis habit.

When he calmed down, I said, "Right, I've got one."

He raised both eyebrows, his dark eyes almost glowing

hazel in the sun. "Okay. Hit me."

"Would you rather have…incurable full body acne…" I paused for comic effect.

"Or…?" he prompted.

"Or, a full body Celine Dion tattoo. Her face was your face. Her arms were your arms. Her legs were your legs."

He dissolved into hysteria again, sitting down on the wall of someone's front garden and whacking his thigh like an old man.

"No…neither."

"You HAVE to choose," I insisted. "I told you about my melon balls."

More hysteria. "Okay, okay, okay… The acne. Oh God, it would have to be the acne."

I sat next to him and laughed too. For one moment, he rested his head on my shoulder. Then his head was gone. We stopped laughing abruptly and earlier's convo napalm descended again instantly.

"I'm almost home," I said. For no real reason.

I felt Guy turn to me on the wall and instinctively turned towards him too. The tips of our knees touched and it made my heart do a…thing. A thing I didn't quite understand. My face tingled with the dappling of oncoming sunburn.

"So you coming to this party on Saturday then?" Guy asked, all serious.

"Yeah. I guess."

"And you're bringing this guy?"

"Oli."

"Yeah."

"Well, maybe, I guess. We'll see."

"The pussy…cat?"

I shot him a look. "Why do you care?"

He leaned back off the wall, balancing his weight in mid-air, and put his hands behind his head.

"I don't care. I don't care about anything." He said it with pride.

"Right, well, see you Saturday."

"See you then."

Fourteen

It was date time. Time for the date. Another actual date! My heart was going boom badda boom badda boom badda BOOM.

"Are you okay?" Rose asked, poking her head around my bedroom door halfway through my wardrobe-meltdown. She was holding a toothbrush and pyjamas, packing for a sleepover she was going to that night.

"No," I told her. "I am supposed to be going on a date but all my clothes hate me."

Rose looked at the fashion concoction I'd draped myself in. "You're not wearing that, are you?" And she made a little face.

"I'm not now you've made that face."

"Flared jeans *and* a dress? Umm…why?"

"BECAUSE I WANT TO WEAR THE DRESS BECAUSE IT'S PRETTY BUT WE LIVE IN STUPID ENGLAND AND IT'S TOO COLD OUTSIDE."

Panic took over – stupid overwhelming panic, over a stupid underwhelming wardrobe crisis. My chest tightened and I flopped back onto the bed, focusing on my raggedy breathing.

Rose instantly rocked into calm-down mode. "Shh, shh," she said, joining me on the bed and stroking my hair. "It's okay. We'll sort your outfit out."

Tears bulged up in my ducts at her kindness. "You're not supposed to see me like this. Mum will go nuts."

"I don't care what Mum thinks."

"I just…I…I know it's just a date. But the other one went so badly…and…and…"

BAD THOUGHT

I'm corrupting my little sister and she'll go mad and it will be all my fault.

BAD THOUGHT

This date is going to go awfully and I'm going to get sick from the filthy cinema and die alone.

"Shh, Evie, it's okay. Everyone gets nervous before dates. You're not going mad, you get that, right? This is normal nerves."

I sniffed. "Is it normal to put jeans on under a dress?"

Rose giggled. "No, that bit's just you."

We laughed together quietly, though not quietly enough for Mum not to hear. She barrelled into my room, cradling a bundle of fresh laundry.

"What's going on in here?" she asked, all suspicious, like Poirot. She spotted my blotchy face and I saw her freak-out face forming. "Evie, have you been crying?"

Mum's eyes flicked from Rose's face back to mine again, like she was analysing Rose for crazy-by-osmosis.

Rose – bless her – kept a poker face. "I'm just helping Evie pick out what to wear."

"Wear where? Where are you going?"

"Umm...to the cinema." I wasn't going to tell Mum about my date. She'd have opinions. Negative opinions.

She still looked surprised though. "The cinema? Evie, that's huge. Are you sure you're ready? I mean, you've not mentioned it... Have you talked it through with Sarah? I mean, the cinema! That's great...but, are you ready for that?" She looked at Rose and then realized she'd hinted at the crazy. "I mean...well, not that it's a big deal..."

"Muuuuuum," I said. "You're not helping!"

"Oh... Okay, but I do wish you'd tell me these things, Evie."

"Mum," I sighed again. Rose and I stared pointedly at her until she took the hint and left.

"Now," said Rose, clapping her hands together. "Take off the dress and show me what lacy tops you have."

I did as she said. "I love you, Rose."

"Yes...yes... Oh my God, Evie, why are you wearing cowboy boots?"

Fifteen

We were meeting at the cinema. Like dates do. My date. And I. For our date. DATE. Rose had calmed me down enough to put some make-up on and shoved me out the door with the strict command of "tell me everything".

Oli'd actually asserted himself when it came to deciding what to watch. I'd had my eye on this new indie comedy called *And Rainbows* but he'd messaged quite firmly saying he'd booked us tickets for the new Tarantino.

BAD THOUGHT

He won't have booked an aisle seat. How am
I supposed to run away if it all gets too much if
I don't have an aisle seat?

I'd been given a new method for dealing with the

resurrection of bad thoughts – courtesy of Sarah. I was supposed to start owning them, rather than the other way round. This involved a process she'd scribbled down for me, with strict instructions to practise.

HOW TO OWN YOUR BAD THOUGHTS

1) PUT THEM THROUGH THE WORRY TREE.

What the heck is a worry tree? Well…it's a bit like those flow chart tests you get in women's magazines that tell you what sort of orgasm you're supposed to be having or whatever. However there are only two branches to the tree.

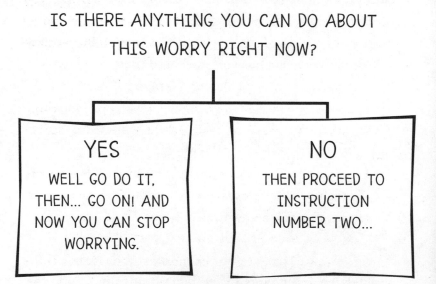

IS THERE ANYTHING YOU CAN DO ABOUT
THIS WORRY RIGHT NOW?

YES
WELL GO DO IT,
THEN… GO ON! AND
NOW YOU CAN STOP
WORRYING.

NO
THEN PROCEED TO
INSTRUCTION
NUMBER TWO…

2) ACKNOWLEDGE THAT YOU'VE HAD A BAD THOUGHT.

Sorta like "Oh, hello there, you fine young man of a bad thought, I can see you, you know."

3) BUT DO NOT "INDULGE" THE BAD THOUGHT.

Example of indulging a
BAD THOUGHT

Bad thought: Hey, you, do you think that maybe you're always going to be mad? That maybe, Evie, darling, you should just give up on this whole "recovery" thing and go back to the unit and get sectioned for ever and never have a boyfriend because you're so fucking crazy?

Evie: Oh my, you're right. I am crazy. How long do you think I have left before everyone realizes and gives up on me?

Bad thought: Hmmm, maybe a year? Then you're screwed.

Evie: A year's quite a long time.

Bad thought: You're right. Six months. Who do you think will be the most disappointed?

Evie: Mum probably…but then Rose…

Bad thought: Yeah, Rose. Man, you're really going to screw her up, aren't you?

Evie: *nods sadly* I know.

* Continue until Evie lies sobbing on her bed for no visible reason.*

What next? Well, after you've successfully acknowledged but not indulged the bad thought, you…

4) RETURN YOUR MIND TO THE PRESENT MOMENT.

Note: Modern psychology is currently OBSESSED with The Present Moment, like it's the elixir of life or something. You do this by either focusing on your breathing, or listening to all the noises around you and concentrating really hard on them. Sort of like meditation, like the Buddha did.

5) WHEN YOU FIND YOUR MIND DRIFTING…

Which it inevitably will, because the present moment is so utterly boring compared to freaking out and fretting obsessively, well…

RETURN TO STEP TWO.

Over and over.

There you go, thoughts owned.

That's about five hundred quid's worth of therapy, right there for you. But does it work? Ha, that's the problem. You have to exert brain control in order to do it, and isn't a lack of control over your brain why you're in therapy in the first place?

As I walked to the cinema to meet Oli, I did try and own them. This was my backlog of bad thoughts so far:

BAD THOUGHT

You look like crap.

BAD THOUGHT

How are you going to eat the popcorn?
You can't seriously dip your hand repeatedly into
something — think of the germs multiplying.
You'll get sick and vomit down yourself and Oli
will hate you.

BAD THOUGHT

Will it be awkward? What if we don't have anything to talk about?

BAD THOUGHT

What if you have a panic attack in the cinema? You've not had one in ages, but you've not been to the cinema in ages...

So I really tried to concentrate on The Present Moment to calm myself down. I looked up at the leaves on the trees and thought how pretty they were, the first tinges of yellow tarnishing the edges. I listened to the steady whir of traffic as cars passed me. I counted my steps on the pavement – up to ten each time. And, soon, Sarah was right... I was almost there and I hadn't spiralled into a sobbing incoherent mess.

The cinema was in the distance, all new and shiny and the-most-exciting-thing-to-happen-to-this-town-in-five-years. Oli was in there, with his basil eyes, and his questions about monkeys, and his tendency to prefer violence in movies...and all of these were good things and things that made Oli Oli. And I was going on a date to find out more about what made Oli Oli, and he was going to find out more about what made Evie Evie because that is what dates are and that is how love begins to maybe happen and I so wanted to fall in love. Because love means someone accepts you for who you are, unconditionally; it's like you've been given a giant "well done" sticker from the universe, and I was well on my way to starting that so why…why…

…despite all my best efforts, did Proper Bad Thoughts start to win things right at the last moment?

PROPER BAD THOUGHT

You may be owning them, but you're having
an awful lot of them.

PROPER BAD THOUGHT

What if you start not being able
to own them?

I stopped dead in the car park and got honked at aggressively by a bald man driving a BMW.

I barely heard him.

WORSE THOUGHT

It's really, maybe, coming back again.

Sixteen

I was late. I found a quiet alleyway round the back of the cinema and I stayed there for a bit, wiping the tears from my eyes the moment they spilled so as not to wreck my mascara, and breathing in deeply for three, and out for six…

I entered the cinema with only five minutes to go before the film began. The cool air of the unnecessary air-conditioning helped shake off the remaining panic and dried up the moist layer of sweat on my forehead.

I could make out the back of Oli's head. His spiked hair gave him away. That, and the fact he was the only one left in the foyer because it was so goddamned late. I reached out and tapped him on the shoulder, tentatively.

"Evie." He spun round and I almost gasped. His face was like looking at my reflection – his eyes panicked, forehead sweaty, his smile strained. "I thought you weren't coming," he said, in a breezy way that didn't have anything breezy about it. I felt so guilty for being late.

"I'm so sorry," I said, the guilt blooming in me like a flower. "I, er…got caught up. We've still got time, haven't we?"

Oli's strained smile became more natural. "Yeah, we've only missed the trailers. We probably don't have time to buy any popcorn or anything though."

"That's too bad."

"I'm so glad you came, Evie." And then, in a fit of courage, he reached over and took my hand and it felt so lovely that all I could do was stare at our unionized fingers.

"Evie…"

"Huh?" I still stared at our entwined digits.

"Evie?" Oli said louder.

I looked up, confused, still riding the tsunami wave of today's emotions. Oli's stark green eyes were scared again. Instantly I panicked.

"What is it?" I asked.

He gulped and took away his hand, scratching the side of his head. "I…umm…there's something I need to tell you."

And just as all the worst-case scenarios catapulted into my brain, we were interrupted…

"Hello," said an unfamiliar voice behind me. "You must be Evelyn."

What?

"Oh, Oli dear, she's just as lovely as you said."

I spun in the direction of the voices and saw two frumpish grown-ups. An older couple, both wearing bobbly cardigans. They beamed at me like I was selling them cookies.

"Evie…" Oli said, his voice shaking. "These are my parents."

PARENTS PARENTS PARENTS PARENTS PARENTS PARENTS PARENTS?!?!?!?

They held out their hands and I found myself shaking them in shock, and saying, "Nice to meet you."

"Lovely to meet you too, Evie," Oli's mum – MUM?! – said. "But we better be taking our seats otherwise we'll miss the start of the film."

We all turned and walked to the cinema door, handing our tickets to the cinema guy, like it was the most normal thing in the world. His parents – PARENTS – walked ahead and disappeared into the darkness before us, their chatter drowned out instantly by the noise of the last trailer.

Oli took my hand again, but oh how different it felt.

He leaned over and whispered, "Don't worry, we don't have to sit next to them."

And we, too, were submerged in the darkness.

Oli was right, we didn't have to sit next to his parents – PARENTS. They sat a grand total of three aisles in front. Just before the film began, his mum turned round, waved, and literally said, "*Coo-eee.*"

Oli stared at the giant cinema screen, rubbing his hands together like Lady Macbeth, offering absolutely no explanation for:

a) Why his parents were there,

b) Why he didn't tell me they were coming, and,

c) WHY HIS PARENTS WERE THERE!

That's the thing about anxiety. You can worry about anything and everything, dream up all sorts of weird and wonderful situations to be terrified of in the hope your fear will control the world somehow...and yet the world remains uncontrollable. Nothing you can imagine is ever as weird and wonderful as reality and what it chucks at you.

Never, in my history of bad thoughts, had I conjured up:

BAD THOUGHT

What if my date brings his parents?

Three minutes into the Tarantino film, the grisly violence began. Guts splattered against the screen and blood spurted from people's heads against the backdrop of clever-but-essentially-meaningless (in my filmic opinion) dialogue. I shuffled in my seat and tried to focus on the movie but it was hard. I really wasn't a fan of this director and I was too distracted by working out what was happening with Oli. I glanced over in the dark. He was leaning right forward in his seat. I looked over at his parents. His mum had already buried her face into his dad's bobbly jumper.

I had a think.

Possible reasons for why
Oli's parents were here

a) They wanted to see the movie too... But then why was his mum's head now right up his dad's bobbly cardigan?

b) They are very overprotective parents... But then wouldn't he have warned me?

c) He has a bee allergy and they've got to be with him at all times in case they have to inject adrenalin into his heart...but he comes to college every day?

Then it hit me...like a cartoon of a light bulb pinging above my head.

Maybe Oli's got anxiety too.

I looked over again in the gloom.

His feet bounced up and down, his legs jiggled like a jelly in a wind-machine. Check.

His hands tapped on his knees, like a drummer who'd been told his entire family would die if he stopped drumming, even for one moment. Check.

He kept shuffling in his seat, moving positions, over and over, like someone'd tipped an industrial-sized vat of itching powder down his jeans. Check.

I looked down at my own body.

My legs were wobbling. My hands were a-tapping. And

I'd readjusted myself more frequently than the director had beheaded a character.

Snap.

BAD THOUGHT

I can't go out with someone with anxiety.

BAD THOUGHT

It would be like two alcoholics dating each other.

BAD THOUGHT

How the hell am I going to break this to him without causing him more anxiety?

The film wasn't my thing – yet I didn't want it to end. I willed it on for ever so the lights would never come up, so I wouldn't have to deal with the situation. How how how? What was I supposed to do? I couldn't even message the girls as my mobile would glow too bright and make everyone in the cinema hate me. I couldn't really explain it to them anyway. What if they laughed and called him a "freak"? Would that mean they'd laugh at me and call me a freak if I let my guard down and wigged out at some point?

The film ended; the lights came on. Oli turned round and grinned, his smile carving more sculpture into his beautiful cheeks.

I wiped my sweaty hands on my clothes. I wiped them again.

"It was great, wasn't it?" he asked, his voice a bit strained. Or maybe I was imagining it?

"Yeah. Very…umm…violent."

His smile dropped. "You didn't like it?"

"No, I loved it," I lied. "I wonder how they got those guts to look so realistic. Impressive, huh?"

Oli didn't look convinced. "Yeah, I guess."

We stood and collected our stuff, letting the people who'd sat in the middle trickle past us. Just as I was wondering what would happen next, I was tapped lightly on the shoulder.

It was his mother. She looked a little bit…green.

"Hey, guys," she said. "Did you enjoy yourselves?" She was talking like a kids' TV presenter – all patronizing and over-enthusiastic.

"I don't think it was for me, but you love this director, don't you, Oli?"

Oli nodded but stared at the carpet as he did so.

"Anyway, Oli, I've had a chat with your father and we're happy to hang about the cafe for a bit if you two want some time to yourselves?"

Oli nodded again.

"Great…" She looked at her watch. "Shall we all meet

back here at half five then? Evelyn, we can give you a lift back if you like?"

"Oh…that's all right. I don't mind walking."

"Walk? But it's cold. We'll give you a lift."

The thought of being in a car, after the chat I was about to have with Oli, was too much. "It's okay," I said, firmly, in a voice far more authoritative than usual. "I'm happy walking. But thanks."

His mother bristled, but straightened and walked back to her husband. "Remember, Oli," she called over her shoulder. "Half five. I've got to get dinner on."

"Okay, Mum."

We stood, not talking, as the cinema emptied around us. When it was obvious only I was going to break the silence, I did.

"So…" I pulled out my phone and looked at the time. "Half five, we've got forty-five minutes. What do you fancy doing?"

Oli shrugged. "I dunno. We could grab a coffee?"

"Riiiight. Do you want to go to the same cafe as your parents, or do you want to go to a different one?"

He blushed, and I felt instantly guilty, though it'd been an honest question. "A different one is fine."

"You sure?" My voice sounded as patronizing as his mother's.

"I'm sure."

It was almost dark when we walked out into the car park, but bright enough to feel disorientated after sitting in the cinema for two hours. Sensing I would have to be The Decider on this date, I steered us wordlessly towards a little coffee house I knew around the corner.

It was winding down for the day – the waitresses looked tired and ready to go home. I ordered us two lattes and took them to the table. Oli's foot was a-tapping like crazy and he wouldn't look at me when I put the drinks down.

"Thanks," he said to the table.

"It's fine." I was surprised by how calm I felt, and in control. Maybe there's such a thing as relative anxiety? If someone else is more nervous than you, you therefore feel calmer or something? Either way, I had an instinct today was A Big Day for Oli and I hoped I could show some compassion.

He stared into the steam of his drink. I waited for him to talk. He didn't.

So I sipped and I waited.

Still nothing. Just the tap tap tapping of his shoe and the slurping of caffeinated beverages.

When we only had twenty minutes left I gave in.

"What's going on, Oli?" I asked gently, putting my hand on his. He flinched initially, and then relaxed into my hand. I didn't even think about the germs on his skin, which was evidence to back up my relative anxiety theory.

I watched as my question broke him, like a grief wave crashing against a cliff. Oli's arm began to shake, his face screwed up. When he spoke I could hear the repressed tears in his throat.

"I'm sorry…" he stumbled. "About my parents… I should've told you they were coming. I'm such an idiot…" The disdain in his words was heartbreaking. The self-hatred. I knew it so well. You can't help getting sick in your head, but, by golly, do you forget that. Daily. You despise yourself for being the way you are, like you're doing it on purpose or something.

"Why are they here?" I asked in my same calming voice. I felt like I was hovering above the situation; it was too surreal to freak out about. Things had got too weird too quickly and all I could do was go with it.

"I… I…"

"It's okay, you can tell me." I realized I sounded like Sarah.

"I find it hard…I used to find it hard…" His voice shook with his hands. "To go out sometimes."

Ah, agoraphobia. That old chestnut. And by "chestnut", I mean misunderstood and totally debilitating clusterfuck of a mental illness. It made sense now, thinking it all through. By the looks of things he was a year behind me in recovery terms.

"That must be hard," I said.

<u>Notice how I didn't say</u>

"I've been there."
"I understand."
"I get it."

> *"I once didn't leave the house for eight weeks.*
> *I really get it."*

Or any of the other things you would think I'd have said. All the things I probably should have said. All the things that probably would've helped. Because there's nothing more comforting than someone who actually gets it. Really gets it. Because they've been to the same hell as you have and can verify you've not made it up.

I didn't say anything like that.

"It's hard..." he continued, both of us utterly ignoring our drinks. "I'm getting better. I'm seeing...someone. I probably wasn't ready to...you know...date, I guess. But when I first saw you in film studies, I just felt something, like maybe you were different... I liked how intense you were when you answered questions...and...well...you look like that..."

I blushed.

"I didn't think you'd say yes if I asked you out. And then you did. And I was so happy, and then, so panicked, and I knew I would screw it up, and I have screwed it up. Who brings their parents on a date? Who? WHO?" He suddenly slammed his drink down on the plastic table. Coffee splashed everywhere.

"Woah, Oli, it's okay."

He bashed his cup down again, more liquid flew everywhere. "It's not okay. It's not. I'm a freak. I'm such a FUCKING FREAK."

And then, of course, he cried.

I know what you want to have happened, or maybe I don't. But I reckon that, at this point, you would like it if I'd reached over and taken his hand again. If I'd opened up and told him all about my brain, and how I was sectioned once, and that he'd get through this and we'd work it out together. And maybe we would kiss, and he would go home feeling amazing about his day, rather than humiliated and broken.

That's not what happened though.

I let him cry. I walked him back to his parents, saying "it's okay" over and over again while he continuously apologized. His mum gave me a dirty look as I delivered her son back. I wanted to grab her face and yell, "I'm not a horrible person, I'm not. But I'm broken too and I've never been on the receiving end of this behaviour before and I can't handle it and I have to look after me first, before anyone else."

I just said, "It was nice meeting you."

Then I turned and left them to tend to their son.

I ran home quickly to change for the party, my phone buzzing with messages from the girls asking how it had gone. I had a horrid feeling in my stomach.

Guilt.

I packed my bag, chucking lipsticks and all sorts into it. Why hadn't I opened up to Oli? It's not like he would judge me. He would get it, much more than anyone else. He wouldn't have thought any less of me, and it would've reassured him so much.

Just as I was about to leave, I looked at myself one more time in the mirror. Really looked. My hair was up, my top clung in all the right bits, a bag hung off my shoulder. I looked like any other sixteen-year-old on her way to a party. From the outside, nobody could tell what had happened to me, and I'd worked so hard to make it that way. Then I understood why I'd done what I did.

I enjoyed being the healthy one. That was it.

For the first time ever, *I* was the normal one.

And it had felt intoxicatingly good…

Seventeen

A couple of hours later and I was getting acquainted with the treacherous world of shots. Sambuca shots to be precise. Screw the medication, I was on hardly any now anyway.

"Woah, Evie, where have you come from?" Guy yelled over the music. He'd just stumbled into Anna's kitchen and witnessed me doing two shots. Alone. Because doing shots alone is a great sign of mental well-being.

"I am doing shots," I told him calmly. "It is a perfectly reasonable thing for a sixteen-year-old to do." I did one more and winced.

Guy took the sambuca bottle out of my hand. "Yeah, but you're not usually like this."

"Like what? Fun?"

"No…like everyone else."

We held the sambuca bottle between us, looking at each other a bit longer than two friends would usually look at each other. Amber came in.

"EVIE," she hollered. "Where's the sambuca? I need it." Her hair was frizzing, a sign Amber was wasted. She said whenever she got drunk, her hair got drunk with her. It was her idea to get trashed tonight. And after hearing how loud she and Lottie laughed when I'd told them about Oli bringing his parents, I was inclined to agree.

They'd really laughed at him. They thought it was funny, hilarious even. I'd found myself laughing along, muttering "yeah, what a freak" with them as my personal guilt turned to anger and despair. I mean, I hadn't told them about the agoraphobia because I reckoned that was private. But they'd wanted to know, obviously, why I hadn't brought him with me to the party and the parent thing had just sorta blurted out. I guess it was freaky if you didn't know why...

As I said before – mental illness, we sure as hell know the words for it, but we still can't have sympathy with the actual behaviour.

I tugged and reclaimed the sambuca from Guy. I waved it in the air in victory but I hadn't screwed the bottle top on properly and treated us all to a sambuca shower.

"Oops," I said, giggling as sticky aniseed splattered in my hair.

"Jeez, Evie." Guy wiped the dribbles off his face, looking peed off. "I think you've had enough."

"Me? Coming from the king of substance misuse?"

"Yeah," said Amber. She wiped the sambuca off her shoulder with her finger and licked it. "Don't you have a spliff to smoke in the corner by yourself or something?"

"As a matter of fact, I do." Guy stormed out the kitchen, knocking an empty bottle over in the process.

For some reason, I found this hilarious and threw my head back laughing. Amber eyeballed me curiously.

"You all right, Eves? It ain't that funny."

"The beer bottle!" I laughed harder.

"Yikes. Maybe you have had enough."

"No!" I protested, and held my makeshift shot glass (egg cup) up. "Please, sir, can I have some more?"

Amber grinned and obligingly poured. "To us," she said, knocking our egg cups.

"To us," I drank.

Joel and Jane just wouldn't stop laughing. They clutched at each other, holding each other's ribs instead of their own.

"Wait," Joel gasped. "So what did this dude say when his parents showed up?"

I tried to remember. It was hard, despite it happening only a few hours ago. I was finding it hard to remember anything though. What people's names were, where I was, how to walk properly...

"Er..." I said, searching for the memory. "Oh yeah! He said, 'Don't worry, we don't have to sit with them.'"

Joel literally cried with laughter. "Here," he yelled at a group of his mates, beckoning them over. "This girl just went on a date today" – he gestured towards me – "and the guy brought his parents with him!"

All of Joel's mates laughed. Well, not Guy. He wasn't there. I hadn't seen him since the kitchen. It was getting out of hand; everyone knew about Oli. Poor Oli! I hoped it wouldn't go around the whole college. I'd already been such a douche today.

"No way."

"What? Seriously?"

"That's mental."

I stood up. My head spun so fast I sat right back down again. I gave myself a moment and tried again.

"I'm off."

People still giggled manically as I left the living room.

Amber was in the hallway.

"EVIE!" Her hair was definitely drunk. It was twice the size of her head. She pulled me onto the stairs for a hug. "I've missed you."

I fell on top of her and we lay there, giggling, until someone asked us to move out the way. "Where's Lottie?"

"Oh, she's upstairs shagging Posh Boy. Has been since we got here."

"Oh…" That didn't seem very like Lottie. This party was supposed to be The Big Moment Where Tim Finally Met Her Friends but we'd only really said "hi" before they'd both disappeared upstairs.

"I know…" Amber answered. I must've been thinking aloud. "I think there's stuff up with them."

"What sort of stuff?"

"I dunno. Did you notice how he hardly even said hello to us? Who knows? I've never been in a relationship."

I settled my face into her moist shoulder. "Me neither."

"At least you had a date today…well…does it count as a date if the boy brings his parents?" And she too, like everyone bloody else, melted into hysteria.

I bum-shuffled down the stairs. "I'm getting more drink."

"Oh! Bring me some," she called.

There were so many obstacles to the kitchen. People, crap on the floor, my own feet not behaving. Everyone was hazy, like they were in an art house movie's self-indulgent scene or something. All slow shutter speeds and blurry limbs.

Movie. I wished I was at home watching a movie.

The bass beat from the heavy metal was all metallic in my ears, my mouth tasted of metal too. Maybe if you hang out with heavy metal people enough you become metal?

Kitchen. Busy. Had trouble getting to the gin bottle.

What is gin anyway?

It tasted like grown-ups.

It was okay if just a shot of it.

Shots.

Sarah would be proud. Shots make you drunk. Being drunk makes you sick. I hadn't been sick in six years.

I couldn't bear the thought of being sick.

Until tonight.

Outside. I was outside.

Cold though. It was proper cold.

Nice down here in this little corner I'd found.

Maybe if I just closed my eyes? Had a little rest. Didn't think about Oli and the hatred in his face, at himself. Didn't think about just how loud everyone's laughs were. Didn't think about how I didn't tell him about me. About who I am. What I'm like. I let him down… I let myself down.

Just like him. I'm just like him.

And everyone thinks he's a freak.

Freak.

Freaky freak freak…freakington.

Man, it was cold.

"Evie?"

"Shh, now quiet time," I told the voice.

"Evie? What you doing out here by yourself?"

It was Guy's voice. I smiled.

"I'd rather have two bollocks the size of watermelons," I told him, and started manically grinning.

"Oh Christ. You're wasted."

"No, YOU'RE wasted." It's more convincing if you say it with your eyes closed. That was my viewpoint and I was sticking to it. "You're always wasted." I put on a voice I didn't know I had. "Oooo, I'm Guy. I think I'm so cool because I play the gee-taar, and I smoke all the weed but what am I hiding from? WHAT?"

I opened my eyes on the "*what?*" for dramatic effect, and his face was right in my face. Smiling.

"Your mate. The giant one. She's passed out. I don't

know where the other one is. Can you please let me take you inside?"

"You said please."

"Yes, well, I have very good manners."

"Not really." And I closed my eyes again.

"No, Evie, don't go to sleep. Come on."

I was lifted and floated through the garden. It was a nice garden, lots of bushy bits, it would be nicer without all the people standing around in circles, playing the music too loud, passing one cigarette between them. Was it a cigarette? I floated past too quickly to work it out.

Floated back into the party.

Floated up the stairs.

"I'm floating," I said, to no one in particular.

"No you're not," Guy's voice came from under me. "I'm fucking carrying you."

"Am I heavy?" I floated past a group of people, strumming a guitar and singing "Wonderwall", at the top of the stairwell.

"Yes, you are."

I scrunched my face up. "I can't believe you called me fat!"

"What? I didn't. Oh for God's sake…girls…hang on… almost there."

Guy turned and used my arse to open the door into a dark bedroom. He turned on the light; no one was there. He did a small sigh, of relief maybe, and then doofed me down on top of the bed. I fell into the mattress heavily, like a tonne-weight.

"Oomph," I said, surprised, looking up at my surroundings. Then I realized where I was. The bedroom. Anna's bedroom. From that awful first date with Ethan. I sat up. "I can't be in here. It's the sex room." I tried to stumble to my feet but getting up so quickly made my stomach lurch angrily.

I felt sick.

Oh no. No. I can't be sick.

"I'm going to be sick!" I yelled, panicked. Why? Why had I done all those shots? My forehead was sweating, I was shivering, panic panic panic panic panic.

"No, you're not." Guy's voice had this soothing quality I'd never heard before. It was the exact opposite voice to all the guttural vocals he sang in his band. "Lie back down… I'll get you some water and crackers."

I grabbed him, wide-eyed. "I can't be sick, Guy. You don't understand, I can't get sick. I can't I can't I can't…" The panic won over and I did what I always did, I cried. There was no build-up, no slow ascent to a crescendo. Just one minute Guy was trying to get me to lie back down, and the next I'd grabbed his hand, squeezing all the blood out of it, sobbing uncontrollably.

"I can't be sick. Guy, what if I'm sick? What have I done? How do I stop it, Guy? Help me. My stomach, oh God, help me. I can't be sick."

I began shaking uncontrollably. Guy, his eyes wide with shock, hugged me into him.

"Shh, Evie, you're not going to be sick. We'll get you

some water. Calm down. Shhh. Shhh. Christ, where are your mates? Shhh, you're not going to throw up. We'll get you some water. Shh, shh, stop crying."

His jumper smelled smoky, but in a sweet fragrant way, like flowers being burned. And his armpit was so squidgy and lovely and his hand was on the small of my back, and no boy's hand had ever been on the small of my back before. Pins and needles erupted around where his fingers met my skin. His voice, his touch, brought me back.

My sobs quietened.

"Evie?"

"Yes?" I answered into his armpit.

"I'm going to go get you some water. Are you going to be okay?"

I nodded into his armpit.

"You're going to have to come out of my armpit."

"I like it in here."

"Come on." Even through my sambuca haze I could hear the impatience in his voice. I was just sober enough to know I'd pushed my luck and withdrew from under him. "Now lie down, take deep breaths. I won't be long…"

"Where are Lottie and Amber?"

He sighed again. "I'll go check they're okay. Now, are you feeling all right?"

I nodded and it made the world go wonky. A late tear slipped out of my eye.

"I'll be back in just a minute."

The sound of the door closing. I lay back, like Guy said,

and looked up at the ceiling. It spun, my head spinning with it. I closed my eyes to stop it but my head just kept on whirring. The bass beat made the room vibrate, steadily, like a heartbeat. I counted the thuds to stop the panic creeping back in.

Breathe, hold on for ten beats.

See if you can go twenty beats without being sick.

Good, there you go. Now let's see if you can make it to forty beats.

People were yelling right outside the door. It could've been Lottie's voice, it sounded a bit like her. Where'd she been all evening? With Tim? That wasn't like her. My stomach swelled, nausea rose in my throat.

No no no. Can't be sick, can't be sick.

Oh how I wished my head would stop circling.

The door opened, the music got louder. It closed, the music got quieter again.

"Evie? You asleep?"

It was Guy. He'd come back. I opened my eyes and looked up at him sideways. I could see right up his pointed nostrils, but there weren't any boogers. He had quite nice nostrils actually.

"You have quite nice nostrils actually," I told him.

He grinned and put the toast-laden plate and glass of water on the bedside table next to me.

"So you've not passed out then? Your mate, Amber, is it? Jane and Joel are looking after her. She's come round and is vomming in the front garden."

I shuddered. How was I going to get out of this party without walking past her sick? Would some of the atoms of it break off and float into my nose and make me sick too? Hang on…I already felt sick. Another tear leaked out.

Guy saw it. "Oh no, Evie, not again. Come on, eat this toast. It will help you not vomit."

"You promise?"

He looked me right in the eyes. "I promise."

I lolled over and made room for him on the bed. He pushed me so I was upright against the wall and then wedged me up with his own body – budging over on the bed so he was right next to me. A whole side of me was touching a whole side of him.

He held the toast up. "Come on." He spoke like I was a baby at feeding time. "Open up."

"Did you wash your hands before you made the toast?"

He rolled his eyes, like I'd instantly become a misbehaving baby. "Yes."

"And is the plate clean? You didn't get it out of the sink, did you? Did you know there are more germs in a kitchen sink than there are in a toilet bowl?"

"Just as well I took this plate out of the toilet then." He saw my face. "Relax, Evie, I got it out of the cupboard. You could say thank you, you know?"

I slowly leaned forward and took a bite of the buttery toast. It tasted amazing. And he'd cut it into triangles.

"Thank you," I said, through a mouthful of crumbs.

He kept feeding me, until my tummy didn't want any

more, then he forced me to slowly sip a pint glass of water…
"I got it straight out of the dishwasher, don't worry."

When I'd finished, I felt…better. Like the worst had passed, though seeing straight was still a bit challenging.

"This is the room where it happened," I told him, my head wanting to rest on his shoulder. I resisted and lay it back against the hard plaster.

"What happened?"

"My date, the nympho…this is the same bed he shagged someone else on."

Guy twisted his head in my direction and grinned.

"So it's a lucky bed then?"

I'd sobered up enough to hear his innuendo. "Hey, I am very drunk right now. You are not to take advantage of this." And I pointed to myself in all my drunken unattractive glory.

He rolled his eyes again. "Where's the 'thank you for looking after me'? No, I get sexual assault allegations…"

I opened my mouth to protest and then realized he was right.

"Why are you so drunk anyway? This isn't the control freak Evie I know and love."

Did he just say love? No. Well, yes, but not like that.

"Bad date."

"Jeez, another one? Hang on, weren't you meeting pussycat boy today?"

It stung somewhere in my foggy mind that he'd forgotten I had a date.

"Yeah, it was him. We went to the cinema."

"And what happened? Why didn't you bring him here?"

I let out a deep breath, reliving the day and tonight like a superfast flickbook of crap. "He brought his parents with him..." I waited for the laughter to start.

Guy didn't laugh though. He just looked concerned. "What? Seriously? Is he okay, like, in his head?"

My mouth dropped open and stayed open longer than was probably necessary in the attractiveness stakes.

"I don't think he is okay. In the head, I mean..."

"Wow, poor guy." He was quiet a moment, before adding, "I had a mate like that. In school..." He trailed off. "He wrote some brilliant lyrics for our band at the time, I'm telling you. But man was he messed up. He moved away. To the sea or something."

I smiled at Guy. We were exactly the same height and my nostrils were right up in his nostrils. I didn't even worry about my breath smelling. Though I did afterwards. Loads.

"Thank you," I said.

He scratched his head and pulled a face. "For what?"

"For not laughing."

"Why would I laugh?"

"Everyone else laughed when I told them."

"Well, people are idiots, Evelyn."

"I'm sorry about your friend." I wondered if he'd ever been in the same facility as me, but I couldn't remember much from that time. I'd totally not-subconsciously blocked it out.

"It's okay. Shit happens..."

I wanted to kiss him. Somehow, suddenly, all I wanted to do was kiss Guy. The urge was insane, like something stronger than me, stronger than any urge I'd ever had before…even all my urges to wash all the time, and not eat, and check sell-by dates, and close my window just so at night-time to control the airflow into my room perfectly.

I caught my breath.

"Evie? You okay? You feeling sick again?"

I made myself look right at him, completely into his eyes, which I'd never done before. They were so blue, how had I never noticed how blue they were before? Guy looked straight back and it was like nothing and everything all at once. My heart practically panicked and ran out of my ribcage to claim asylum. I'd never been looked at like that before. And even though I knew nothing about kissing, I knew Guy wanted to kiss me too. I could feel his own urge pulling him to me.

He leaned his head forward.

He hesitated and licked his lips.

There was not one bad thought in my head.

He came closer.

And closer.

I felt his stubble almost tickling my face.

Then the noise of the party got louder.

"EVIE?!"

And he had pulled away.

I blinked and looked in the direction of the voice.

Joel and Jane stood with Amber held up between them.

She looked like an abused rag doll. Her head flopped forward, her knees bending weirdly.

"Can you help us get her home?"

Eighteen

I woke up with my very first hangover.

"Ouch," I said aloud on waking, because, well, it summed up exactly what I felt. I put my hand to my clammy thumping head. "Ouch ouch ouch ouch ouch."

Hang on, where was I?

I looked around me; just turning my head hurt. I was in my bedroom, on top of my duvet. I looked down. I was still wearing last night's clothes.

Had I passed out? How had I gotten home? What had happened?

And... Ouch ouch ouch ouch OUCH.

I lay back on my pillow – OUCH! – and tried to remember.

Shots. I'd done shots... And Amber too. And everyone had been laughing about Oli, that was horrible. Poor Oli. God, I was such a bitch... Would it get out at college? He'd know I'd been taking the piss. That would be horrific.

Why was I so stupid?! And where had Lottie been? Had there been a fight? I vaguely remembered a fight. And then…nothing. Blank. Zilch. Nada. I bit my lip. This was pretty scary. I hadn't ever forgotten a part of my life before – though there were huge gaping wounds in my life I wished I could forget. I reached round my body for my phone and found it nestled under my spine – OWW.

One message. From Amber. Received that morning at about 6 a.m.

EVIE WHAT HAPPENED? I'VE WOKEN UP
COVERED IN SICK AND WEARING ONE OF
JOEL'S BAND T-SHIRTS?????????

Joel?

A vague memory lazily pinged into my brain. Amber. I'd walked her home with Joel and Jane. Well, they'd carried her and I was too busy…singing? Had I been singing? Another memory pinged in of Jane and me undressing Amber in her bedroom. She'd been covered in sick so Joel had lent her his T-shirt as we couldn't find any of her clothes in the dark. I distinctly remembered that, I'd been cringed-out by the sight of Joel topless.

What else had happened? And why did it feel like a hoover had sucked all the moisture out of my mouth?

My bedroom door opened and I cowered in the beam of light like a scared vampire. *Don't be Mum, don't be Mum, don't be Mum…*

It was Rose – thank God. Carrying a glass of water!

"Morning, waster," Rose said, all bright-eyed-and-bushy-tailed. "You're alive then?"

I eyeballed her water glass. "That better be for me."

"It is. I'll go make some toast in a min if you want me to?"

"Have I ever told you I love you?"

She handed the water over and I glugged it back all in one go. I needed at least twelve more, I reckoned, and a time machine so I could go back to yesterday and not do those last couple of shots.

"Thanks," I moaned, handing the glass back. Then I crumpled back into bed, my head hammering angrily in my skull. Rose smiled and sat on the end.

"So what happened then?"

I groaned. "I drank too much."

"Well that much is obvious. You couldn't get your house key in the lock. I only knew to come let you in because you woke me up screaming that African bit at the very beginning of 'The Circle of Life' from *The Lion King*."

I searched my memory bank for any glimmer of a reminder that that had happened... Nope, nothing.

"If that was real, I would definitely remember it."

"Oh, it was real. You are SO lucky Mum was out late last night."

Mum – the thought of her made the water in my belly freeze. "Hang on? She went out?"

"Yeah. She and Dad were on their monthly date night." And she pulled a face.

That was lucky. Mum was pretty…puritanical. We'd had so many lectures from her about the perils of drinking and smoking and drugging and funning and, well, living really. Thus why fun between her and Dad was scheduled into a monthly box on the calendar, like enjoying time with your husband was a dentist's appointment or something. She was almost as unspontaneous as I was…almost. I smelled my duvet. It really didn't smell very nice. I wondered if I could get away with washing it on the sly. Usually I was only allowed clean sheets every Tuesday, once a week, just like Sarah ordered.

"Weren't you supposed to be out last night?" I asked her.

Rose shrugged. "Yeah, but I came home."

"Why?"

"So what happened last night? Was the party any good? And how was the date?"

It was such an obvious change of subject that I should've challenged it. But my head hurt and Rose never opened up unless she wanted to, so I just closed my eyes and made a dramatic "EGH" sound. "I did shots," I said, my mouth prickling all metallic and gross at the mention of them. "And then, I'm not sure. And the date… Oh, Rose, it was awful. He brought his parents with him, then broke down and basically told me he had agoraphobia."

"What, seriously? Is he…"

"Mental, like me? Yes."

"That's not what I meant."

"Yes, well… I was shite. I didn't help him at all. I just

freaked out and handed him back to his parents. And then, at the party, everyone was laughing their arses off about Oli…and what if he finds out I told everyone? Lottie went off somewhere…I dunno. Alcohol ruined it. What did I tell you last night?"

Rose smiled a little. "Well, you wouldn't stop droning on about some guy. I thought it must've been Oli."

I sat up in bed. "Guy?"

"Yeah."

"No, it wasn't Oli. Guy's his name. He's a guy, called Guy."

"Ahhhh. From Joel's band?"

"Yeah. What was I saying?"

Rose snuggled up to me, using my bum as a pillow. "You just kept wittering on about how sweet he was and how he took care of you and didn't laugh like everyone else… You were quite soppy, Evie. I don't have to emotionally prepare you for yet another first date, do I?"

Guy. Guy…Guy…GUY!

Oh my God, GUY! We'd almost kissed. The memory came crashing back like it'd been waiting for me all this time. He carried me up the stairs, and was so lovely, and I'd got feelings. They resurfaced instantly. And I was there again, on the bed, wanting him to kiss me so much and so hard and he almost had. Hadn't he? My heart started tap-dancing on my insides.

I smiled to myself as a metaphorical packet of fizzing candy erupted in my stomach.

"That smile," Rose said, all holier-than-thou, "tells me everything I need to know."

I grinned again. "It's nothing. Nothing happened." But it would've happened, wouldn't it?

"You're not behaving like nothing happened."

"Stop being so wise. I'm sick."

"You're not sick, you're hung-over."

"Same thing."

"No it isn't."

"Can you bring me some more water?"

"Only if you tell me what happened."

"I told you – nothing. But if you bring me water, I'll play with your hair while we watch a DVD."

"You're on."

Rose returned with water and carbs and we cosied up in my smelly duvet to watch *The Virgin Suicides*. Her head was in my lap, and I stroked her hair, rubbing my fingers over her scalp. Rose was like half human, half Labrador when it came to getting her head rubbed. She utterly blissed out and went all trance-like whenever you did it.

I only half-watched the film. I'd seen it countless times. Sofia Coppola was probably one of my favourite directors. Though I didn't know how much of that was down to her being female, and me wanting to support a girl doing well in Hollywood...without taking her clothes off or starving herself. The dreamy highlighted shots were just what my hangover needed, but Guy was never far from my mind. Did I like him? What would've happened if the others hadn't come in? Did he like me? Was it normal for me to keep getting crushes on every boy who showed interest in me? Was that bad? And what would happen when I next saw him? Was he going to ask me out? I didn't deserve to be asked out again, did I? Not after how awful I'd been with Oli.

I wanted Guy to ask me out though.

He would, wouldn't he? I mean, he'd been about to kiss me. Me. That's how it worked, right? You like them, they like you, they want to kiss you, you start going out. Right?

Rose dozed off and I soon joined her, the film playing as backing vocals for our nap. I was just on the brink of utter unconsciousness, when my phone rang.

I sat up blearily. "Huh?" I answered, instead of hello.

There was no answer, only sobbing.

"Hello?" I asked. More sobbing. I looked at my screen. It was Lottie.

"Lottie? Is that you?"

It prompted a massive howl, a heartbreaking one, one that rips through your soul.

"Evie?" I could just make her out through the snot. "Evie? Can you come over?"

"Sure. Are you okay?"

"He...he... Can you just come round? Bring Amber."

"I'll be right there."

Nineteen

Lottie's mum answered the door, her big owl glasses poking around the gap. She looked – and dressed – exactly the same as she did when I was eleven.

"Evie? Is that you, darling? I haven't seen you since you were yay high."

She opened the door and Amber and I pushed past the beaded curtain, setting off five wind chimes as we did so.

"How are you, Ms Thomas?" I asked as she pulled me in for a hug. She smelled of hemp – I think. I'd never really smelled hemp before. I was proud of myself for remembering the "Ms". Lottie's mum always refused to be called "Mrs", despite being married.

"I'm good." She released me then waved her hand around my body – cleansing my aura. Yep, just like when I was eleven. I remembered then why I used to be scared of going round.

"And this must be Amber." She pulled her in for the hug

treatment and Amber's hair practically obliterated Ms Thomas's face.

"Nice to meet you," Amber muttered into her shoulder.

"I'm glad you're here, girls," she said, releasing Amber. "Lottie's in a state; she won't leave her room. I can hear her crying but, of course, she won't tell her mother what's happened."

I headed up the stairs to Lottie's room. "We'll look after her," I reassured Lottie's mother. It'd been so long since I was here, but everything was the same. The weird seventies style wallpaper, the big painting of the words "THIS IS IT" hanging over the stairs that a monk had painted for them on an educational family holiday somewhere. I knocked softly on Lottie's door, already able to hear her cries through the thin plywood.

"Who is it?" she croaked.

"It's Evie and Amber. With freshly cleaned auras."

The door opened and a puffy-faced Lottie appeared, her eyes almost gone from crying.

"Oh God, sorry about her." Lottie's back was already to us as she stumbled over to her unkempt bed. She slumped down on her belly and buried her face in the pillow.

Amber and I sat gingerly to the side of her.

"Lottie," I said gently, putting my hand on her back. "What's wrong? Where did you go last night?"

"He…he…" she stammered into the pillow, her voice muffled. "He broke up with me."

Both of us leaped into action. I rubbed her back more,

while Amber provided the indignant outrage. "What? Why? How? What a bastard."

Lottie slowly raised her head, leaving at least half of her hair sticking to her face.

"That's not even the worst of it," she said. "He was confused…he didn't even think we were going out in the first place!"

And we sat there as she sobbed and cried and sobbed some more.

Twenty

"I'm such an idiot," Lottie announced to the pillow. "I'm such a goddamn idiot."

I rubbed her back. "I think he's the one we should be calling an idiot."

"No, it's me. I'm so stupid. Thinking we were falling in love...when it was just me."

"There's nothing idiotic about having feelings," Amber said, who was on hair-stroking duty.

"Yes there is. Feelings are for losers."

Eventually Lottie turned over. She looked so different with all her heavy eye make-up cried off, her face much softer.

"Sorry, guys," she hiccupped. "I feel so stupid, crying like this over a stupid smelly boy."

"What happened?"

"Ergh, it's so clichéd."

"Tell us."

"Okay."

What happened between Lottie and Tim

She'd agreed to meet him at the house party. She was looking forward to us meeting him properly, since they'd been seeing each other for a few weeks.

But he was weird from the moment he got there.

"Well, you saw him," she said. "He barely said hello to either of you, and wasn't interested in the party at all. He kept trying to whisk me upstairs."

I could hardly remember meeting him, but then I had killed about twenty million brain cells in the last twenty-four hours. I remembered him trying to shake mine and Amber's hands, and we didn't really know what to do with something that posh. Amber and I had disappeared into the kitchen to start our drunken oblivion mission, leaving them alone to make small talk with people.

"It was awful," she said, curling her knees up, tucking them neatly under her delicate chin. "He seemed to get posher and posher, and all judgemental of our friends. Like, I know Joel and that are a bit odd to look at...especially with Joel's new nose ring thingy, but he'd been to their gig, he knew what they were like. It was like the louder the music got, the more upper-class he got. I bet he was probably wishing we were all chinking champagne glasses, wearing blazers and yelling 'tally ho' to each other or something." I giggled and Lottie smiled weakly. "I got so wound up. I just wanted things to be better. And he kept whispering into my ear, saying we should go upstairs. And I thought maybe that would help, I dunno, get him out of his weird mood."

Amber and I each raised an eyebrow at each other over her head.

"So we went upstairs. And then he…we…" Amber bristled and my hand went tight on Lottie's back. "We had sex. Right there in the toilet. Argh… God." She picked up the pillow and buried her face in it again. "It was awful. He was all rough, not like usual. Like he was just doing a job. And then…then…afterwards…" She started to cry again, a really hollow cry, from the very pit of her stomach.

"What?" I asked.

"It felt so weird and unromantic, so I panicked, and said something like 'Hey, my parents really want to meet you' and, I'm not kidding, guys, his entire face dropped. Like I'd announced I was the secret love child of Hitler or something. He…he…just pulled up his fly and said, all posh and blustery, 'I think you've got the wrong idea here, Lottie.'"

Amber's mouth gaped open. "What? Just like that?"

Lottie nodded, more tears spilling. "He looked so shocked, and then he started apologizing. Which made it even worse I think. 'Oh, Lottie, sorry, you're a great girl but…well…I thought it was just a bit of fun. I thought you agreed. Oh, I'm so sorry.' I felt like a charity case! I'm so stupid. I was really falling for him, you know? Argh, Christ, I'm such a bloody girl. I'd even practised telling people how we met – 'Oh, he spilled drink down me'…it all seemed so romantic."

"So what happened then?" I asked, returning to rubbing her back.

She sighed. "Well then, of course, I went stark raving mental. I started yelling at him, all drunk and totally unladylike, screaming, 'What? Are you serious? What? You arsehole, you led me on.' I swear the whole party heard. And he just apologized even harder, coming up with all this stupid crap, about how we never said it was anything official, and that he liked spending time with me but… And I was like, 'But what? BUT WHAT?' I was chasing him out onto the street by then, like a rabid dog, screaming. I just remember yelling, 'BUT WHAT?' I didn't get it. I still don't get it."

"Did he answer you?"

Lottie sat up suddenly, and wiped her curranty eyes. Her face morphed from grief into anger, like someone had pointed a remote at her. "He said he didn't understand why I was so upset. That we were just seeing each other. And why would he want to be tied down at sixteen anyway?"

Amber and I went to the local corner shop. Chocolate was purchased.

"I'm such a cliché," Lottie told us on our return, half a Dairy Milk hanging out of her mouth. "I'm eating chocolate and moaning about men."

"Sometimes clichés are helpful," I offered.

"I hate how he's made me do this. I hate how much chocolate is genuinely helping."

I broke off another square of the Whole Nut and passed it down to Amber, who leaned against Lottie's bed, her long legs sprawled out on the carpet.

"I just can't believe he said that," she said, taking the chocolate and popping it into her mouth. "*I don't want to be tied down.* I hate that. That they think girls are just obsessed with having relationships. What do they want us to do? Shag them but not expect anything in return?"

"Er, yeah, basically," Lottie answered.

"No, that's not right either," I said. "They call those girls sluts."

They nodded in agreement.

"So we're damned if we do, damned if we don't, basically?" Amber looked utterly depressed.

Lottie stood up on the bed, slipping a bit in her fluffy socks. "No, there's another way. We can pretend to be a Manic Pixie Dream Girl."

"A whatta whatta what now?" I asked.

"You know? A fraud. A boy's dream. Especially the indie boys that we hang out with."

"What's a Manic Pixie Dream Girl? Why do you know all these words all the time?"

She sat back down, and scrolled on her phone, pulling up a few movie stills on Google. Zooey Deschanel came up. And Kirsten Dunst. And this indie film I really liked called *Ruby Sparks* that came out a few years ago. "*Voilà,*" she said. "Manic Pixie Dream Girl. Or MPDG if you wanna sound, like, so four years ago."

"Huh?"

Lottie jabbed at the screen. "She's like this invention in men's imaginations, but girls pretend they're real. It's all basically a recycle of the Madonna-Whore complex, but with vintage dresses."

"The Madonna whatnow? Seriously, you know all the words," I said, my head spinning.

Lottie ignored me and just explained. "The Manic Pixie Dream Girl is pretty but she doesn't really know it. She's kooky and makes you feel alive, but she knows when to shut up and just let you watch the football. She drinks whisky or beer and doesn't ask anything of your relationship because she's too busy doing whacky leisure activities or at band practice. She likes casual sex, but just with you, not with anyone else."

Amber twisted around and grabbed the phone. "Oh, I SO know what you mean." She turned to me and helped explain. "I did a whole topic about Madonnas for my art GCSE, it's basically paintings of the Virgin Mary. The Madonna-Whore complex is this idea Freud came up with that men get all sexually confused because they want us to be virginal Madonna types they can bring home to meet their parents… but they also want us to shag them like we're insatiable whores. They can't make up their mind which one they want. Ideally both, because, you know…" She shrugged. "Because boys. I made up my own phrase for the ideal combo of both," she said proudly. "For modern times. I call it The Girl-Next-Door Slut."

Lottie cackled. "LOVE it! The juxtaposition of two feminine ideals, i.e. a complete lose-lose stereotype."

I pulled a face. "And you think guys want this?"

"Sure," Lottie took back her phone. "I swear the only way you get a boyfriend these days is to pretend you're a Girl-Next-Door Slut."

"Pretend how?"

"Oh, you know. Say stuff like 'Do you mind if we keep this casual, I kinda get freaked out by the whole commitment thing?' It drives me mad. Boys always think I'm like that because I'm quite sexual, I guess…" Lottie didn't look sexual right then. She had melted chocolate all round her mouth. "But then they realize I sort of want them to only put their organ into my body, and nobody else's, and maybe even have a chat about our feelings and stuff in-between and – bam – they get all jumpy and moody, like I've let them down."

I pulled a face. "Aren't you being a bit sexist? Boys aren't all like that."

"Yes they are," Amber said.

I thought of Guy, and how he always picked me up on it when I got double-standardy. Thinking about him felt good… "You can't just lump all boys into the same turd lump."

"Why not?" they both asked.

"Well…look at Jane and Joel. He's not cheated on her, has he? He seems to really love her."

"He loves a lie!" Lottie stood up again. "Jane is totally

playing the Manic Pixie Dream Girl. Didn't you say she's changed loads since they got together? That you feel she's made herself a product? A girlfriend product?"

"I guess…"

"I swear to God, if she pulled out her clarinet and started saying 'I'd rather you not blow me off for band practice at the last minute', Joel would up and leave."

"I…guess…"

Amber came and joined us on the bed, flopping down and making ripples on the mattress. "Sometimes I don't care if I am sexist, you know? We have to deal with it all day every day, why not fight fire with fire?"

"Girls should rule the world," Lottie said.

"Totally."

I always felt I learned something when I was with them. They had such strong opinions, such high opinions about being a girl and how it's amazing, it was hard not to get swept up in it. Especially with Einstein Lottie teaching me all these new thoughts and words. I did feel a bit glowy about girlfolk. I mean, we are really cool, aren't we? And the world is, like, totally against you if you have a fanny, isn't it?

"Shall I tell you what annoys me?" I asked, wanting to join in. "About Tim?"

"Go on."

"It's the language boys use, the language all of us use when we talk about girls. It's so screwed up. Like, there are all these horrid words for being girls with no male equivalent – like 'slut' or 'psycho girlfriend'. Like Tim saying 'being tied down' implies we're a burden, that we, as a species, tie boys down and take away their freedom. Why do they get freedom and we don't? Why does everyone assume boys want freedom and girls want to be attached to someone?" I took another square of chocolate and it helped my dulling hangover. "Think about it," I continued. "When boys get older, if they don't find someone they get called bachelors. We get called spinsters. There isn't a word that means male spinster. Just like there isn't a word for a guy who sleeps around – whereas there are TONS for girls. The English language itself is sexist – it reinforces these overgeneralized, screwed-up notions about how boys and girls are allowed to be…" I trailed off when I noticed them both staring at me.

"What?" I asked self-consciously.

"You're quite smart, aren't you, oh quiet one?" Lottie said, grinning. "I forget sometimes."

"Well…umm…"

Amber re-flopped on the bed, causing another mini-earthquake.

"I hate the word spinster," she said. "I'm already worried about becoming one and I'm only sixteen. And then I get mad at myself for worrying so much about meeting a guy."

"Why don't we reclaim it?" Lottie asked, grinning wider. It was the first time she'd smiled all day and she looked gorgeous – all lit up from inside. I felt proud that Amber and I were able to turn her round so quickly. "We can reinvent the word 'spinster', make it the complete opposite of what it means? Like 'young' and 'independent' and 'strong'? She yanked out her phone again, tapping away madly, pulling up photos of a protest in London – mostly of women, waving placards and wearing miniskirts. "Look, a couple of years ago some feminists tried to reclaim the word 'slut'. And they organized these protests called 'slut walks' all around the world. It didn't completely work, mainly because slut is such a horrible word it can just never be empowering. But why don't we try and reclaim 'spinster'?"

Amber smiled. "I like it."

"At the moment, spinster, technically means, what? An older unmarried woman? But it also means more than that. It's the scary fairytale word girls are told about so we fear being unattractive to men from a young age. It means left on the shelf. It means a life wasted. It means cat lady. It means lonely and sad and bitter just because a man doesn't want you... What if we reversed it?"

"To what?" Amber asked.

And I answered.

"Being a spinster means you value your female relationships as much as your male ones." I thought of Jane. "Being a spinster means not altering who you are, what you believe in, and what you want just because it makes a boy's life easier."

They both smiled wider and Lottie took over. "Being a spinster means you're not afraid to look at society and say loudly, 'I don't agree with this, this is wrong.' Being a spinster means not worrying that boys won't find you cute or sexy for saying those things."

I smiled as Amber finished up. "Being a spinster means looking after your girlfriends and supporting them through whatever they need."

I grabbed their hands – one each – and raised them to Lottie's ceiling. "I formally announce us...SPINSTERS through and through." And we clapped and cheered and whistled ourselves and, for the first time ever in my life, I felt strong.

RECOVERY DIARY

Date: 23rd October

Medication: 10mg Fluoxetine

Thoughts/Feelings: Don't let them find out, otherwise you'll lose them. Look what happened with Oli...

Do I like Guy? Is this the sort of thing I'm supposed to write about in my recovery diary? Who cares? Sarah doesn't see it. Hahahaha...

Homework:
- Keep doing regular exposures to ensure you're still tackling your fear
- Tell me or your parents if any rituals start to creep back in

Twenty-one

At my next appointment with Sarah, I told her about the party. She wasn't impressed, funnily enough.

"I can't believe you're not proud of me for doing all those shots."

Sarah narrowed her eyes over her pad full of notes.

"I work for the NHS, i.e. the institution responsible for keeping people alive and healthy. Do you know how much of our budget is spent each year looking after underage binge drinkers in A&E?"

I flung the wooden caterpillar I'd been playing with back into the toy bin. "But I willingly did something that could make me sick. I did an exposure all on my own accord!"

"I don't think you drank all that, sambuca, was it?"

I nodded, defiantly at first, then a bit meek and ashamed.

"Well I don't think you drank all that because you wanted to try an exposure."

"Well I've told you that's why and I don't care that you don't believe me."

I crossed my arms.

I did care.

Just a bit.

Sarah left us in silence for a while, her favourite trick. Then she said, "One, you know you're not supposed to drink alcohol on your medicine, even if your dosage is really low now." She ticked it off on her finger. "Two, I find it unlikely you'd do an exposure that extreme, of your own accord, in an environment like a house party. And, three, you just told me about your date with that Oli guy and it sounds like you're pretty upset by what happened with him, and by how your friends reacted."

"So?" I bet she thought she was Miss Marple. I bet she was imagining herself in an ITV Agatha Christie drama.

"So," Sarah said, all calm as always, "I think you did all those shots to escape the bad thoughts you were having about your friends."

I shook my head, all no-no-no. "I didn't have bad thoughts about my friends. They are cool and understanding and awesome."

"And where do they think you are this afternoon?"

I blushed. I didn't reply.

"Where?"

"Well, it's half term."

"Where do they *usually* think you are on Monday afternoons?"

"They think I've got last period free," I said to my toes.

Sarah did a triumphant face. It involved a tiny eyebrow raise and a smug grin she struggled to hide.

"I do have a free period last thing on Mondays! That isn't a lie."

"But you don't go straight home, do you? You come here and see me."

"So, it's not the whole truth, so what?"

My skin was all prickly. I felt like a hedgehog, my spikes up, ready for a fight, or protection, or whatever it is that makes hedgehogs put their spikes up. Or are they always up and they just roll into a ball? I was too busy pondering this to initially realize Sarah had produced a sandwich.

She put it on the table in front of me and instantly, every other thought – about Oli, about Guy, about the girls – vanished.

I felt sick.

"No, Sarah, not today, come on."

She gave me a small smile. "I warned you we needed to keep doing exposures – to see how you handle them on your lower dosage. Now, have you had lunch?"

"Yes," I lied.

"Well, you can still manage a sandwich, can't you?"

I didn't want to touch it. I could already see its poison, glowing, invisible to everyone else, through the cardboard triangular box. I reached out slowly and took the packaging. With my fingers shaking, I turned it over and looked at the sell-by date.

I dropped it instantly. "TWO days past? Sarah, seriously? There's meat in it."

Sarah picked it up off the floor and put it back on the table. "What's your number right now, Evie?"

"Why are you doing this? You didn't warn me. You didn't say it was today. Put it away, please!"

"Your number, where are you on the anxiety scale out of ten?"

My palms were already damp with sweat. My throat felt like I was wearing a boa constrictor as a necklace. And I was quite sure I would've felt less doom-filled if the four horsemen of the apocalypse had cantered in.

I gulped, hating her. "Eight out of ten." It came out all raspy.

"Okay, eight, that's quite high. Breathe with me, Evie." She did an exaggerated breath in and out. I tried to copy her but the snake around my neck tightened.

"Why?" I asked. It came out in a whisper.

"Why are you so scared? You've done it before. Nothing bad happened."

I went from scared to angry almost in a second. "That wasn't the same! That was only one day past, and it was ham, not chicken. Not even normal people eat chicken past its sell-by. And something did happen, I felt sick all day!"

"From the panic, not from the sandwich."

"There is no way of proving that. I definitely felt sick, and I'm sure it was from that sandwich. And if I did it then, why do I have to do it again now?"

Tears were on standby, threatening to jump out at any minute. My heart felt like it had been plugged into a generator. A generator powered by The Earth's Inner Core.

Sarah got her uber-calm voice out of its box. "I've explained to you before that you're going to experience heightened anxiety now you're cutting back on your medicine. It's really important we continue with exposures, so you can prove to yourself things are still okay even when you're not on your medication."

"Why don't I just stay on them?"

"You can," Sarah soothed. "But you told me you wanted to come off them. It was your decision."

She was right. I hated being on them.

Why I wanted to come off my medication

I hated worrying that I wasn't sure who I was. What was Evie? And what was a chemical I took that changed my brain? I hated the way they made my feet burn at night. How, in summer, I had to soak flannels in ice water and wrap them around my toes, just to cool them off enough to get some sleep. I hated that I wasn't sure if I was better, or if I was just dependent on a mind-altering medication. I hated that I'd started taking them way below the age you're medically supposed to because I was so sick. I hated that I'll never be entirely sure what impact that may've had on my brain. I hated how they'd made me puff up. I hated that it was too dangerous to just come off them suddenly, and that therefore I was technically "trapped" with them. I hated how if I ever had children and I was still on them, it might damage them in the womb. I hated how I felt weak for going on them in the first place. I hated how I never felt happy or sad since I'd been on them, more just…numb…

But at that moment, in that dankish therapy room, I didn't hate anything as much as the idea of eating that sandwich.

"Not the whole thing," I bargained, my voice wobbling, all my emotions desperate to tumble out like the traitors they were.

"Just one triangle."

"Three bites."

"One half, you've done it before."

"I wasn't so utterly terrified then."

"That's the point. Come on, Evie, you're strong, you're brave. What's the worst that could happen?"

"I'll…I'll…get sick." And then the tears came and I sobbed them out so hard I could hardly breathe.

"So, you get sick, so what?"

"I'll throw up."

Sarah shrugged. "So? You'll still be alive."

"Stop it."

"Stop what?"

"Using logic with me. It's never worked before, it won't

work now." My hands shook so hard I swear their energy could register on an earthquake machine. My voice got louder. "Do you not think I know it's unreasonable? Do you not think I don't spend all my time telling myself it's stupid, bullying myself: 'Stop being so bloody illogical, Evie, you're ruining your life.'" I smashed my hands on the table just to use up some energy. I was shouting now. "Just because it's illogical doesn't mean it's any less scary."

Sarah kept her voice calm; it was the utter opposite of mine.

"Just one triangle."

"Oh, fuck it." And I picked up the disgusting, smelly out-of-date sandwich, ripped open the packaging and shoved as much as I could in my mouth.

"Good girl."

I started to chew but my mouth was so full. Two days out of date, two days out of date, TWO DAYS OUT OF DATE.

I choked.

"Come on, Evie, just keep chewing, then swallow."

There was no saliva in my mouth. The mayonnaise tasted sour. I heaved.

Poison poison poison poison poison.

"Keep chewing, keep chewing."

I thought of everything in the world other than what was in my mouth. I attempted to picture a calm lake. When that didn't work, I pictured all the people in the world who have worse problems than me. Real problems. Sick people. Lonely people. Poor people. Starving people. Starving people would eat the sandwich instantly. Starving people would be grateful for the sandwich. They wouldn't even know about sell-by dates. Because they had real problems whereas I was just a self-indulgent, selfish, stupid, stupid, WEAK, self-indulgent brat.

Oh God, the sandwich, it was still in my mouth. Turning to a sludgy paste, wedging itself around my gums, sticking in a lump between my tongue.

Two days out of date.

I pictured the bacteria growing in the chicken flesh; I pictured the microbes in the sauce multiplying, the lettuce wilting. And now it was all in my body, my weak stupid body.

No. I couldn't. No. How much had I swallowed already? No. No. NO.

I spat it out, right there, onto the table. All over the tissue box. I heaved, dry retched. A piece of bread that had wedged in my throat spilled onto the wooden top, thick with mucus. I gagged, I really was going to be sick. Hold it in hold it in hold it in. I hated Sarah. I hated the world. I grabbed her water glass, downed it. I tried swilling my mouth out but I'd had too much water and it spilled down my chin. I knocked the glass over as I choked, spilling it everywhere.

Then I dropped to the industrial carpet, gasping for breath. I tried so hard to breathe but the sobs…the sobs wedged in my throat, stopping the oxygen.

"Evie. EVIE? Calm down. BREATHE, EVIE."

My eyes bulged out of their sockets. I could hear this odd

donkey-like heehaw breathing. It was me. Where was my air? I was going to black out.

Sarah's hand was around my hand. Squeezing tight.

"Listen to me. Listen to my voice. Let's breathe in for three. Come on, one, two, three…"

I tried, but another sob erupted, blocking my windpipe.

"Stop crying, Evie, listen to me. In for three, one, two, three…"

I concentrated on her voice and managed to grab a quick gasp of air.

"Good girl. Now out for five. One, two, three, four—"

I managed till four but another sob bubbled. I coughed on nothing.

"In for three…

…out for five…

…in for three…

…out for five…

…in for three…

…out for five…"

Soon my sobs dulled to a whimper.

Soon my breathing came back.

Soon I was able to get up off the carpet.

Soon I'd meet my friends for coffee and pretend that it hadn't happened.

Twenty-two

I went home to change before I went to meet the girls for a half-term catch-up. I had dried phlegm all down my jumper, I'd cried my make-up off, and my fringe had separated into tear-drenched clumps.

I prayed Mum was out before I unlocked the door. She did admin for the small estate agents down the road and I could never work out her hours, as it was sometimes mornings, sometimes afternoons. She didn't appear to be home so I tiptoed inside. Rose wasn't in either. All I could hear was the ticking of the grandfather clock on the landing.

For once, luck was on my side.

I hovered over the loo, letting the smell of stale bleach turn my stomach and coughing up any remaining sandwich. When I was satisfied, I lay on my bed and observed myself for signs of illness. This is hard when, generally, signs of anxiety are the same as signs of illness. It's such a torturous circle. I eat something, I start to worry

I'll get sick, this releases adrenalin which makes my stomach churn and my hands shake. That, of course, makes me think I am actually sick, so I get more scared, and feel more sick.

Over and over. Day after day. So much life lost.

I focused on my breathing, trying to slow my body down. With time, it slowed. I wasn't ill, I didn't think. I'd spat the chicken out in time. Or maybe it was never going to make me sick in the first place. Maybe the sandwich was fine. Maybe sell-by dates are ridiculously over-the-top and I shouldn't live and die by them.

Maybe…the word of hope.

Maybe I won't ruin my whole life, just my teens.

Maybe one day I'll be like everybody else.

Maybe one day I'll be happy.

I brushed my teeth until I spat out blood. I stood in the scalding shower until my skin turned tomato. I brushed my teeth again. With a dash of make-up and a quick blast with the hairdryer, I left the house once more. I would just about be on time.

As I walked, kicking up piles of soggy leaves, trying to get the last bit of angst out of me, I thought about how Sarah'd finished our session.

When I'd finished crying, she'd sat on the arm of my chair, asking prying questions.

"Your new friends, Evie, what are they like?"

I thought of yesterday and managed a small grin. "They're spinsters."

"What? Aren't you a bit young to be calling yourselves that?"

I smiled again. "It's a private joke."

"I see." She paused. "Why haven't you told them?" she asked.

Because I'd lose them. They wouldn't get it. They'd treat me differently. I wouldn't be "normal" to them any more, even if I never freaked out ever again. Once they knew, they'd always be watching…waiting…wondering if I was going to lose it. I didn't want anyone else to look at me like that. I'd had enough with Mum, Dad, Jane and everyone at my old school.

"It just hasn't come up, that's all."

"Have you talked to anyone at college, about coming here? Have you even hinted to anyone?"

And even in my state, I felt a goo when I thought about Guy. I smiled again. "There's this one guy."

"Guy?"

"That's his name actually. Guy. Guy the guy."

Sarah didn't comment that I'd brought up another boy. She must've been losing track. It was *my* life and *I* was losing track. Things, life, just kept happening. Was it always like this? Or had my life been on pause for so long that I was on fast-forward now to catch up with everyone?

"And what did you tell Guy?"

"I didn't tell him as much. He was at the party, when I did the shots you don't approve of. He looked after me. And I got in a state about being sick, and he was…nice.

He mentioned he had a mate with head problems once."

So nice. So unlike-Guy nice.

"Maybe you should think about opening up more, Evie? People are much more understanding these days."

I thought about meeting the girls for coffee later. How we'd chat, and laugh. How much I enjoyed feeling normal around them.

"Hmm."

And I retched again, just to get her off the topic.

Twenty-three

Oli wasn't in film studies the first day back after half term. I came in late and found his seat next to mine glaringly empty. It should've had a neon sign on it, flashing, "you're a bad person, you're a bad person".

I could've messaged him to ask how he was.

I didn't though.

I just sat there, torturing myself with how selfish I was, imagining how much he was hurting. And yet still not messaging.

A film played on the screen at the front of the classroom. We weren't supposed to watch films during the classes – that was our homework. But Brian was hung-over – on a Monday – so he turned off the lights and put on *Dogville*, this totally screwed-up film with Nicole Kidman in it.

Of course, there was rape in it, which pissed me off. "Important" films had a tendency to do that. Like a storyline can't be meaningful unless there's been violence against women. It was like the rule of films. If an actress makes herself ugly for a role, she automatically wins an Oscar. If a scriptwriter shoves in a rape, the film's automatically "important".

Time sludged on by and I tapped my foot on the carpet – excited for lunch, excited about seeing Guy again. I hadn't heard from him at all over half term…but maybe he was shy? Thinking about him distracted me from my self-loathing around Oli. Would it be awkward? It would definitely be awkward, but in a nice way.

The bell finally went and I made my way to our usual spot on the grass next to the college smoking area. It wasn't as busy as normal, the biting wind putting everyone but the most determined smokers off. I wondered how long we'd be able to keep this up – it was getting colder every day. There he was. Wearing his beanie again. All alone as the others hadn't arrived yet. I put on my prettiest grin – the one where I close my mouth and tilt my head down, and because I'm short I look all demure.

"Hey," I said, sitting next to him, my knees all bandy with nerves.

He didn't look up. "Oh, hi," he said, with the least amount of enthusiasm in the world.

I bit my lip. "Umm, did you enjoy the party? I've not seen you since… I was so drunk." I found myself giggling in a really dumb way. Guy opened his rucksack and pulled out his rolling tobacco and Rizlas.

"Yeah," he replied, with even less enthusiasm than

before, which was a scientific feat let me tell you. "You were, I guess."

"Thanks for looking after me…"

"Whatever." He sprinkled some tobacco onto his papers and began to roll while I stared at the back of his hat. Completely stunned.

Awkward silence descended. Or maybe it was only awkward for me? Guy just sat quietly, smoking.

Had I made the whole thing up? The thought made me want to cry. My ribcage seemed to tighten, like it was squeezing my heart in on itself. I kept opening my mouth to say something, but shame kept closing it again.

"Er… Guy?"

"What?" He looked at me, but he may as well not have bothered. There was nothing in his face – no warmth, no affection.

"Umm… Oh Amber's coming."

I blinked back the first stirrings of tears and watched her approach. She was shivering and pulling the arms of her coat down – bless her, she said no coat ever fitted her long body. She was grinning from ear to ear.

"You'll never guess what!" she called, completely ignoring Guy, as I wished I had.

"What?"

She jogged over and chucked her bag on the grass next to us. "Where's Lottie?"

"She had philosophy with Jane and Joel at the other end of college."

Amber plopped next to me and gave me a giant smile. "She needs to get here NOW!"

"Why?"

"Because...I've made these!" And she reached into her bag like a magician into a top hat and withdrew some small laminated cards. She chucked one at me.

Guy peered over. "What is it?" he asked.

"It's our spinster membership card," Amber answered.

"Your what?"

I turned over Amber's masterpiece in my fingers. I knew she did art but I'd never seen her stuff before. The small card in my hand was stunning. She'd used black calligraphy and inked intricate designs of cats all over the front, all of them with tiny speech bubbles saying, "I'm ironic."

"Wow," I told Amber, ignoring Guy. "Girl, you are so talented. I love the ironic cats."

Amber turned the same colour as her hair. "Turn it over."

I flipped the card and found my name on the other side. *Evie – Spinster number two.*

"Oi," I said. "Why am I number two?"

She laughed. "I'm number one. I made them."

"I love them," I told her truthfully. "This may be my new favourite thing."

Guy leaned over and every hair on my body stood to attention. He glanced at the card as I resisted the urge to hide it. What sort of spinster would I be if I wasn't proud of my membership card? Especially around blokes like Guy, who I'd decided was The Epitome of Bell-ends. He didn't seem that bothered anyway...

"Girls are weird." He removed his space from my space, making me feel the gap.

I evilled him. "Oh, we're not the weird ones, believe me."

Amber shot me a questioning look and I just shook my head. Maybe I should tell her about Guy and the party? But that would make me fail the Bechdel test. It was all very well being a strong independent woman, but it was hard when boys' confusing behaviour kept making you lose your focus.

"Your mate's here," Guy announced. "Is she sick?"

The shadow of Lottie lumbered over, with Joel and Jane behind her. Lottie did look different, mainly because she wasn't wearing any make-up when she usually used eyeliner like face lotion. She wore just a plain checked oversized shirt too, rather than her usual lacy beady get-up. She'd been moping all half term, and didn't look like she was going to stop any time soon.

"You're sick," I muttered to Guy under my breath.

"What?"

"Nothing." And I turned my attention to Lotts.

"You all right, Lottie Botty?" Amber asked, as she sat between us, letting out a sigh.

"Hey, guys, yeah, I'm fine."

"You don't sound fine," I told her.

"Well, you know, my boyfriend still turned out to not be my boyfriend."

I saw Guy look interested but he didn't say anything. I knew this because I'd been sneaking glances at him every fifteen seconds to see if he'd been looking at me. He hadn't. Because obviously I'd dreamed up all of it in my stupid little brain.

Amber pulled out a third membership card. "Here, this will cheer you up."

The moment Lottie saw it she lit up a bit. "This is awesome," she declared, holding it up to the light. Jane and Joel rocked up with their arms around each other.

"What's awesome?" Joel asked, without saying hello.

Amber answered. "Our spinster membership cards."

They looked at each other in unison. "Your what now?"

"Our spinster cards," Lottie repeated. She held it up to the couple who were now in the process of sitting down and putting Jane's head in Joel's lap. "We are reclaiming the word."

"Cool, I guess," Jane said, before twisting her head around to check her reaction matched her boyfriend's.

"I don't understand," Joel said. "Aren't spinsters like old cat ladies?"

Amber rolled her eyes. "Tell me this, Joel. Is there a male version of an old cat lady?"

"I don't get what you mean."

"Is there a horrid word used to describe men who don't find anyone?"

"Er…" Joel looked bored already but that didn't deter Amber. She was on fire; I'd never seen her this happy.

"Exactly! Which is why we're reclaiming it. Spinster is the new cool word for awesome girls who don't let their lives revolve around men." She gave Jane a special look – Jane didn't notice, as she was busy tracing the outline of Joel's jaggedy eyebrows with her finger.

"Oh, cool," Joel said, in a dead way that made it obvious he didn't find it cool. "Anyway, good party last week, wasn't it, everyone?"

My skin prickled. Had Guy told Joel what almost happened between us? Was this what he was alluding to?

"Man though, Amber, you were wasted," Joel continued. "I never knew it was so hard getting vom out of curly hair."

Amber crumpled then brazened it out. "Whatever."

Jane twisted around and looked at Guy, who was smoking his second roll-up. "You have a good time, Guy? I barely saw you."

I looked at him too, my heart thud-thudding. He was annoyingly good-looking in the autumn sun. It lit up all the concaves in his cheeks; it made his dark hair look almost golden rather than black.

Good thought

Maybe he's going to turn around, look deep into my eyes, and say, "Actually it was one of the best nights of my life. If only we'd been given five more minutes, Evie."

Guy blew a plume of smoke directly upwards into the crisp air.

"It was okay. Pretty boring."

He didn't even look at me.

BAD THOUGHT

You imagined the whole thing. You're delusional.

I lay down on the grass, like I'd just been shot in war, not even caring about the chill seeping into me from the ground.

What had happened? Why was he behaving like this? Had I really imagined it? Was this my karma for Oli? And why was this making me like him more?

I didn't hear what Joel said at first.

"That's amazing, you'll so win," Jane told him.

I sat up, dazed. "What?" I asked.

Joel's eyes were dewy with excitement. "I said they're doing a battle of the bands at college. In a few weeks' time. In the canteen. The winner gets a free day in a professional recording studio."

Guy expressed his first display of emotion since I'd sat down. "Really, man? We're totally going to smash it."

"I know, right?" They leaned over and high-fived.

"You girls coming?" Joel asked. "You can bring that fella if you want to, Lottie?"

Lottie didn't look up. "Oh, great," she half whispered.

Jane's eyes were as excited as Joel's. "We could all get ready at my house," she said to us girls. Amber rolled her eyes, ever so slightly so Jane didn't see.

"Oh, great," she said. I shot her a look.

"That sounds fab, Jane," I said. I looked at the others. "But…umm…I'm not sure if we're going…"

It didn't sound like our thing, especially after the church hall gig. How would this be any different? The college canteen was hardly a more exciting destination. And I really didn't fancy listening to "Die Bitch Die" again, or having to watch Guy onstage when he was being like this…

…as if on cue…

"Bullshit," Guy interrupted me. I turned and he was finally looking at me – his eyes staring directly into mine, a half-smile on his face. "You are definitely coming, Evie. I wouldn't have it any other way."

He winked, and I didn't feel like crying any more.

Twenty-four

I told them.

Not about me, obviously. But about Guy, in our Spinster Club meeting at my house straight after college.

"Man your room is tidy, Evie," Amber said as she walked in. "Do you guys have a cleaner or something terribly middle class like that?"

I'd actually run up to my room before them and scattered a few bits of laundry on the floor but it obviously hadn't made a difference.

Lottie was just as gobsmacked. "Are you Jesus? Only Jesus could have a room this clean." She sniffed. "Everything smells of pine."

That would be my antibacterial spray. I was down to only one spritz a day, but, yeah, I guess the tree smell lingered. To me, it smelled of safe.

"It's not usually like this," I lied. "Mum made me tidy this weekend."

Actually the opposite was true. Mum was in charge of me *not* tidying.

Luckily they were distracted by my wall of film. Amber stood with her head back, straining her neck to see up to the top of my gigantic film cabinet. It dominated the whole wall – floor to ceiling jampacked with movies. "Christ, Evie, how many movies does a girl need?"

"I do film studies," I said, all breezy. "You have to watch a lot of films."

"Yeah, but, wow... You have like every one ever made. How do you ever leave the house?"

Well I didn't, that was the point.

They started digging through my collection, pulling ones out and asking to borrow them. I nodded and went downstairs to make hot chocolate. Mum and Dad were in the kitchen. They both had glasses of red wine in front of them.

"Woah, hey, guys," I said, bending down to give them a quick hug at the kitchen table. "What are you doing home so early? I've got some friends upstairs, is that okay? They're not staying for dinner or anything." Mum was going to be cross, and I inwardly prepared for it. She got stressed if I invited people around without loads of pre-warning; she never said why. Only that it was "disrespectful".

Dad gave me a weak smile from behind his glasses. Every facial expression he made was weak. A side-effect from working sixty hours a week. It also didn't make for a very patient person. I still remember the day I tied myself to the bed with a skipping rope so they wouldn't make me go to school. Mum had tried pleading, crying, begging, dragging in Rose to make me feel guilty.

Dad had just come in with a bucket of water, yelled, "If you wanna be so clean, I'll make you clean," and chucked it all over me.

Afterwards, in our family therapy sessions, he'd said he'd thought it would shock me out of it. But I'd stayed on the bed, my teeth clanging together, until Mum caved and promised I didn't have to go in. It took a two-hour bath to get warm again.

Now, both of them sat at the head of the kitchen table, business looks on their faces.

"It's nice your friends are here," Mum said. "Though I do wish you'd asked me first."

I tried not to pull a face. "We're just chatting in my room."

"Still though, it's my house. I like to know what's going on. You know that."

"Well I'll ask them to leave then."

My parents gave each other the look they'd honed to perfection, the one they use when I'm being difficult.

"Don't talk to your mother like that," Dad said, sounding resigned.

I sighed. "Like what?"

"Like that, with the attitude."

"Should I ask them to leave or not?"

"There's no need for that, just ask next time."

"All right, I will." I walked past them to the kettle and

brought it to the sink to fill with water. As it boiled, I noticed them both staring at me.

"What is it?"

"We had our catch-up with Sarah today," Dad said, not looking me in the eyes, the way he always did when he mentioned Sarah.

"Oh…"

I'd agreed confidentiality-wise for my parents to have regular meetings with Sarah, so they could be kept up to date on my goals and strategies.

"She told us about the sandwich," Dad said.

"We're really proud of you, Evelyn." Mum gave me her first smile of the day, like I'd just got an A in a test or something. I guess I had, an A in "Undercover Normal". Although no one normal would eat that sandwich.

"Thanks." I got out the cocoa powder and heaped it into three mugs. Whenever I glanced over, they were watching me…

"Now, she wanted us to discuss your medication some more…" Dad said loudly.

"Shh," I interrupted, somewhat desperately, pointing to my bedroom directly above. Dad's voice had always been rather boomy. "My friends are upstairs, they might hear you."

Dad looked nonplussed. He turned to Mum who shrugged. "So?" he asked.

"So…" I said, pouring the now-boiled water on top of the chocolate. "They don't know about stuff…"

"Why not? Why haven't you told them?"

"Just because…"

There was an awkward pause.

"I came home especially early to talk all this through with you," Dad said. "I was really hoping we could put a plan together." He put his wine glass down and it clanked.

"But you didn't tell me about it!" I protested.

"Well you didn't tell us you were having friends round."

"Ergh!" I poured too much milk into a cup and spilled some onto the counter. I grabbed a kitchen towel to mop it up. Both of them looked shocked by my yelling. "When I was really sick, when I never left the house, didn't you guys *dream* of me bringing friends back from school? Didn't you worry that would never happen? That I'd never even go back to school, let alone make nice normal friends? Now I've done it, your wish has come true, and all you wanna talk about is me being sick!" I dumped the soggy towel in the bin and stared both of them down. We stayed like that for a moment, standing off, then Dad crumbled, screeched back his chair and stood to give me another hug.

"You're right, darling." He squeezed so hard it hurt my ribs. "Go back upstairs, have a good time with your friends."

I looked at Mum over his shoulder. "Mum?"

Mum softened too. Not quite as much though. It had been so long since I'd had anyone round, I'd forgotten what an issue it was.

"Have a good time, dear. Dinner's at eight though, so can

you have them out by the time I start cooking? And you still should've asked."

"I know, I know."

I came back to my room brandishing hot drinks.

"You were aaaaaages, Evie," Lottie said, the most bright and cheerful I'd seen her all day. "We've put *Thelma and Louise* on, rather fitting for our first meeting I thought."

BAD THOUGHT

You've not put the film that was in the player back into its case. Now it's going to get scratched. What sort of person would do such a thing?

I smiled, "Great thinking."

Amber was sprawled out on the floor as was her custom, her long legs taking up half the rug. "I've never seen this movie," she admitted sheepishly.

Lottie chucked a cushion at her. "What? You haven't seen *Thelma and Louise*. It's like… the Bible."

"The Bible's a book," I pointed out. "And religious."

"Whatever, it's like the film version of the Bible. The Bible for strong women."

Amber ducked from the cushion. "My little brother

always chooses our films," she said. "You don't want to know how many times I've sat through *Star Wars*."

I pulled a face. "Kids still watch *Star Wars*?"

"What can I say, my brother's a moron."

"AMBER," both Lottie and I yelled.

She shrugged. "I'm not even sorry."

I carefully picked my way over my friends' bodies, dispersing their drinks, before tucking myself up on the bed and wedging myself in the corner. We half watched, half slurped as Thelma and Louise got drunk at a bar. When it got to the rape scene, Lottie chucked another cushion at the screen. "Aww, man, I forgot about this bit."

"What bit? The entire motivation for the characters' actions?" I asked.

"Yes, oh, can we talk through it? I'm down on men enough at the moment."

"Hey," Amber said, "I've not seen it."

"That bloke attempts to rape Thelma so Louise shoots him," Lottie told her.

Just as she said it, Susan Sarandon arrived on the telly and shot the guy dead.

"Well, thanks for ruining it for me."

"You'll live." Lottie turned away from the screen. "I feel bad," she announced. "It's our first meeting as spinsters and I want to be empowered and talk about the glass ceiling or whatever, but I can't stop thinking about Tim. It's like he's dancing on my brain." She stopped and thought about it. "Dancing on my brain, and pissing on my heart."

I gave her a sad smile. "With metaphors like that, Cambridge is going to let you right in."

She returned my smile with a sadder one. "I know, right? Well, there's never been more potent a creative force than heartbreak."

I budged nearer on the bed. "Is your heart really broken?"

"I dunno. Yes, maybe. Maybe it's just been maimed. Really horribly maimed."

Amber twisted around and patted her leg. "Do you want to talk about it?"

"Yes, maybe...no. Ahhh, I'm not a very good spinster, am I?"

"Spinsters don't judge other spinsters," I said, surprised by how wise my voice sounded. "You're allowed to talk about what you're going through – it's what friends are for."

Even I could see my double standards then, without Sarah there to point them out.

Lottie's eyes welled up again. "What would I do without you guys?"

I put my arm around her. "Go batshit crazy, skin a rabbit, drape it over your head and go stand outside his window, singing 'I Want You Back' by the Jackson 5?"

She giggled, her tears subsiding instantly. "That sounds like so much fun."

"Revenge is always fun," Amber said. "Just ask my adopted brother."

"AMBER!"

"I'm not even sorry."

And we all laughed like maniacs.

"You know what's the best revenge, of course?" Amber said, finishing off her hot chocolate and putting the mug down on my wooden floor…without using the coaster I'd given her. "Moving on with your life, and becoming absolutely fabulous so he can see what he's missing."

I shook my head, biting my tongue about the coaster. "No, I don't agree. You should become fabulous for you, because you want to be fabulous, not because you want some idiot to kick himself for rejecting you in a year's time."

"Ahh, but this is why it's the best revenge," Amber said. "By the time they're kicking themselves, you're so fabulous you've forgotten all about them."

"I like to think I already *am* fabulous," Lottie wailed, and we giggled.

"Of course you are," I said.

"So, how do I get revenge then?"

"By not caring."

"That's what I want, but my heart won't let me. It's got Stockholm Syndrome."

"Give it some time. It only happened a week ago."

We turned back to the movie and Lottie seemed to get lost in it. She turned onto her stomach and put her feet up against my wall. But now my head wasn't in it. I was still going over this morning with Guy – the way he'd acted like nothing happened, the way he'd tortured me with his silence, the way he'd known I was getting pissed off and then told me to come to Battle of the Bands...the way I kept imagining what would have happened if we hadn't been interrupted at the party.

Maybe I should open up? Maybe I should talk it through with my friends. It wasn't about me, as such. Maybe I could test them with this?

I sighed. "Something sort of happened between me and Guy." I surprised myself by blurting it out.

Immediately Thelma and Louise were forgotten. They both whipped around in unison.

"No way?" Lottie said, her hand over her mouth.

"Ergh, why?" Amber asked in disgust.

So I told them. About our strange walk home, about the way he'd looked after me at the party. I neglected to tell them just how much they'd upset me about Oli. "And, then," I said, "we were about to kiss but Jane and Joel burst in with Amber...and then, today, well you saw him today, he acted like nothing happened. And I didn't hear from him at all over half term."

Lottie grimaced. "What a jerk."

"It's Guy," Amber said. "What did you think would happen? He's good-looking, yeah, but he's also got trouble written all over him."

Lottie gave me a wry grin. "That's why she likes him."

"Hey, that's not why I like him. I don't even know if I do like him."

"I certainly don't like him," Amber said. "Evie, he's soooo up himself, especially now all those younger girls fancy him after that awful gig. And he's a filthy stoner. I mean, why?"

Lottie nodded solemnly. "Amber's right. I mean, love, he does drugs. How much bigger do the words 'BAD NEWS' have to be scrawled on his forehead?"

"It's only weed though…" I wasn't sure why I was defending him. "That's not like real drugs, is it?"

"Try telling that to the police," Lottie replied, picking up her hot chocolate and taking a sip. "Try telling that to the homework he doesn't do, the activities he's probably given up, his brain cells that are lying in a brain cell morgue somewhere, dead as dead can be."

"I…I…" I didn't know what to say to that.

Amber untangled her limbs and sat with me on the bed. "Why do you even like him anyway? Be honest, did you even like him before you realized he might like you?"

"I…er…"

"Because it sounds to me like he's playing you…" she continued, not letting me finish. "There's nothing more attractive than having someone think you're attractive. Unless they're like facially-challenged or whatever. Sounds like he made some poxy move, dangled a carrot, and then when you were about to bite, hid the carrot, and now you want the carrot even more."

"Er…I…er…what's the carrot?"

"His penis," Lottie interrupted and she and Amber burst out laughing again.

I didn't laugh. I hadn't thought about Guy's penis before.

It was weird, but I guess he must have one, tucked in his jeans the entire time. That must be strange, having one THERE all day, every day. I'd never really even thought about any penises before, I certainly hadn't ever seen one. Apart from in diagrams. I assume Jane had seen Joel's by now. And Lottie had certainly seen a few. Was I supposed to want men's penises? Wouldn't I just giggle? For the millionth time I wished I'd had a normal teenagehood so I could've encountered penises during drunken parties in people's garages at the age I was still allowed to giggle at them. Now, I would have to act all mature around one…that is, if I ever got to see one… Would I have seen Guy's if we hadn't been interrupted? No, no way I would've let him.

Penises have diseases.

"Evie, you're blushing," Lottie teased, her face red from laughing.

"No, I'm not."

"Yes, you are."

"Not."

"Are."

Amber interrupted. "I can't keep up with you, Evie. First Ethan, then Oli, now Guy…you have a flaky heart. It's like puff pastry."

"Hey," I said, hurt. "That's not fair. Ethan was a sex maniac… Oli, well, you know what happened there, and, well, I don't know what I feel for Guy yet." I crossed my arms huffily. I wasn't *trying* to be puff pastry, I just sort of wanted to date someone and have a boy think I was half-decent and not mad. That's normal, right?

Amber raised a gingery eyebrow. "Calm down, Eves, people might start to think you really like him."

I sighed. "I don't know. How are you supposed to know. Why can't God come down from the sky with a giant foam finger, point at some bloke, and say, "That one, Evie, you're supposed to fall in love with that one. He's not a douche, I checked for you.""

"God," Lottie turned around too, her head blocking the film, "…has more important stuff to do."

I grinned wryly. "Oh yeah, like what?"

"Like mending the world."

"Not doing a very good job, is he?"

She grinned too. "True, that's why we need to help. By fighting inequality with our kick-ass spinster meetings…"

"True," I said. I thought about Guy, again. "Do you think it's all part of inequality's plan? To mess us about lovewise so we're too busy waiting for text messages to burn our bras and run for Prime Minister?"

"If that's the case," Amber said, "you two are playing right into inequality's hands."

I rolled my eyes at her. "Oh you, so noble. Just wait until *you* almost get kissed at a house party."

Amber looked sad. "I should be so lucky."

And we accidentally spent the rest of the time we had before mum kicked them out, trying to convince Amber she was pretty instead of fighting the patriarchy…

Twenty-five

Rose shuffled past my room as I cleared up afterwards.

"Why are you using antibacterial spray all over your bed?" she called over the threshold. I stopped spraying and looked up, blushing.

"I had friends over. They were eating biscuits on my bed."

Rose drew a pained smile, the sort you usually see on grown-ups, not tweenagers. "You know what I'm going to say."

"No, what are you going to say?" My voice sounded sulky, like someone Rose's age.

"Logical things – like it's fine to just brush the crumbs off the bed and leave them on the floor. That you won't get sick from people eating on your bed…that you could probably even leave the crumbs on the sheets and the world wouldn't stop rotating."

"You never know, it might."

"No, Evie," she came in and perched on the end of my bed, "it wouldn't."

I did one last quick spray, on my pillow, for good measure. My room stunk of pine. If I opened the cupboard I wouldn't be surprised if Robin Hood was squatting in there. I gave Rose a pleading look. "You know how I feel about logic."

"The thing about logic is..." Rose curled herself up like a cat. "Is that it really is rather logical."

"Screw logic, it's just not imaginative enough."

She giggled.

I put the spray away in the box under my bed and sat next to her, pulling her in for a free head rub. She groaned and wiggled into my fingers.

"Did you have a nice time with your friends?" she asked.

I smiled. "I guess. We were supposed to be talking about feminism but we ended up just whinging about boys not calling us. I wish I was your age again."

"No you don't." I felt her tense under my fingertips.

"Everything okay, Rose?"

"I heard you and the parents talking about you reducing your medication again."

"That is called changing the subject. *Is* everything okay, Rose?"

She sighed. "It's fine. So, how do you feel about the medicine?"

"We're not supposed to talk about this together. You're impressionable, remember?"

"You're cleaning a bit more than normal."

"Well you're avoiding my questions more than normal."

"Touché." She rolled over and looked at my films. "How about we just watch a movie and stop interrogating each other?"

I nodded. I could finish after she went to bed. What she didn't know wouldn't hurt her. Or Mum, or Sarah. It was just a bit of spray.

BAD THOUGHT

But it's not just a bit of spray though, is it, Evie?
You plan to finish the whole bottle.

I smiled down at Rose and gave the side of her face one last stroke.

"A movie sounds fab."

I waited until everyone was asleep before I crept out of bed and slowly drew the box out from underneath it.

A floorboard creaked. I paused.

Silence again.

I fished out the spray, and, okay, a bit of bleach and a J-cloth from my hidden stash – I mean, they ate in here! My phone went off. It sounded far too loud in the quiet of the house, vibrating angrily against my bedside table. I grabbed it to shut it up.

It was a message.

A message from Guy. Otherwise known as Ignory Norington.

You are coming to Battle of the Bands, aren't you?

A smile started in my teeth and spread out across my face. If anyone walked in, I would be quite the sight – crouching in the dark, grinning like a madman, clutching a bottle of bleach.

I hid the bleach back under my bed and crawled under the covers.

I fell asleep smiling.

RECOVERY DIARY

Date: 6ᵗʰ November

Medication: 5mg Fluoxetine

Now in a disgusting-tasting liquid form as the tablets are too small to chop up any further

Thoughts/Feelings:

Does Guy like me?

Could I fall in love with him?

Will anyone ever fall in love with me? Could he?

Love = acceptance. Will anyone ever accept me?

...Hang on, what sort of shite feminist am I?

It's coming back, isn't it? But I can't tell anyone.

Homework:

- Let me or your parents know immediately if you experience any suicidal thoughts.
- Keep your recovery diary religiously, if you can. Record your thoughts and feelings, and keep an eye out for new rituals and bad thoughts. Then we can work on them together.
- Keep up the good work, Evie! :)

Twenty-six

Autumn had barely put in an appearance before winter arrived, basically overnight. It swept through our town like a late party guest, one who overcompensates for their bad timekeeping by drinking too much too quickly and making an embarrassment of themselves. One day it was all warm and golden, the next all bitter and grey. Within days dresses were pushed to the back of wardrobes, put into hibernation until April. Girls trawled online shopping sites for the perfect pair of ankle boots that didn't exist. We pulled out our long-forgotten winter coats and found last year's receipts and used tissues still snug in the pockets.

I didn't have any old used tissues in my winter coat. I would never be that disgusting.

Oli still hadn't come back to college. I worried about him. I worried about him but I still didn't message him.

As abruptly as the change in season, they'd lowered my medication again. To almost nothing.

"Now, if you start suddenly feeling really low and potentially suicidal, you are to ring me immediately," Sarah said, as she chatted through the new recovery plan. "It's a really rare side effect of withdrawal, but it can happen."

"Thanks," I said, dryly. "Give the anxious girl coming off her medication something more to worry about, why don't ya?"

"I'm proud of you," she said. And the way her face looked made me think she really meant it. "Now, I'm going on holiday for a week, so we'll miss a session. I know this isn't great timing, but you've got the emergency contact number, haven't you? And you can always go to your GP."

I felt my tummy sink… I hated it when Sarah went away. It was weird to think of her having a different life, a normal one, with holidays, and people she could talk to without using medical training.

"I'll be grand," I said, smiling. Thinking, *I don't know if I will, but I like how proud you look right now.*

Mornings took longer, as I had to carefully pour out a liquid form of my medication onto a spoon. Very soon, I would stop completely.

Rose told Mum about my cleaning box and it was removed from under my bed. I didn't talk to Rose for two days and spent all my spare time with the girls instead. Amber was enough to bring anyone out of a bad mood.

"Guys," she announced, on a windy Wednesday, smashing her bag on the table. We'd relocated to a cosy corner of the cafeteria. "Guess what? I've made an agenda for today's Spinster meeting."

Lottie and I looked up from our game of noughts and crosses.

"An agenda?" Lottie asked.

Amber nodded, her face as red as her hair. "To give us focus. You two spent most of the last meeting whinging about boys. That is all fair and well, but I think we need an agenda too."

I poked my tongue into the side of my mouth in amusement.

"Item one: History of the Suffragettes – discussion topic: *Were they terrorists or heroes?*" I said, in a BBC news presenter voice. "Item two: *Why won't Guy reply to my messages?*"

Lottie rolled her eyes. "Has he done it again? Messaged you then not replied to your reply?"

I nodded. "Yep. He messaged the other night, asking me about the new Wes Anderson film. I know, right? Guy? Wes Anderson? Anyway, I thought he might ask me to go see it. But when I replied – after a good half-hour of waiting time I may add – saying it had good reviews, nothing. Nada. Not a sausage."

"You need to stop replying."

"I know."

"So why do you keep replying?"

I put my head down on the table. "I don't know."

Amber bashed her bag on the table again, like a judge with a gavel.

"You see!" she said, her face even redder if possible. "*This* is why we need an agenda!"

I looked up and smiled at her. "I couldn't agree more."

As if he knew I'd just made a conscious effort to stop talking about him, Guy barrelled through the double doors of the cafeteria. Why do guys like Guy look so good in duffel coats? It really is terribly unfair. He had Joel and Jane with him – their hands in each other's coat pockets – just like the saying. They spotted us and headed over.

Guy sat next to me and I felt outside's cold air coming off him. He stank of smoke.

"Smoking in winter is such a mission," he announced, without even saying hi. "It's so effing cold outside."

I sat up straighter in my seat, realized I should look casual, and slouched again. "So why smoke?" I asked.

He looked right at me. "Because it's cool."

"I don't know if lung cancer would agree with you on that one."

He shrugged. "I'll quit before I'm twenty-five."

"Being cool?"

I watched him struggle not to smile. "No," he said. "I'll be cool for ever."

Joel and Jane went up to buy some chips to share while Amber handed Lottie and me some paper. "Here's my agenda."

"Jeez," I said, scanning it. "You've actually made an actual agenda."

Guy gave her a look. "Is this for your lezzer club again?"

Amber's prickles went up. "It's for the Spinster Club, yes! And that's a totally offensive word anyway, dickwad. We're meeting at my house after school." She gave me a *what-the-hell-do-you-see-in-him?* look over the top of his head. It involved lots of pointed glaring.

I scanned the page and it made me love her more. She'd even scheduled in a fifteen-minute break for "cheesy snacks".

The topic for tonight's meeting, I wasn't expecting though. "We're going to discuss periods?" I asked.

Guy almost choked on his Diet Coke.

Amber nodded while Guy looked at us in horror. "You girls are dedicating an evening to talking about being on the blob?"

Amber gave him a pointed glare while I went as red as a...well, a period I guess.

"It's not our fault we bleed."

We all grimaced. "Unnecessary usage of the word 'bleed'," Lottie whispered and we both burst out laughing.

"That is disgusting," Guy said.

"You're disgusting."

"I'm not the freak who can bleed for three days without dying."

Amber gave him another glare. "I'm not going to continue this with HIM here."

Guy looked all faux innocent. "Who me?"

"Yes you."

"Well, quite frankly, Amber, I'm gutted. I really felt like

openly discussing menstruation while I ate lunch." He pulled out an unhealthy looking white bread sandwich and took a satisfied bite.

Amber waited until he was chewing. "Your mum menstruates you know."

Guy almost choked on his mouthful.

"She might be bleeding right this moment," Amber added and looked on contentedly as he disintegrated into a proper coughing fit.

Worried, I thumped him on the back until he stopped. Every time I touched him it sent little fireflies buzzing up my arm. Jane and Joel returned with their chips and surveyed the hubbub.

"What's going on?" Jane asked, looking at Guy's bulging eyes and Amber's smug grin.

Lottie answered, not looking up from her agenda where she'd been colouring all the "o"s in with pencil. "Amber here has just been reminding Guy that his mother has periods."

"Gross," Joel said, at the exact same time Jane said, "Eww."

Amber grabbed back her agendas, making Lottie accidentally scribble on hers as it was torn from her grasp, and stood to leave.

"Your mums have periods too. All of ours do. One of the things we're discussing tonight is society's immature attitudes towards menstruation. Girls, I'll see you at mine after school."

She walked off, leaving us stunned.

Guy readjusted his chair so his leg touched my leg.

Even through my jeans it felt damn good.

Twenty-seven

Lottie examined the plate of biscuits and took her time choosing one.

"I know the theme of tonight's meeting is periods, but did you really have to get themed biscuits?" she asked.

Amber looked down at the plate of Jammie Dodgers, arranged thoughtfully in a circle.

"Oh," she said, looking dismayed. "I didn't think of that."

Lottie and I creased up laughing.

"Thanks," I said. "Jammy Dodgers have now been ruined for the rest of my life."

And Amber joined in.

Her room was a disgrace to all bedrooms everywhere. I literally had to pick a pathway to the bed through discarded clothes, dried-up palettes of oil paints, and crumpled-up bits of paper. How could someone so organized be so messy?

BAD THOUGHT

What sort of pig lives like this?

BAD THOUGHT

When was the carpet last hoovered?

BAD THOUGHT

You're going to get sick, you're going to get sick,
you're going to get sick.

I stopped laughing, my heart already racing.

Shut up, brain, I told myself, and I forced myself to rub my hands on the carpet as a private exposure. I didn't eat anything after that though. I didn't eat for the rest of the evening. Just in case.

Amber pulled her duvet around us so we formed a big lump.

BAD THOUGHT

When was this duvet last washed? Do I really
need to have it touching me?

I wanted to jump out of it, but how would I do that without attracting attention? Amber had already divvied out the agendas and, sensing this really meant something to her, Lottie and I didn't take the piss, and I did deep-breathing about the duvet.

She cleared her throat. "So," she said, a little nervous. "I'd like to declare this meeting of the Spinster Club officially open. Tonight's topic for discussion is periods." Lottie put down her Jammy Dodger. "Now, you may think it's weird I've brought this topic up, but can you understand why?"

Lottie and I looked at each other. "Are we supposed to answer?" I asked.

Amber nodded. "Er…" I wracked my brains. "Because all women have them? I guess that's what makes us girls?"

She beamed at me. "Yes! Exactly right."

"Do I get a sticker?"

"Shut up. No. As you said, periods are what make us girls. Half of the population have them. Our let's-face-it incredible ability to menstruate and grow babies makes us responsible for every single person on this earth. And yet, the sole thing that makes us women, the sole thing that creates life, isn't allowed to be talked about. What's up with that? You saw Guy this lunchtime, he thought I was uber-gross for even talking about it. How screwed is that?"

I rubbed my cheek. "It is a bit gross though, isn't it?"

She shook her head adamantly. "No, we've just been conditioned to think that."

"We have?"

"Yes."

Lottie put her plastic plate down. "She's got a point, you know. Take sanitary towel adverts. Like, why do they always use blue goo to represent period blood? If I found blue goo in my sanitary towel I'd ring the NHS helpline straight away."

"Ha," I said. "I guess I never thought about it. Why don't they use red goo? Or brown?"

"The whole sanitary/tampon world is such a minefield of wrongness," Lottie said. "Think about how they're marketed. They're all made to look like sweet wrappers advertising how 'discreet' they are."

I nodded, thoughtfully. "You're right. I always buy the compact ones, so I can hide them in my hand on the way to the loo so no one can see what I'm carrying."

Amber pointed at me aggressively. "Absolutely right."

"You almost poked me in the eye."

She ignored me. "Think about it. We all do it. Buy these flowery tiny things to hide the fact we're on. But three days a month, nearly every woman in the world is on and we're all hiding it. It's weird. Something we all do, something that's so natural, something that we'd freak out about if it stopped happening…is still seen as shameful."

Lottie giggled. "Have you seen that TV advert for tampons? The one where they call a period 'Mother Nature' and she's this old prudish hag wearing a twinset and pearls that keeps ruining fun stuff like music festivals?"

I smiled with her. "Well have you seen that new painkiller they're advertising specifically for period cramps? I looked at the label and it's just plain old ibuprofen, nothing else. It costs two quid more and the only difference is they've made the box pink."

Amber pointed again.

"Seriously, Amber, I need protective goggles with you about."

She ignored me again, too excited. "It's such a disconnect, isn't it? They market periods themselves as this horrible frumpy awful thing, and then the stuff we buy to deal with it is all pink and girly and 'hey, girl, it's okay, you can still smell of roses and go kickboxing'."

Lottie nodded. "You're right. Why not just go the whole hog? Periods suck, why make them scented and flowery? I'd much rather they put tampons in black boxes that came with a free chocolate bar."

"With little slogans on each one that says stuff like, 'Blame Eve' or 'This is your burden'," I added.

The others laughed so hard that I didn't stop feeling proud for ten minutes. Which was fortunate really because, punctual as ever, Amber called our break for cheesy snacks. I watched as they dipped their hands into the bowl of Wotsits, the neon yellow gunk sticking to their fingers. Lottie licked it off eagerly before delving back into the bowl. My stomach lurched. Bile rose up in my throat.

"Do you not want any, Evie?" Amber asked, a smear of orange dust around her lips.

I shook my head. "I'm stuffed, thanks."

"You sure?" She picked up the bowl and wafted it under

my nose. My tummy lurched again, spiralling in on itself, twisting itself into tangles.

"I...I..."

I was saved by her brat of a younger brother bashing through her bedroom door. He was all wrapped up in a post-bath towel, his hair all wet and sticking up on end. He would've looked cute if it wasn't for:

"Amber is a big fat LESBIAN!"

"CRAIG! GET OUT OF MY ROOM." Amber was already on her feet.

"Lesbian lesbian lesbian."

"OUT!"

"Ginger lesbian! You never have boys in your room, do you?" he cackled. "Lezzer lezzer lezzer."

Lottie and I looked at each other hopelessly.

"GET OUT, YOU LITTLE BRAT."

"At least I don't have ginger pubes. She leaves them in the bath. GINGER PUBES GINGER PUBES."

That's when the bowl flew through the air, sending the Wotsits cascading to the carpet. I ducked. So did Lottie. But Craig was hit right in the face with the bowl. His mouth hovered in an open "o" from shock. Then the howling started.

"MUUUUUUUUUMMMMMMMY."

Amber's stepmum was at the door in a second. When she saw him crying, and the tiny graze above his eyebrow, she went into overdrive. She dropped to her knees. "Oh my God, Craig. Are you okay? What happened?"

He shakily pointed at Amber, who stood, staring at where the bowl had been in her hand. "I didn't mean to hurt him. It's a plastic bowl!"

"AMBER. Out here now."

And she was half-dragged from her bedroom. The door swung shut heavily behind them. We heard yelling. We heard screaming.

Lottie and I didn't know where to look. We couldn't even look at each other for a bit. We just stared at all of Amber's oil paintings, pinned haphazardly to the walls. I didn't know much about art but they were very good, very Vincent Van Goghy, all swirls and spirals, but a bit darker. There was one in the corner of what must be her mum, judging by the hair. Her face took up only the smallest corner of the canvas; the rest of it was painted black.

"Should we leave?" I whispered as the yelling got louder.

"YOU ALWAYS TAKE HIS SIDE."

Lottie looked around for means of escape.

"How? We have to get past…them. God, her brother is a brat."

"Stepbrother," I corrected.

"EMBARRASSED ME IN FRONT OF MY FRIENDS."

"Let's just sit here quietly and hope it goes away," I said. We both started playing with our phones.

"YOU CAN'T GROUND ME, I'M SIXTEEN."

"SHUT UP SHUT UP SHUT UUUUUP."

"I HATE YOU. NO I WON'T SAY SORRY. I HATE HIM. YOU HEAR THAT? I HATE YOU, YOU LITTLE GIT."

My phone beeped and I tapped it quickly, not wanting Amber's family to hear it.

It was a message. From Lottie.

This is so awkward, I could die.

We both dissolved into hushed laughter.

The argument died down and Craig's howling quietened. We heard resentful apologies muttered through the wood of the door. When Amber re-entered, her face was pink and her cheeks were all splotchy. The front bit of her hair was matted from tears.

"So, guys," she said, all breezy, like nothing extraordinary had ever happened in the history of her life. "I was thinking we should each write letters to our local MP, and ask him to cut tax on tampons."

Lottie and I shared another meaningful look over Amber's curls and nodded in unison.

"Great idea."

"Brilliant."

"Why should we pay tax on tampons anyway?" Lottie said. "It's a tax on women. It's not like we *want* to buy them."

Amber picked her way through the clothes piles to her laptop, which was hidden by a heap of rubbish.

"Great, I'll just pull up his address. You guys got pens and paper, right?"

We sat and wrote in semi-contented silence. Amber scribbled eagerly, her biro almost ripping through the page.

I felt sorry for the assistant who read her letter. I reckoned a lot of misplaced anger was heading in their direction. She stopped for a moment, and Lottie and I looked up at her, waiting for her to talk about it.

"I'm not a lesbian," she said, sadly. "If you thought what Craig was saying was true. There's nothing wrong with being gay of course, but I'm not one. It pisses me off that just because I get angry about women's rights, and I don't want to date all the porn-obsessed runts at college, people automatically put me in that box. It's messed up on so many levels, like it's not even a bad box to be in…"

"I don't think you should listen too much to your brat of a brother," I said, though I felt guilty, because I had wondered a bit about Amber myself.

"Guy thinks it too. He calls this the lezzer club."

Lottie made an angry sound with her tongue. "But Guy is a moron. Isn't he, Evie?"

"Umm," I stuttered.

Amber blew out her breath. "Let's not get into this. Come on, back to our letters."

I wasn't sure what to write. I'd never written a letter to an MP before.

My letter to the MP about periods

Dear Chris Briggs MP,
I know you're probably very busy, fielding angry

letters about bin collections and such — our town is a bit like that. Everyone's always whinging to each other about the green belt.

I know all this stuff is important and that you have to listen to them to get re-voted in, but I was just wondering if you could put all that aside for one moment? And think about how difficult it would be to make decisions and keep everybody happy whilst your penis was bleeding for four days a month...

My phone beeped and I accidentally scribbled in the margin. It was a message from Guy.

How's your blob meeting going?

The girls looked up from their letters. "Who is it?" Lottie asked.

I pulled a face, pretending I wasn't delighted. "Just a message from Guy."

Amber rolled her eyes. "Message him back saying you're too busy fighting The Man right now to deal with his shite."

I read the message again, suppressing a smile.

"You know what?" I said. "I reckon I'd have a lot more time and energy to fight The Man if I wasn't dealing with Guy's shite."

"So don't deal with it then."

I shrugged. "I can't help it. It's hormones or whatever."

Lottie gave me an all-knowing smile. "Pheromones more like."

I began to blush but my cheeks were humbled by Amber's death stare. "I swear we can't go an hour without you two talking about boys. I thought my agenda would boy-proof the evening."

"Hey, we're trying," Lottie said. "But I thought spinsters didn't judge each other?"

"I know. It just makes me angry."

"We can tell," I said, and Amber laughed at herself.

"So," she said, standing up again. "What have we got in our letters?"

We talked about periods for another half-hour – the other two reminiscing about their first ones. I stayed silent, just laughing at their stories. We then discussed the rules of the Spinster Club and decided to take it in turns to chair each meeting with a feminism-related discussion topic that interested us. Amber went off to sneak some stamps from her dad's office to post the letters.

Lottie yawned and lay back on the bed.

"I don't think I've ever thought that much about my period before," she said.

"Me neither," I lied.

My first period and what I didn't tell them

I got it pretty late. I hadn't eaten properly in so long that my body delayed it. It still came though, while I was sleeping. I woke up to find my sheets smeared with a brownish-reddish stain. I'd been lying in the blood all night.

Mum was woken by my screaming.

"It's natural," she said. "Come on, Evie, it's womanhood. You should be proud. You're a woman now."

I could control the germs from outside. I'd learned how. Hiding how often I was washing my hands, using my pocket money to buy antibacterial spray to stockpile under the bed. But how could I control these new germs inside me?

I dreaded it each month. The blood. What was I supposed to do with the blood? The packet said you could leave tampons in for eight hours? Eight? Leave blood congealing inside you for eight hours? I used towels. I changed them the moment they were stained. On heavy days I set my alarm clock to go off every hour during the night so I could get up and change them. I had to allocate more pocket money to buying sanitary towels. I didn't have much cash left each month. It didn't matter really. It wasn't like I was leaving the house that often.

After each period was over, I cleaned myself inside out – to ensure I'd gotten rid of the blood. I sprayed the showerhead up there. I used spare change to buy feminine hygiene wash. I didn't trust that to do the job, so I used soap too. I once even used fairy liquid in the bath…

… One day it started to smell down there. I washed it more. By the end of the day, it stank. And it hurt. Just pulling down my knickers was agony.

Mum overheard me whimpering in the bathroom. "Evie, let me in," she'd yelled through the bathroom door. After an hour of her begging, I scuttled over and unlocked it, crying with shame, sobbing in pain. She took me to the doctor and I got diagnosed with Bacterial Vaginosis.

"What were you doing, Evie?" the GP asked, all stern, looking over her half-moon spectacles. "Putting all that stuff up there?"

"I just wanted to be clean."

"Well there's no need."

I looked up from my balled-up tissue. "What do you mean?"

"To clean yourself, up there I mean," the doctor said. "Your vagina is the most sophisticated self-cleaning organism there is. It cleans itself, beautifully, like a team full of housewife ninjas are up there all the time."

I was too upset to smile at the word "ninja". "Tell me more, please."

She smiled sadly and explained words that make people – especially men – wince. Words like pH balance, and discharge. "All you're doing when you shove soap up there is mucking the cleaners up," she said. "Making it worse. They start attacking all the weird new chemicals."

"So, how should I clean it? How often?"

If my intensity concerned her, it didn't concern her enough to do anything other than write a prescription for antibiotics. She got in trouble for it a few months later. When I was sectioned and diagnosed with OCD.

I carefully wrote down her instructions on how to clean myself – just the outside, with a damp flannel every day.

I had a new problem.

I was on antibiotics.

Everyone knows they destroy your immune system.

I hardly left the house for weeks.

I ate so little, my periods stopped completely. I didn't have to worry about them any more.

Lottie and I said goodbye at the end of Amber's road. Lottie's whole face looked orange under the street light. With all her eyeliner, she looked like a jack-o-lantern.

"So it's your turn next then," I said. "To pick a topic for the meeting?"

"I think I'll pick something less…graphic."

"That's a good idea."

"It was interesting though."

"Yeah."

"God I hate my period," she said. "I'm due this week. Don't you just hate it too?"

I looked down at my red buckled shoes – they'd also turned orange in the artificial light – and nodded.

"You going to message Guy back?"

I looked up. Her face didn't go as automatically judgy as Amber's whenever his name cropped up.

"I guess. I'll wait a while first."

Lottie cocked her head. "It shouldn't be hard, you know?

Love? It shouldn't be games and unknowing and waiting for calls."

"I know."

I messaged Guy before bed.

Meeting great. What you get up to this eve?

I'd checked my phone twenty times before I turned off my light to go to sleep.

He didn't reply.

Twenty-eight

If I was one of those people I hate, I would've called Guy's behaviour in the week leading up to Battle of the Bands "bipolar". Messages then no replies. Prolonged eye contact followed by an afternoon of completely ignoring me. He was more up and down than a kangaroo on a spacehopper. And much less fun.

On Monday after college he ran down half a street to catch up with me as I walked home since I had no appointment with Sarah. He skidded to a halt by my side, his face bright red and hair all sweaty.

"Hey, Evie," he wheezed. "You walking home?" He bent over on himself and coughed violently.

"You should give up smoking," I replied, still angry he'd not replied to my last message. "You sound like an old man." I looked him up and down, in my best attempt to look all hoity-toity. "You look like one too. Are you balding already?" Guy's hands shot frantically to his hair. "Ha, made you stress."

"That's not funny, Evie." But he was smiling and we fell into step towards our homes. He was all childlike, kicking up big piles of leaves, grabbing handfuls to chuck them at me. I squealed, not even worrying about the dirt on them.

"Did you ever used to play conkers?" I asked, as we passed a group of schoolkids chasing each other.

His face got even more childlike. "Oh my God, CONKERS! I was the conker champion at my school. Nobody could beat me."

"How can you manage to be up-yourself about conkers?"

He shrugged. "I hate fake modesty. If you know you're great, say you're great."

"I don't think you got bullied enough at school."

"You're supposed to get bullied at school?"

I nodded. "Just a little bit, to cut you down to size."

"Were you?"

I thought of the rumours about me when I came back to school after the time on the ward. I remembered the whispers, the names they deliberately said too loudly. "Psycho girl". "Weirdo". Jane comforting me in the toilets after someone called me "Bertha" when we were studying Jane Eyre in English.

"Not really," I lied. "Maybe it's because, I too, was a conker champion."

Guy did his should-be-illegal grin. "You couldn't beat me."

"Wanna bet?"

His smile reached right up into his eyes, making them all slitty, like a Cheshire cat's. "I hereby challenge you, Evelyn,

257

to a duel. Weapon of choice: conkers."

I put my tongue in the side of my cheek. "I don't want you to get upset when you lose."

"Oh, trust me, I never lose."

And his hand was in mine, tugging me down the road. His fingers felt earthy, worn from years of guitar, rough, like a boy's fingers should be.

I giggled. "Where are we going?"

"To my house, to get supplies for the duel."

We were going to his house? Guy's house? Like where he lived? His home? My heart kick-started its adrenalin-fuelled dance. He was taking me to his house!

He only lived two roads away, on a street that looked just like mine, with lines of sausage-factory townhouses, all identical, apart from when people showed off their identity by painting the door an unusual colour. Like neon green!

Guy's front door was just a normal red. Was he going to take me to his room? Would I have to meet his parents?

BAD THOUGHT

His parents will hate me.

BAD THOUGHT

His room will be an atrocious mess and
I'll go off him.

BAD THOUGHT

What if I go to his room and he thinks that
means we're going to have sex?

He let go of my hand. "Wait here, I'll be five minutes." He disappeared through the Average Joe door.

"Oh okay," I said, basically to myself.

WORSE THOUGHT

He didn't invite you in. He's ashamed of you and
he hates you.

"Shut up," I told myself out loud.

I pulled out my phone to waste time re-reading our messages. I counted the amount he'd sent me versus the amount I'd sent him. I'd sent exactly two more, which meant I needed to not reply to two in order for him to think I wasn't too keen. I rubbed my toe in his gravel, drawing little swirls, covering them, and redrawing them.

Guy had changed clothes, into a navy-blue hoody that made his eyes jump out of his head and do a dance. Not literally of course. He held up string, a screwdriver and some scissors.

"To the nearest park."

I giggled again, and covered up the heart I'd drawn with a swoosh of my Converse.

We discussed rules on the walk there. We were each to pick one conker and one conker only. "This is Sudden Death Conkers," Guy said seriously. "You have to pick your soldier wisely. He will triumph or he will die."

"My conker's going to be female not male."

He burst out laughing. "That cat lady club is rubbing off on you."

I kicked him.

"I probably deserved that," he said.

There are days in early winter when the sun forgets it's supposed to be tucking itself up with a good book and hibernating until April. Though the ever-reliant earth obligingly turns leaves yellow and orange, the sun is occasionally a floozy. And when this happens, you're rewarded with the most beautiful day of days – with the sun hitting all the different colours, giving everything a silver lining, even crappy parks in suburban towns like ours.

We could already see a flurry of kids under the park's best and biggest conker tree.

"Race you," Guy yelled and we both thrust ourselves in the direction of the sun, pulling each other back using the straps of our rucksacks, trying to laugh through our breathlessness. I dropped to the ground the moment we got there and started scouring – ignoring the looks of the children around me. Their pockets bulged with the brown conkers, the last of the season probably, their hands packed full of them, a conker wedged in-between each webbed gap of their fingers, cramming as much conker into their being as possible. They were amateurs though – all their picks were massive. Every conker champion knows big conkers are the weakest.

"You have three minutes to pick your warrior," Guy yelled solemnly, from the other side of the tree.

"Who made you rule master?"

"The universe."

I spotted a likely-looking conker nestled amongst a pile of browned leaves. It had been out of its pointy cocoon for a while by the looks of the skin. Nice and tough. I dived my hand into the pile of decomposing leaves and retrieved it.

BAD THOUGHT

Shouldn't you be worrying about your hands, Evie?

Good thought

Nope. Bugger off.

I squeezed the horse chestnut between my fingers, checking it for weaknesses. There were none. I used to bake mine in the oven when I was younger to make them harder.

But this game was hardcore conkers, vanilla conkers, conkers without the CGI.

"Found one," I called in a sing-song.

Guy held two in his hands, inspecting them closely and muttering to himself.

"Are you the conker whisperer or something?"

He grinned and dropped his spare one to the ground. "I am the whisperer of many things."

"Yeah. Bullshit. You're the whisperer of bullshit."

"Let's play over there." Guy led me to this copse-like bit, right at the side of the clearing. Some trees had grown in on each other, forming a circle. Half the leaves still clung stubbornly to the branches, surrounding us in dappled sunlight. A log provided a makeshift bench and a scorched mark on the ground was a sign of bonfires past.

"This place is so cool," I said, looking up at the sky through the gaps. "It's the sort of place I imagine an Enid Blyton story being set – you know? With goblins and fairies and such?"

Guy sat himself on the log and took his screwdriver out of his pocket. He held his conker up to the light, choosing the best place to pierce it. "Joel and I get stoned here quite often."

I rolled my eyes. "Enid Blyton would be so proud."

"Oh, she would. Her books are blatantly all about drugs. Who was that guy, Moonface? Blatantly off his tits. Chomping down all those pop biscuits – bet he had the munchies. And I bet the Magical Faraway Tree grew marijuana at some point."

I was surprised he had read her books as a kid, though I guess Enid was pretty universal. "The problem with people who do drugs," I said, "is that they think the rest of the world is taking drugs too." I sat next to him on the log – just far away enough so our bums weren't touching.

"You should do drugs, they're amazing."

"Trust me. My brain gives me enough of a rollercoaster ride without the aid of extra chemicals," I said.

Guy nudged over so we were sitting cheek-to-cheek. He looked up from his half-pierced conker to give me one of his special smiles. "You know what? I can believe that."

I blushed while he finished his conker off – threading the string through and tying a firm double knot at the bottom. I took his tools off him and got to work on my own conker.

"Hey," I said, catching him trying to cook his over his lighter. "No cheating."

Soon we were ready. We stood up, facing each other, our conkers braced for combat.

Guy cocked an eyebrow at me. "Is this weird? This is definitely weird."

"Shut up, loser," I replied, and I took aim and smashed my conker into his. It was a straight-on hit and it whirled round on his string. "Gotcha," I yelled, delighted.

Guy bent over like he'd been shot. "Oooo, help," he said. "She got me, she got me."

I did a triumphant air punch and spun round, twirling through the air.

"Right, my turn. You hit me but you didn't destroy me." Guy faced me again and I suddenly felt a bit scared – worried for my conker, wanting it to be okay. I looked up at his face and found him staring right at me. I caught my breath and stared back. There were flecks of grey in his eyes, flecks I never saw because they were usually so bloodshot. But today Guy's eyes were clear, intense, searching mine. I wanted his face nearer mine. I wanted the tip of his nose to brush against mine, nuzzling me gently, making room for his mouth.

Nobody's mouth had ever touched my mouth before. Sixteen and never been kissed. And not because I couldn't get a date for prom or whatever, but because the thought of brushing lips with another person had always horrified me… Until now.

Now my own lips thumped from the blood speeding into them. Guy tilted his head a bit, grinned cheekily and leaned in further.

I closed my eyes and felt the dappled sunlight burning through my eyelids.

SMASH.

My entire hand reverberated from the impact. Splinters of demolished conker rained down on my fingers like hailstones. My string swung emptily.

Guy whooped in delight.

"HE'S DONE IT. HE'S ONLY GONE AND BLOODY DONE IT. THE CROWD GOES WILD. THE CONKER CHAMPION IS GUY SMITHFIEEEEEELLLD." He ran a victory lap around the copse, his arms raised above his head.

My body parts didn't know which was more confused – my brain, my heart, my empty lips, my shaking hands. In my humiliation, all I could do was laugh. "Rematch!" I yelled, loudly, hoping the noise would bury my disappointment. "I demand a rematch."

"NEVER."

He rugby tackled me, scooping me up and holding me upside-down over his back, repeating his victory lap.

"Put me down," I squealed, in a voice so girly I should be thoroughly ashamed of myself.

Guy flung me down and I landed with a thump on my back on the soft grass. He landed on top of me – catching his body weight with his hands. His face was directly above mine, his body pinning me down. I could feel every blade of grass on my back, every beam of light on my face; I could see every pore of his open sculpted face.

His mouth was even closer than before. This time though, I didn't dare close my eyes. I looked at him, asking him questions with my stare.

What are we doing? Do you want to kiss me? Are you going to kiss me?

Guy looked lost. He readjusted his weight onto an elbow and used his spare hand to very slowly brush my face. From my temple, trailing down my cheek, lingering at the side of my mouth. My breath deserted me…

Was he? Was he?

Guy sat up. "Told you I would win."

Disappointment seeped through me, like I'd wet myself with too much hope. I blinked a few times then I got up too and brushed my jeans off. "You just got lucky."

"I better be going."

With a quick gathering of his stuff, a "see you at college" and a wave, Guy stopped being the boy who was about to kiss me and became the spot in the distance.

I shouldn't have messaged him. He was two-up. I was two-down. It wasn't my turn. I sat in the copse for a while, watching the sun set, the day draw to a close. Reliving what'd happened. I *could* message, I supposed. After what had happened, surely it was fine.

Before I overthought it, I fired one off.

Hey, Conker Champ, I had fun today.

No kiss. I purposely didn't leave a kiss – well he hadn't. As I walked home through the chilled air, I had a thought.

New thought

If I touch every streetlamp on the way back,
he'll reply.

I brushed each one with my hand as I passed, regularly checking my phone as I did. No message. So I started brushing each street light twice.

My phone remained undisturbed.

By the time I'd got through my front door I'd been tapping each post six times, muttering "message message message message message message". I don't know why it was six. But six just felt...right.

Rose was in the living room when I got in, watching TV.

"Where have you been?" she asked.

I evilled her. I hadn't forgotten her betrayal just yet. "Why? Want to tell Mum about that too?"

Her face crumpled. "I told her about the cleaning box for your own good, Evelyn. I'm worried about you. You seem... a bit wired."

"I'm fine."

"Want to watch a film together? It's still early."

I did, I really did. I was just about to suggest a few titles but I stopped myself. I wasn't quite ready to stop being mad. "Not tonight." I said it kindly, and sisters being sisters, she understood. She still looked sad though.

"Okay."

No message by dinner. No message after dinner. Nothing at bedtime.

All the goodness that had been bubbling in my belly fizzled out. All the haze in my brain cleared. The bad thoughts launched themselves at me as I sat in bed, trying to read my book.

BAD THOUGHT

You touched leaves. Leaves! A dog could've
peed on them!

BAD THOUGHT

He didn't kiss you because you stank of dog pee
from the leaves.

BAD THOUGHT

Conkers are poisonous. You held them and then you had
dinner and you only washed your hands once, and you
may have passed some unwashed-off poison from your
finger to your mouth.

BAD THOUGHT

You're going to get sick. You're going to get sick.
You're going to get sick.

I got up and clambered desperately into the shower to
wash the sweat bucketing from me. My legs were too shaky

to stand so I huddled in the corner, the scalding water pouring down my face, smudging my make-up into my eyes. I grabbed my loofah and scrubbed and scrubbed my hands. I kept retching up tiny bits of nothing and watching it spiral down the plughole.

I was crying so hard I was surprised my family couldn't hear me over the drone of the pouring water. There was no knock though. They can't have heard. I knew I didn't have long to pull myself together – I couldn't stay in the bathroom for longer than twenty minutes without raising suspicion. I forced myself to stop blubbing and started to work on brushing my teeth, flossing my teeth, using two types of mouthwash.

As I padded back to my bedroom, cleaner than I'd been in ages, it really hit me.

WORSE THOUGHT

Oh, Evie, it really is coming back, isn't it?

Twenty-nine

The next day. No message. No sighting. If Guy was at college, he wasn't hanging in our regular spots.

The next day he sat with us at lunch but said nothing. He just slumped next to Joel, who was loudly discussing their set list and droning on about boring amps.

Guy didn't look at me once.

Next day. Two days before the gig. Another day of stony silence.

Then, at exactly 1 a.m., my phone buzzed and woke me.

You are still coming, aren't you?

I didn't reply. I did smile at my phone.

Maybe my mental health condition was chronic stupidity.

That, or delusion.

That, or plain old hope.

Hope is a mental health condition, right?

Thirty

I was touching every street light I passed six times – glad Jane kept flaking on walking to college so I could do it in peace. I'd started having to leave the house twenty minutes earlier to fit it all in.

I raided my purse and bought a vat of antibacterial hand gel which I hid in my college locker.

I was twitchy, and uncertain and within days I'd lost weight as I worried away all my calories.

I should've rung the emergency doctor person. I should've told my family. I didn't even have to tell them in person, I could've left a note on the kitchen table.

Dear family,
It's back. I'm not coping. Send help.
Evie.

But I didn't.

Rational reasons I didn't tell anyone

1) Er...

Irrational reasons I didn't tell anyone

1) They were all so proud of me, of how I was doing. The other morning, when I was carefully pouring my medicine onto the spoon, Dad actually slapped me on the back, making me spill some down me. "You're doing so well, Eves," he'd said. "Not long to go."

2) Maybe it wasn't "back". I was still functioning. I was still going to college, seeing my friends, doing my coursework. Yes, okay, I washed a bit more but I was still living an outwardly normal life. Like a swan gliding on a pond, from the surface I was a regular person – swimming through life – it was just my feet paddling madly under water, pummelling hard to stop me drowning. If I was still doing stuff, then the OCD wasn't really back, was it?

3) And it's not like I was doing all the same things as before. Especially after my cleaning box was confiscated. I'd never touched street lights before. I'd never counted to six before. And think how dirty street lights are – I mean, dogs pee on them like literally every day. I was still touching them. Maybe this was a sign of progress? Maybe I was doing my very own exposures?

Maybe I should insert a joke here about Denial being a river in Egypt?

4) If it was back, I'd have to up my medication again. I'd failed. I'd always be on it. I'd never know who I was.

5) If it was back than all the therapy hadn't worked. If it was back it meant it would never truly go away. If it was back I would always be like this. I would always have to fight, every day, to stop myself slipping down the slope to Crazysville. Just the thought of that was exhausting. If it *wasn't* back, then I was cured. I was normal again. I was just like everybody else. Everybody else, with their easy lives and normal problems and lucky lucky lucky lucky lucky.

6) If it was back, my friends might find out. They might not want to be my friends any more. Like what happened with Jane.

"Evie? Evie? You all right?"

BAD THOUGHT

If I just run my finger around the whole rim of Jane's mirror, tonight will go well.

"Evie?" Jane asked again.

"Huh?" I jolted back from my own reflection and spotted her in the corner.

"You all right, Evie?" Jane asked a second time. "You've been stroking my mirror."

Amber catapulted into the reflection alongside me, slinging an arm around my neck.

"It's because she looks so bloody gorgeous, don't you, Evie?" she said.

I looked at Amber and me – we couldn't be more different. She was so long and wild-haired, with clashing green eyeshadow smudged around her eyes. I was so short and curvy (well, used to be curvy), my blonde hair sleek as always, no matter how much I washed it with volumizing shampoo. Which was a lot at the moment.

"I…I'm fine, Jane, I've almost finished with it," I said.

"Good," Lottie butted in. Her face was more eyeliner than anything else. "I need to apply my all-important eighth coat of mascara."

I didn't know how to finish touching the mirror with them all looking so I reluctantly stepped away, letting Lottie have her turn.

BAD THOUGHT

You've ruined it, tonight is ruined now.
Everything is going to go wrong.

No it won't, I told myself. *I'll finish it when no one's looking.*

BAD THOUGHT

No, you have to do it now. Now now now now
NOW.

I tip-tapped on my arm with my fingernails, letting them dance a nervous jig of scratches across my skin. "Have you decided what to wear yet?" I asked Jane, who'd been fretting all afternoon.

Jane shook her head mournfully. "No. I look fat in everything I try on."

"You're not fat, you idiot. Saying that is being really mean to actually-fat people."

Jane had upheld her invite to all get ready for Battle of the Bands at her house. In a surprising turn of events, Amber and Lottie had agreed to come and we'd all eaten takeaway pizza together – I hid my share in my handbag. I mean, have you seen the grubbiness of people who make takeaway pizzas?

It was weird being back in Jane's bedroom. I used to spend most days here, getting lost in her butterfly wall stickers, picking my way through her collection of musical instruments. Now, her butterflies had been replaced with angry black posters of hairy bands I'd never heard of. An electric guitar sat where her clarinet used to be. "Joel's teaching me," she'd said. The air hung thick with hairspray and perfume and not enough spare oxygen for everyone.

I was desperate to open the window but it had been so cold walking here it'd hurt my lungs.

At least cold air is clean. And crisp. As air should be.

"I think you should wear the red top," I offered.

"Won't it clash with my new hair?"

"Oh, yeah, that's a point." Jane's new do was blood red, which really didn't match her blonde eyebrows and English Rose colouring. It really was a blood red too. I didn't have the heart to tell her it looked like her head was bleeding. I probably would've told her in the past, but it would seem mean now...now that we weren't really mates any more.

"Black? I could wear my black lacy top, I guess."

"Yeah, that one's really nice," I said.

"I won't really stand out for Joel in black though, will I?"

Amber rolled her eyes as she dowsed herself in perfume. "And that's the whole point of the evening, isn't it? To stand out for Joel."

Jane bristled. "What band is your boyfriend in then?" she quipped.

"Girls, come on," I groaned.

Amber ignored me. "I don't judge my worth on having a boyfriend and what he does."

"GIRLS."

"Just as well," Jane said.

"STOP IT. NOW."

They did. But there was an awkward silence and at least two evils exchanged.

"Riiight," Jane said. "Black top it is." Her face was all pinched.

"It's really lovely," I said, glancing at the mirror again, wondering if I could get to it.

"Yeah, it is," Amber said, surprising us all. I smiled a weak *thank you* at her and she smiled back meekly. "Sorry, Jane," she added genuinely.

Jane looked relieved. "I'm sorry too."

Lottie – who'd been ignoring the whole thing – threw her mascara wand back into her bag. "*Voilá*," she declared. "Jane, we've got some wine. Do you have a bottle opener?"

Jane nodded, pulling her top over her head. I saw her marshmallow stomach – she *had* gained weight. Why hadn't I noticed? "Yeah, downstairs in the kitchen," she answered from inside her top.

"I'll come with you," Amber said. "We'll bring up some glasses."

They left. With Jane's head still inside fabric, I saw my chance, jumped across the room and quickly trailed my hand over the circumference of the mirror. My stomach melted in relief and I savoured it for a second…before it knotted up again almost instantly.

BAD THOUGHT

And again. You need to touch the mirror again.
Just in case.

I reached out to it, like that scene in Disney's *Sleeping Beauty* when Princess Aurora keeps trancing out and trying to touch the spinning wheel.

"Evie?"

I whipped round. Jane was right behind me.

"Evie? Are you really okay?"

I dropped my hand guiltily. "I'm fine…" My voice squeaked. "Why wouldn't I be?"

Jane's eyebrows pulled together. "You seem…on edge. Twitchy. Is everything okay? You know?" She tapped her head. "In here?"

It was Jane's old face, the one I remembered. Open and caring and chewing her lip as she worried about me. It would've been so easy to tell her then. To tell my best friend that I thought I was maybe losing it, that I didn't know what to tell my parents. And that, more than anything, I couldn't stop thinking about a silly boy. Guy Guy Guy Guy Guy, on a loop.

It may've been old Jane's face, but it was still new Jane's personality…

"I'm fine," I said, in that halting way you deliberately use to say "I'm not fine!" – testing her.

Jane failed the test. She didn't even press me on it, she just cast her eyes to her new black rug and said, "They hate me."

I instantly felt so alone.

"Don't be silly, they don't hate you," I replied hollowly. Though I gave myself away by not asking who she meant.

"They do. They just think I'm a Stepford Girlfriend. Amber, like, really hates me."

"Amber hates the world." I wasn't sure why I was consoling her still. Default maybe? "She's funny with all of us about boys. She's made spinster membership cards, remember?"

Jane tugged at her top, trying to get the edges pulled over her muffin top. "I just thought if I invited them round, they'd see I was cool, you know?"

"And they will…I mean, they have."

"I dunno." She looked sadly at the rug again. Maybe I was reading too much into it but it seemed like, for the first time, Jane was jealous of me. Jealous of the friendships I'd made, the identity I was carving out for myself, independent of anyone else. Despite the odd Guy blip.

We heard a clattering of glasses downstairs and some giggling. The wine was on its way.

Jane walked past me to the mirror to check her reflection. "My new hair's okay, isn't it? I've got this patchy bit at the back where I missed some across my parting. I had to do it by myself…"

"Oh…yeah, well, it doesn't show."

She pouted and turned her head side to side. "When Joel saw it he said we should try and spend more time with our friends. He said we spend too much time together."

A-ha! Joel was steering her sudden burst of friendliness. I felt suddenly angry at her – that this change had come from Joel, not her. Angry that she couldn't see that I was hurting…or that she was just choosing not to see it. Because she'd seen too much already. She'd reached her threshold.

"Ahh, well, I mean, it's important to have friends, isn't it?" I tried to make myself feel sorry for her, to calm down the inner anger.

"Yeah. I don't know what I would do without you, Evie." It came out empty. Forced. I looked at my friend's reflection with her. She'd changed so much in the past few months. Different hair, new piercings, crazy outfits – but that didn't stand out to me – that didn't make me really look. It was the way she carried herself now – none of her sass, none of her attitude. It was like someone had slowly turned her from Technicolor into sepia tone.

"How are things with you and Joel?" I asked.

"Why?"

"Just asking."

"Well, they're fine. Great. Wonderful. Just wait till you fall in love, Evie." I sneered slightly at the back of her head. "But, as Joel said, it's important to have friends too. That's why I invited you all around tonight."

Because Joel suggested it…

The bedroom door opened and Lottie and Amber came in brandishing wine and glasses.

"We've got Merlot!" Lottie announced, setting it clumsily on the carpet and pouring it slapdash into four glasses. Some splashed on the carpet. Nobody said anything. Maybe nobody else but me noticed. "I stole it from my parents. We're going to class-up the college band night by drinking red wine. We will be the most sophisticated girls there."

I pointed to Amber who was carefully pouring another bottle of red wine into an empty plastic Coke bottle. "Not if anyone sees us swigging from that."

"Nonsense," Lottie said. "That's for the walk there. Nobody will see us drink it. We'll be walking through the alleyways."

"Classy as hell."

"Too right. Come on, let's chink."

The overly-full glasses were passed about and we cheers-ed each other.

"To Joel's band winning tonight?" Jane suggested.

Lottie cackled. "No chance. Let's drink to the sisterhood." And we chinked again.

I was on an even lower dose than I'd been at the house party. And this wasn't shots. So I drained my glass as quickly as you can drain red wine without making little wincing faces that give away you're not really a grown-up yet.

It took ages to leave the house in the cold, what with ten layers of coats and scarves to put on. We were glad for them though when we filtered out onto Jane's front porch.

Lottie let out a little squeal. "It's colder than liquid nitrogen! Pass me that bottle of wine."

Amber obliged and Lottie drank some and passed it over. I pretended to drink, not letting it near my lips. I just couldn't share. And anyway, I already felt a bit fuzzy from the wine I'd had at Jane's, from a nice, safe glass.

"It's so cold," I said, to cover my lack of drinking, "that it is scientifically impossible for me to unclench my buttocks right now."

Amber and Lottie cracked up. "That's sophistication, sister."

"Don't pretend your arse cheeks aren't hiked together with freezingness right now."

"Oh, mine are so tight, I could crack walnuts between them," Lottie said, and we laughed again. We bobbed between side-streets, dodging from lamplight glow to lamplight glow, the wine disappearing from the bottle.

Jane launched into some monologue about Joel's set list. We listened dutifully without really listening until she said, "Guy talks about you a lot, Evie."

I almost stopped walking. If I was a rabbit, my ears would've shot right up. If I was a meerkat, I would've rocked up onto my hind legs. Lottie and Amber groaned before I could reply.

"Aww, Jane, don't tell her stuff like that," Lottie said.

"Yeah, she's managed to go two whole hours without bringing him up."

"Shut up." I turned to Jane and tried to keep my voice casual. "Oh, really? What does he say?"

I thought I sounded disinterested and vague but the other two groaned louder. "Oh, man, now you've done it."

"What did he say, Jane?" Amber said, in a high squeaky voice. "Can you tell me again? Can you write it down? What do you think of this full-stop he used? What does it mean? Do you think he likes me?"

I thumped her on the head with the empty Coke/wine bottle. "Shut it. I'm not that bad."

"Yes you are."

"Well, maybe I am. But he makes me that way."

Jane watched us with a puzzled face. "What's going on?"

Amber flailed her arms dramatically. "You mean Evie hasn't told you about her romantic game of conkers?"

"Followed by an all-out communication blackout," Lottie added.

"Or the almost-kiss at the house party?" Amber asked.

"Followed by an all-out communication blackout," Lottie added.

"Or the unnecessary deviations from his walking-home routes so he can sit on a fence with her and chat about nothing."

"Followed by an all-out communication blackout."

"Or how he slags off every guy she considers dating…"

"Before an all-out communication blackout."

I hit them both on the head with the empty bottle.

"Oww."

"If you were trying to make a point," I said, "you could've stopped a while back."

"Hang on," Jane said. "Stuff's been going on with you and Guy?"

Why did I like hearing his name so much? Why was I so pathetic?

"Have you not been listening?" Amber asked. "He's been so changeable with her I'm surprised he's not been accepted to Hogwarts for his transfiguration skills."

We exited an alleyway and came out on the road next to college. Cheap cars were parked everywhere, students pouring out of them, heading towards the light of our school.

"He does talk about her a lot," Jane insisted.

"I'm sure he does," Amber said. "But that doesn't make him a nice guy."

"I am under no illusions that he's a nice guy," I protested.

"Then why are you so hung up on him?"

"I'm not…well…I can't help it. And I told you, enough's enough. I'm not messaging him any more. He is dead to me."

Jane walked up close to me and whispered like we were old friends. Which we were, I guess. "Well, you're certainly not dead to him."

I hung back a little as we walked towards college. In the darkness, walking just behind them, I tapped every remaining lamp post six times.

I would have to wash my hands before the music started.

Thirty-one

It was weird, being in college at night. It felt unreal, or forbidden or something. All the same old faces were there but everyone seemed stranger in the darkness.

"Yikes, it's packed," I said, as we turned into the college car park and spotted the crowd.

"Tell me, Jane," Lottie said. "You've known Evie a long time. Has she always used ye-olde Milly Molly Mandy words like 'yikes' or is this just a recent issue in her literary development?"

"Hey," I said as Jane spoke over me, the teeth from her smile shining in the moonlight.

"Always, her favourite used to be 'crikey'."

"*Crikey* is a vastly underrated expression," I argued. "Anyway, it's not my fault. I watch a lot of old romantic movies. They talked properly back then...with class."

Jane's phone buzzed and she wrestled with her coat to retrieve it. "It's Joel," she told us, though none of us had asked. "He says they're second-to-last on. They're backstage but he may be able to come out and meet us."

"Backstage?" I could see Amber raise an eyebrow, even in the dark.

"Well, in the photography block. That's what they're using as a Green Room."

"Green Room?" Amber's eyebrows went into overdrive.

I linked arms with both of them, holding one on each side like squabbling siblings. "Let's go get our tickets."

We queued, paid our fiver entrance fee that was going to a local charity, and got our hands stamped. The cafeteria looked so much bigger with all the tables pushed to one side. I was pretty impressed – there was a proper stage and lights and speakers everywhere that the music tech students had set up.

"Oooh, look, there's a bar," Lottie said, pointing to where pizza and chips were usually on sale.

"It's only for Upper Sixth," Jane said. "The ones who've turned eighteen already."

Lottie screwed up her face. "Stuff that." She peered over the queue. "I think I know the guy who's working on it. He's in my philosophy class. He's in the year above but is taking philosophy as an extra AS level. His name's Teddy."

"Teddy?" I asked. "Seriously?"

"Deadly. His mum is obsessed with *Little Women*. He's quite cute, isn't he? If you all give me a fiver, I'll try and get us served."

We all obligingly handed her money and Lottie steered

through the crowd. Teddy was instantly smitten when she got to the bar, trying desperately not to look at her exposed midriff. Five minutes later she handed us all plastic cups filled with vodka and lime.

"I think I like him," she announced. "Just the name Teddy makes me want to bury myself into him for the world's largest cuddle."

I took a sip of my drink.

BAD THOUGHT

How do you know the plastic cup is clean?

BAD THOUGHT

You've still not washed your hands.

My sip turned into a gulp and I winced at the acidy nothingy taste. "Do you think he has a hairy chest?" I asked, hoping to distract myself.

"Only one way to find out." She grinned and chinked her plastic cup with mine, contaminating my cup further with her lip juice. Reckoning on alcohol that strong being self-sanitizing, I drained the rest of my drink, swilling it around the insides of my mouth. Like mouthwash, I guess.

Jane opened a programme and squealed at Joel's photo.

"Look," she said, pointing. "They've been given more space than anyone else." I followed her finger and saw Guy's face staring back at me, from the grainy depths of the bad photocopy.

"I just need the loo," I told them and I worked my way through to the bathroom. I didn't need to go but a clump of girls took up all the basins, redoing their make-up in the mirror. It would look odd if I just stood waiting for a sink, so I went into a cubicle and stood there, waiting the amount of time it usually takes to wee. Then, knowing I'd be instantly washing my hands afterwards, I pulled the chain and watched the clean bowl flush itself.

The music started just as I pushed past someone to wash my hands. A warbling, the sort that can only come from a middle class white person with dreadlocks strumming an acoustic guitar, echoed off the white tiles. I pumped the soap dispenser six times.

How to wash your hands – the Evie way

- Pump the soap six times. One, two, three, four, five, six.
- Rub your palms together to create a rich lather.
- Concentrate first on scrubbing the thumbs, and then individually around each finger.
- Interlace your fingers and rub your palms together roughly – wincing at where the soap seeps into the

few open sores on your skin.

- Rub the backs of your hands together thoroughly.
- Finish on your wrists, creating an "o" with your clean fingers to whoosh the soap around like a bracelet.
- Then rinse. First with hot. Then with cold. Then with as hot as you can stand. Turn the tap off with your elbow.
- Use the elbow to start the hand dryer and leave them under it until your hands are bone dry.

I picked up a programme on the way back and flicked to the page with Guy's photo. There he was. His stupid no-message-replying face all tortured and shaded and sexy. I noticed my hands shaking. I found the girls in the crowd near the front. Lottie was covering her ears dramatically while Amber laughed at her.

"This girl," Lottie called over the music, "needs to be told that listening to music should be a pleasurable experience."

We all winced as the girl onstage failed to hit a particularly high note. I looked over at the source of the noise. My guess was correct, the girl's blonde hair was matted into dreads and she wore an actual real-life shawl. Her guitar was painted with sixties flowers.

Amber looked over too. "I think she suffers from OCD," she said, and my blood stopped in its veins. She paused before delivering the punchline. "Obsessive Cliché Disorder..."

I pretended to laugh while considering going back to the loos to cry.

The song finished, followed by half-hearted applause. "Thank you," dread-girl said, beaming. She tried to bow but was pushed offstage by the next band. They were a group of guys, all wearing smart suits with skinny ties.

"Wait," I said to the others. "It's Ethan."

Amber and Lottie's faces both whipped round to the stage. "I didn't know he played the drums," Amber said as Ethan settled down behind his electric blue drum kit.

I shrugged, watching him play about with leads and twizzling his drumsticks. "Yeah, he does. And violin too. I wonder where he finds time amongst his sex rehab."

"Is that the guy you brought to Anna's party?" Jane asked, her phone still surgically attached to her hand.

"Yep."

"He is cute, isn't he?"

"Yep."

Maybe it was the wine. Maybe it was the vodka. Maybe it was seeing Ethan's annoyingly-sexy ferret face up on a stage – but I went a bit hot and woozy. The lead singer came up to the mike and said, "Hey everyone, we're The Imposters." And they launched into a rip-roaring cover of "Back in Black".

"AMAZING," Lottie yelled, her face swelling with excitement. "Music we can dance to." Before any of us had time to think of valid excuses, she'd pulled us towards the front and began dancing crazily.

It's hard not to dance to a decent AC/DC cover and everyone around us had the same problem. It's also hard not to dance to AC/DC like a pissed old person at a wedding and everyone else had the same problem. We dipped and twirled and formed a girly shrieky circle where we all flicked our hair about to the "hey hey hey hey" bits. Mid-flick, I looked at the stage and met Ethan's eyes. I grinned and he winked at me. I stuck my tongue out and returned to my hair flicking. It was then I noticed Amber. She wasn't joining in. She had her arms clutched around herself as she awkwardly nodded her head. I joined my hands with hers and waved them about, grinning madly to get her to smile back – but the moment I dropped them, her hands fell back to her chest. Which meant, to be honest, that I'd dirtied my hands for no reason.

"What's up?" I yelled over the music. "Why aren't you dancing?"

"Nothing wrong," she said in that girl way meaning there's definitely something very wrong indeed.

"Tell me."

"I just hate dancing. I'm too tall. Everyone's looking at me."

I looked around at the room full of people not looking at Amber. "No they're not."

"Yes they are."

"Back in Black" finished and the band lurched into another rock-a-cheesetastic cover of "Walk This Way". Everyone screamed and cheered.

"Come on," I yelled at her. "It's Aerosmith. Lottie is attempting to moonwalk." Lottie cleared a space on the dance floor and was wiggling backwards while Jane took pictures on her phone.

Amber gave a strained smile. "I'm fine. I'll go get us some more drinks."

I tried to feel bad for her but the band was too good – the music too infectious. I shuffled over to Lottie and started a weird hip-hop move that had everything to do with alcohol and nothing to do with dancing ability.

"Woooo, go, Evie," Jane yelled, and I pulled her in and we wiggled around each other – jumping up and down. I was having so much fun I didn't really log I'd now touched two people's hands.

"I love cover bands," Lottie said, her matted hair swish-swishing. "It's so much better listening to music you know."

"Yeah, but a cover band can't win, can they?" Jane said, leaning in close so we could hear her. "That's not fair. Joel's band writes all their own songs."

"I'm sorry, Jane," Lottie said smiling. "But 'Die Bitch Die' ain't a dancey number."

Even Jane laughed. Until Amber stormed back, looking even more miserable."Your mate wouldn't serve me," she said to Lottie, her face as red as her hair again.

"Fret not, I will mend this," Lottie said, and she sauntered over to the bar, doing her own hop skip. The three of us watched her dazzle Teddy into submission. He kept laughing at her and pushing his dirty blond hair off his face. Then Lottie crawled over the countertop and dropped to his side of the bar, helping herself to drinks. He just laughed harder and helped her pour. She planted a dizzying kiss on his lips before leaping back over the counter, clutching four plastic cups between her fingers.

"*Voilà*," she announced, handing us each a cup of ill-gotten gains.

"I think Teddy may be a bit in love with you," I said, taking my drink and downing most of it. We all looked over and saw him staring longingly at Lottie, ignoring the queue of thirsty people around him.

Lottie gave a smug side smile. "Well, he's not bad, is he?"

"You over Tim yet?" I asked.

She stuck her tongue out. "Who?"

"That's my girl."

"Let's dance."

Ethan's band launched into their third and final cover – Bon Jovi, "Living on a Prayer". Everyone erupted, even reluctant Amber. I downed my drink, tossed the plastic cup over my head with abandon and did the most energetic hair flicking the world has ever known. I love love LOVED this song. It was all about making the most of what you have, and hanging on, even when the odds aren't in your favour.

"Take my hand," the lead singer sang, and Lottie and Amber and I, and even Jane, put our hands into the middle of our makeshift circle and clutched at each other before releasing our fingers into the air.

"WOAH-OOOH," we screamed over the music.

You're going to make it, Evie, I thought and I lost myself in the crazy guitar solo. Vodka and wine and cheesy rock pulsed through me and I twirled and jumped and grinned at my friends.

"OOOON A PRAYER," I screamed at everyone, euphoria ripping through me like tearing sheets of tissue paper.

Then I was hugged from behind and it all went dark. He whispered into my ear, so close I could hear him over the band.

"Guess who?"

I lifted his hands down and turned to face him. "Hi, Guy," I beamed. I was so glad to see him. I was so glad to see anybody.

"You look happy, gorgeous," he yelled at me, giving me a full body scan that would've been leery if he wasn't young and good-looking.

Gorgeous? He called me gorgeous?

"Dance with me," I yelled back, grabbing his hand and twirling myself under his arm. But he stayed stiff and upright, giving me a weirdo look.

"I'm not dancing to Bon Jovi. Don't tell me you're enjoying this crap?"

I was, I really really was. But then I wasn't.

"Everyone else is," I said, gesturing to the girls behind me who were holding hands and spinning in circles, and all the people behind them who seemed just as dedicated to screaming along to every word as I was.

Guy did his best sneer. "I can't believe they let an actual cover band into the competition."

"It's not really a competition, it's a charity gig at college." I realized instantly that that was the wrong thing to say. Guy's sneer got sneerier, his nostrils all pinched.

"Well in that case, I don't need you to wish me luck then, do I?" He turned and dissolved into the crowd.

My euphoria drained out of me, like a plug being pulled in the bath, and I sagged on the dance floor. Amber's arm was around me first. "So, what did Mr Bell-end want?"

"Umm…nothing."

Lottie's arm draped on my other side. "Wow, Evie, it's like you've had an instant mood transplant."

Amber evilled the bit of the crowd Guy had disappeared into. "Guy is a professional mood transplanter. He should be a surgeon in mindfuckery."

I shrugged. "It's fine. He just doesn't like Bon Jovi."

"Which further proves his idiocy," Lottie said. "Come on, love, there's only a chorus left."

They enveloped me into a hug and screamed the lyrics so loudly into my eardrums that I thought they would burst. I giggled and sang along and pulled Jane in with us but my heart felt like one of those balloons you buy at theme parks that sags halfway to the carpet in the drab interior of your house the next day.

The band was encored, despite it being against the rules. They pulled out "Mr. Brightside" by The Killers and there was no roof left to raise by the end of it. When they finished, the whole of college exploded into applause and wolf-whistles. The band bowed. Ethan rose up from behind his drum kit, smothered in sweat. Through the crowd he somehow found my face and, though we hadn't talked in ages, he winked at me again.

Surprised, I waved back.

The lights came up and some dull background music came on whilst Ethan's band dismantled their equipment and Guy and Joel's band started assembling. The crowd recovered, blinking in the bright lights, and began swamping Teddy at the bar.

Jane flung her arms around me, her body all sweaty. "They're on next, Evie, I'm so nervous for him."

I looked over her shoulder at the stage. Joel didn't look nervous, just bored by everything, which was standard. Guy wasn't looking at me. At any of us. His lip was all pouted out like a toddler who didn't get the Christmas present he wanted.

Sensible thought

Why do you fancy him, Evie?

But the vodka pushed it away. The vodka, or lust, or love, or his carrot dangly penis or whatever.

A sudden urge twinged in my stomach and I pushed Jane away, aware of all the things I suddenly needed to do.

"I need to go to the loo again," I told the others.

"Oh, cool," Amber said, "I need it too."

No no no no no no no no no.

I smiled through my teeth. "Great."

She whinged on as we made our way to the college toilets and it grated on me. I was already mad at her for joining me, for ruining my plan…

"I hate that I'm so tall, it's like I can't enjoy any gigs, you know? I just know everyone behind me is thinking 'oh great, we're behind the ginger giraffe'… And yet I can't get served by that Teddy bloke. It's 'cause Lottie has tits, isn't it? But then it wouldn't work if I had tits, they'd just be right at everyone's eye level…"

There was a queue, as always. Never, in the history of the universe, have there been sufficiently-sized ladies toilets.

"That band was good though, wasn't it? Don't listen to stupid Guy. I'd much rather listen to covers than his crap. Oh God, they're on next. Are you going to fall for him even more once he's up onstage?"

"Amber, I'm not that predictable."

"You're a girl, he's a guy onstage. Everything that happens afterwards is predictable."

A cubicle came free and I locked myself in, counting to sixty under my breath. It usually took about sixty seconds to pee, didn't it? Then, without having done anything, I unlocked the door and washed my hands. But not properly. I couldn't do them properly, especially with Amber washing hers right next to me. She didn't even use soap. Just water. What was water going to do?

I could hardly hear her as we emerged back into the cafeteria.

BAD THOUGHT

*Go back, go back, you're not finished,
you need to go back.*

"...Oh look, they're about to start. Christ, Jane looks like she's going to piss herself. Thanks for breaking it up between us earlier. I'm sorry I was a bitch...she's just so...I dunno... but I get that you're friends..."

"Oh no," I gasped, whacking my hands to my face dramatically, stopping me in my tracks.

Amber stopped too. "What is it?"

I hit my pockets, all over-the-top. "I'm such an idiot. I think I left my purse in the loo."

My purse was in my clutch bag. It had been there all night.

"Do you want me to come back with you?" Amber said. Just as she said it the lights dimmed again. A scratch of chords ripped through the air. I looked up, it'd come from Joel's guitar. They were starting.

"No, it's fine, I'll meet you there."

Before she could argue, I'd been swallowed by the crowd and deafening music.

The angry start to "Die Bitch Die" echoed dimly around the toilet walls. I pumped the soap, one, two, three, four, five, six…hang on, did I count right? Stupid vodka. I sighed, scraped the soap off and began again.

One. Two. Three. Four… Did I pump on three? Really? Was I sure? I had to be sure.

I scraped the soap off and started again, counting out loud with each push of the soap dispenser.

"One," I said, slowly and deliberately. "Two. Three…" Thank God no one was in there and they were all watching the band. Then I swished and circled and rubbed the backs of my hands together and interlaced my fingers and did all the things you're supposed to do if you don't want norovirus if you work in a hospital.

I felt so relieved. Yet, just as I was about to push through the door…

BAD THOUGHT

Do it again, Evie, just to make sure.

That was the point where I was supposed to use my "coping strategies" – to put things through my "worry tree" again. To acknowledge the thought, bring myself back to the present moment, and walk back out into the band competition – anxious, yes, but knowing I wasn't letting it win.

Have you ever noticed that sentences that begin with "that was the point where" never end with someone doing the point?

All the relief of ten seconds ago drained away, replaced with an urgent need to wash again. It was like when you need to pee so badly you're hopping on one leg. But I knew that if I did it again, the relief wouldn't last long. And the next time, it would last even less.

My face crumpled in on itself and I let out such a hollow empty sob that it didn't even sound like me. My sob drained slowly down the white shiny tiles of the empty bathroom before dissolving into the thudding music of Guy's band.

Another sob erupted in my throat and tumbled from my mouth. I doubled over, clutching my stomach, twisted in knots of nerves and disappointment and feeling lost – just so lost – and there was only one way to make it go away…

I used the back of my hand to push tears back into my eyes and walked slowly to the nearest basin.

I washed my hands again.

It felt so good. So so good.

I finished and smiled at myself in the mirror. There – all done, Evie – out you go now, go back and have fun with your friends.

BAD THOUGHT

Touch the tap of every basin six times and then you'll have a good night.

The tears sprang back. I watched my reflection cry – this wretched girl staring madly at the mirror, her arms wrapped around herself.

"No, I won't," I told the girl in the mirror. It came out like a whimper. If anyone came in they would've probably sectioned me, straight away.

BAD THOUGHT

Go on, it's just touching a few things. Then you
know you'll have a good night.

I was too exhausted to fight. I watched myself as I moved from basin to basin, tapping the taps, counting under my breath.

The relief settled in my belly once more. I was all done now. I was going to have a good night. I was going to go out there and be with my friends and listen to the not-very-good band and pretend *yes-they-are-actually-okay*, just like everybody else.

I fluffed my hair, blew myself a kiss and went to – finally – leave the bathroom.

Just as I pushed open the door…

BAD THOUGHT

You've made your hands dirty touching all
those taps. Go and wash them again. Go on,
just once more. Just. In. Case.

I cried for ten minutes before I gave in again.

I missed most of the set.

I missed yet more of my life, because of myself.

And yet, when I emerged from the bathroom, my make-
up was perfect.

Thirty-two

Guy and co were on their last song. The crowd were… umm…sort of into it. There was a bit of a divide. Some hardcore metallers, i.e. Joel and Guy's mates, had claimed the area in front of the stage. Some actually held onto the edge as support as they tried to dislodge their brains through their noses using violent force…or "head banging" as it's otherwise known. The rest of the hardcores had started a mini mosh pit – swooping around in a violent circle, pushing and grabbing each other's T-shirts. Lottie and Amber stood reluctantly on the edge of the pit, trying their best to look after Jane, who kept flinging herself into the centre of all the unnecessary violence, screaming, "Joel, I love you."

But the rest of the crowd appeared bemused, or plain unimpressed. There was a long queue for Teddy's bar, and the cafeteria was much emptier than when The Imposters was playing.

My eyes travelled to the stage. To Guy. His eyes were

closed, his fingers gripping the microphone. My stomach dived in on itself. I stopped really hearing the music, which is just as well because, of all the things I fancied about Guy, His Music wasn't one of them.

I was just contemplating joining my mates – weighing up how likely it was I'd be splattered with a stranger's sweat, when I was poked on each side of my ribs.

"Hey." I spun round to see Ethan. His stubbly face glowed with post-gig high. His smile was more contagious than norovirus.

"Hey, stranger," he said, lighting the entire northern hemisphere with his grin.

I couldn't not smile back, even with our history. "All right, sex maniac? Great set by the way."

"I've been meaning to talk to you about that."

"WHAT?" Guy's drummer attacked the cymbals repeatedly for some sort of "interlude" and I could hardly hear a thing.

Ethan leaned in close, his black tie hanging undone around his neck. "I SAID I WANTED TO TALK TO YOU ABOUT THAT." He cupped his hand over my ear, his breath tickling my hair. "I wanted to say sorry. I was a douchebag. Not a sex addict."

I couldn't help but laugh. "I'm over it," I yelled back.

"I can see that. You're looking good, Evie." He cocked his head, cockily.

"You should've seen me ten minutes ago," I said, knowing only I would get the joke.

"Why, were you touching yourself?"

"Yes," I deadpanned. "That's what girls do. The moment boys leave the room, we all start touching ourselves up, just to spite you."

He laughed so wide I could see he had two fillings, which helped put me off him a bit.

"I've missed you, Evie."

"I'm still in your sociology class."

"Yeah, but you're always scowling at me. Whenever I hear about an odd mental condition, you're the first person I want to tell about it."

I suppose Ethan wasn't to know that was hurtful, so I smiled at him. "Gee, Ethan, and whenever a boy doesn't boff someone else on a first date, you're the first person *I* want to tell about it."

"Did you just say the word 'boff'?"

"What's wrong with boff?"

"Not even my mum uses the word 'boff'," he said.

"Well, maybe if she had, you wouldn't have such an urgent need to boff people. People who aren't your date. On a date."

He laughed so hard, I could see another filling on the other side of his mouth. "You dating anyone at the moment, Evie?" He asked like a friend would, but he'd now put his sweaty arm around me.

"Umm, not really." But my eyes instinctively went to Guy.

He was staring right at me. From the stage, a grim look on his face. Our eyes met before his went to Ethan.

Then Guy turned his back so I couldn't see his face.

Ethan saw it all. "Wow, what's going on with you and that guy?"

"What guy?"

"That crappy singer you just eye shagged."

"He's not a crappy singer. And, nothing. What's it to you, anyway?"

Ethan wiggled his eyebrows. "I can help you make him jealous?"

Guy was looking right at me again. "Huh? What? How?" I half-asked, distracted.

"Like this!"

He tugged my waist and spun me round and Ethan's lips were on my lips, just like that. I'd always worried my lips wouldn't know what to do but they kissed Ethan's right back and I didn't even think about germs or when Ethan would've last brushed his teeth.

Until afterwards.

I pushed him away. Hard. Though it had felt nice.

"Ethan, you can't just kiss people!" I yelled. "That's sexual assault."

He grinned and shrugged. "No it's not, it's me repaying the karma I owe you." He grabbed me once more and spun me. "See, it worked."

The band was finishing their last song and Guy's face was dark, his eyebrows screwed up. His fingers shook on the microphone and he missed a note, wrecking the climax of the song.

I couldn't bring myself to make eye contact with him. I was shaking. "Ethan, what the hell have you done?"

He shrugged once more. "You. A favour. Promise me you won't go after him. Let him come to you."

"Are you writing self-help books, as well as molesting people?"

"Whatever. I'm off to win this stupid competition and then take my pick of the girls here."

"You may not win," I called after him, but he'd already become part of the massive crowd.

My hair was pulled from behind. It was Amber, grabbing my head into her.

"WHAT THE HELL ARE YOU DOING KISSING ETHAN?!"

Thirty-three

"Oww, you're hurting me."

"I don't care," Amber replied, still dragging me by the hair back to her spot near the stage. "What are you doing? It's Ethan! The sex maniac. He's supposed to be dead to you, remember?"

"He kissed me," I grumbled.

The last throngs of metallic chords vibrated to a standstill. The band was finished. Amber let go so we could join in the lacklustre applause. I clapped, desperately trying to make eye contact with Guy but he'd stormed off the stage.

Good thought

He's jealous? Ethan's sexual assault...worked?

We clapped and walked at the same time, arriving back at the side of Jane, who was screaming and wolf-whistling.

"WOOOOO, YOU GO, GUYS!"

The rest of the pit joined her, yelling "ENCORE". Joel stood right at the front of the stage, drinking it in. He ripped off his T-shirt.

"I LOOOOOOVE YOU, JOEL."

I looked behind us to see everyone else in the cafeteria had stopped clapping politely.

"No one else is clapping," I told Amber.

"That's because they sucked. My ears have taken a restraining order out against me. I mean, I know it's not my kind of music anyway, but they were much worse than in that church hall. Did you hear how many notes Guy missed?"

"No…I was…"

OCDing the hell out of the college toilets.

"Attaching yourself to Ethan's face?" Amber suggested.

"I told you. He kissed me!"

"Yeah yeah. I can't keep up with you. Or Lottie…who apparently isn't heartbroken any more." Amber pointed. To the bar. Where there was a queue. And no Teddy.

"She went to get another round in and never came back. Leaving me with Courtney Love here." She pointed to Jane, who was throwing devil signs and was the last one screaming. "I wish you two would stop running off and leaving me alone like an actual spinster rather than a reinvented spinster. It is bad enough being six foot and ginger, without standing around like Loner Lonington of Lonersville."

"I'm sorry. I just got…held up in the bathroom. And then Ethan attacked my face."

"Well, if it was to make Guy jealous, it worked."

IT WORKED!?

"You think?" I said.

"Well he's stormed offstage, hasn't he? I watched the whole thing. Because that's what I do, watch other people find one another attractive."

I gave her a sympathetic pat on the shoulder. "Please don't tell me you're jealous of Ethan attacking me."

"Please don't tell me you're going to do anything about Guy."

"I…"

"He's bad for you, Evie." She said it with such venom I felt I was being told off.

BAD THOUGHT

It's just because she's jealous.

NASTY THOUGHT

It's just because no one wants to kiss her.

BAD THOUGHT

She's trying to control you.

"You know what else is bad for me?" I snapped. "Having you ALWAYS telling me what to do."

Her mouth fell open.

"Evie...come on." Her auburn eyebrows drew together in hurt. "I'm just looking out for you."

"Well stop!" I turned on my heel to leave.

"Where are you going?"

"I'm getting some air."

"You are coming to the Spinster Club meeting tomorrow, aren't you?"

But her sad voice was lost in the air.

Thirty-four

Guilty guilty guilty.

Horrid horrid horrid.

I was a horrid person. I should feel guilty.

I was also SO angry.

Why did she keep going on about Guy? Why did they keep teasing me about him? I just wanted a boy to like me, one that I liked too. It was such a normal thing to want – why did they keep barging in? All judgy? If they were so judgy about this, then imagine how awful they'd be if I ever told them about me.

I wormed my way through the crowd. I needed to get out of that stuffy cafeteria.

I imagined my friends' reactions to me… I got mad just picturing it.

What Amber would say

"Oh, Evelyn, snap out of it. Just don't wash your hands – simple."

What Lottie would say

"Sorry, Evie, we were going to invite you, but you can't… handle that sort of thing, can you?"

What everyone always says

"Pull yourself together."
"That doesn't make any sense."
"You're only doing it for attention."
"Just stop. It's easy."

By the time I stepped out into the cold night air, I was almost gasping. I ran around the corner of the cafeteria and found a dark patch. I leaned against the wall and took five giant breaths.

In, out, in, out. Come on, Eves, don't cry now. Remember what Sarah said… If you get into the habit of falling apart, it's a hard habit to break.

Stupid Sarah. Stupid Sarah with her stupid normal brain. I hated her.

I dropped my back against the wall, sliding downwards until I sat on the cold wet grass.

Don't cry. I wasn't even sure why I was upset.

"Well, fancy seeing you here."

I jumped at the voice. His voice. Guy's angular face emerged from the blackness.

"Guy, you scared the hell out of me."

He walked closer, more of him coming visible as the lights from inside hit him. He had a roll-up hanging out his mouth and a can of beer in his hand.

"What are you doing sitting here by yourself?"

I looked around. I was basically in a hole in the wall – I could've asked for a PIN number and dispensed cash. There was no reasonable reason to be wedged into a hole in the college wall on a Saturday night.

I answered truthfully. "Hiding from the world."

He smiled – a sad one – and sat down next to me, putting the can of beer between us.

"And why would you want to do that? You seemed to be having a good night…" His voice trailed off. It was as sad as his smile. He picked up the beer and offered me the can. I shook my head.

"I've had enough."

"Fair enough."

"Ethan kissed me. I didn't really know what was going on."

A slight nod of his head showed he'd heard it. He didn't answer. Not right away. He stubbed out his cigarette and took a swig of beer – looking out into the blackness.

I couldn't help but stare at the side of his face – it was mesmerizing. I'd already forgotten all about yelling at Amber, and wondering what Lottie was up to, and stressing about my malfunctioning brain. When I looked at Guy, it was like my brain was on a dimmer switch and the rest of the world was twisted down to mute.

Finally, he spoke. "I wish I didn't care."

"You care?"

Silence descended once more and I tried to find the darkness as interesting as Guy. Then he sighed and reached out an arm. It dropped around my shoulder and pulled me into his body. My whole right side was touching his left side and it sent bursts of static rushing through my body. I could smell him, all smoky and honeylike. My face was nudged into his neck.

"I care," he whispered.

Guy's hand found my face and pulled it to his. My lips were quivering. And then, in a crevice of a college outbuilding, my lips met a boy's for the second time. Everything around me went hazy. Guy's kiss was soft at first but his lips got harder and harder. His hand reached to the back of my hair, pulling my face right into his. Then he moaned and effortlessly grabbed me and put me onto his lap. Instinctively, I wrapped my legs around his waist. When his tongue strayed into my mouth, I didn't even worry about it. In fact, I let out my very own small moan.

Kissing Guy made up for every kiss I missed out on over the past three years.

Kissing Guy was like all the good bits of a hundred okay kisses, piled into one amazing one.

Kissing Guy made me feel like I wasn't Evie any more. It marked the end of All That and the start of Normal.

Or so I hoped, I hoped, I hoped.

A loud clang of opening chords broke us apart – by lips only. Our faces were still crowded into each other's. I turned in the direction of the college cafeteria, and saw the lights dim once more through the giant floor-to-ceiling windows.

"We're missing the last band," I said.

"I don't care."

He kissed me again – raining them down on my cheeks and my nose and my neck. He pushed back my hair to gain further access to my skin. I loved the look on his face – like he couldn't believe his luck that he got to kiss me. That he was trying to make the most of it. I laughed and pulled back.

"Don't you want to go back and see if you win?"

His face dropped slightly and my stomach with it. "We won't have won."

"You might've. You were really good."

"How would you know? You missed most of our set." I looked up at him and a twinge of pain danced behind his eyes. "Because you were with that bloke."

"I wasn't!" I protested. "I was…in the bathroom… I drank too much. I felt a bit sick."

Guy twisted his body away and leaned back against the wall.

"Whatever."

Instantly I went into panic stations.

BAD THOUGHT

You've screwed it up. Of course you have,
you always screw it up.

BAD THOUGHT

You missed his set because you were OCDing
in the bathroom. Because you're a massive freak.

BAD THOUGHT

Why did you think you could be normal?
Why did you think you could have
something good?

"I…I…" I didn't know what to say. Guy used silence as punishment. My tummy tightened with the need to make it better, to make it right again. My hands already missed him and wanted to claim back their permission to touch him. My eyelids blinked in overtime, working hard to repress the tears banging on the door.

Please make it better, make it better, make it better.

He wouldn't look at me. Before he could see me cry, I stood, dusting the mud off my jeans. "I'll go back inside then," I said.

"Whatever."

No movement. I really was going to cry.

"Bye then...?" I hovered a few more seconds, just in case.

"Bye."

I stumbled over the grass, letting the light of the cafeteria guide me back. The effort of holding in tears made it hard to breathe. I would just tell Jane I was leaving, then I would go home. And I could cry all I liked. And digest whatever the heck had happened.

Just as I was about to step out into the light, onto the courtyard, I heard him.

"Evie."

I turned round, a bit pissed off. "What do you want, Guy?" I turned before he saw me cry.

"You."

He grabbed me back and I swirled like a dancer into his arms. He pulled me right up against his chest and, with no introduction, he kissed me again. It was rough and delicious and he pushed me against the college wall, pinning me with his body. His hands started in my hair but moved down until he was stroking up my arms, pinning them behind me effortlessly with his. We kissed and kissed and kissed to the backdrop of an unknown band inside. I'd never been lost in any kind of moment before. I'd always noticed everything, my brain was always tick-tocking wherever I went, whatever I did. But, then, there, I was drowning in the moment. There were no thoughts, just feelings and tastes and sensations and me giggling so hard in Guy's mouth all of a sudden that we had to stop.

He pulled back – looking half annoyed, half smiling at my laughter. "What is it?'

I giggled again. "Aren't Joel and the others going to wonder where you are? You're supposed to be in a competition."

He trailed a finger up my arm to my shoulder, leaving a Hansel and Gretel trail of goosebumps as he went.

"Yeah, they're probably wondering." He broke into a grin. "That's why we should leave. Now." He pulled me away into the darkness. I laughed harder.

"Where are we going?"

"Away."

"Where away?"

"To darker locations with more privacy."

I felt a thrill build in my toes and echo up my back.

Hands held, we walked back in the vague direction of our houses, the same way I'd walked with the girls. But this time we stopped at every lamp post to kiss, not for me to touch it six times. When we got near my house, Guy pulled me through a hedge into this pretty little grassy place with a war memorial in the middle. It was bathed in moonlight, the silver from the sky reflecting off the stone. A few soggy paper poppies from last week's Memorial Day were scattered on the steps. In the darkness, they almost looked real.

"I've never been here before, it's so pretty," I said.

Guy didn't reply. He just squeezed my hand and manoeuvred me onto the damp grass. I was on my back, his weight on top of me, and he was kissing me like the world would implode the next day. It felt so gorgeous – the sky above my face, his tongue in my mouth, his hands creeping up the sides of my top – every inch of my skin covered with goosepimples now. I ran my hands through his hair and he did that weird groan again. It was surprising, in a nice way, that I seemed to be quite good at it. Maybe it was all those years watching people kiss in the movies. I'd learned by Hollywood osmosis.

Things with Guy were getting a bit past 12A by then. His hand strayed dangerously close to my chest, and my bra, and my bra's interior contents which weren't quite ready for him.

How do you say "stop" when you're busy kissing someone?

Then, just as he was an inch away from my underwire, his phone went off.

Guy rolled off me and got his screen up, while I lay there, looking at him. It was a little bit like the meadow scene in *Twilight*, apart from the empty beer cans on the grass. Oh, and, well, the graffitied bench over there. And, I guess, yeah, I was quite sure Guy had a boner right then because something had been sticking into my leg and I really didn't think Edward Cullen had a boner in the meadow because that would've ruined it, quite frankly.

"Who is it?" I asked, rearranging myself and feeling shy. Guy's face was lit up by the artificial blue light. He didn't reply, just started messaging.

I can do that too, I thought. I got out my own phone. There was a message from Amber. I'd forgotten all about her.

Evie, I'm sorry. Where are you? How are you getting home? I'm with Jane and Joel. You coming to Lottie's Spinster Club meeting tomorrow?

I frowned at it. I was still a bit mad, I guess. About what she'd said about Guy. She didn't know him, not like I did. He'd been so sweet this evening... I think.

I'm with Guy. I know you have opinions but please don't share them right now. I'll see you tomorrow... I paused for a moment before adding, **I'm sorry too.**

I put my phone back in my bag and looked up at Guy. His face was dark again. My stomach did an uncomfortable flip-flop. "What is it?"

He shrugged. "We didn't win. Your boyfriend's band did." His tone made the uncomfortable flip-flop do a backflip.

"He's not my boyfriend. I told you, I..."

Guy interrupted me. "I mean, who lets a cover band win a battle of the bands? They've not even written a song. What did they contribute?"

"Well, I...nothing, I guess."

His lip curled. "Oh shut up, Evie. I know you loved them. I saw you dancing to their stupid set. You didn't even watch ours."

"I…I…"

He stood up abruptly. "Joel's parents are out so he's having a few people back to his. I'll walk you back then I'm heading there."

"Oh…okay." I stood too.

He stormed off through the bushes and I had to half run to catch up with him.

What had happened? Was it my fault? Why wasn't he inviting me to Joel's party? Was I a bad kisser after all? Was he really that upset by not winning? Ethan's band was much better… Were we boyfriend and girlfriend now? Why wasn't he holding my hand? What did he want from me? Should I maybe try and make the first move? Make it back to how it was fifteen minutes ago?

I matched his pace and gently took his hand. Guy looked down at it. He squeezed it a bit and then dropped it like it was the wettest fish in the fish shop and kept walking.

We stormed through the darkness in silence – my mind whirring ten million miles a moment.

What's going on? What have I done? Is it my fault? It's usually my fault. Does he still like me?

When we got to my house I was resigned to the fact I'd ruined everything. I held back tears, my jaw wobbling with the sheer effort. Rose's light was still on. Oh God – how was I going to get past without her seeing me cry? Then she'd tell Mum and Dad and they'd put me back on the medicine and I would've failed once again, like I fail everything, like life is just one big test I keep flunking.

"Well," I said, not able to look at him. "Bye then."

I went to leave – the tears right in my ducts now, just waiting for the command to fall uncontrollably for the next two hours…

"Evelyn."

Guy kissed me hard again. And all my tears turned to gasps of breath. And my heart…it was beating so hard, it was so filled with relief and happy.

He grinned at me, his teeth almost bumping into my teeth.

"I had such a good night," he whispered.

And he was gone.

Rose was reading one of my film magazines in bed. She saw me tiptoe past the gap in her bedroom door. "Evie? What's happened? I can see your smile from here."

I stopped and put my head around the door. "Oh, hey, Rose. I'm fine. How are you? Did you have a nice evening?"

She put the magazine down. "Why are you talking to me like you're at a job interview?"

"Oh – am I?"

"You are. You just did it again." She smiled, though it was a bit sad. "Something happened with you and Guy, didn't it?"

"I don't know what you mean."

"Get in and tell me everything."

She looked so happy for me – so genuinely buzzingly happy for me, that I forgave her for the cleaning box and clambered under her duvet.

"Well…" I said. "It all started when Ethan kissed me."

"ETHAN?"

"Yes."

We whispered and giggled until time lost all meaning. Rose was so lovely about Guy. She got it, I guess. What a big deal it was.

Just as she was falling asleep on my shoulder, I remembered something.

"Hey? Weren't you supposed to be staying at Rachel's tonight?" Rachel was her best friend and I vaguely remembered Mum talking about her ice-skating and sleepover party.

"Oh…that…" Rose said sleepily. "She got sick… I'm so happy for you, Evie."

Rose fell asleep.

I carefully untangled our limbs and tucked the blanket up around her. Her little face was so peaceful. Is that what I looked like when I slept? Was it the only time my face looked that serene? Without my conscious brain to bully me about? I crept to my room and clambered into bed.

I had rolled in grass, I'd danced in a sweaty mosh pit, I'd had Guy's tongue in my mouth, his unclean hands on my body.

I didn't feel like washing any of that away.

Unhelpful thought

Say thank you, Evelyn.

I should, really. My good night. My gorgeous perfect night – it was my reward. For touching the mirror, for touching all the lamp posts on the walk in. I'd done what the universe had told me to do and it had rewarded me.

You should always say thank you.

I pulled out every film individually from my shelves and touched it six times, whispering *"thank you"* as I did.

By the time I was done, the sun was rising.

RECOVERY DIARY

Date: 19th November

Medication: 5mg Fluoxetine every other day

Thoughts/Feelings: Why does it even matter??!!

Homework:

- Call the emergency surgery number if you need help while I'm away
- Keep up your Recovery Diary
- Practise your mindfulness

Thirty-five

I woke up to no message from Guy.
  Then I remembered.

BAD THOUGHT

You've not washed since yesterday.

BAD THOUGHT

You were lying on the GROUND.

BAD THOUGHT

Get in the shower, Evie. Get in, get in, GET IN.

I wrapped my bath towel around myself and pattered out onto the landing. Mum was waiting for me, a pile of laundry in her hands.

"I didn't hear you come back last night," she said.

"I made curfew, but it was still late."

"Thank you. Did you have fun?"

"Yes." I tried to sidestep past her. "I'm having a shower."

She sidestepped too, blocking me like a bouncer. "Evie, I'm trying to talk to you."

"Mum, I'm in a towel!"

I'd been pretty frantic already, but with her stopping me, the need was urgent. I need to do it, I need to do it. Now now now now now.

"I can see that." Her eyes fell on my hands. Bugger! I'd forgotten to hide them under the towel. I went to pull them away but she'd already grabbed them.

"Evie, what the hell have you been doing to your hands? They're red raw."

"Mum, I'm going to be late."

"Have you been washing them again?"

"Everyone washes their hands, Mum, unless they're gross."

Shower shower shower, I needed to get in that shower. Why was she stopping me, why? WHY? Tears pricked in my eyes. My hands shook in hers. They stung.

"You know that's not what I mean."

"It's just the change in season!" I protested.

"Evelyn, I'm ringing Sarah first thing tomorrow to tell her.

Thank God you've got an appointment booked in already."

My mouth dropped open. "No!" Sarah would find out I was losing it again, and then they'd put me back on my meds and then I would've failed, and then I'd have to start recovery all over again. And that would mean they'd make me stop touching street lights...when I'd just worked out how to make my life good... The worst thing of all, they'd make me stop cleaning things again and I couldn't, I wouldn't. Not now. Not yet. Not when I'd just started living.

"I am."

"Please, just let me take a shower." I was crying now. She gave me this look, the one I hated, of trying to be kind but secretly hiding her disgust and disappointment, like she still couldn't believe I couldn't control myself. "I'm going to be late to meet my friends."

"Do you *need* a shower?" Her voice was all stern. I hated her so much. I swear she enjoyed this tough-love thing.

"Yes, I do. Please!"

Begging, I was begging. How was I so happy just last night? If everyone would just leave me alone, and let me do what I wanted, then I'd be happy.

"When did you last shower?" she pressed.

No – she wasn't going to do this. She wasn't. "LEAVE ME ALONE." I yelled it so loud she released my hands in shock. I took my chance and barged past her into the bathroom.

"Evie? Evie, NO."

I locked the door, my heart thumping like mad. I dropped my towel and turned the water on. I was under it before it'd even warmed up, crying into the water streams, mixing my tears with my shampoo down the drain. Mum banged on the door but I started humming, tuning it out.

Now, Evie, you just need to make a really good lather, don't you? The soap is antibacterial, so you'll sterilize the top layer of your skin, and get rid of all yesterday's horridness. Then, maybe if you use that apricot scrub? All over? You'll open up your pores more, won't you? Then use more antibacterial soap and that will get into the pores, making sure you're getting it all out.

I did it, and it felt amazing.

I wanted to do it all over again. So I did.

The banging stopped, my crying subsided. I thought of perfectly valid reasons why Guy hadn't messaged to keep my brain busy.

Perfectly valid reasons why Guy hadn't messaged

1) His phone battery died.

2) He crashed at Joel's, so has no access to a charger yet.

3) He felt no need to message because he said, "I had such a good night", and that's usually the sort of thing you would message.

4) He's overwhelmed by the strength of his feelings and needs some space.

I lathered up for a third time, this round focusing on right under my fingernails and toenails. I sat on the floor of the shower so I wouldn't lose my balance as I scrubbed viciously.

5) He…

The water ran stone cold and I gasped. It sent shockwaves through my body. I screamed. It was so cold. It had to stop. I tried to get to my feet but slipped over, icy cold water raining down on me as I clambered up again. I had to get to the tap – to make it stop. I leaned up and got there, pushing the tap towards the hot side, trying to make the warm come back. If anything, the water got colder. The door banging started again.

"Evie, get out before you freeze!" Mum yelled.

She'd turned the hot water off. The horrible horrible bitch.

My hands shook so hard I could barely push the tap off. With one last tug, I did, and dropped to the floor again, shivering uncontrollably.

"Evie, get out of there, right now!" My teeth chattered. I was still covered in soap. I hated her, I HATED HER. I wobbled out onto the lino, grabbed my towel and used it to scrape off the worst of the suds. The door banged again.

"All right, all right." I could barely breathe I was so angry. I wrapped the towel around myself and flung open the door.

"HAPPY NOW?" I screamed into Mum's face, before pushing past and padding angrily to my room.

"Evelyn, come back here. I'm worried about this. We need to talk."

"No, I need to put some clothes on before I die of hypothermia," I shouted, before slamming my bedroom door shut. The first thing I went for was my phone. Just in case he'd messaged when I was in the shower. It would all be fine if he'd messaged. It would all be okay if someone cared for me.

My phone screen was tauntingly empty.

I screamed and chucked it across my room. The screen smashed at the side as it clattered on my wooden floorboards.

Rose came in without knocking. "Evie, what's going on? Mum's crying in the hallway."

"You better get away from me!" I yelled, loud enough so I knew Mum would hear. "Isn't she scared I'll give you ideas? That just being in my proximity will make you CRAZY TOO?"

"She's just trying to help, Evie," Rose said quietly.

"Oh, I knew you'd be on her side." I chucked clothes onto myself – layer after layer to warm up. I caught a glimpse in the mirror and had a fleeting thought that was soon lost in the rage.

Fleeting thought

You're looking a bit thin again, Evelyn.

I was supposed to maintain my weight, supposed to eat three meals a day. And, yeah, maybe I hadn't been eating that much recently but I just wasn't hungry. That, and, well, food can make you sick, can't it? I pulled on an extra jumper and wrapped my scarf around myself six times.

"I'm on your side, we all are," Rose said.

"You sound like a hostage negotiator."

Her face crumpled up with hurt but I didn't care. Anyway, I was more hurt! I could hardly see I was crying so hard.

"Where are you going?"

"Out." I put on a bobble hat.

"Where out?"

"To see my friends." We had a Spinster meeting planned at Lottie's.

"Can't you just sit and chat to us for a bit? Until Mum calms down? We're worried about you, Evie."

"No."

"You're making it worse."

"Christ, Rose! Can't you act your age for once? Can't you be a normal sister and help me escape down the drainpipe? You're such a goody-goody!"

Rose started crying and it made my heart ache – but it was aching for me more. For the soap flaking off my skin, for the skin flaking off my hands, for the message that wasn't on my phone, from a boy who took flaking to a whole new level. I couldn't bear it, I couldn't feel guilt on top of everything.

I picked up my cracked phone, stepped past my crying sister and blasted out of the house, with Mum calling, "Evie? EVIE?!" behind me.

Thirty-six

"Evie!"

Lottie's mum opened her arms for a giant hug. She smelled of herbs and I didn't want to touch her. I stepped back instinctively and faked a cough.

"Oooh, better stay away, Ms Thomas, I've got a horrid cold." I smiled sweetly and sniffed a hammy sniff.

"Oh, poor thing. Yes, your eyes do look a bit red. Do you want me to make you an echinacea tea? Amber is already upstairs. I can bring it up for you?"

"Oh, thanks, but I'm fine really."

I smiled again, and pushed through the beaded curtain leading to the staircase. Before I stepped into Lottie's room I took a moment to calm myself. My face didn't look too cry-ey any more, not after I'd walked twice around the block till my sobs ran out. And my hands had stopped shaking quite so much. I needed this, I needed the girls. I needed to be normal and laugh with my friends and talk to people close to me without making them cry about how screwed up I am.

Lottie had stubble rash.

"Teddy's fur is a bit rougher than an actual teddy bear's?" I asked, announcing my arrival by clapping her on the back. Amber gave me a small anxious smile and made room for me on the beanbag. I didn't want any bad feelings, so I sat right next to her and gave her a warm smile.

Lottie, however, rolled her eyes. "There are no teddy jokes left! Amber made them all before you arrived."

I nudged her with my foot. "So…?"

Lottie whipped out a hand mirror, sighed, and rummaged on her bedside table for a tube of moisturizer. "So…I think my period of mourning for mine and Tim's imaginary relationship is officially over."

"And yours and Teddy's relationship is beginning?"

She grinned. "Maybe. Anyway…what's this I hear about you and Guy? And Ethan? Did you go completely mad last night or are you just stupid?"

I wasn't sure if I was stupid or not yet. I was definitely completely mad – but outwardly suppressing that was working okay. He still hadn't messaged – but then, he never said he would.

"Yeah, well, last night was sort of dramatic, I guess." And this morning, but I wasn't going to tell them about that.

Lottie rubbed some cream into a particularly rashy bit of her cheek. "Sort of dramatic? Getting off with two guys in one night? Even I've never accomplished such a feat.

Were you wearing that illegal pheromone perfume I read about online, that makes all men want you?"

"Oi, rashy." I chucked a bit of exploded beanbag at her. "Maybe it's my natural wonderfulness, charm and sex appeal?"

Lottie checked herself in her compact again. "Or one guy's a self-confessed sex addict and the other has some weird sadomasochistic obsession with you. Anyway, have you and Amber made up yet?"

Amber stiffened next to me. I turned slowly to her. "I, I guess."

To my surprise, a tear slid down Amber's cheek. "I'm sorry, Evie. Please don't stay mad at me. I'm sorry I told you what to do about Guy. I just don't like him but I'll stop telling you that." More guilt trickled into my belly and I played with my hands. Why was I making everyone cry? Was I evil? Was I one of those bitches who doesn't realize I am a bitch? I was just trying to get a normal life together – I didn't mean to hurt anyone. But people wouldn't leave me alone.

"It's okay," I said awkwardly. "Don't cry."

I wanted to hug her.

BAD THOUGHT

You can't hug her, that would mean touching her.
And you've seen the state of her room.

I patted her lightly on the back instead and made a mental note to wash my hands as soon as I could. Lottie smiled at us.

"Well this is awkward, isn't it? Just as well I've got the world's most appropriate agenda for today's meeting." She stood up and rummaged in a discarded pile of clothes. "Hang on." After a bit more rummaging she yanked out a clipboard. "Here it is. Right..." She cleared her throat. "Today's topic of discussion for the Spinster Club is...drum roll, please... *Feminism and Dating.*"

Amber and I gave each other *what-the-hell?* looks – our first conspiratorial glances of friendship since last night. It already made things better.

"I don't understand," I said.

"Me neither," said Amber. "This sounds like a huge excuse for you and Evelyn to share snogging stories from last night."

Lottie pointed at her. "But this is precisely the point! You were the one who gave me the idea. You get so mad at us for moaning about boys, and so mad at Jane for hanging around Joel like a determined virus. When, actually, Evie is the one who should be most upset – they're the ones who were best friends." Lottie waved her hands about like a university lecturer. "There is something going on here – and I reckon it's something to do with feminism. Because when women hate each other and judge each other's choices, it's usually inequality's fault."

"I thought women were supposed to be the victims of

inequality?" I said – not quite sure where Lottie was going with this one.

"We are," said Lottie wisely. "But we are also one of inequality's biggest bad guys too. Our own worst enemies. Here, let me explain." She flipped over a page of her clipboard. "Have you guys ever heard of the phrase 'benevolent sexism'?"

"Stop it with your long words already, Miss Cambridge," Amber said. "I do art, not linguistics."

"I'm going to explain."

"Make it simple."

"Okay." Lottie pushed a bit of hair off her face. "So we all know about blatant sexism. It's stuff like when boys say, 'girls should stay in the home' or 'you can't play football' or 'you're a dirty whore who has to let me do all this weird sex stuff on you because I watch too much porn and please don't tell me about your thoughts because you exist only as a sex object'. That's blatant sexism, isn't it? It's obvious. Okay?"

"Oooookay," I said, smiling.

"But I was reading about this thing on my phone called 'benevolent sexism'. It's like Undercover Sexism, Hidden Sexism – and both boys *and girls* are guilty of it. The thing is we don't think we're being sexist when we do it, which makes it even more dangerous."

"Sexist how?" Amber asked. "What sexist thoughts and actions do we all unknowingly do?"

"It's how we think about the sexes that's wrong," Lottie

said, turning another page of her clipboard. "We believe that men and women are inherently different. So, like, women are meeker and need a bit more looking after than blokes. And we're kinder and more fragile – and that's our biology and we can't help it. Lots of us think that but... that's benevolent sexism because, actually, those kinds of attitudes can really pull us down. Just say we all get high-flying jobs when we grow up. If Evie's boss openly said in a meeting, 'Oh, Evie, you can't get that promotion because you're not as smart as men.' Well then you could sue his arse for sexism and everyone would agree with you." Lottie took a deep breath. "But, if you were up for promotion, but the process involved being really pushy and...well, if you were too embarrassed to do that in case they thought you were 'butch' or a 'bitch' or 'unfeminine', so you just smiled nicely instead and then didn't get the promotion... That's benevolent sexism holding you back. You thought, because you're female, you shouldn't behave a certain 'male' way. See, it's hidden! And women are just as sexist – even though it makes their lives worse."

BAD THOUGHT

If you don't get a job, Evie, it's because you're a screwed-up nut job who can't leave the house. It will be nothing to do with benevolent sexism.

"I think I get it," I said, mulling it over. Envious – once more – of Lottie's superior brainpower.

"I do too," said Amber. "But I don't see what it's got to do with boyfriends or dating."

"Well this is what I've been thinking about. What if we're all actually benevolent sexists? Without realizing it?" Lottie said. "You know how much I fancied Tim? Well, that's because he was all manly and loaded and I felt protected. I felt men should be that way. It was sexy. So reading this thing, I thought, 'Oh God, I'm a benevolent sexist!' Well, my sex drive is anyway. And it got me to thinking, 'How can you be a feminist if you're going out with someone? Is it possible?' Because we all have screwed-up ideas of how boys and girls are 'supposed' to be and it affects who we fancy and how we behave in relationships."

Amber crossed her arms. "It's definitely possible. I would never let myself fall for an alpha dickhead. Not after I got stood up by that football idiot."

I tilted my head. "Yes, Amber, you say that. But, no offence, have you ever been in love?"

Amber's mouth dropped open. "What's that got to do with anything?" she snapped.

"I'm not saying that to be mean," I backtracked. "But, like, it's easy to have morals before you've got a boy you really fancy making you compromise them without you even realizing."

Lottie nodded excitedly. "Exactly, this is what I mean. Our need to be loved, fanciable, desirable – whatever.

It messes up our judgement. Take Evelyn for example…"

"I'm not sure I want to be an example."

"Well, I'm using you as one. Look at her – she's helped us form this club. You're a feminist, right?"

It was my turn to nod. "Of course. A feminist and a fellow spinster." I gave Amber a little grin, nervous I'd upset her again with my comment.

Lottie continued. "But then look how you behave around Guy…"

"Huh?" I said, suddenly flustered. "What do you mean 'how I behave'?"

"No offence, Eves, and I've not heard yet what happened last night but I can probably guess. He treats you like crap. He's controlling and all alpha…and you can't help but fancy him more because of it. Because you're a benevolent sexist too. You find his arrogance and his alphaness sexy – because you've been conditioned into thinking that's how boys should be. If he started crying and getting all soppy and feminine over you – like that Oli bloke – you'd go off him."

If Guy's lack-of-message was a scratch in my already-dented sense of self, hearing that was like a stab wound. And any reminder of Oli hurt too much right now. He'd still not come back to college.

"Hey!" I wailed. "That's so unfair."

Lottie shrugged. "Look, I'm the same! I'm just as broken. This is what I wanted us to talk about today. How can we fix it? How can we keep Amber's determination to be true to ourselves, when being distracted by sexy boys with bad values who, despite ourselves, we really really fancy?"

"I know how," Amber said. "Grow to be five foot eleven and die your hair ginger. Then none of those sexy boys try to distract you."

"Ahh," I said, laughing, though her pain was quite sad. "So you're just a perfect feminist by default?"

She looked miserable. "Probably."

Lottie's eyes were shining, her smile massive. "This is great guys, great!"

"I don't feel very great right now," I said.

"Me neither," said Amber.

"But that's the point. It's hard to realize unpleasant truths about ourselves. But it's the first step towards making things better."

"So, what do we do?" I asked.

"First things first, we eat the biscuits I've got in the kitchen downstairs. Second, we all come up with a rule we think we can incorporate into the way we date. Then we put it all together into a manifesto. Then we try our best to follow it…even when the guy has floppy hair and sexy eyes and does that cupping-your-face-in-his-manly-hands thing."

"That was what Guy did to me last night," I admitted.

"See!" Lottie looked so proud of herself I almost wanted to kick her. "I promise you, Evie, by the end of this meeting, you'll never want to see Guy ever again."

But that's not what I want, I thought.

*   *   *

Amber and I walked a bit of the way home together. I dawdled, not wanting to face my parents. I'd also have to redo the whole route later when Amber left – but this time touching each lamp post six times.

"So," Amber said, pulling her beret further down to keep out the harsh cold air. "What *did* happen with you and Guy last night?"

My cracked phone still lay dormant in my coat pocket. "I told you guys already."

"You told us you kissed. But you kept adding aggressive rules to our dating manifesto."

I pulled our makeshift rules out of my pocket.

The Spinster Club rules
of feminist dating

1) If we expect all men to have six-packs and biceps, we can't get mad when they expect us to be stick-figures with DD boobs. Try and fancy decent men with decent HEARTS, rather than pricks with abs.

2) Do not be afraid of being any of the following in a relationship because you want boys to like you: bolshy, naggy, opinionated, ambitious, intolerant and independent. Don't be a bitch, but don't pretend to be a passive cupcake-baking robot either.

3) Do NOT drop your friends/life once you're loved-up.

4) Do not pretend to like the following because you

think you should: football, rugby, action films, anal sex (Lottie added that one), metal music... Like what you like.

~~5) If a boy kisses you then doesn't message, you're allowed to puncture his face with a compass.~~ (Amber and Lottie wouldn't let that one of mine in.)

"I still stand by that last one," I said, stubbornly.

"So, what? You kissed and now he's ignoring you?"

My eyes welled up, with the frustration, as well as confusion and hurt. "Yes. I'm such an idiot. You're allowed to tell me I'm an idiot. I know you've been dying to."

Amber took my hand – which would've been nice but I knew she didn't wash her hands with soap. I'd have to scrub mine when I got home. I didn't know what to do first – the lamp posts or the washing. The lamp posts, I guessed. My parents wouldn't let me out after the Big Talking To I'd no doubt be getting. My phone had been going off all through the meeting and I'd ignored it.

"You're not an idiot," Amber reassured. "And, anyway, remember the bit of the manifesto we let through... *Girls must try not to let blokes pee all over their hearts – but matters of the heart are complicated, so you should always be there for each other.*"

I gave her a sad smile. "That won't fit on a bumper sticker."

"Good. I hate bumper stickers. They're always so bloody patronizing."

I squeezed her hand and let go promptly. "You're right. We kissed, I thought it was wonderful. Now he's not messaged. I really am an idiot." The rejection stung so much and it didn't make any sense. I'd been so normal around him – apart from that blip at the party I'd been utterly usual. Was me freaking out at the party enough to put him off? And, if so, why did he kiss me?

"Oh, Evie." She put her arm around me and I let her because our coats were thick and therefore no skin was touching. "He's the idiot, not you. I wish you could see that."

"It's because he thinks I'm crazy. And he doesn't want to go out with a crazy idiot."

She laughed through her aww-noise. "What are you talking about? You're not crazy! Yes, you watch weird films I've never heard of, and sometimes you talk like my grandma, but you're fine. Perfectly normal otherwise. Why would you say that?"

I started to cry and she hugged me, looking confused. Not knowing anything.

"Evie, hey, it's okay. What's wrong? You can tell me."

It would've been the perfect time to tell her. To tell anyone. To say, "I'm drowning and I need someone, anyone, to be my life raft." To say, "I thought it had gone, and it hasn't and I'm so scared by what that means." To say, "I just want to be normal, why won't my head let me be normal?"

But I couldn't. It would be confirmation I *wasn't* normal. I wasn't better. I'd failed at boring everyday existing that everyone else finds so easy.

"Nothing's wrong," I said into her bustle of hair,

wondering when I could wash it off my face. "I just really liked him."

My hands were filthy by the time I got in. Filthy from a mile of street light touching, and freezing from cold.

BAD THOUGHT

You must wash them. Whatever goes down with your family, you must wash them.

URGENT THOUGHT

And you really need to finish the shower too.

URGENT THOUGHT

Are you sure you touched every single street light? Maybe you should go back and do it again, just in case?

I hesitated on the doorstep, unsure of what to do first. My hands were so dirty…but I wouldn't get a chance to go back to the street lights again. Maybe if I touched twelve times, rather than six, that would make Guy message? Or at least make me better? But my heart beat so fast about my hands…

…The front door opened, making my decision for me. Mum's face appeared through the threshold – her face grim.

"Evelyn, get inside."

"But…"

"No arguments. Get inside. Now."

She yanked me into the house, getting her germs all over my arm.

"Oww, Mum! There's no need for that."

"We're having a family meeting in the kitchen."

URGENT THOUGHT

YOU HAVE TO WASH YOUR HANDS NOW, EVIE.

"Okay, great," I said, as breezily as I could. "I just need to go to the bathroom…"

"No. I'm not letting you lock yourself in there and make your hands bleed again."

NO NO NO NO NO NO NO NO NO, I screamed inside.

"I need a wee! You're not going to let me wee?" My voice broke.

"No. Because you don't need to. You're just trying to ritualize."

"Fine then. I'll piss myself. Let your own child piss herself."

"That's okay. The kitchen has lino."

"This is child abuse."

"No, Evie. This is called 'caring about you'."

I was sobbing before I even got to the kitchen. When I saw Rose sitting at the table, finally but tragically let in on my pathetic non-secret, I wailed. Dad's tie was loosened, his hair standing on end from running his hands through it. Only my dad would wear a tie on a Sunday.

"Evelyn, sit down," he said, talking like he must do at work before he sacks people. That's what his job is. A professional sacker – or "performance expert", as he calls it. Companies hire him to decide who they can dispose of to save money, then let Dad do all the dirty work for them. That's why he charges so much. And probably why he has a sick daughter. Karma.

I bet he wished he could sack me...

"I just need to wash my hands," I pleaded, in a small voice. "They're...cold?"

He leaned back in his chair and took some drying socks off the kitchen radiator. "You can warm them here."

I made a run for it, it was the only way. I bolted for the kitchen sink and Dad kicked his chair backwards, chasing me. I got as far as turning the tap on before he grabbed me around the stomach, pulling me back.

"Noooo," I yelled, crying so hard. "Please let me, please let me. Please. Please!"

He smoothed down my hair, trying to calm me. "Evie, this is for your own good. Remember that? You don't need to do this. You're not dirty. You're not going to get ill."

"I am, I am. I AM! Please let me, please. I'll scream…" What an amazing idea. I screamed as loud as I could – it rang off the walls, pierced all our eardrums. Dad dropped me instinctively and I took my chance, running for the kitchen sink. In a second my hands were underwater. Oh the relief, the sweet relief. I could feel the germs dripping off me, splashing down the plughole, leaving me alone. I tipped a generous gloop of fairy liquid into my hands and rubbed it into the bad places.

…Wash wash wash…up in between every finger… spend lots of time around the bottom of the thumbs…palm to palm…back to back…

I'd stopped crying. I felt okay.

Then I realized no one was stopping me.

I turned around to my family, the water still running.

They all stared at me, watching me attack my skin frantically, looking like a meth addict. Mum had slumped to the floor – her hands over her ears, trying to block out her daughter. Dad was shaking his head slowly – disappointment bleeding all over his face.

And Rose…Rose…

Her eyes were wide with shock, shiny with worried tears. One lay suspended on her cheek.

"Evie?" she whispered. "What are you doing?"

I turned the tap off. Shame echoed and bounced off the inside of my bones. "Sorry about that," I said. "I just needed to…"

"Rose," Mum whispered. "Go to the living room. I was wrong, you *are* too young for this."

"But I want to stay." Rose got off her chair and hugged me hard. I felt the warmth in her body, her arms around my back. Huge waves of grief crashed through me.

"Rose, Mum's right. I'm fine, honest."

"But, you're not fine, are you?"

"I am," I insisted, hugging her back hard.

Dad stood up. "You're not fine, Evelyn. We think you've had a relapse. We've rung Sarah; we're all going to see her together after college tomorrow."

Relapse…

"No," I whispered. "No no no no no."

What they tell you about relapse

It's all part of recovery, they say.

It's nothing to be ashamed of, they say.

It doesn't mean you've failed, they say.

It doesn't mean you'll never get better, they say.

Watch out for those triggers, they say.

It can happen very quickly, they say.

"No," I said, louder this time. "I've not relapsed. You're wrong."

Mum covered her ears further. "Evie, look at you. Look at your hands."

I did. They were bleeding.

"So what? So I keep clean so I don't get sick – doesn't everyone else wash every day? Don't people buy bottles of that antibacterial hand gel and tip it over themselves whenever they get a train? The world is filthy, Mum. What's wrong with keeping myself clean?"

She shook her head in an *I-can't-believe-we're-here-again* way.

"We've been through this before, Evelyn," Dad said, taking over. "It's the amount of times you do it, the fact it's controlling your life again."

"It's you who is controlling my life," I yelled, so loud Rose unwrapped herself and sat down on a kitchen chair. "The only interference is YOU. I'm going to college, I'm doing okay in my coursework, I've got friends, boys like me. I'm only going crazy because YOU'RE STOPPING ME."

"FOR YOUR OWN GOOD," Dad yelled back.

"Oh shut up, and go fire some more people. Is that for their own good too, eh? Is that what you tell yourself?"

"We're seeing Sarah tomorrow and we're going to increase your dosage again. Just until this blip is over."

"No." Not the medicine. I'd finally almost come off it.

"Yes."

"You can't make me go."

"We're picking you up straight after college."

I wasn't going, I wasn't going to go.

"Fine," I said, to shut them up. And while they were all still reeling – Rose still crying, Dad still fuming, Mum still rocking on the floor…I saw my chance.

I ran out the kitchen, up the stairs, and into the bathroom to shower.

Once the water hit me, I felt so much better.

Why I didn't want to admit I was having a relapse

I really thought I'd got better. I really thought it had gone away. Coming off the meds was the last chapter of the book of nightmares I'd picked off the shelf three years ago. It was the epilogue to a one-off story, the one-night-only performance of *When Evie Went Crazy*.

If I was having a relapse now, that meant, in time, I'd have another one. And another…

If I was having a relapse, this meant it was "chronic".

I was stuck like this.

I would always be like this.

This is who I was.

"Sick" was who I was.

"Crazy" was who I was.

And I just wanted to have one shower in the morning, like everybody else. And go to college without it feeling like the world's biggest effort, like everybody else. And brush my teeth twice a day, like everybody else. And get the train, like everybody else. And not feel sick with fear all the time, like everybody else. And relax occasionally, like everybody else. And have fun with my friends, like everybody else. And get kissed, like everybody else. And go on holiday, like everybody else. And fall in love, like everybody else. And not cry every day, like everybody else. And not have stiff muscles and be in constant pain from stress, like everybody else. And eat hamburgers with my hands like everybody else. And to…

My phone went – buzzing dully on my bedside table.

It was him. Finally it was him.

I can't stop thinking about last night.

I didn't think I was capable of smiling that evening. But this made me smile and I was so grateful for the pitter-patter of light in the clunking mess of my life.

That's when I decided it. If they were going to drag me back to Sarah, if they were going to label me with diagnoses you can find on NICE guidelines where "who you are" is defined as a list of symptoms, if they were going to confirm my worst suspicions...

...*Evelyn, you're not like everybody else. You are wrong. Who you are is wrong. It needs treatment.*

Well then, I'd make the most out of pretending to be normal while I still could.

I wrote back – not even waiting the obligatory five hours you're supposed to.

Me neither. What you doing tomorrow?

An instant reply.

My parents are out all evening. Come over?

Thirty-seven

I pulled back my bedroom curtains the next morning and squealed. The frost had come! The frost had finally come.

Good but unhelpful thought

It freezes all the dirt. It makes the air clean.

I loved winter – with its fresh cold air and its jewelled blades of grass and how everyone shut themselves away and left each other alone.

I also hated winter. Flu season and the yearly norovirus stories bombarding the pages of local newspapers, making me stop eating anything from the cafeteria, or touching doorknobs without covering my hand with my jumper first.

I wiggled out of my pyjamas and started the treacherous

business of deciding what to wear to Guy's house… Skirt? Too obvious? And tights would be a nightmare to get off. But then so are jeans…and would I be taking anything off anyway…? There was a soft knock on my door.

"Hang on," I said, from inside a checked shirt I couldn't decide was "girl-next-doory" or just plain "farmy".

"It's Mum." She marched straight in without waiting and sat on the bed. "You'll freeze to death in that shirt."

"That's why I'm taking it off."

"Your dad and I are picking you up from college at ten past four. We'll meet you in the car park and we can all drive to Sarah together."

"Cool," I said.

I won't be there, I thought.

Mum picked up my pillow and stroked it absent-mindedly, which meant now I'd have to find some way to wash it.

"I'm really proud of you, Evie. I've noticed you've not had a shower this morning. That's really brave."

Most people would think that was really gross…

Plus, it wasn't quite true. I'd set the alarm for 4.45 that morning, snuck into the family bathroom and thoroughly flannelled every bit of my skin while they slept. It hadn't been easy – as I'd predicted, all the shampoo and soap had been confiscated, just like last time – but I'd searched right at the back of the cupboard under the sink, and found an unopened bottle of hand soap.

I now stunk of honey and oatmeal hand wash.

"Uh-hur." I pulled on this cool see-throughish jumper I'd forgotten I had and it was actually perfect. Guy would love it, especially if I backcombed my hair to match...

"It would be great if you could talk to Rose. She was really upset about last night."

I tried not to rise to the bait – focusing instead on combing my hair upside down.

"I was upset too."

"I know...but you could've been more thoughtful."

I bit my lip.

BAD THOUGHT

It's been years, and your own mother still thinks it's something you're able to control.

BAD THOUGHT

She cares more about Rose than she does about you.

BAD THOUGHT

Because Rose isn't broken...

"I'm sorry, Mum. I'll try and control myself next time."

My clipped delivery was lost on her.

"Thank you. We're going to get through this, Evie, it's just a blip. That's all. Have a good day, see you at four ten."

"No, you won't," I said to the door, when I was sure she wouldn't hear me.

I couldn't wait to get outside. I couldn't wait to get to college. Guy was there! And I was going to his house. And my friends were there – and I could be normal all day. God, the frost was beautiful. I skidded on icy patches and watched my breath crystallize as it left my mouth.

And then Guy was literally there – waiting by a lamp post I had no desire to touch because I was so happy about the frost. I skidded to a stop.

"Guy?" I asked, even though it was definitely him.

He looked up and smiled in a way that's illegal in several states of America.

"Morning, Eves."

He kissed me right away with no grand introduction. His lips were cold, which made me even happier and even more desperate to keep kissing him. He pulled away and draped an arm around me, steering me past several lamp posts I didn't even notice. "So you're on for mine later?"

I nodded, my heart fluttering like mad.

"It's going to be great." He squeezed my hand which

could've been romantic, or could've been aggressive, depending on what mood you were in.

I was in mood "both". I gulped.

"Great," I echoed.

I watched him as we walked to college, fancying him more with each step. He was a boy, and he had his arm around me. That was the sort of thing I saw happening to other girls. And he was a good-looking boy…with his weird – but fit – pinched nostrils and his weird – but fit – dark circles under his eyes.

He didn't talk. Were we supposed to talk?

I tried, nervous about using my own voice. "So, how was Joel's party?" I asked.

He grinned. "Epic."

"Right."

Silence. Paranoia descended.

"I wish you'd been there."

Paranoia evaporated.

He had weird but fit arms too – all veiny and bulgy and cold in his band T-shirt and no coat on. I wanted to stroke his arm – the urge to touch him was overpowering. I lightly stroked it, sending ricochets of electricity running up my hand.

Guy coughed and took his arm away.

Paranoia descended.

I pretended I hadn't noticed and watched him from the corner of my eyes. He rummaged in his jeans pocket, withdrew a battered-looking roll-up, lit it, and took a deep pull. He blew the smoke into my face and laughed while I coughed.

"That's not funny, arsehole."

He laughed harder and put his arm back around me.

Paranoia evaporated.

Just as we got closer to college, he pulled me into an alleyway.

"We're going to be late," I said, but Guy silenced me with his mouth. For someone so permanently stoned, he had a lot of energy. He pushed me back against a moss-covered garden fence and kept pushing my body further into it as he kissed my mouth and my face and then my neck – which was basically the best feeling that had ever happened to me. I kissed him back – tentatively copying what he was doing and responding to his moans.

"Today can't go quick enough," he whispered in my ear. "I can't wait to get you in my bed."

Initial thought

DOOOOOOOOOOOOOM

Next thought

This is what you want, Evie. To be like everybody else. He is treating you like a normal girl, and normal girls get into bed with guys that look like Guy.

I tried to whisper back but croaked on the first word. "I can't wait either."

More kisses. The warning bell – signalling college started in ten minutes – echoed in the distance. I reluctantly pulled Guy's mouth off my neck. "We need to go."

"No, we don't." His lips returned right back to where they had been.

"We'll be late."

"So?"

"So, I don't like being late."

He stepped back and gave me a smirk. "You're such a geek."

Guy turned and walked off towards college. I stood, panicking – my neck thinking, *Oi, where have those lips gone?*

"Hey," I called, paranoia descending around me again. "Where are you going?"

"To college," he answered, looking ahead. "Model student Evelyn can't ever be late."

"I can be late! I can *so* be late."

I didn't want to be late, but I didn't want Guy not-looking at me either.

"Well I don't want to be late now."

He didn't put his arm back around me and – when we got through the college gates – I swear he stepped away from me. Or maybe he didn't. That was the thing, I could never trust my judgements. There was, at least, a person-sized gap between us though – that was a fact. Guy walked quickly and soon we were inside, pupils trickling past lockers, clutching folders as they funnelled down the corridors. I stopped, waiting for a romantic farewell, or at least a goodbye.

Guy walked straight ahead, down the corridor, until he was swallowed by people.

I touched my lips. "Bye then," I said to myself, not knowing what to make of it all.

The bell rang. Classes were beginning.

I got a feeling in my tummy. An urge to wash it away.

I was late to sociology.

Thirty-eight

Oli was back.

He sat in his usual chair in our film studies classroom, next to me, all rigid and poker-straight.

My heart cut free from its arteries and plopped down to my feet, like it was filled with molten lead. Guilt took its place and began pumping turmoil around my veins.

I took my time getting to my desk, feeling awful with every step – replaying our date...my shameful behaviour.

"Hi," I said shyly.

"Oh, hi, Evie."

Oli looked up and it was like looking at myself. His eyes were overly wide with earnest *me?-I'm-all-right-really* false conviction, his hands twisted in and over themselves like he was holding an invisible fireball, his eyes darted and flitted as he overloaded on all the new information, and his leg jiggled so hard under the desk he kept accidentally bashing it with his knee, making his biro roll off.

"You're back," I said, knowing how hard today must be, how he would've counted down the date on his calendar with his therapist, how exhausting it would be...though of course it wouldn't be as knackering as the realization you have to keep doing it, again and again until, hopefully, it's not scary any more.

"Yeah, I'm back. I...er...wasn't well."

I nodded and sat down. "That sucks, are you feeling better?"

A big beaming fake grin. "Oh, yes, much better, thanks."

Brian bowled in and launched into an inappropriate monologue about how hard he'd partied over the weekend. Oli's leg was like jelly next to mine. He must've been burning about five hundred calories a minute by jittering it so much.

My leg started bouncing too. This is what I was worried about.

BAD THOUGHT

It's contagious, you're catching his crazy.

WORSE THOUGHT

Or maybe he's catching yours?

Brian started half-lecturing us about product placement. I absent-mindedly reached into my bag and got out some antibacterial hand gel. Mum'd forgotten to check my bag.

Oli saw me rub it into my hands. My chapped, flaking hands.

"You, er, got a cold?" he whispered.

"Me?" I looked down at what I was doing; I'd barely realized. "Oh, no. It's just my hands...they're, er...not taking to winter very well."

He stared at them in a way that made me feel naked. They really were a mess – when had they gotten like that? There was hardly any skin left around my thumbnail – I'd picked it all off. My hands were just peeling skin and open, weeping, angry sores. The skin that was left was so dry it was almost reptilian -- scaled with white dusty bits of flake. Angry red skin glistened through thin patches I'd worn down through washing.

How hadn't Guy noticed this? My hands had been all over his body, all over his hands?

"Evelyn? Are you okay?"

Oli's basil eyes pierced into me and I wanted to cry. His own nerves had vanished, transferred into concern for me. He wasn't looking at me in disgust, or confusion. He looked from my hands, to my terrified face, in complete understanding.

He'd worked it out. He knew. Broken people are like homing missiles to one another.

But I wasn't broken, I was fine. And I couldn't handle him staring at me like that.

I pushed my chair back and stood abruptly.

"Evie?" Oli asked.

"Where you off to?" Brian barked.

I couldn't stay. I was suffocating, in Oli's pity, in the thought of everyone's pity. When they knew...when they found out – the pity always comes first...followed by the annoyance that you're not better yet, even though they've been so understanding.

"I don't feel well." I gathered everything back into my bag and hoicked it onto my shoulder. It wasn't a lie.

"Well, go on then." Brian dismissed me with a flutter of his gnarly hand.

I fled.

I paced the empty corridors, trying to make peace with my thoughts. It was strange wandering round with everyone in lessons – living their lives, not worrying about touching street lights and washing the filth off them. I peered into a few windows and just watched classes taking place. I stared at students, wishing I was them, wishing I had their brains, wishing I had their inconsequential problems. Wishing I even had their totally consequential problems. As long as they weren't mine.

If my mum had cancer, or Dad got hit by a car or something, it wouldn't be my fault. It would be horrific but it also wouldn't be anything to do with me. It would've happened because life is cruel and unfair and shit happens sometimes. But me... Me and my problems, they only existed because I wasn't strong enough. Because I was weak and couldn't pull myself together like everyone else did. I know Sarah wouldn't agree, but that's how it felt...

I pushed through some fire doors and paced through the frosted college grounds, startling some squirrels.

What would happen at Guy's tonight? I vaguely knew his plan...to get as close to having sex with me as I'd let him. Why was I going? Why wasn't I going to see Sarah?

I wasn't sure.

Maybe if I just convinced everyone I was normal I would convince myself and get better?

And I really liked him...I guessed.

I'd kissed him and not freaked out about germs. Was that love? When I was with him I forgot about rituals. Maybe love was the answer? Maybe if I slept with Guy and fell in love it would mend me, as love always mends everyone? I mean, look at all the movies I'd watched. Love always sorted those people right out. In *An Affair to Remember*, she gets all uncrippled because of love. In *The Notebook* love makes the old couple die at exactly the same time. In *The Matrix*, Trinity admitting she loves Neo brings him back from the dead. Let's ignore *Titanic*... All stories are based on truth, so maybe someone loving me could mend my glitchy brain? Maybe just having that security would make me feel less insecure about the rest of the universe?

It was worth a try.

Bad but sensible thought

STI test STI test. How do I find out if he's had an STI test?

Argh! I bent down on the jewelled grass and put my hands over my ears. My stupid brain! With its constant CONSTANT barrage of thoughts and what-ifs and worries and bullying.

I wished I could scream. I wished I could scream, right there, near the college smoking area, disturbing all the lessons. Just letting it out. Screaming. Getting rid of it all.

But I couldn't.

So I made my hands bleed into the suds of the cheap soap from the college toilets.

Thirty-nine

It was so cold that nobody batted an eyelid when I came into the cafeteria with my gloves still on. Jane sat on Joel's lap, playfully tugging his long hair into plaits while he pretended he didn't like it. Amber and Lottie giggled over a sheet of paper, their art supplies spread out all over the table.

Guy wasn't there.

"Hey," I said, dropping my bag down. "What's so funny?"

Lottie looked up and smiled hello. "We're painting Jane and Joel's love child."

Jane beamed over the table. "They won't let us see until it's done."

I pulled up a chair next to Amber and looked at their masterpiece. I almost snorted. They'd drawn this hideous baby with Joel's gross ponytail and given it Jane's full lips. The baby had a speech bubble that said, "I worship the devil."

Jane picked up on my almost-snort. "What? Is it bad?"

Amber gave me a look. "It's lovely," I said, my voice all high-pitched from lying.

"Our children would be so cute," Jane told Joel and his eyes bulged a little with panic. Or maybe I imagined it.

"Where were you this morning?" Amber asked with a sigh. She put white paint on her brush and carefully dabbed over the most offensive bits of her painting.

Umm, kissing Guy in an alleyway.

"I walked in with Guy. He lives round the corner from me."

Joel looked up and peered at me inquisitively. I stared back, trying to read his mind. They were best friends. Had Guy ever mentioned me? Told him he liked me?

Amber just looked unimpressed. "Did he manage to make it until 9 a.m. before he got high?"

"Umm, no," I admitted. "Where is he anyway?" I asked, as naturally as I could. The result was an operatic voice that squeaked.

"Around," Joel answered. He paused for a moment, really looking at me. "I'd be careful, Evie…" he started to say, but we were interrupted by Lottie's giggles. I looked at the painting again, wondering what Joel had been about to say. Careful about what? Guy? Why? *Did* he have an STI? Lottie giggled again. Amber'd just given the love child a Hitler moustache, though they'd painted over the rest of the bad stuff.

Jane looked over. "What is it? Let me see," and she grabbed it from them. She was quiet for a moment, then she burst out laughing.

"Joel, honey, look! Our child is Adolf."

Joel looked away from me, glanced at it, and chuckled.

"I love it," Jane said, beaming at both of them.

"Ahhh, man," Amber said. "If I knew you could take a joke so well, I would've left the 'I worship the devil' speech bubble."

Jane laughed harder. "You should've given it Joel's ponytail."

Amber went red. "I did!"

"I can't believe you lost your nerve. Our love child feels let down."

"I...er..." Amber struggled for words. It was nice to watch her like Jane against her will. Like Amber was an iceberg and Jane was a hairdryer – slowly melting chunks off her.

I looked around for Guy. I felt sick when I thought about the upcoming evening. I also felt determined. And a little bit excited. Mostly sick... Maybe I was coming down with something? The air in the canteen was muggy with crammed-in bodies, condensation dripped off the giant glass windows and obscured the view of the frosted football fields outside. Did someone just sneeze? Did they have a cold? Would I catch it? I couldn't have a cold. I couldn't be sick for tonight.

I sniffed. It did feel a bit blocked. Oh God – I was getting a cold!

Lottie looked up at me – I hadn't realized I'd been drumming my gloved hands on the table.

"You okay, Evie? You're playing the drums of inner distress."

"I'm fine."

I wasn't fine. Nothing was fine. I was going to get a cold and then be too snotty for Guy and lose my chance to sleep with him and make myself normal. And then I'd go home and they'd march me back to the psychiatric clinic and drug me up and tell me I'd had a relapse and that would mean I'd always get sick and I'd always be sick…

My chest rose and fell dramatically with short sharp breaths.

"Evie?" Lottie put her hand on top of mine to stop the drumming. Maybe she had a cold? Could she be putting it on my gloves? I couldn't wipe my face now. Her germs would jump from my gloves and incubate in my nose and make me sick and ruin everything. "Seriously, are you okay? You've gone white."

I ignored her. I needed an action plan.

My action plan

1) Go into town and buy that nasal spray stuff that kills colds in their tracks,

2) Put half of the bottle up each nostril, just to be safe,

3) Take some ibuprofen to ward off the headache the overdose of nasal spray will no doubt give me,

4) Burn the gloves,

5) Find something to cover my scabby hands with once the gloves are burned,

6) Maybe go to my English lesson,

7) Message Mum and Dad to reassure them I'll meet them in the car park,

8) Maybe skip English so I can wash myself in the college bathroom and smell nice for Guy,

9) Meet him after English,

10) Escape out the back way of college so parents don't see me,

11) Go to Guy's. Dazzle him with my effortless charm,

12) Somehow get him to show me valid proof he doesn't have an STI,

13) Sleep with him?????

14) Realize I'm just like everyone else,

15) Walk home with a loving boyfriend, knowing I'm miraculously cured. Explain to Mum and Dad that I don't need to see Sarah any more,

16) Be like everyone else, for ever.

I couldn't feel Lottie's hand on mine. My mind was raced and jumped and bullied and hurt. I watched Jane and Amber giggling across the table. I watched Joel playing on his phone. I watched groups of friends, scattered on tables, joking and studying and chatting and piss-taking and just living living living.

It was like a thin veil floated between Me and Them.

They were on one side – Side Normal.

I was on the other.

"Eves?" Lottie jolted me back.

I batted her hand away and gave her my best "I'm fine, really" smile.

"I'm all good, I promise."

Then I left. I had some nasal spray to buy.

Forty

He didn't message all day. I panicked about why that might be.

- He's gone off you.
- He's changed his mind.
- It was all a joke.
- He saw you throw a perfectly good pair of gloves into a public bin.
- He saw you tap every street light in town on the way back from the pharmacy.
- He doesn't think you'll put out.
- He ran into Oli and Oli told him you were crazy.

I didn't go to afternoon lessons. Instead I paced the empty corridors of college – wringing my ruined hands, dashing to the bathroom to check my hair and make-up and rub stinging soap into my open sores. Wincing, crying. Having to put my make-up back on again. My stomach was in knots – the type you get a scouting badge for. Maybe I really was getting ill? I kept needing the loo, which meant re-contaminating myself and having to wash again.

There was no sense left. It had deserted me. Fled. Run away to claim asylum in a neighbouring body. In last period, when I should've been in English, I walked the halls, running my newly gloved finger along the wall.

BAD THOUGHT

If I can make it round the whole English block without my finger leaving this wall, Guy and I will work out.

I didn't see Amber heading straight for me. We collided like snooker balls, her mass of fiery hair flicking into my face. My hand lost contact with the wall.

PANIC PANIC PANIC.

I dusted myself off as quickly as possible and put it straight back, hoping a two second blip didn't undo the spell.

"Evie? What are you doing? Why aren't you in lessons?" Amber asked, straightening her coat that had got crumpled in the collision. "And, oww, by the way. That hurt. For someone so small, you have really hard bones."

"Amber, hi." I leaned back into the wall so she couldn't see me holding onto it. "What are you doing out of class?"

"I've got the dentist." She narrowed her eyes. "And I asked you first."

"Me? Oh…I just felt like skiving, that's all."

"You? Skiving? Miss Goody-Goody A-Star Lady."

"Yeah."

"Evie." She grabbed my coat and I flinched, backing into the wall. "Can we talk?"

"Don't you need to be getting to the dentist?" My voice wobbled.

"In a sec. Evelyn, what are you up to tonight? Guy turned up after you left at lunch. I heard him tell Joel you're going round his later."

"Well maybe I am."

"What? How? Even though he didn't message you the whole weekend?"

"It's fine."

Amber got closer, her hair almost tickling me. "Is it though? I'm trying to back off, Evie, I really am. But you're not making it very easy. I was chatting to Joel about Guy, and he said he's been a bit weird after his parents divorced last year. It might not be the wisest thing to get involved with him. And Lottie and I are worried about you. You seem really wound up…"

"You guys have been speaking about me behind my back?"

BAD THOUGHT

Discussing what a freak you are.

Discussing how to ditch you without
hurting your feelings.

Laughing.

Jeering.

"Yes, we have," Amber said simply. "We're both concerned about what Guy's doing to you."

"He likes me."

"He has a funny way of showing it."

I didn't agree. He'd kissed me, hadn't he? That was showing it. He'd looked after me at that party – that was showing it.

"I'm fine," I repeated, tapping the wall desperately behind my back. One two three four five six one two three four five six.

"Look, you know we're here for you whatever. Just, be careful, okay?"

"I'm always careful."

Too careful. That's the problem.

She gave me a weak smile and let go of my coat. "Well, I'd better go get my mouth attacked by a sadist wielding a drill."

"Make sure your dental practice sterilizes the equipment properly," I said, suddenly worried for her. "You don't want them putting a glove covered in someone else's saliva into your mouth." I went to grab her, to get her to realize the urgency of it…but I couldn't bring myself to touch her.

Amber screwed up her face. "Eww, gross. Now I'm *really* looking forward to going to the dentist. Cheers, Evie."

She turned to leave but I changed my mind and grabbed her at the last moment, pulling her back. This involved letting go of the wall.

BAD THOUGHT

You're going to have to start all over again.

"Wait," I said. "You can ask them what their sterilization procedure is. They'll tell you. And if you really kick up a fuss, they'll show you their cleaning machine and you can check for yourself."

"Riiiiiight."

BAD THOUGHT

Weirdo weirdo weirdo. You're being a complete weirdo.

I let go. "You know…just some people worry about that sort of thing."

"Evie, are you really all right?" Her voice was so calm, so full of care, it made me look right at her. Her eyes were soft.

With the low winter sun streaming through the hall window, it lit her red hair up like an angel in a stained glass window. She put her hand on my arm. I was trembling.

"I…I…I dunno."

"I don't have to go to the dentist, you know?" she said quietly. "It's not like I'm looking forward to it. We can get a coffee somewhere? Chat?"

"I…"

Amber's eye's flickered past my head and she frowned. I turned and saw the object of her disgust.

Guy sauntered down the corridor, all swaggery, with bloodshot eyes. My heart went mental. I completely let go of the wall.

"Well if it isn't Evelyn Crane," he said, drawing to a halt and draping an arm over me. His touch was like a calming tonic. The day's nerves melted away and dripped into a puddle on the polished squeaky floor.

Well, most of my nerves.

"You ready to go, Eves?" I couldn't believe he had his arm around me. In front of Amber. Like he wasn't embarrassed.

Amber!

"Evelyn?" Amber's voice sounded like a teacher's – the "lyn" bit all harsh. "We can still go for a coffee."

Guy looked confused. Just as he was about to say something, I jumped in.

"Amber's just going to the dentist," I said, all bossy, like it was a command. I mouthed "*Thank you*" at her over his shoulder.

She'd understand, right? I'd made plans with Guy first. And she did need to go to the dentist. It sort of grossed me out she was due to go. That meant it had been at least six months since Amber had got her mouth professionally cleaned. I'd used a glass at her house once.

The bell went. And though it went off every day, it still startled us. Classroom doors opened and students spilled out like an upturned carton of milk.

"Yes," Amber said. "I'm just on my way to the dentist."

"Gutted." Guy drew me in close with his elbow, pushing my head into his neck. "Come on, Evelyn, let's go."

"Right," I said and my heart became a drumbeat of nerves and confusion and fear. "Can we go out the back entrance? I need to pick something up from my locker."

And my parents are waiting out front for me...

"Sure thing."

He steered me away from Amber.

"Bye," she called. The way she looked at me, I felt like I was in that film, *The Green Mile*, where this man gets led to the electric chair.

"Bye," I waved.

The next time I saw her, I was in hospital.

Forty-one

He kissed me the moment we were off college grounds.

"Come here," he said, all gruff, pulling me into him. His hands stroked my back as his mouth explored my mouth. If all my craziness was a sore throat, then Guy was a Strepsil, melting the crap away in my head. A nicely flavoured Strepsil at that, the sort you pretend you have a sore throat for so you can nick one out of your friend's packet.

When he pulled away, he cupped my face in his hands and stared right at me. I could only stare back – feeling love – or whatever the hell this was – jumping through my tummy.

"I've been looking forward to seeing you all day."

"You could've told me as much," I said, without thinking.

"What was that?"

"Me too."

"Great." He took my hand and pulled it to start walking. He swung it back and forth too hard, making me giggle.

The low winter sun was bright, but it was still so cold

that the morning's frost hadn't melted. We crunched our way through alleyways, melting icy leaves with our footprints. It was perfect. I couldn't stop smiling. The air was clean, I was falling in love with a boy, we were holding hands and I was too happy to worry about whether he'd washed his hands...

I'd done it. This was normal. Preferable even. Other girls may even walk past us and ENVY me – rather than the other way round.

As we got nearer his house, the jumping beans in my stomach started some sort of sponsored jumpathon. Guy sensed my hesitation and stopped, right on his driveway.

"What's wrong?" he asked, squeezing my hand.

The real answer

I'm terrified.
I'm not sure I'm doing this for the right reasons.
Do you care for me?
Will I regret this?
Will it hurt?
Am I even ready?

What I said

"You sure your parents are out?"

He grinned and squeezed harder. "Yep. My mum and her boyfriend are at the theatre in London."

"Oh, great." There was no chance of an interruption… which was good, I supposed.

"Plus they're pretty okay about me having girls around the house."

WHAT?!

"Oh…"

What girls? What girls? How many? Had he used a condom? Did he still love them? Did he even like them? Had he washed his sheets?

My breath caught in my throat. Guy had dropped my hand to unlock his front door, which was just as well because it was shaking.

He beckoned me inside, with a bow and a flourish. "Welcome to my humble abode."

"Cool," I squeaked, and stepped over the threshold.

He led me straight upstairs to his bedroom. No tour of the living room, no kissing on the couch, not even a polite question about whether I wanted a glass of water. Just up the stairs, my hand gripped in his, and through the doorway.

I didn't get to take in much of his room before he slammed me against the door and started kissing me. The walls were red, the bed unmade, it smelled a bit of stale… something. Guy's kisses were different to usual – angrier, more urgent. He kept nipping my lip and his stubble scratched my chin. It was nice, but it wasn't. I felt aroused, terrified and confused in equal measures – like a Victoria sponge recipe…for losing your virginity.

I made myself focus on the present moment and all the different sensations erupting over my body to keep calm. There were Guy's kisses, which made my lips tingle and my intestines go limp with how good they felt. There was the weight of his hand on my left boob, gently squeezing it through my top. There were the sounds he made, the moans and groans. There were the sounds I was making – the odd gasp, as he tried something new.

And, gradually, I got lost in the "now" and let life happen to me.

He steered me to his bed, bending me over it backwards until we fell, limbs entwined, into the sag of his mattress. He pinned my arms behind my head and showered me with kisses – on my face, my neck, up my arms.

I let out a sigh.

I found myself pulling his top over his head, letting the weight of his body crush me, trailing my fingernails down his back. He didn't notice the state of my hands… Next he was tugging my top up and over my head, covering my cold skin with his warm mouth.

"You have such great tits," he said, before kissing them through my bra. And I winced, because that wasn't the most romantic thing to say.

Things Guy could've said instead

You're beautiful/gorgeous/stunning/perfect.
I'm falling for you.
Are you ready?

He reached round my back and, like magic, my bra was undone, and fell on the bed between us.

BAD THOUGHT

How did he undo your bra so easily?

BAD THOUGHT

You can't even undo it that quickly, and you undo your bra every day. You usually have to pull the straps down and swivel the damn thing to the front in order to unclasp it.

BAD THOUGHT

This means he's done it loads of times before... and...

BAD THOUGHT

YOUR BOOBS ARE OUT IN THE OPEN!
GUY FROM COLLEGE CAN SEE YOUR BOOBS!

Sheer instinct made me cross my arms over myself, trying to cover as much of my chest as I could. If Guy noticed, he didn't react. Though he did leave my WIDE OUT IN THE OPEN boobs alone a bit and concentrated on pulling down my jeans instead. They didn't slide off like in the movies. I didn't know not to wear skinnies, so they got stuck halfway down my calves and I had to kick them off, turning the bottom bits inside out in the process. One sock came with off with them, the other didn't.

At the sight of my purply-from-the-cold legs, Guy groaned and stroked them, making them warm with his mouth. I tried to lose myself again but I was too busy covering my breasts with my arms and crossing my legs though I knew I should be doing the opposite. Guy ran his hands up and down my skin. He kissed me deeply again then, using that as a distraction, he wedged his hand between the gap of my clasped legs, like a key in a stubborn lock. He began touching me through my knickers. Then he took my hands, guided them to his unzipped jeans, and coaxed me into touching him back.

My eyes flew open.

Thoughts became wildly obvious.

Perfectly reasonable thought

You're not ready, Evelyn.

And another

You're not doing this for the right reason.
You know you aren't.

And one more

If he really likes you,
he'll understand.

And, for once, I trusted my thoughts.

In a moment, my hand was off his groin and I'd backed away on the bed, pulling my knees up to cover my chest. Guy's mouth hung open, looking lost without my mouth covering it.

"What the fuck?" He half-opened his eyes. "Where'd ya go?"

"Guy? Aren't you going to court me?" I asked, before I really thought what I was going to say.

His eyes narrowed...in confusion...annoyance? "Huh?"

I scrabbled for my jumper and pulled it over my head.

He watched me, his mouth slowly melting into a cartoon sad face.

"Like shouldn't we at least go for a date before we sleep together? In the olden days, men used to 'court' women. Or 'woo' them. You know? Like in the old movies? They'd sweep them off their feet and work really hard to get their hand in marriage?"

"Marriage?" His face went even whiter than normal.

"I mean, I don't want us to get married, but don't you think you should court me a little? Just to be polite. You know, like, work for a bit before you get in my knickers?"

He looked like he was figuring out a very hard maths sum. He also looked pissed off. I was so scared. I liked him, I really really did. But I needed to know he liked me, and that meant asking.

"Do you like me?"

"You know I do."

"But what do you like about me?"

"I just told you, you've got great tits."

"What else?"

He scratched his head, he actually scratched his head, then gave me this horrid look. "Well, until two minutes ago, I liked that you didn't ask these sort of questions."

"What sort of questions?"

"You know…" He put on a high squeaky voice. "Do you like me? Why haven't you messaged me? Can't we go to Pizza Express before we go back to yours? Can I sing in your band? Are we going out now?"

"What's wrong with wanting to go to Pizza Express before you let someone sleep with you?" I asked.

Guy threw up his arms. "See! I knew this would happen. I liked you, but I worried you'd do this. Why does it always have to get so serious so quickly?"

"And having sex with someone isn't serious?" I felt like my world was breaking.

"Well yeah, it is…I suppose… But, why does it always have to be…I dunno…so full on emotionally?" He gave me another weird look. "I thought maybe you were different. You seemed all breezy, you didn't nag when I didn't message you. You've been seeing different guys, like I see different girls. You didn't seem that bothered about that Ethan guy or that pussycat boy. I thought maybe it could work…you know, casually?"

I listened in horror to his description of a girl called Evelyn who wasn't anything like me at all. "Oh God," I said, almost to myself. "You think I'm a Girl-Next-Door Slut."

Guy squinted. "A girl next what?"

An urgent need to put on my jeans. I began scrabbling into them, desperate to cover my skin, to get some of my power back. I'd tried *too* hard to be normal for Guy. I'd tried too hard to be carefree and breezy, like I thought other girls were. But they're not…

It couldn't just be casual for him, could it? It didn't make sense. He'd, like, proper stared at me before kissing me, and he'd told me, to my actual face, that he cared… None of it made any sense.

"I think I'm falling in love with you," I told him, desperately, trying to coax some feeling out of him.

The whites in his eyes doubled. If we were in a cartoon, they would have rocketed out of his skull on stilts. "What? Evie? Seriously? What's going on?"

Emotion raced up my throat, catching in the back of it. "I thought you really liked me..."

"I do like you. But...love...what? Are you crazy?"

"You were so nice at the party."

"What party? What? When you were off your face? Well someone had to look after you. I didn't know that meant you'd go all psycho..."

Everything I said bothered him more, like my words were stink bombs I was lobbing in his direction. "Fucking hell," he muttered to himself, running his hands through his hair. "This is mental. You're mental..."

That word. That ruddy word. Tears leaked from my eyes. I'd fought so hard to dodge it... He saw my tears. "Oh God, you're not fucking crying now? I can't handle this." He stood up and put his T-shirt on. I cried harder.

Were these my options? Easy lay or mental? A lie, or alone? Were these the only options boys gave you? Was it mental to want someone to love you? Was it mental to want to be courted before you let a guy put an actual piece of his body inside your body? Was it mental to want a message after you'd kissed someone? Was it mental to want the most normal thing in the world – a relationship? One that didn't make your heart feel like it was full of bogeys?

Was it mental to not want your heart stamped on until it shattered?

Or was it my fault? Had I just fallen for an alpha-jerk, casting a lovely boy like Oli aside, because I was a screwed-up benevolent sexist and Amber was right all along?

Guy watched me cry with growing impatience. "Evie, stop. My mum will be back soon."

I let out a gulp. "You said they were at the theatre."

"Well, they're not. They're out for dinner. They'll be back by eight."

I calculated it through my sobs and threw my hands down when I figured it out. "So, what was your plan? For after we'd had sex? To send me home once you'd got what you wanted?"

"No," he said, but his face said yes.

My tears turned into angry ones. "You're pathetic," I said, knowing it was true but my ribcage still exploding. "I know you have more feelings than you're letting on! You're messed up!"

Guy just shrugged – his attitude towards everything. Shruggy-shrug shrug in *a well-if-you-don't-like-it-don't-fancy-me* way.

"And your band is really pants," I added.

"Pants? What are you, twelve?"

"I'm going now."

"Fair enough."

No "please don't", no "I've made a horrible mistake".

No "but I've loved you ever since we played that game of conkers".

Just a "fair enough".

It wasn't fair though. Feelings never are.

I gathered up my stuff and dashed in humiliation from his red smelly room.

Forty-two

I was filthy.

I couldn't believe how contaminated I'd allowed myself to get. I ran home in the early winter darkness, skidding on ice, sobbing whenever I stumbled.

Filthy filthy filthy filthy filthy.

His duvet – duvet! It probably hadn't been washed in months. Months! And that room, the smell! What had caused that smell?

I fled past street lights, ignoring them. I'd touched them all before and it'd done nothing. I wasn't normal. Guy didn't see something special in me. He just thought he was going to get laid.

He'd called me mental…

My foot slipped on a patch of black ice and my ankle twisted violently in on itself. I screamed and fell face down, my hands breaking the fall, grazing the pavement, scooping up gravel and dumping it inside my palms.

"No…"

I stayed there, splayed across the pavement and whimpered.

He'd touched me.

I'd let Guy's filthy hands touch me. I could feel the imprints of his poking fingers all over my body – they throbbed with germs, with filth, with wrong. He'd known how to undo my bra. That meant he'd undone other bras. That meant his poking fingers had poked other girls. Did they have diseases? How would I know? Guy hadn't asked me any questions about my sexual health before undoing my bra. That could only mean he hadn't asked the other girls either.

BAD THOUGHT

You could have HIV now…

I whimpered once more and tried to get to my feet, wobbling like Bambi on the ice.

Reasonable thought

You won't, Evie, you can't catch it like that.
You know that…

BAD THOUGHT

All right, herpes then? That's contagious as hell
and transmitted through touch.

BAD THOUGHT

And HPV. You'll definitely have HPV now.

BAD THOUGHT

And you missed out on the jab for that
because you didn't trust them to sterilize
the needles properly.

The dirty bits of my body throbbed again. I could feel the
bacteria multiplying, the infections digging into my skin.
What had I done? How had I allowed this to happen to me?
I had to get home. I had to get clean. Now. Maybe if I was
really quick I could stop all the germs in their tracks?

So I ran. With a busted ankle and two bleeding hands
splattered with gravel, I ran.

Rose was in the hallway, her face blotchy as I exploded
through the door.

"Evie! Where have you been? Mum and Dad have gone

nuts. They're out in the car looking for you."

I ran past her, up to my room. She followed.

"What's happened to you? Have you been attacked? Let me call them. They phoned your friend Amber. She said you were with a guy?"

My sterile little room was unwelcoming and unhelpful. I tipped the duvet off, chucking it to the floor. There must be some cleaning stuff here. Something my parents hadn't found.

Rose was on the phone behind me. "She's here. She's in a state, I don't know what happened. Okay, I'll try…"

I didn't have much time.

"Evie?" Rose called softly, watching me turn my bedroom upside-down but talking like I wasn't doing anything extraordinary at all. "Mum and Dad will be back in ten minutes. Let's have a chat? Tell me what happened…"

I opened my bottom desk drawer…the germs…I could feel them growing…my tiny hidden bottle of antibacterial hand gel wasn't there. They'd taken it.

BAD THOUGHT

You're going to get ill and die… Get clean.
Find a way! Now nownownowNOW!

"Rose." I grabbed her with my eyes wide. She jumped. "What?"

"You have to help me. Something dreadful has happened. Where do Mum and Dad hide the cleaning stuff?"

Her mouth fell open, her eyelashes shaking. "Evelyn, no. There's nothing here for you. It's all gone. They don't keep anything here."

BAD THOUGHT

She's lying. Your own sister is lying to you. She hates you and resents you and wants you to get ill and die so she doesn't have to put up with your craziness any more because you're ruining everyone's lives.

"You're lying," I screamed. "There must be something. They must have cleaning products somewhere."

"No," she repeated, but I watched her scared eyes flicker in the direction of our parents' bedroom.

The en suite. I pushed past her and ran down the corridor. "Evie, no. Please. Stop."

I ran past their bed and into the little alcove that was their extra bathroom. Like a frenzied girl – well, I was one – I dived into the cupboard under the sink. And there, there it was. What I needed. Spray bottles and rubber gloves and disinfectant spray and all the wonderful lovely cleaning products that wipe away dirt and germs and all that's wrong with the world.

I pulled out a bottle of bleach...

Evie's logic that wasn't logic really

If I could use something strong enough, I would stop all of Guy's germs before they had time to breed. Simple soap wouldn't cut it – he was too dirty and the viruses had had too much time to spread.

Bleach though. Bleach kills everything. Everybody knows that.

If I could just bleach the bits where he touched me... then everything would be okay and I wouldn't get sick and I'd go see Sarah to keep my parents happy and things would get back to normal because normal is all I'd ever wanted.

But bleach burns... Maybe if I diluted it, it wouldn't burn me? Like one of those acid peel face masks. I plunged my hand down on the safety cap, unscrewed the top and tipped some into the plugged sink.

Rose burst in just as I was adding water to dilute it. She looked so in pain – if there was any reasonable part of me left, her face would've broken my heart.

"Evie, please. Stop. Whatever you're doing, stop!"

"I can't," I sobbed back, honestly, watching the bowl fill with water, willing it to fill faster. If I could just apply one layer before my parents came back and wrecked everything...

"What are you doing?"

"I'm just washing something off."

I needed to put it on, I needed to stop the germs, I needed, I needed, I needed...

I sank a flannel into my diluted bleach mixture. The bleach seeped into the open sores of my hands.

I screamed.

The pain... The stinging.

"Evie!"

If I could just break through the pain... It'll scab, but it will be free of germs, free of filth, free of dirt.

"Is that water, Evie?"

"Yes!" I wrung the flannel out and howled again. Then, with my hands shaking uncontrollably, I pulled my trousers down, right in front of Rose, and dabbed the skin at the top of my legs, erasing where Guy had been.

"Evie. Oh my God, is that bleach?! Have you put bleach on you? Oh God, Evie. Help! Someone help!"

Relief.

Relief flooded through me like a tidal wave of gorgeousness. My legs sang with relief. I let out a deep breath.

Then the burning started. First a tingling, then a hot fire coursing up me. I looked at my withered hands – blisters had erupted all over them. It hurt so much I could hardly see.

I sank to the floor, sobbing, wanting so much to do the rest of my body.

"Mum? Dad? She's in here! She's done something. I think she's put bleach on herself."

Crashing. Worried shouting.

"Get her in the shower. Now."

"Evie? What have you done? What the hell have you done now?"

Cold water hit me – it rained down on my head, ran down into my eyes, joining with the tears.

Just before I passed out, I remember having one thought.

The thought

Well this isn't normal, is it now, Evie?

Forty-three

What the doctors said

"It's a good thing she diluted the bleach."

"You did the right thing, getting her in the shower that quickly. It stopped the burn."

"She doesn't need a skin transplant."

"But she may struggle to feel temperatures in her palms."

"The scar on her leg will fade with time."

"Your youngest daughter, Rose, may need some counselling."

"How did Evelyn find the bleach?"

"We're transferring her to the psychiatric ward, just for a week or two. Evelyn, do you understand what that means?"

"Evelyn, we're putting your medication back up. We're also prescribing you some diazepam, to help you feel calm again."

"Your daughter has suffered a significant relapse of her Obsessive Compulsive Disorder…"

RECOVERY DIARY

Date: 5th December

Medication: 60mg Fluoxetine, 5mg Diazepam twice daily

Thoughts/Feelings: ....

Daily schedule:

8 a.m. Wake up

8.30 a.m. Breakfast and meds

9 a.m. – 11 a.m. Therapy

11 a.m. – 1 p.m. Free time

1 p.m. – 2 p.m. Lunch and meds

2 p.m. – 4 p.m. Visiting hours

4 p.m. – 5 p.m. Group work – art class, group therapy, etc. etc.

5 p.m. – 6 p.m. Stare aimlessly at the television

6 p.m. Dinner

6 p.m. – 10 p.m. Stare aimlessly at the television

10 p.m. Meds and bedtime

Forty-four

Mum's visit

Mum was the first. She was allowed to bring chocolate, and clothes.

I sat in my tiny room, playing with my bandages, staring at the clock.

I burst into tears the moment I saw her. "Mum, I'm so sorry."

She gave me a sad little smile and sat on the hard-backed chair next to the bed, placing some folded jeans and a bar of Dairy Milk on the mattress. "How are you feeling?" she asked, to the pair of jeans.

"I'm so sorry."

"It's okay, Evelyn." But it wasn't okay. I could tell by her face. Pain bled all over it.

"Where's Dad and Rose?"

"They're dropping by tomorrow."

"I'm so so sorry."

Mum brought her face up to look at me, to really look at me. At my skinny frame and bandaged hands and the sterile box room. It was her turn to cry.

"Oh, Evie," she sobbed, sitting down next to me and smothering my face into the nook of her neck. "What happened? You were doing so well!"

"I know," I sobbed back. "I'm sorry. I let you down. I let everyone down."

She cried harder. "It's not your fault," she said. And, for the first time, I really believed she meant it.

We hugged and cried and hugged and cried some more.

"What's going to happen to me?" I asked her, wiping some snot on her blouse by mistake. The snot didn't upset me. It already didn't bother me. I didn't know if it was the drugs, or the intense therapy sessions, but I looked at the slimy trail and just thought, *Oh, there's some snot.*

Mum smoothed down my hair. "You're going to get better."

"You said that last time."

"And you did get better."

"But then I got worse."

"Well, that's life. That's not just you. Life is better and then it is worse, over and over, for everyone."

It was like I'd climbed Everest, had the summit in my sight, the flag in my hand, all ready to pierce it into the top of the mountain and say, "Whoopdedoo, I made it," and then an avalanche from out of nowhere swept me right back to the bottom of the mountain again.

Was it worth bothering to try and climb it again? I was exhausted. I'd already climbed it. I didn't want to…but, then, what other choice was there?

I extracted myself from her shoulder dent. "How's Rose?" My voice quivered, with shame and guilt and worry.

Mum sighed, rubbing her eyes. She looked knackered. I guess she'd just fallen down a mountain too. "She's not great, Evelyn."

"I'm so sorry. I know you never wanted her to see me like that."

"It's not just that… She…never mind." Mum picked up the jeans she'd brought and refolded them for no reason.

"What?" I asked, sitting up on the bed.

"I shouldn't tell you. You need to rest."

"I'm fine." I looked at my surroundings. "Well, obviously I'm not fine, but I'm fine enough to care about Rose. I'm okay handling other people's problems – it's just my own I'm not so good at."

Mum gave me another sad smile. "All right then. Maybe you can help. I don't understand a lot of it anyway. I don't get technology."

"Technology?"

"She had a counselling session," Mum continued, her eyes filling up again. "To, you know, make sure she was okay with what she saw…" More guilt free-fell down my throat. "And, well, she got very upset. Not about you. Well, about you a little bit…but, well, she's being bullied at school…

She broke down on this counsellor and told him everything. We've had to have a meeting with her school."

"What!?" I asked, in complete shock. "I thought she had loads of friends?"

"Your father and I did too. But they're not her friends. They've set up this silly website where they call her names, I don't quite understand that bit. But she's been coming home from school every day to an inbox full of horrible emails and text messages."

"Saying what?"

"She showed us some." Mum's voice cracked again. "They call her a geek. Or up herself. Or ugly. They invited her to this sleepover and then said at the last moment it was cancelled. Then they rang her mobile that night and giggled down the phone, saying the sleepover was happening and they just didn't want her there."

My mouth was wide open. The guilt in my stomach lit an ember that grew into a fire. A fire of rage. Every defensive mechanism in my body ignited. I clenched my fists and winced. My hands still really hurt.

"I was there that night," I said. "I should've noticed something was wrong. Well, I did, but she convinced me it was all fine."

"You had other things on," Mum said kindly.

"That's not an excuse. She's my little sister. I should look out for her, not the other way round." I burst into tears again.

So much is lost when you lose yourself. Not just your pride, or your hope. But worse things, things that affect others. Like your ability to help them when they need you, to notice when they're hurting. You're too wrapped up in your own hurt, your own mess. It wasn't fair. I didn't want to be selfish, I didn't want to be a crap sister…and yet I was…because I wasn't strong enough.

Mum cooed and let me cry. I thought about Rose – perfect, lovely Rose.

"Why would anyone bully Rose?" I asked.

Because it should've been me. I was the freak. I was the abnormal one. I was the annoying one, the needy one, the crazy one, the one to point a big finger at and say "ho ho ho, look at that loser". I was the one who could never eat spare ribs with my fingers, and never stay the night in other people's houses because I didn't trust how clean they'd be, and couldn't go ice-skating for someone's birthday party because you have to borrow shoes… Those were reasons to get bullied. Yet there was no flaw in Rose – no unredeeming quality to pick on.

"Because people do," Mum said simply, putting the jeans down. "People are broken, so they bully others."

"But there's nothing to bully Rose about?"

"They find something – even if you're near-perfect, they find something. You can't protect yourself from the world, Evie. God knows, I know you try. But bad stuff happens, people are mean, there are no steps you can take that ensure the world leaves you alone. All you can do is try not to be one of those people who contributes to the bad. And that's why I'm proud of you…"

I looked at her. "Proud of me? For what? It's not like you can hang a sectioning certificate above the stairs?"

"Yes, proud of you. Because, despite all you've been through, you're still good and kind. You're not bitter. Well, you are, but only at yourself. You may feel broken, but you don't break others."

"I make your life hell."

She grinned and gave me another hug. "But you don't mean to! You hate what you do to us. And maybe we all need to have a big chat about how we can handle each other better. We've been talking to Sarah and she's been giving us some tips. You didn't tell us about your relapse symptoms. You tried to hide them instead. And that must be mine and your dad's fault too. Not just yours. Maybe this whole tough love thing isn't entirely working?"

I laughed. "You can't just *let* me go doolally. Otherwise I'll never get better."

"Maybe. But your father and I could be more accepting... because this" – she gestured around the room and to the bandages on my body – "this isn't your fault."

"But, if I could've just been stronger—"

"No!" she interrupted. "It's not your fault."

"But..."

"Evelyn." Her voice was so stern it shut me up. "Look at me, listen to me." She cradled my face in her hands. "None of this is your fault."

And I cried so hard I thought I'd never stop.

Forty-five

Rose's visit

I hugged her so hard I almost killed her.

"Why didn't you tell me?" I asked, hoping if I squeezed hard enough all her pain would ooze out.

She hugged me back. Hard. "Why didn't you tell me you were getting worse?"

"Who are the girls? Tell me. I'll kill them. I can easily plea 'temporary insanity' at the moment and get away with it."

"Evie, you can't ever do that to me again, promise me?"

Dad stood over our hug, smiling wryly. "Do you not think," he interrupted, "you should both answer each other's questions?"

Rose and I unhugged and grinned at each other.

"All right, I'll go first," I said. "I am so so sorry for what I did to you…" I looked at Dad. "For what I did to all of you. I thought I had it under control. I thought I was just like everybody else." I looked down at my ruined hands. "I guess I was wrong."

Rose hugged me again. "You're forgiven, on one condition," she muffled into my shoulder.

"What?" I asked nervously, tapping her back. "I don't think I'm ready to start cleaning your room for you."

She only half-giggled. We both knew I was a long way away from doing anything normal with cleaning. My care team still let me touch the light switch six times. Apparently I could do whatever I wanted, rituals-wise, until I'd "adjusted to my new lifestyle", i.e. the ward, my ruined hands, the trauma of the relapse.

"I won't make you clean my room. But I want you to promise me that you'll stop comparing yourself to everyone else."

"What?" I broke off the hug, not understanding.

"You. Evelyn. You're always like, 'I wish I could be like this' or 'I wish I could be more like so-and-so'. You're so obsessed with being normal, but that's well boring, and you're extraordinary, Evie. Promise me you'll stop trying to stop being you."

Tears collected in my eyes for, like, the millionth time that day.

"I'm going to sound like a fortune cookie, but you've got to love you before worrying about anyone else loving you."

Dad and I looked at each other over Rose's unruly mop of hair.

"I've said it before, and I'll say it time and time again," I said. "You are TOO WISE for someone so young."

She shrugged and wiggled her eyebrows. "I know, I'm basically Gandhi."

"Well, that's taking it a bit far."

We both giggled until Rose's face fell. I put my hand on hers and she didn't even flinch at the rough touch of my bandages.

"How are you?" I asked softly. "Mum says you've gone through hell...I could kill them."

"We're looking into changing schools," she said.

"It's that bad?"

"It's that bad."

And there was nothing I could do but hug her, as only sisters can hug. Each of us clasping the other as tightly as possible, hoping that love, somehow, would seep through our embrace and cure each other's pain.

It was a surprise to both of us when Dad joined in.

Good thought

I am so loved and so lucky...

The nurses came in and said visiting hours were over. Dad picked up his briefcase, put some extra chocolate on my chair and smiled goodbye. Rose stayed behind a moment.

"Your friends," she said. "Amber and Lottie. Mum and

Dad rang them when you went missing. They want to know how you are."

"You didn't tell them, did you?" I tried not to sound accusatory.

She shook her head. "No, but *you* should."

I couldn't, could I? They would think I was so stupid. That I'd just done it because of Guy or something, like some melancholic lovesick saddo teenager. Guy... Funny how quickly love can turn to anger.

"I don't know, Rose, they wouldn't understand," I said, picturing telling them and them not being able to handle it.

"How do you know that?"

"I just do."

"Is this because of Jane?"

"What about Jane?" I asked, though I sort of knew.

Rose rolled her eyes. "I do share a house with you, I have seen what she did to you. She was your rock, and then she dropped you like a rotten fish at Christmas dinner."

"Is that even a saying?"

"I dunno. But it's what happened. I saw her let go of you, when you weren't quite ready to be let go of."

I scratched my eye and looked around my tiny room, wondering for the billionth time how I'd got here. "It's because I was so annoying. She couldn't put up with me any more. She'd had her fill of my crazy."

"Or..." Rose said. "She's got ridiculous self-esteem issues and clings onto whoever worships her the most."

I went quiet and digested what she'd said. Sometimes

there's a nail that needs to be hit on the head but you don't have the tools to do it yourself. Right there, right then, my terrifyingly-wise little sister's words banged the *what-the-hell-happened-between-Jane-and-me* nail right into the wood. It finally made sense. The hurt, the rejection…they weren't just my issues, but Jane's too.

I gave her one last massive hug. "What are you going to be like as an old woman, if you're this wise already?" I asked. "Are you The Oracle from *The Matrix*?"

"There is no spoon," she laughed.

"I bloody love you." I hugged her tighter. "And I bloody love that you know that line! You are truly my sister. No matter what happens, I'll be there for you…even more so when they let me out."

"I love you too." A nurse came up behind her and gently put a hand on her back, in a caring but *please-go-now* way. "I still think you should tell your friends…"

"Maybe."

Forty-six

Sarah's visit

Sarah came the day they took my bandages off. I'd already had a two-hour therapy session to help me come to terms with the state of my hands. But when she found me in my room, I was still staring at them like they were the Ring of Mordor.

"How are they?" she asked, without a "hello", perching on the edge of my bed and putting her file down.

I turned them over at the wrist and watched her try not to wince.

"You know those baboons with the really gross arses?" I answered, thinking maybe if I made it a joke, it would hurt less. "I have a baboon's arse where a palm should be." And I cried harder than ever – because Sarah was there and she could take it better than the others.

"They'll heal," she cooed, letting me cry myself out.

"The doctor said they'll get better. You were lucky your family washed it off so quickly."

I looked at her through my blurry tear vision. "I can't believe you just called me lucky. And I can't believe you sectioned me."

She cocked her head. "Well, that's not quite accurate, is it, Evelyn? You agreed to come here of your own accord… You're only sectioned if you refuse help. You came here willingly."

"Otherwise I'd get sectioned."

"Well…"

"How did it come to this?" I interrupted with a hollow wail, that I could tell made even a seasoned therapist feel uncomfortable. She sat and listened, and made sympathetic faces while I, once again, relived the last month or so. The battle of the bands, the fight with my parents, Guy's bedroom…

"I became a mess so quickly." I tried to explain my sadness. The pain in me that wouldn't dull, no matter how many paintings the art therapist made me paint. "It was, like, so quick, Sarah. I was doing okay, I was getting better, and then – BAM – I lose my life again, I lose my mind again. That means that, even if I get better now—"

"Which you will," she interrupted confidently.

"Even IF I get better now, what's the point? I'm always a week away from potentially losing it again. On the cliff edge of normal. Then what? Then what do I do?"

"You remember how far you've come, you get the help

you need, and you continue fighting."

"I'm so tired of fighting," I cried. "It's exhausting – trying to be like everybody else."

"Do you not think everybody else finds it exhausting too, trying to be them?"

"No," I said sullenly, crossing my arms and wincing as my newly exposed hands scraped the wool of my jumper.

Sarah was quiet for a moment, then she said. "What does normal look like to you, Evie?"

"Just being like everyone else," I answered without thinking.

"And what does this great 'everyone else' do? Tell me specifically, what do they do?"

"Well…they…umm…they don't get sectioned."

Sarah actually rolled her eyes. "You've not been sectioned. You came here willingly."

"Yeah, but they don't end up here."

"Maybe not…but when they go through bad patches – which everyone does – they end up in other bad places… down the pub…in a casino…in a stranger's bed…in a bad relationship. If they know what's good for them, they may end up in a yoga class…or running in a park."

"What's your point?"

"Everyone's on the cliff edge of normal. Everyone finds life an utter nightmare sometimes, and there's no 'normal' way of dealing with it." Sarah sighed. "There is no normal, Evelyn. There's only what's normal to you. You're chasing a ghost."

I thought about it. "If there is no normal then, if we're all just massive freaks in our own special ways – why am I here? Why am I on medication? Why do I see you every week?"

Sarah put her tongue in the side of her cheek. "Because, Evelyn, your behaviour isn't making you happy. If you were cleaning the house ten trillion times a day but thought 'well, that's just me' and whistled while you did it, well, it's not so much of a problem, is it? But you're miserable. You're wasting hours each day living in fear, trying to control everything around you. Trying, ultimately, to control who you are. You've got to stop hating yourself, Evie."

I burst into tears again, huge weeping peals of tears. I cried for where I was, I cried for my hands, I cried for Guy, I cried for the life I'd never have, the worries I'd always have, I cried because it was all so horribly unfair.

I cried because, as always, Sarah was right.

I thought about my logic the day of the accident, the day in Guy's room. "I...I..." I stumbled through sobs on my words. "I really thought if someone loved me, then maybe it would be okay..."

Sarah rearranged her skirt. "There's two things to say about that," she said. "One...about teenage boys, I bloody told you so." Mum had obviously filled her in on what happened with Guy. I'd broken down and told her at the first hospital, after the doctors had picked the gravel out of my warped hands. "And the second thing to say is, people do love you, Evelyn. Maybe not randy seventeen-year-old lead singers – but your family do. And…well, your little sister tells me you've got two friends who won't stop bugging her with calls. That's love."

I caught a stray tear. "They won't love me once they realize who I really am."

She picked up her file, making to leave. "I'm sure they will. But *you've* got to love you first, that's the most important part. Anyway" – she tucked her file under her arms – "visiting hours are up, I'll leave you in the very capable care here. You know you can call me anytime?"

"I know."

"Well, bye then."

"Bye." She turned to leave me in my lonely little room.

"Sarah, wait!" I got off the bed and caught up with her in the doorway. "Do you…do you think you could arrange for me to have non-family visitors come here?"

She gave me a huge, proper, no-protective-barrier-up grin.

"I'll see what I can do."

Forty-seven

It started with a house party.

I don't know if you can call a get-together in a private room on an adolescent psychiatric ward a "house party". But there were definitely biscuits – and at least one attendee was on mind-altering drugs – just of the medical, safe, anti-depressant variety.

I was so nervous that morning I shook all the way through my psychiatrist's assessment. He peered over at me, from the depths of his red bulging file.

"You've been doing very well in here, Evelyn. We're happy with your progress and I think it's time to start discussing a schedule for your discharge."

"Oh, that's great," I said, barely taking in what he'd said.

BAD THOUGHT

They won't come.

BAD THOUGHT

They'll never see you in the same way
after today.

Good thought

But they'll know who you are...and if they
don't like it, why would you want to be friends
with them anyway?

"Are you all right, Evelyn?" the psychiatrist asked. "You seem very nervous. This is good news!"

I looked back at him distractedly. "Oh, yes, I'm fine. I'm...er...just, having some important visitors today."

He gave a small smile. "I've heard. Good luck, Evelyn."

He sounded like I was about to go on a mission to the moon or something. Maybe I was really.

Fifteen minutes. Fifteen minutes until they were here.

BAD THOUGHT

Your room is too gross, you should tidy it.

Good thought

No, Evie, you've worked hard to make
it this scruffy.

BAD THOUGHT

They're not going to believe you have OCD if you
leave that banana skin in the bin.

Good thought

You can't control what they think, so why
bother worrying?

I left the banana skin where it was – though it did start
to smell and made me very nervous. I paced the length of
my room, muttering, hands shaking, stomach somersaulting.

This is it.

No going back.

You might lose them.

They might not handle it properly.

They might not come.

What's going to happen?

Back and forth, back and forth. Sweat dripped down my

forehead. I sat on the bed. I stood up again. I sat down again.

Lottie and Amber arrived with a nurse at the door.

"Miss Crane? Your friends are here."

I gave myself a moment, before I looked up at their faces. It was like GCSE results day and you're holding the envelope in your hand. The tests are over, there's nothing else you can do, the results are in there, unchangeable, and yet you wait a while with the envelope – savouring that moment of not-knowing, before you rip apart the glue and see what the future has in store.

I raised my head.

They both held a giant handmade poster, with the words "Get Well Soon, Evelyn" painted on it in massive letters. Amber had used her amazing artistic talent to create a collage of famous female icons around the lettering. There was Marilyn Monroe, Thelma and Louise, Queen Elizabeth I, Emmeline Pankhurst, Germaine Greer, Eleanor Roosevelt, JK Rowling, Sofia Coppola and dozens more – cut out carefully and stuck around the poster, all of them wishing me well.

Lottie and Amber's hands shook at the top of it. They looked so scared and sad – but also like they were trying their best to brazen it out. For my sake.

A lump rose in my throat and I coughed to get rid of it. I smiled at them, so wide my face hurt.

"Ladies," I said, with a confident voice that didn't really belong to the situation. "Welcome to the official Spinster Club meeting number four. Come…" I beckoned to the two beanbags I'd borrowed from the common area. "Take a seat."

They handed me my poster and I couldn't look at it or I'd cry uncontrollably. I hugged them both and put the beautiful piece of paper down.

"I've got biscuits," I said, passing out a plate of pink party rings Mum and Dad had brought in. They looked at each other first, raised an eyebrow and then took two each. "Great, now, today's topic for discussion is…" I coughed again. "Women and mental health: *Is the patriarchy literally driving us mad?*"

Lottie and Amber exchanged another look, turned to me, and then burst out laughing.

"What a fitting location you've picked," Lottie said, "for such a discussion."

I knew then that everything was going to be just fine.

"Shh," I said. "I've prepared a talk."

What I learned about Sarah

Sarah helped me research all the information for the meeting. She'd brought in her iPad and we'd poured through health reports and historical records, compiling what I needed. She'd known exactly where to look. After a long afternoon reading Victorian hospital records, I asked her why. She gave me a cheeky smile. "I actually did my dissertation on this at university."

"On what?"

"On women, specifically. And how much society is to blame for their 'madness'."

My mouth dropped open.

"Sarah, are you…?"

She grinned. "A massive feminist? But of course! If it wasn't breaking our patient confidentiality, I'd have a good mind to set up my own Spinster Club. Such a great idea, Evelyn. Like a book club, but for women's rights. The antidote to the WI. It could go places."

"Really?"

"Really."

"Sarah?"

"Yes."

"I give you my permission. To set up a Spinster Club, I mean."

"Thanks, Evie. I may well just do that."

I handed out my sheets to the girls, and began my meeting.

"Statistically," I started, "women are crazier than men. If you look at the numbers, the simple act of having a vagina makes you more likely to have a depressive illness, post-traumatic stress disorder or be unipolar, and we're more likely to self-harm. Now, you could blame our DNA. You could blame our hormones. You could criticize the statistics themselves. But I think this…" I paused for dramatic effect. "We are not just a crazier sex. I believe the world, our gender roles, and the huge inequality we face every day MAKES US crazy."

I took a deep breath and Lottie and Amber took the opportunity to whoop, clap and cheer. "Wooooo, go, Evie."

"Shh," I smiled. So glad they were here. So glad they were my friends. "I'm only just getting started." And I stood up and pretended I was in a TED talk.

"Madness and femininity have been linked throughout history. By the mid-nineteenth century, records show the majority of patients in mental health wards were women. We were considered more vulnerable to 'madness' because of our biology. Actually, the term 'hysteria' comes from the Latin word for womb, *hystera*. I.e. if you've got a vag, you're hysterical." The girls smiled. "The thing was, these women being shoved into asylums weren't always 'crazy'. They just didn't fit the repressed notions of how women were 'supposed to be' at that time. You were called 'mad' and chucked into an institution if, say, you had a temper. Because women are supposed to be docile and meek. If you were sexual, you were mad because women back then were supposed to be pure... Think things have changed? Think it's all better now? Think again. Just look at the language we use when we talk about women..."

I had drawn some cartoons for this bit so I handed them out. Lottie and Amber took them, and giggled at my shite art. "Think about it, today a girl gets angry about something completely legitimate, and she's called a 'mad bitch'. A girl gets upset about something upsetting, and she's told to 'calm down, dear, you're hysterical'.

"The other week, Guy called me 'mental' when I dared ask him if he was only interested in sex. Girls get called 'mental' all the time." I smiled sadly. "Yes, in Guy's case, he may've been onto something…" I looked around my little room again and Amber and Lottie laughed nervously. "But…he wasn't having a go at me for being mental because I have OCD. He called me mental because, again, I wasn't playing the part I was supposed to. Because…now… women are also 'mad' if we want boys to treat us properly and with respect. We're called 'high maintenance' or 'psycho exes'…"

I trailed off. Mainly because Lottie and Amber were elbowing each other and giggling.

"Are you finished?" I asked, sounding like a school teacher. "You know, you could give the sectioned person a bit more attention."

"You weren't sectioned," Amber said, still smiling. "That Sarah lady told us you'd try and say that you were."

They dissolved into giggles again.

"You tell her."

"No, you tell her."

"What are you guys talking about?" I said, worried they were laughing at me.

Lottie coughed and stopped herself laughing. "Sorry, Evie, this is interesting, really it is. It's just Guy…" And she burst into peals of giggles again.

"What? What about Guy?"

Lottie was laughing so hard she couldn't talk. Amber took over.

"We…er…umm…well Lottie and I…we swapped his weed for some kitchen herbs and he's not noticed and still pretends to be stoned."

Then they were both unreachable for a good two minutes. I laughed too, in disbelief. "You did what?"

"It was stupid," Lottie squealed, tears running down her face. "But totally worth it. Jane helped actually. She really wants to visit, Eves, you should let her. I think she's pretty worried, and she was amazing with the prank. God, Guy's a loser."

I smiled, with a warmth in my tummy that porridge advertisements would love to be able to describe.

"You really did that, for me?" I blinked back some threatening tears.

Amber beamed at me. "Of course," she said. "We're not going to let some dickwad get away with treating you like that."

"We're here for you, Evie," Lottie said shyly. "If you'll have us, we're so here for you."

"I'll have you."

"Good," Amber said loudly. "Now, before we all start blubbing – Evie, finish your talk."

I sniffed and attempted to pull myself together. "Right," I started. "So it got me to thinking – women are always thought of as the weaker ones, the ones more prone to craziness…and I was trying to work out why. I came to two conclusions. One, being a woman, in this world, ultimately makes you crazy. And, two, you're more likely to be labelled crazy anyway if you're female." I pulled out some sheets from the World Health Organization. "Look, these guys are in charge of the health of the entire WORLD. And they're basically saying gender is the cause of loads of mental health problems. People don't wake up one day and think, *Oooh, I think I'll go completely gaga*. It's usually a case of spiralling circumstances. And, if you're a woman, think about it, we have a shitload of spiralling circumstances. We're paid less, we're told we have to be beautiful, and thin, but we're also told to eat chocolate all the time otherwise we're not 'fun', and we're constantly being objectified and told to calm down when we care about something… Isn't all this likely to make us a little mental? Isn't being subjected to daily inequality going to be a spiralling circumstance?"

"Here here," Lottie called through her hands. "Evelyn for prime minister."

I took another deep breath. "And then we go to the doctor for help and, because they're all warped by our twisted worldview, they're more likely to label us mad too. You know, they did this study and, say a boy and a girl both go to a GP's surgery about depression – the girl is statistically much more likely to get prescribed antidepressants than the boy."

"No way."

"It's mad, isn't it? And that's not just hurting girls. It's hurting boys too. Feminism is all about equality, right? But how is this helping men? How is a society so broken helping anyone? I looked at the Samaritans website..." I handed them both a printout. They were both so engrossed I could've jumped on them with love. "Boys are more likely to die by killing themselves. Forget fast cars, forget cancer, forget getting attacked by a gang. Every boy at college – if they die – it's statistically most likely because they took their own life. Sorry, am I talking too much? Sometimes a side-effect of my medication is mania – tell me if I've gone manic."

Lottie rolled her eyes playfully. "You're not talking too much. It's interesting, honestly. CALM DOWN, DEAR."

"Oi!"

We all cracked up laughing. "So, anyway," I continued. "See how it's hurting everyone. How we're told to behave as boys and girls is breaking all of us. Girls are under extreme strain and are more likely to be diagnosed and labelled as mad. Whereas boys aren't allowed to open up and talk about their feelings because it isn't 'manly' so they bottle it all up until they can't take any more. Something needs to change."

Amber took a bite out of a party ring and sprayed crumbs all over the floor as she spoke. It actually didn't bother me that much. "So what's the answer, Evie? What do we do?"

I pulled a face and scratched my head. "Er...yeah...I'm not so sure. Maybe riot on the streets, raise a revolution and overthrow the entire system?"

"Careful now," Amber replied, spraying more neon pink icing crumbs onto the floor. "Talk like that gets people thrown into psychiatric institutions."

I was initially too shocked to laugh, so was Lottie. But then it sank in and I giggled. The giggle turned into a laugh. Lottie joined in, and then a relieved Amber. We laughed and laughed and laughed until all Lottie's remaining eye make-up had run off, Amber's face was the same colour as her hair, and I felt like "me" for the first time in weeks.

With time, we laughed ourselves out. I felt pressure on my hand. Lottie had taken it gently, turning it over and examining my scarred skin. A tear ran down her cheek. Just one.

"Evelyn," she asked quietly. "Why are you here?"

I looked at them both. My new friends. Who would inevitably become old friends. The sort of friends it's worth going to Hell and Back for, as long as you find people like them along the way.

"I'll tell you," I said.

And I told them.

Epilogue

Hi Oli, it's Evie. How are you? Long time, no see. I was just wondering if you fancied meeting for a coffee? I think we've got a lot we could talk about...

Q&A with Holly

What does feminism mean to you?

Equality for everyone, regardless of their gender. IT REALLY IS THAT SIMPLE. I know some people think feminists want to win power from guys, walk them around on leashes made from our plaited grown-out armpit hair and then lock them all in cages. But that's not it. Feminism is for all genders. Feminism benefits all genders.

What was the inspiration behind writing AM I NORMAL YET?

I really wanted to write about relapse – and how being labelled with a mental health problem changes how you view yourself. I used to work for a charity website, TheSite. org, and we were launching a sister website called Madly In

Love. It's all about how mental health impacts relationships and vice-versa – and Evie just came to me! I loved the idea of exploring how much "crazy" is "normal" when you're dating someone who never lets you know where you stand.

What first got you interested in feminism?

I always had this feeling growing up that something was… wrong…but couldn't quite work out why I was feeling so icky. I had this constant conflict inside of me between feeling something wasn't right, but then also wanting to partake in the wrongness. I remember one rainy day at school, the boys decided to spend their lunch-hour lining all us girls up in order of who had the nicest arse. Half of me thought, "this is disgusting" and the other half thought, "I hope I win".

It was only in my twenties, when the fourth wave of feminism hit, that I was like – hang on – I LIKE THIS. I LIKE WHAT YOU'RE SAYING VERY MUCH. And, *How To Be A Woman* by Caitlin Moran really did change my life. It made feminism FUNNY, and approachable, and it was like a big fat fire was lit inside of me. I really think humour is the best gateway drug into feminism. Start with the ridiculous, like, *I know, I'll spend forty quid painfully waxing off all my pubes, even though no one ever sees them*…then build up to the big stuff – rape culture, abuse, female genital mutilation, rights to education…

Evie, Amber and Lottie call themselves "The Spinster Club" — did you ever take part in a similar group growing up?

When I was sixteen, me and two friends were the only single girls on Valentine's Day. So we had a sleepover and called ourselves The Spinster Club as a joke. It really was the best fun ever. But it more involved dancing to a band called Feeder (yep, I'm old) and eating raw cookie mixture than making strategic plans to overthrow the patriarchy.

When I knew I wanted to write a trilogy about a feminism grassroots group, I pondered for ages about what they'd call themselves. That's when I remembered my own Spinster Club, and dug out all my old stuff. I wish my sixteen-year-old self could've known that her singleton Valentine's Day would inspire a trilogy of books I'd have published over a decade later.

Even now, just meeting up with my female friends and having a chat is where so much of my love of feminism comes from. Just a cup of tea, some cheesy snacks, and a natter about HOW FREAKING WEIRD it is to be a girl in a patriarchal world. It doesn't have to be serious, either. I literally cried laughing recently, having an argument about whether it's "unfeminist" to be scared of pooing at your boyfriend's house.

What's your go-to cheesy snack?

Nachos. Life's just better with nachos.

What research did you do for the book?

A lot. I spent a lot of time grilling Cognitive Behaviour Therapists and psychotherapists, and young people with OCD, to make being in Evie's head as real as I could. I felt a huge pressure to represent OCD accurately and sensitively. This is incredibly difficult as OCD manifests itself in so many unique ways – I'd never be able to cover everyone's "version". But, when Evie came alive in my head, the key thing was how annoyed she was that she had the "clichéd" version of OCD and I had to pay homage to that.

Did writing the book change your own ideas about feminism and mental health?

My ideas about feminism and mental health continue to change and grow as I learn more. And that's what needs to be embraced more. Enlightenment is a journey – we can't expect to know it all and get it all right the moment we decide to fight for something we believe in. We shouldn't yell at people for "getting it wrong" if they're at a different stage in their learning. We shouldn't be yelling at anyone identifying as a feminist, period! When feminists start in-squabbling, I'm always reminded of that scene in *The Hunger Games* when Finnick yells to Katniss about remembering who the real enemy is. I've grown so much as a feminist in the process of writing these books, and I really hope my readers will see my own learning and development as they make their way through the trilogy.

Did you have a "film that got you into films"?

I am a huge film geek. And, like Evie, I have a top five list honed to perfection:

1) *The Usual Suspects*
2) *American Beauty*
3) *Eternal Sunshine of the Spotless Mind*
4) *The Matrix*
5) *Thelma and Louise*

Are there any specific books that inspired you to write this book?

The Georgia Nicolson books will always be a huge inspiration to me – and they'll always make me want to write books about hilarious girls having hysterical friendships.

Another book that influenced this is an odd one – *The Beach* by Alex Garland. I loved how the reader goes mad with him, as he goes mad in the book… I really wanted to capture that too. I want my readers to feel disjointed and uneasy and attacked and fragmented as they read *Am I Normal Yet?* to get a sense of what it's like when your brain is like that all the time.

Can you give us a hint of what's next for the Spinster Club?

The Spinster Club is GOING INTERNATIONAL. In the next book, Amber is going to have All The Things happen to her at an American summer camp. Plus, there are NICE BOYS in the next book. As I'm aware of all the über-douche male characters in *Am I Normal Yet?*

And Lottie is going to take on the ENTIRE PATRIARCHY in book three. I'm so excited I can hardly type.

Are there any messages in particular you would like readers to take away with them?

That's not up for me to decide – it's up to you guys.

…but if any of you do read this, and do decide to set up your own Spinster Club – please let me know. Because it would make my day/week/life!

Find out more about Holly:
@holly_bourneYA
www.facebook.com/Holly.BourneYA
www.hollybourne.co.uk

Don't miss Amber's story

From the author of AM I NORMAL YET?

HOLLY BOURNE

HOW HARD
CAN
L♡VE
BE?

From the author of AM I NORMAL YET?

HARDER THAN YOU THINK

DO I WANT TO KNOW?

WAAY
TOO
HARD

W·A·A·Y
TOO HARD

EASY WITH
the RIGHT
PERSON?

ISBN: 9781409591221
EPUB: 9781474915588 / KINDLE: 9781474915595

So I'm spending the summer in CALIFORNIA, with the mum who upped and ABANDONED me — and I think I'm falling for a guy guaranteed to BREAK MY HEART. This is a SITUATION DESTINED TO FAIL.

All Amber wants is a little bit of love. Her mum has never been the caring type, even before she moved to America. But Amber's hoping that spending the summer with her can change all that.

And then there's Prom King Kyle, the serial heartbreaker. Can Amber really be falling for him? Even with best friends Evie and Lottie's advice, there's no escaping the fact: love is hard.

"Holly is the pure, real, honest voice of YA."
Never Judge a Book by its Cover

And see Lottie take on the world in:

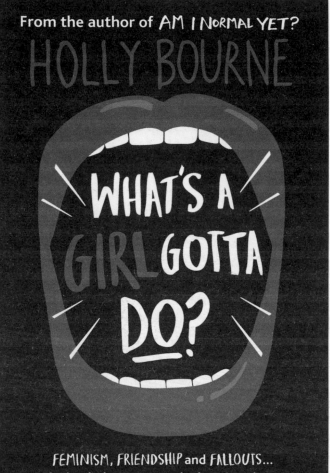

ISBN: 9781474915021
EPUB: 9781474919364 / KINDLE: 9781474919371

HOW TO START A
FEMINIST REVOLUTION

1. Call out anything that is
unfair on one gender
2. Don't call out the same thing twice
(so you can sleep and breathe)
3. Always try to keep it funny
4. Don't let ANYTHING slide.
Even when you start to break...

Lottie's determined to change the world with her
#Vagilante vlog. Shame the trolls have other ideas...

"A book to press into the hands of every
teenage girl you know."
The Bookseller

EXCITING NEWS!
The girls are back in a
SPINSTER CLUB special

...AND A HAPPY NEW YEAR!

Out November 2016

Acknowledgements

I would firstly like to thank Andy*, for sleeping with someone else on my very first date. And then blaming it on having nymphomania. Us writers need emotionally-scarring things like that to happen to us at sixteen – thanks for obliging. I couldn't have made it up.

I'd also like to thank the original spinsters – Rachel and Emily – for Valentine's Day 2003. Who would've thought our singleton sleepover would become a trilogy of books? Thank you for always being hilarious and mad. I still treasure my Spinster Club membership card.

Finding Evie took me to A Very Dark Place, and I want to express my enormous gratitude for everyone around me who yanked me back into the light. Mum, Dad – I owe you everything. Thanks for teaching me to question everything, and how to be strong. Thank you to my beautiful sisters, Eryn and Willow. Ruth, thanks for taking my late-night phonecalls. Owen, you were incredible and I am so grateful. And thank you to my girly gang, Amy, Katie, Lisa – for keeping me upbeat with crisps, dips and poo stories. I couldn't have got through it without you. Particularly the poo stories.

This book wouldn't be here if it wasn't for my always-incredible publisher Usborne. A HUGE thank you for being the sort of publisher that lets me write a trilogy about feminism. Cheers to my incredible editors, Rebecca, Sarah, Becky and Anne. And my amazing marketing ninjas, Amy, Anna and Hannah. And thank you to everyone at Usborne who helped with this book who I don't get to see. I love you ALL. As always, thank you to my agent, Maddy, for being excited by this and giving me the courage to see it through.

I've met some incredible people in the UKYA community, and I am so grateful you all exist. Particularly kudos to CJ, Lexi and Carina – for being my go-to authorly types whenever I have a writer wobble. You are the greatest. But thanks to ALL the brilliant authors, bloggers, booksellers, readers and librarians I've met along the way who champion my books and champion UKYA. You are all the awesome. Thanks to Harriet Hapgood, for letting me shamelessly steal our Twitter jokes about black velveted tampons for part of this book.

And finally, I just want to say thank you to anyone reading this who considers themselves a feminist. THANK YOU. Fighting for equality is not always fun, it's never easy. But it's the right thing to do. And, as a woman, I am so grateful to anyone who dedicates any time whatsoever to fighting for gender equality.

Now, let's go kick some patriarchal ass.

*Yep, didn't even change your name. SORRY (not sorry).

For more fabulous Usborne YA reads,
news and competitions, head to
usborneyashelfies.tumblr.com

To Mum and Dad (again), for making me strong

First published in the UK in 2015 by Usborne Publishing Ltd., Usborne House, 83-85
Saffron Hill, London EC1N 8RT, England. www.usborne.com

Text © Holly Bourne, 2015

The right of Holly Bourne to be identified as the author of this work has been asserted
by her in accordance with the Copyright, Designs and Patents Act, 1988.

Author photo © Dannie Price, 2016

The name Usborne and the devices 🏆 🌐 are Trade Marks of
Usborne Publishing Ltd.

A CIP catalogue record for this book is available from the British Library.

JFMAMJJ SOND/16 ISBN 9781409590309 03573/8

Printed in the UK.